Woman on Top

By Brenda L. Thomas

Woman on Top © 2015 by Brenda L. Thomas

Phillywriter LLC www.brendalthomas.com

www.brendalthomas.com

brendalthomas@comcast.net

First edition August 2015

Second edition November 2018
ISBN Print: 9781729354346

Dedicated to a true artist, my nephew

Eric N. Brown

1968 – 2013

Also by Brenda L. Thomas

NOVELS
Every Woman's Got a Secret
The Velvet Rope
Fourplay, The Dance of Sensuality
Threesome, Where Seduction, Power and Basketball
Collide

NON-FICTION
Laying Down My Burdens

SHORT STORIES
Bewitched
Secret Service
Every New Year

ANTHOLOGIES
Four Degrees of Heat
Maxed Out
Kiss The Year Goodbye
Every New Year
Bedroom Chronicles
The Experiment
Indulge
The Watcher

Prologue

An Evening in Paris
Tiffany L. Johnson-Skinner

The party was just getting started, but little did I know, it would never end.

Why I've been dreaming about him, I don't know, but tonight I can feel him, here at the Mayor's Charity Ball. Peering up at my handsome husband, I can't imagine why I'm even thinking about another man. Yet, he's managed to stay in my head, like a stained memory recalling itself at will. However lately, the memory is there at times when it shouldn't be. Like tonight, while I'm in the arms of my husband, the most powerful man in the city.

Gazing across the ballroom, with guests dressed in Parisian attire, tables adorned with Eiffel Tower centerpieces, and replicated paintings by Claude Monet and Paul Cezanne hanging on the walls, it feels like I'm walking through a cheesy Parisian museum. Nonetheless, it's for a good cause and people seem to be enjoying themselves.

As First Lady, I enjoy every aspect of what my position allows me, whether it's supporting my husband's initiatives or building my own platforms. All of this, of course, is preparation for Malik's future, another term as mayor, then governor, and final stop, The White House.

"You okay?" my husband asks, his fingers tickling along the deep opening at the back of my dress.

"A lot on my mind," I say in response, all while checking the movement of the heavy red velvet drapes to see if he might be lurking there.

"Thinking about your event tomorrow?"

"No, thinking about me and you skipping this party, and going up to our suite."

"Well then who," he asks, turning to look behind him, "do you keep looking around for? Are you waiting on somebody?"

I want to tell him that the person I'm waiting for, I fear, is already here; instead I hold my head up toward him for a kiss.

"That's what I'm talking about," he says, giving me a smile that comforts me, the same way it does the people in this room.

Mayor Malik D. Skinner

My life is good and if things continue to go as planned, it'll only get better. Tonight's gathering has brought out the best of not only my constituents but also those with pockets deep enough to finance my re-election campaign.

Only a man who loves Philadelphia could be the mayor of this city, with all it's grittiness, drug wars, union strikes, and organized crime, I've learned to leverage it all. We have the best restaurants and retail shopping outside of New York and no other city can quite match our historical culture, which is proven by the hoards of tourists who visit every year. But even with all that, it's this woman right here in my arms, who's always got my back.

"You know I had the DJ play this for us," I tell my wife as Eric Benet begins to sing *"Chocolate Legs."*

"Malik, don't you start singing in here."

I tighten my arms around her, bending my head to her ear and croon, *"The memory of my day will quickly fade away, when you come wrap them chocolate legs 'round me."*

You know you can't sing, right?" she says, but her smile tells me she loves it.

"I'm the Mayor, I can do anything," I whisper in between verses.

"Yeah, well it's been three weeks since we..."

"I need you to understand and make me glad I'm your man…" I continue to sing to my wife who, when I brush my hand over her backside, I realize isn't wearing any panties.

"You're a bad girl, Mrs. Skinner."

Again, that smile.

However tonight's festivities are dampened with thoughts of having to demote my longtime friend, Wesley

Lawson. I see him over at the bar, nodding my way, giving me that innocent grin he's been using all his life to get over.

When I took office, Wesley had been disappointed that I hadn't appointed him as my Chief of Staff. Instead, I'd placed him in the role of Senior Director of Community Relations. But even in that position, his self-ingratiating ways and back door deals caught up with him, and threatened to not only tarnish my reputation, but my bid for re-election as well. Luckily, we got wind of his shenanigans before they were made public, so I'm reasoning that having to demote him from my staff is far better than losing him as a friend.

I look over Tiffany's shoulder and down at my watch and that's when my Chief of Staff, Constance Barnes sidles up next to us on the dance floor and says, "I'm sorry to interrupt, sir, but you're going on the air shortly."

"How much time do we have?"

"Eight, maybe ten minutes, but Deacon Brown would like to see you beforehand and DA Leander would also like a minute."

Deacon Brown has been vying for a private audience with me on a subject that I'm not ready to broach. I'm already committed to speak at the Concerned Black Ministers Brunch in the morning, and he's pushing me to do a series of Town Hall meetings in February for Black History Month. I don't mind, but at every public forum I attend, it's the same thing; everybody wants taxes cut yet they want the full services of the city. Nobody, believe me nobody, wants to hear or see the ugly side of this city; the child porn ring we busted, the murders that don't make the papers, and corruption that runs through to the city's core. If they heard about all that really goes on, the residents would flee Philly faster than a mouse in the cold.

Mr. Gregory D. Haney II

I'm not one to go out and celebrate New Years; my preference is to keep it private with the people who have tastes similar to mine. Tonight being no exception, I head straight for the bar in the crowded and noisy Marriott lobby.

"Cold out, my friend?" the bartender asks as I pull off my gloves, stuffing them into my coat pockets.

"I'm not complaining, anything is better than where I spent the past few New Years."

"What can I get you?"

"Old Grand Dad, neat."

An exquisite Asian woman two stools away from where I stand, slithers over toward me.

"You sound like a man that enjoys a good drink," she muses.

I nod.

When the bartender settles my glass on the bar, I watch the brown liquid swirl against its sides, but I don't want to rush the first drink I've had in over six years.

"Been a long time since I had one of these," I say, taking a whiff of the whiskey that used to cap my nights.

Offering me her well-manicured hand, she says, "Sato."

Licking my lips I prepare for the sting of the warm liquid; but instead of savoring it, I down the entire glass.

"Haney," I respond once I finish, confirming that I'm the one she's here to meet. At the same time, another woman, tall, bronze, and statuesque, moves to stand in front of me. *"Felices Año Nuevo, Haney."*

"Give them both what they're drinking," I say to the bartender, before laying a crisp hundred dollar bill on the bar.

Smiling, the bartender surmises, "Guess you ain't headed to the Mayor's party?"

Looking from the Asian beauty, to the sultry Latina, each standing with a hand on my shoulder, I say to the bartender, "Mine will be a private party."

With our glasses refilled, I begin to engage in conversation with the ladies when I hear the bartender exclaim, "Now that's a beautiful black woman right there!"

Turning his way I see him smiling at the flat screen above the bar where First Lady, Tiffany Johnson-Skinner is standing beside her husband, as he's being interviewed on the news. Unable to hear what they're saying, I watch her hands, her lips, and the contour of her breasts against her dress, which are fuller since she had the baby. But most of all, I wonder about the scent that lingers between them.

All those years in federal prison and it wasn't my ex-wife who I wanted back, nor did I have fantasies about regaining control of this city. It was only her, the First Lady, that I craved.

I mumble in response, "She tastes even better."

"Sir?"

"What's your name, bartender?"

"They call me Reds."

"Well, Reds," I say, taking notice of his Mohawk of red hair, "make sure these ladies don't go thirsty while I'm gone. And while you're at it, pour one for yourself, it's New Years."

Placing my room key on the bar between the two women, I walk away in what I know is the wrong direction.

Tiffany

I didn't see him enter the room, doubt that he came through the main entrance, probably slithered along the perimeter. Yes, that's how he was, the slithering type, only being seen when he was ready to be seen or better yet, when he was ready to pounce. That's why we'd put him down, locked him away, for what had to be at least six years.

I wish Kamille and Julian could've come to the party tonight, because they surely would've made a long night more bearable with their comic banter. However, my brother was celebrating New Year's in Prague, and my sister was bringing in the New Year at home with her family, probably in front of that huge stone fireplace. But for my New Year's, there's no other place I'd rather be than right here, in my husband's arms.

"What time can I take you away from all this?" I ask him when Eric Benet's voice fades out and the tempo of some version of a line dance begins to play.

"With this dress, you can get me to do anything. *Faire l 'amour Ce soir.*"

I vaguely hear Malik's attempt at speaking French, promising a night of overdue lovemaking because I'm distracted by a figure I see thorough the haze created from the pale glow of the gas street lamps placed throughout the room.

"Hey, woman?"

"Yeah."

"The song's over. You okay?"

"No. I mean yeah, I need to go to the ladies room."

"You want one of the guys to escort you?"

"No, I'll be fine by myself."

Mayor Skinner

With Constance beside me, and my security detail tailing behind, we head toward a smaller room to where my interview will take place, but not before we're stopped.

"Mayor Skinner, do you have a minute?"

I turn toward the voice of the CFO of Children's Hospital. "Dr. and Mrs. Pope, how are you? Enjoying yourself this evening?" I ask, shaking his hand, then, kissing his wife on the cheek.

"*Oui, Oui*! We're having a delightful time," Mrs. Pope says. "Having been to Paris, I must say you did a great job replicating the city."

"I see tonight has brought out the French in all of us," I respond, it being obvious that Mrs. Pope is slightly intoxicated, "but I owe all the credit to my staff."

"Mayor, I'd like you to meet our daughter," Mrs. Pope offers, nudging her daughter out from behind her.

"Yes, the Naval officer. Welcome home," I say, turning to shake the hand of the stunning young woman.

"*Merci*, Meryl Pope, sir."

"Officer Pope, hard to see you standing on the front lines."

"I'm protecting my country, which includes you, sir."

"What are your plans now that you're home, for what, six months?" I ask, glancing at her father for clarification of what he's told me.

"Yes sir, six months before I deploy out again."

Having put her arm through mine, Mrs. Pope speaks up, "Mr. Mayor, you know we've been in full support of your wife's fundraising, and we're hoping that perhaps our Meryl might intern at your office."

Dr. Pope gives her a disconcerting look and I feel embarrassed for him as my mind immediately goes to the reputation of interns and their infatuation with men in power. However, for me, besides being unable to trust them, the lure of beautiful women isn't worth what I would stand to lose. Plus, Tiffany isn't the type to stand beside me through an affair and she told me that on several occasions when I was running for office.

With Meryl now poised directly in front of me, before I respond, my eyes briefly take in her well-toned body. "I'm sure we can find something to fit your skill level. I'll have my chief of security give you a call this week to see how we can fit you in."

"Thank you, Mr. Mayor. It would be my honor to protect you."

Mr. Haney

Heading up the escalator to the mezzanine level, I move down the wide hallway, where men in those stupid berets stand with palettes, attempting to paint drunken partygoers on canvasses. I'm humored with the knowledge that the majority of these people have never even been out of the country.

Careful not to be noticed, (as if anyone would notice me), I stand off to the side of the ballroom, hoping for a simple glance of her in the flesh. It's hard to see through all the bullshit decorations, yet my eyes find her dancing in his arms. I'll admit seeing her in that dress, knowing those warm chocolate thighs are hidden underneath, makes my mouth water. Even her scent from that far away fills my subconscious.

Unbeknownst to Philly's First Lady, I've been following her for days, if only to see what type of woman she's become. She'd been so young and vulnerable back then, unknowing of the depths of her sexuality, and how eager she'd been to use every part of herself for my satisfaction.

As for him, Mayor Skinner, it has taken me a long time to get over wanting to put a bullet in the back of his head; but for Tiffany, my only revenge would be tying her up for days, taking what I wanted and giving her what she needed - she'd like that. However, cautiously I mutter to myself, "Haney, this isn't what you've come for."

Tiffany

Easing around the perimeter of the ballroom, I make my way toward the exit, but then I hear, "Mrs. Skinner, hello Mrs. Skinner, do you have a second?" It's the annoying voice of a guest trying to get my attention.

Knowing I can't ignore anyone, I turn and face the woman, who I know is a pastor's wife, but whose name I can't recall.

"*Bonjour*, Mrs. Skinner, *Bonjour*. You remember me?"

"Yes, of course," I lie, which is often when people expect me to recall their names and faces.

"You look beautiful tonight. That dress is perfect for your skin tone," she tells me, her voice soaked with envy.

"Thank you, but if you'll excuse me for a moment, I'm headed to the ladies room," I respond, while still in motion.

"Let's take a picture," she adds, while waving over Lou Mendels, a city photographer who's been following Malik and I around all night.

"Sure, you ready?" I ask, smiling for the quick photo op.

"Mrs. Skinner, I was checking to see if you'd be coming with your husband to the brunch tomorrow. Some of us wives would like to meet with you."

"Of course, I'll have a moment," I say, now headed toward the elevator to rid myself of her. "We'll chat then."

"That's wonderful, but Mrs. Skinner..."

"Yes?" I answer, irritated.

"The ladies room is that way."

Mayor Skinner

Once again we head in the direction of my interview, scheduled to air live on tonight's eleven o'clock news and I now have exactly two minutes to spare. I tell Constance to reconfirm my attendance with Deacon Brown, however that's when my security captain, Keenan Wright, informs us the DA has been called away on an emergency.

Lowering my voice, I ask, "Anything I need to know?"

"Not yet, sir. I'm waiting to hear from the Deputy."

In the adjoining room, my press secretary, Cyndi Kilrain, greets us, then begins affixing a microphone to my lapel.

"Has it been all work for you this evening?"

"Actually, Mr. Mayor, I tried to get your attention earlier, but you've been on the dance floor all night," Cyndi tells me.

"Yes, with his wife," snaps Constance.

"Who else would he dance with?" Cyndi retorts.

It has become quite comical seeing the tension between these two women because it's no secret in my office that Constance wants Cyndi nowhere near me, especially when no one else is around. Being in my position, I've learned that women will go to extreme lengths when battling for position, and for the attention of a man that wields power.

A grimacing Constance interrupts, "Cyndi, did you bring a date tonight?"

While adjusting my bowtie, she quips, "Isn't it obvious I'm working?"

Constance stares blankly at Cyndi until someone else distracts her.

Inconspicuously, Cyndi whispers, "Malik, I need to see you, tonight," she glances back at Constance, "alone."

"That's difficult."

"All I want is twenty minutes, please."

Mr. Haney

Making haste to the elevator, I'm stopped head-on by a woman saying, "Greg Haney, is that really you?"

Shit.

"Dr. Ennis, how are you?" I unfortunately have to ask of the aging and most likely, drunk woman.

"No need to be formal. I think we passed that years ago, but I will say you certainly have retained your looks," she tells me, while blocking my path, forcing me to hug her.

"And as always you still have that girlish bounce," I lie, having no interest in ever bouncing with her again, well not unless she can be used as leverage, but I can't talk to her tonight. Through my peripheral vision, I can see Tiffany posing for pictures, and now she appears headed in my direction. I can't let that happen, her seeing me here is not part of the plan.

"We should have dinner, catch up. You could come to my house in St. David's."

Winking at her I ask, "Same number?"

"Yes but…"

"You'll hear from me," I say, swiftly walking away.

Hurrying through the open elevator doors, I pray that the women waiting in my hotel room are prepared to be pushed to the limit but after seeing Tiffany so close up, I already know they won't be enough. However, as the doors begin to close, a hand reaches in and I know I'm in trouble.

Tiffany

I make it to the corridor, but there's no sign of him. I'm relieved, but also annoyed as to why his image was so vivid. Glancing back into the ballroom, I see Malik headed in the opposite direction, off to his interview. Instead of returning to the party, without paying attention, I slip through the closing doors of the elevator to make a quick retreat to our suite.

Without looking up, I push the button repeatedly for the doors to close, and then PH for my floor, but as the doors begin close I know that what I'm feeling is not my imagination. I tell myself, maybe I'm paranoid, that the sensation I'm feeling of him being near me, being in this elevator can't be real, but who am I fooling?

Mr. Haney

Damn, what the hell is she doing in here? I knew I shouldn't have come here tonight but it's too late. I must quickly find a way to adapt, and in this case take advantage of the moment.

Sensing her panic, I close the short distance between her just to calm her fears but I go too far. Reaching around her, I accidentally brush against the unmistakably soft skin of her back, and having no choice, I pull the elevator's stop button. This won't take long.

Tiffany

I attempt to make out his reflection in the smoky mirrored doors and when I do, I am filled with dread. Don't turn around I tell myself, don't look the devil in his face.

Keeping my eyes on the doors, I ask, "What are you doing here?"

No response.

"What are you doing here?" I ask again, hating the sound of my own pitiful voice.

I feel him lightly pressed up against me, feel his eyes burning through my skin and I know he's inspecting me, my clothes, my hair, my body, all of me. Why won't he say anything? Why won't I turn around?

My breathing has hastened to the point that I fear I may have a panic attack, that is until he touches me, one finger tracing the outline of my dress along my lower back. Letting out a sigh of relief, he easily slips his hand through its opening, traveling down my stomach until his fingers touch the throbbing moistness that awaits him.

"Turn around," he tells me, but I don't because the sound of his voice is paralyzing.

When I don't do as I'm told, he gingerly bites down on my neck until I no longer have a choice but to allow his lips to meet mine, and that's when I feel the familiarity of his mouth, his tongue tasting of Old Grand Dad, mixed with the scent of the aftershave that lingers on his mustache. I attempt with all I have to pull away, until with a slow but steady thrust, his fingers penetrate me and my juices overflow down my thighs.

"Please," I moan, not knowing if it's for him to stop or keep going, but he allows them to linger, until slowly he removes them one at time, only to smear their fragrant and intoxicating taste across my lips.

Mustering all the strength I have, I reach for the button and the elevator slowly begins to move.

"How. . . how'd you get out," I cry, my raspy voice signaling a woman whose body has betrayed her.

"Good behavior."

Chapter 1

Happy New Year

Waking up, I could hear Malik on a call in the other room. He hadn't disturbed me yet, giving me time to nuzzle in deeper under the comforter. But in an effort to drift back to sleep, the dark reality of New Year's Eve returned. Mr. Haney was home and he'd let me know in his very own way.

I'd never gotten the opportunity to tell Malik because before we'd even made it upstairs to our suite, he'd been called away to the scene of the first murder in the New Year; actually it had been a murder-suicide, and he hadn't returned to our suite until daylight. But what would I have said? I couldn't tell him the truth then and I can't now, yet I have to let him know the man is home.

Even now, laying here, my mind goes from last night to that first night many years ago, the first time he'd taken advantage of me.

Six years ago, while Malik and I were broken up, I'd lost my way and started dating G-Dog, Mr. Haney's son;

however on this particular evening his father had to come to Club Teaz, to personally deliver our permits. Why he came I never knew. But I was packing up to leave when he arrived and after some small talk, he asked for a drink. The bottles were all still crated, but he was the District Attorney, my boyfriend's father, so I opened one and even though he'd never admit it, I'm certain he slipped something into my drink. That's the only explanation for having allowed him to stretch my naked body over a drop cloth on a concrete floor, where he'd ravished me unmercifully as if he were punishing me for a crime I hadn't committed. From then on I'd been drawn to him, making myself collateral damage between a father and son. And now that man was back in my life and if I wasn't careful, this time he could destroy me.

"What time is it?" I asked from the bed to where Malik stood in the mirror knotting his tie in the adjoining room.

"Nine-thirty. We have to be downstairs by 10:47. Brunch starts at eleven."

"Can we talk? It's about last night."

"Tiffany, I didn't have a choice, I had to leave."

"You know I understand that; it's something else."

"What's up?" he asked, coming to stand in the doorway, as he fastened his watch around his wrist.

I sat up in bed and said, "Last night when. . . " I couldn't finish before there was a knock at the door.

"Who's that?"

"Listen baby, I have a meeting before the brunch, then afterward I have to head over to the Mummers Parade. I'll see you downstairs, that okay?"

I nodded, knowing that I couldn't blurt out that his arch nemesis had been released from jail.

"No problem. I'll see you down there."

An hour and two Advil's later, I was seated beside Malik on the dais, along with several ministers and their wives. It was hard to concentrate because I had my eyes out for Mr. Haney, hoping he wouldn't make himself known before I could warn Malik.

While Reverend Shoulders talked about the mission of the organization, my eyes canvassed the audience. Perhaps he was lurking about for another opportunity to catch me alone. Maybe he'd come to harm Malik. I checked the room for Malik's security detail. Keenan was to Malik's right and Phinn was near the entrance.

There were about 150 people in the audience, half of whom had attended last night's party and were easily recognizable from their red eyes and excessive coffee drinking. Then, of course there were those whose full attention was on the dais, appearing to stare right through us.

My mind drifted back to the elevator, and how he'd touched me. I stabbed at the food on my plate, mixing the scrambled eggs into the potatoes. Meanwhile my husband was chowing down on his food.

Unable to wait any longer, I took the moment before they introduced him and whispered in his ear, "I saw Mr. Haney."

The muscles in Malik's face tightened, but he kept his

face fixed on the audience and the television cameras that were stationed throughout. Leaning in closer to me, he asked, "When?"

"Last night, here," I replied, afraid to mention the closeness of our encounter.

Reverend Shoulders was in the middle of the introduction. "At only 38 years old, Malik Skinner is not only the city's youngest mayor ever, but also one of the most successful it's had in generations. . . a God fearing man. . . "

Not to draw any undue attention to us, he smiled up at the Reverend, but asked through tightened lips, "Why didn't you tell me?"

My throat felt dry, so I paused and took a sip of orange juice. "I never had the chance. You were being interviewed, then you had to leave."

I must've been speaking too loud because Deacon Brown, who sat to my right, hunched closer to listen in on our conversation.

"Did he approach you?"

Now would've been the time to tell him at least half the truth.

"Not really," I lied.

Over our conversation Reverend Shoulders continued. "Mayor Skinner has emerged as a rising star among the nation's African-American political elite..."

"Why would he come here?" Malik asked, more to himself than me.

That wasn't the reaction I'd been expecting. Shouldn't

he be concerned instead of so indifferent? Where was the outrage?

I slammed my eyes shut, then squeezed my hand over his and with my voice low and shaky, I asked, "You knew he was out? Why didn't you tell me?"

"Our Mayor has revitalized this city's infrastructure and displayed a preternatural gift for bringing business into Philadelphia and its surrounding counties. He is a proud representative of the African-American community and we are proud to present the Honorable Mayor Malik D. Skinner, with the prestigious President's Award."

"We'll talk later," he said, then stood as the crowd thunderously applauded.

For the first time in our marriage, my husband had kept a secret from me. Why hadn't he told me that Haney was out? And how long had he known? Did he forget that if it hadn't been for me, he would've never been able to put Haney behind bars, thereby putting himself on the fast track to the mayor's office? Then again, if it hadn't been for me. . . maybe a lot of things would be different.

"Thank you, Reverend Shoulders and thank you to the Black Clergy of Philadelphia and the vicinity. . . It is an honor and a privilege to stand before this great religious body. . . "

I barely listened as Malik spoke about what it meant to receive the award because I was fuming. What my husband didn't know was that it was me who'd paid the biggest price. Haney had seduced me into an intensely erotic relationship that was wrought with alcohol, cocaine, and ecstasy, thereby making me a willing participant.

". . . My job, as your humble public servant, is to do everything in my power to make you feel safe strolling the streets of our city. . . to ensure our children are educated in a school system built to compete. . . navigate to decrease crime and to provide respectable employment for men, women, and young adults. . . in this New Year, I also ask that you pray for my administration, as they support me in guiding our city into greatness. . . because with a city of 1.5 million people," he paused, then said, "what can we do, Philly?"

"We can do better!" replied the now awake and enthusiastic audience.

Smiling broadly and with his hand to his ear, Malik shouted again, "What can we do, Philly?"

"WE CAN DO BETTER!"

'Now folks, you know I wouldn't be receiving this award if it weren't for my wife, the beautiful Tiffany Johnson-Skinner, whose love, support, and God knows patience, allows me to be available wherever and whenever Philadelphia needs me. I would ask, if you're able, that's if you didn't party too much last night, to tune into her TelEvent later today, and consider a donation to the Blessed Babies Wellness Center."

Hearing him say my name, I offered my painted smile in acknowledgement, while secretly seething, and praying that he didn't ask me to say a few words.

Twenty minutes later with his speech finished, he began working the room, shaking hands and promising meetings.

And me? Well, I did much of the same, committing to attend various charitable events and church functions. Another twenty minutes passed and we were finally headed toward the escalator.

When we reached the carport, two black tinted Tahoes with municipal tags awaited us. I made my way in the back seat of the first vehicle, while Malik stood outside shaking hands and wishing passersby Happy New Year.

He leaned inside the open door and said, "I'm going to have Phinn drive you today."

"What are you talking about?"

"Haney. I don't want you feeling uncomfortable; Phinn will keep an eye on things."

Phinn Baker was second in charge of Malik's security detail. He was a nice young white guy, but was a bodyguard really necessary?

"Malik I don't. . . "

"Hold on," he said, turning to shake the hand of a homeless woman, in which he enclosed a few dollars.

With his attention back to me, he said, "Listen, until I speak with some people, I want to make sure you feel safe."

"If you're worried, then why didn't you tell me he was out?"

He glanced at his watch. "When have you seen your husband worried about anything?"

"Then why are you sending a detail?" I stated, colder than I intended.

He slid in next to me, and closed the door. Holding my hand in his, he calmly responded, "Tiffany, please, relax;

I'm doing it because this is how *you're* reacting."

Shaking his hand loose, I told him, "Don't patronize me, Malik, I'm not your constituent, I'm your wife!"

"All right wife, then let your husband do his job. I promise you, he won't be a problem."

One of his staffers tapped on the window.

He kissed me on the cheek. "I love you, Tiff. We'll talk tonight and good luck with your fundraiser."

If he would've stayed in that back seat one more second, I would've told him that Mr. Haney had already gotten too close.

From the driver's seat, Phinn asked, "Excuse me, Mrs. Skinner, are you ready?"

"I don't need anyone watching me."

"I have orders from the Mayor," he said pulling into the Race Street traffic.

"This is ridiculous. Take me to my sister's restaurant, please."

On the ride to 18th and Walnut, I tried to think more of Kamille than myself. The only thing worse than my being involved with the Haney men, was that it was at this same time that Kamille discovered that the then-Philadelphia District Attorney, Gregory D. Haney II was her biological father. It was no secret that me, and my two siblings had been adopted, but it was Kamille who'd been obsessed with searching for her parents, and unfortunately, she found him. As for our younger brother, Julian, the only thing he cared about was professional baseball and women.

The Halfway House Café located in Rittenhouse Square

was a breakfast restaurant, whose normal hours were Tuesday through Sunday, one a.m. to eleven am. By it being a holiday, they'd extended their hours until two p.m. and justifiably so because the New Year's Day crowd had a line that careened down Walnut Street.

Not being in the mood to play First Lady, I rang Kamille's mobile before getting out the car.

"Sis, I know you're busy, but I really need to talk to you," I blurted out when she answered.

"Happy New Year! How was the party?"

"It was fine, but I need to talk to you."

"Where are you?"

"Circling the block in a city car."

"Come through the kitchen. I'll meet you downstairs in my office."

I hung up, then said, "Phinn can you pull around back, please."

"Certainly."

Phinn eased down the narrow street, referred to as Hope Alley, lined with dumpsters, a few sleeping homeless men, and the ever-present, Halfway Hal, who lived between two recyclable bins in a cardboard tent.

Not waiting for Phinn to extend the courtesy of opening my door, I climbed out into the trash-strewn alley and went inside.

Entering the kitchen, I was overcome with the aroma of freshly brewed coffee, mixed with the undeniable scent of pork bacon, and my growling stomach reminded me that I hadn't eaten.

Well-groomed wait-staff hurried about tending to diners, bus staff flipped tables, and three cooks yelled out orders, all while music blared from overhead speakers. Through the open kitchen, I could see into a packed dining room where New Year's revelers ate in hopes of curing a hangover.

Obviously it wasn't a good time to interrupt my sister, but I didn't have a choice.

"Happy New Year, First Lady," said one of the waitresses, as she passed by me with a mouth-watering tray of home fried potatoes, smothered in onions and green peppers.

"Tiffany, what's up?" shouted Chef Haak, the grill man, who not only wore a net on his baldhead, but one covered his Lihyah beard as well.

I smiled back, wished them a Happy New Year and kept moving down the hallway lined with boxes and five gallon drums of oil, toward my sister, where she stood at the end of the hall talking with one of her hostesses and waving at me.

Years ago, Kamille and I had been opposite in our views of the world. I thought I was the one who had it all together, and as it turned out Kamille had been the one who'd led me out of a difficult and dark time. My sister had gone from being a crazy and wild young mother of three, to a business owner and married woman. She was the only real friend I had, and probably the only one I could trust.

Kamille was taller than me, curvier, and opposite of my Hershey bar skin; she was French-fry yellow. Having recently chopped off her thick wavy hair, which had almost hung to her butt, she now sported a short bob that she covered in an LA Angels baseball cap.

"Happy New Year, sis," she said as we embraced.

"Not that happy," I responded.

"C'mon, let's talk, you look like somebody died," she joked, with a roll of her eyes before pushing me into her office.

"Here sit down and don't talk about my office," she joked, making space for me on the cluttered and cracked leather love seat.

For as much as my sister's restaurant was orderly, her office was not. I'd offered several times to organize it for her, but she refused, insisting that she'd get to it. I remained standing, my back against the closed door.

"You guys are really busy."

"We might be feeding the entire city and Chef is talking about he doesn't want to close the door until all the food is gone. What's up?" she asked, poised against her metal desk, with her hand succinctly placed on her hip.

"I really, really hate to spring this on you, but Mr. Haney is out of jail," I said, my eyes searching for her response.

"How'd you find out?" she asked, not looking at me but instead moving around to the other side of her desk.

"I ran into him at the party last night."

"He came to your party? What was he doing there?" she asked seemingly more interested in what was on her computer screen, rather than what I was saying.

Her placid response caught me off guard because she of all people should've known why he was there. "What do you think?"

"I mean what did he say?" she asked, now sifting through the disarray of papers, and receipts overflowing from a wire basket on her desk.

Walking to where she stood, I pulled her hand away from the mess. "Kamille, are you listening to me? He was at our party; he was in the elevator with me. Why are you acting like this isn't a big deal?"

"Sis, I swear, you're overreacting," she remarked, absentmindedly pulling the bib of her cap further down over her eyes.

Holding back a scream, I covered my mouth with my hands, then said deliberately quiet, "I don't believe it. You already knew."

Holding her head down, I watched as Kamille drew a deep breath, then blew it out slowly before saying, "You're right, I'm sorry, I should've told you, but I'm pretty sure my father doesn't want any trouble. He's an old man, hell he's 59. He just wants to get on with his life."

I backed up, knocking over a box of menus before taking a seat on the arm of the couch and asked, "Did you say, your father? What the hell are you talking about, Kamille? Your father? You can't seriously be referring to him like that. You only found out he was your biological father right before he went to jail and you hated him then. And now you think it's okay to keep it from me? Remember, we're not sisters who keep secrets."

"Slow down, nobody's keeping secrets. I never said anything, but he wrote me while he was in jail," she said, her tone slightly apologetic.

There was a knock on her door, it opened a crack. "Boss, customer wants to see you out here."

"I'll be right out."

I waited until the door was closed before I asked, "How could you not tell me that he was out?"

She squeezed in beside me on the arm of the couch and continued. "Brandon kept pushing me to tell you, but I needed to get to know him first. He doesn't have an ax to grind like you think."

Brandon was my sister's husband of the last two years. He bragged about being lucky to have a wife and three sons, and even though they weren't biologically his, he'd gladly taken on the role of Daddy.

"I don't understand, you knew, Malik knew, and your husband knew, but nobody bothered to tell me? That's wrong, Kamille, how could you do that? You know the kind of relationship I had with him," I cried, my voice beginning to crack, realizing that I was in this alone.

She looked at me with a smirk and said, "Now sis, we both know that wasn't a relationship."

My mobile rang. I glanced at the caller ID; it was my assistant, Janae. I needed to be on my way.

Taking my hands in hers, she said, "Tiff, I admit, I was wrong not to tell you we were communicating but when we found out, you remember it was a bad time, and now, well I wanna give him a chance. Please try and understand. I mean things are different; when he went to jail I could've cared less after that crazy stuff you two were into, but you're married to Malik and you're not that vulnerable and reckless woman anymore."

At that point, my sister's face was begging for my understanding, which meant I couldn't possibly tell her how I'd allowed him to touch me in that elevator. There weren't many things I kept from my sister, but somehow I wasn't inclined to tell her the truth about our interaction.

My mobile rang again; this time it was Phinn. I sent it to voicemail.

Standing up to face me, and maybe even moreso to let me know she'd made her decision, she said, "Listen sis, my relationship with him has nothing to do with you and Malik. He's been to my house, met Brandon and the boys, and we've talked about what happened. He only wants to make amends. As for seeing you in the elevator, I'm sure that was a coincidence."

Kamille's reaction was making my head hurt. I had to get out of there. As much as I hated that he was in her life, I certainly wasn't there to make her choose.

"I'm not sure what's going on, but we need to talk about this. Are you going to be around later?"

"Sure I'll come over if you want, but like I said, he doesn't want any trouble. Believe me. What did Malik say?"

"Same as you, no big deal. But, Kamille, he doesn't know about what was going on with me and Haney, he only knows about the relationship I had with his son."

"And he won't know, okay? Stop worrying. Now get on your way."

I left the restaurant thinking that there was no way anyone could convince me that Mr. Haney didn't want trouble. My husband had put that man, and his son in jail; how could he not want revenge?

Chapter 2

Blessed Babies

We were back in the Tahoe, headed to the CW studios at 16th and Callowhill Streets. This afternoon I would be hosting a TelEvent for my organization, Blessed Babies, which I'd founded after witnessing the horrifying effects of a newborn addicted to crack.

Initially with the guidance and support of the nurses at Children's Hospital and University of Pennsylvania, I was able to corral volunteers to simply sit and hold newborn babies, rocking them through their tremors. Then after a considerable amount of research and strategizing, I came up with the idea of an actual facility to provide services specific to their needs. I presented it to Malik, thinking the city's Public Health Department could help, but he pushed it onto my plate, making the Blessed Babies Wellness Center (BBWC) my first project as First Lady.

In the six years since I began this project, I'd been able to bring together a very prominent board of directors, in addition to securing a four-story building at 38th and University Avenue. The entire project, from renovations to operating costs for the next ten years totaled approximately $40 million. To date we still needed $25 million. Our goal was to keep BBWC a non profit center, where newborns and children could go for extended treatment once they left the hospital, especially if they didn't have an initial home or foster home to go to.

We were also kicking off our first crowdfunding campaign specifically to raise money through what we'd named the Cuddle Campaign. For each person who posted a video cuddling a baby for 10 minutes, they were to donate $10.00.

Phinn pulled into the parking lot on 16th Street and this time I let him get the door for me, probably because I was preoccupied with my thoughts.

Holding the door open he asked, "Mrs. Skinner, you have my number, right?"

"Yes Phinn, I'll text you when I'm ready."

In the lobby, a jubilant Craig Ernst, chairman of our finance sub-committee, welcomed me. Craig was a nurse anesthesiologist at the Perelman Center, but he was also a good friend whose wedding Malik and I recently attended when he married his partner of 12 years.

"Happy New Year, Mrs. Skinner," he said, kissing me on both cheeks.

"Yes, Happy New Year, Craig. How's it going up there?" I asked, before stepping into the elevator.

"We're at $75,000, Moosh & Twist performed, then remotely from London, Eve hosted for an hour; she pulled in a good $15,000 and Tina Fey dialed in with a $5,000 donation. And lest I forget, the Smiths signed on as patron donors, which would give us $10,000 a year for the next five years."

"The Smiths?"

"Will and Jada?"

"Nice, very nice."

"But everyone is waiting to hear from you, so I hope you have your game face on."

"I'm ready," I answered, realizing it was time to put my personal life aside.

When the elevator doors opened, Janae stood waiting with a clipboard in her hand. I'd been trying to get her to use the iPad I'd given her for Christmas, but she was making slow progress.

"Happy New Year, Mrs. Skinner."

"Happy New Year, Janae," I said, realizing that not only was I sick of repeating that greeting, but thus far, the New Year hadn't been happy. "I swear, I remember telling you that you didn't have to be here today."

"You're here, I'm here. What can I get for you?"

"Can you get me a Mountain Dew, please? I don't think coffee is going to do it and I'm starved."

"Already got it. But we only have about ten minutes before you go on. I also jotted down a few notes to get you started," she said, while showing me to a table where she'd set me up with a bagel and Mountain Dew.

Ten minutes later the spotlight was on me.

"Happy New Year! Thanks so much for tuning in today. I'm Tiffany Johnson-Skinner. I'm sure you're aware that I'm the First Lady of Philadelphia, however this afternoon isn't about politics, or campaign endorsements, it's about our children. . . Blessed Babies and The Wellness Center. When I first started this project, these babies were labeled with the awful term of crack-babies and nobody cared that they lay crying in the hospital. Like everything else, it was regarded as an urban problem and maybe for the most part it had been. But in the last three years that's changed. The definition, Neonatal Abstinence Syndrome, simply refers to babies born addicted to any type of substance. . . whether it's heroin, crack cocaine or prescription drugs. No matter how you spin it, our babies are suffering and it's not their choice. The BBWC will help these children and their parents with managing the physical and emotional issues surrounding NAS, and for that we need your help."

For intervals during the next three hours I spoke, interspersed with performances by local and national entertainers, poetry readings, a Skype with Kevin Bacon, some humor from Kevin Hart, and a final performance from Meek Mills, appealing to the young audience to whom many of these babies were born. We even had parents and grandparents sharing personal stories.

Finally, with less than an hour left in the show, I slipped into the green room, hoping to find something to eat. The Mountain Dew had burned a hole in my empty stomach, and the catered food had shriveled and dried, leaving me to munch on a bag of Doritos and a bottle of water.

The television was playing clips of my husband waving to the crowd at the Mummers Parade, Philly's 100-year-old folk festival, with its elaborate costumes and string bands. That, of course, followed with clips from the previous night's murder scene, where reporters questioned how he planned to make good on his campaign promise of keeping Philly safe. No matter how hard they pushed Malik, he never appeared surprised by a question and always had an appropriate response.

I did, though, catch the slight shift of his eyes as he stole a glance at the worn Bulova watch he'd been wearing since law school, a gift from his grandmother. I'd been after him to buy a new one, but Malik never wanted the public to think he was grandiose. However, by giving his constituents full access to our lives through social media, it also gave them reason to comment on every aspect of our lives, which sometimes to me was quite intrusive.

Three taps on the green room door interrupted my thoughts.

"Come on in."

"Mrs. Skinner, you won't believe the gigantic surprise waiting for you," Craig exclaimed, spreading his arms open to indicate how big it was.

"If you don't stop calling me Mrs. Skinner," I replied to my friend, who was ten years my senior.

"All right, all right Tiffany, but you're hardly going to believe this! It's fifty thousand dollars!"

"You can't be serious?"

"Yes, yes, isn't it wonderful?" he squealed, all while clapping his hands and twirling around the room.

"Is it someone my husband knows? A celebrity?"

"It's a law firm, Spevak or something, he's on his way up in the elevator so you have to get back on camera to formally accept it. Please hurry before it gets away!"

"That'll be the easiest thing I've had to do this year!" I said, before applying a fresh dab of lipstick, popping a mint to freshen my breath, and making sure my bun was still neatly in place.

When I reached the phone bank to stand with Craig, we held hands in anticipation. Usually we knew beforehand about a contribution of this size, so this really was a surprise.

"He's here. Two minutes to action," yelled the production assistant.

The PA was right, he was here; our donor was Mr. Haney.

I felt myself shrinking into a dark place mixed with desire and fear; there was no way I could be face to face with that man on television. My mouth went dry, my scalp tingled and I had to clinch my thighs together to stop the awful pulsating between my legs.

Having recognized who Mr. Haney was, Craig exclaimed, "Looka here, prison sure did him well, that man is one handsome old man."

We both stared as Mr. Haney straightened his tie and moved toward us. Under the glare of the studio lights, as he sauntered my way, our eyes locked.

I hadn't noticed it so much on New Year's Eve but this man appeared even more distinguished than before he'd gone away. Flecks of gray were sprinkled throughout his hair and his perfectly trimmed mustache and beard accentuated his wrinkle free skin.

And that's when it happened, without warning, my mind momentarily drifted back to that night he uninvitingly showed up at my house and dripped hot candle wax all over me, and for two days he used my body over and over until I'd literally passed out. How could I desire such a horrible man, whose lovemaking knew no boundaries?

"Craig, you have to handle this, I can't," I mumbled, squeezing my friend's hand a little too hard.

Turning to me with concern, he asked, "Tiffany, it's money, who cares about his being an ex-con."

"I need you to accept this, please," I begged, while fumbling to remove the microphone attached to my dress collar.

"Get it together, First Lady, this is your baby."

"I can't. . . " I stammered, but it was too late, Mr. Haney was a mere ten steps away, and the cameras were focused in my direction.

Having no idea who he was, Janae proudly introduced

us. "Mrs. Skinner, this is our most generous supporter, Mr. Gregory D. Haney, the second, of Wallus, Spevak & Rule, Attorneys at Law."

With a wary smile on my lips, I said, "Good evening, Mr., we're so grateful for your gift," I responded, unable to say his name, as I'd said it too many times in the throes of passion, most recently in that damn elevator.

"It's my pleasure, First Lady," he answered, his warm outstretched hand grasping mine in a double-handed handshake.

The PA instructed, "Thirty seconds. I need you on your spot, please."

All eyes from the studio audience, cameramen, stagehands, assistants and those manning the twenty-person phone bank were on Mr. Haney and me. I couldn't come unglued.

When the cameraman said, "Roll it," the last thing I saw out of my peripheral vision was Phinn on his mobile phone.

"As the chairwoman for Blessed Babies, we at the foundation thank you for the generosity of Wallus, Spevak & Rule."

Mr. Haney stepped in closer; his shoulder brushed against my arm and I felt my nipples harden.

"Often people don't want to think about the babies who are born addicted to drugs and sometimes abandoned by parents who aren't equipped to deal or who are struggling with their own addictions. But because of your firm's generous donation, the doors of the Wellness Center will soon open. Again, we thank you."

"Mrs. Skinner, if I may take a moment to say that we at the firm understand how hard you're working for this worthy cause and want you to know that we are here to provide not only financial support, but pro-bono legal advice to your center and its parents when needed. All you have to do is give me a call and I'll generously give of my services."

Chapter 3

Restitution

"Good job this evening," Malik whispered when I walked into the family room where Nylah lay asleep across his lap.

"Malik, we need to talk about Haney, right now," I fumed.

"Let me put her to bed first."

"Why are you avoiding the subject? This is important. I'm worried about what he's up to, and why'd that law firm give him their money to donate anyway."

"You worry too much," he said, then lifted Nylah and headed toward the back stairs.

I followed him and stood outside Nylah's room, watching as he tucked her under the covers and gave her a kiss goodnight.

"I'm confused. If you're not worried then why did I have to ride with Phinn?"

He stepped out the room, leaving the door slightly ajar.

"Woman listen, if I thought for a minute he was out to hurt you or me, I'd take care of it. Now yes, I knew he was out. He was in a halfway house down on Erie Avenue. That law firm is letting him work there as an advisor. He sure can't practice law anymore."

"Yeah, Malik, but you were the one who handed over the evidence that put him in jail and you benefited tremendously from that. You'd been a partner at your firm for what, three years, and then you hit a goldmine by uncovering dirt on the city's most powerful man and you don't think he's coming for you?"

"He went to jail because he was taking money from crime bosses in South Philly. Did I uncover it? Yes, but it had nothing to do with you, it was Haney who violated his oath of office. And his son, G-dog, that you were running around with well, everybody knew he was trafficking drugs from Miami and you, my sweet thing," he paused for a moment, then laughed and said, "all you did was snitch."

"That isn't funny."

"Honestly, Tiff, if I hadn't been so bullheaded back then, you wouldn't have been dating that jerk anyway."

"And you don't think he wants revenge?" I asked, while following him down the hall to our bedroom.

"I don't think he wants to risk returning to the federal pen," he said, taking a seat on the footstool of his leather recliner. "Last night at the party was pure coincidence and as for the donation, maybe it's his way of making restitution."

"That's not good enough for me," I said, standing over him.

"Listen, I know you have a lot going on right now, the opening of the Wellness Center, this fool reappearing, and your stupid husband not telling you, but it's not as if his son came home to win you back."

"And my sister."

"Kamille knew?"

"Yes, she's now referring to him as her father. They were communicating while he was locked up."

He shook his head. "Okay, we were both trying to protect you, and went about it the wrong way. The last thing I want is to see you on edge like this, so take a few days off, relax."

"Time off? How is that even possible?"

He pulled off his socks, unbuckled his belt, then said, "One weekend isn't going to make that big a difference."

Taking a seat on the footstool, I said, "Both our schedules are in high gear right now and you're able to take a few days off?"

"I'd love to, but you know what's going on. I have to finalize the details on Wesley's reassignment, then be prepared for any repercussions."

Wesley and Malik had been friends since elementary school. Malik had gone to Clemson and Wesley to Temple, both majoring in criminal justice. Unfortunately after several attempts, Wesley had been unable to pass the bar, but Malik never gave up on him and with every move up the political ladder, my husband had made, he'd brought Wesley along. He was the closet thing Malik had to a brother, and confidant.

"Exactly what position are you offering him anyway?"

He pushed back into his chair and told me, "He'll still be in community affairs, as Community Liaison, reporting any issues to Jason Wu, who will be our new Senior Director of Community Affairs."

"Isn't that the guy who ran against you?"

"Even more reason why I can't up and go out of town right now," he told me while glancing at the time on his watch.

"Then what are you suggesting?"

"I was thinking more like you and your sister going away to one of those spas, my treat. I'd even throw in some shopping. You could ask your mom or even Nanny to look after Nylah for the weekend."

My hope for a getaway turned into disappointment. "That's crazy, I have too much to do. Did you forget everything that's on my plate? I have to meet with Huli's realtor, speak at that Women's Resource Center luncheon you signed me up for, and there's Blessed Babies."

"I know this Haney thing caught you off guard. And you're right, I should've told you, and if you want me to, I'll tell him to stay away from you."

"I'm not a fuckin' child!"

"Tiffany!"

"I'm sorry," I said, apologizing for cursing.

"You're my wife, the First Lady of this city, and I'm telling you to take a break."

I stood staring at him in disbelief.

He tapped his watch. "Now look, it's ten-thirty. I have a few calls to make, then I'll come back up to tuck you in," he said slapping me on the backside, before retrieving his vibrating mobile from the chifforobe.

The next morning after dropping off Nylah at Crème de la Crème preschool in Mt. Laurel, I gave some thought to Malik's suggestion of going to a spa. Maybe it would be a good idea to get away for the weekend. It had been so hectic lately with the holidays, the New Year's party, and now Mr. Haney's reappearance that I could use some time to regroup.

I phoned Kamille to see, if in fact she could get away. "Hey sis, you busy?"

"Walking out the restaurant, what's up? You okay?"

"I'm fine, but listen my husband is offering to treat us."

"Really, to what?"

"A spa weekend," I said after paying my toll on the Ben Franklin Bridge.

"You serious, cheap ass Malik?"

"Stop, you know he's not cheap, he's frugal," I joked.

"Yeah, okay, so you say."

"He said he'd treat us to some shopping," I added, knowing she didn't need Malik's money to shop.

"That means he wants me to take *you* shopping. But hey I'm in, what's the date and where we going?"

"Where, I have no idea, but I was hoping to get away this weekend."

"Can't this weekend, Brandon's coming home, he's been in Minnesota for three days on some secret Homeland

Security crap. Next month is better for me."

"Worse for me, I have two board meetings, about five social engagements with Malik, and the Blessed Babies Gala to plan. You still have that on your calendar, right?"

"We'll be there. But you should go without me. It'll be good for you."

"I don't wanna go by myself and we never get to hang out anymore."

"Stop complaining and take advantage. By the way, great show yesterday!"

"Thanks. You watched?"

"A little bit. We went out to dinner with. . . " she lowered her voice, "with Haney."

"You mean your father?" I asked, my voice filled with sarcasm.

"C'mon sis, I don't want this to be an issue with us. I'm trying to give him a chance."

"Do Mommy and Daddy know you're trying to build a relationship with him? Daddy's going to think you're trying to replace him."

"I went over there yesterday and talked to them. Mom tried to understand, but Dad was a little pissed, I could tell."

"He was hurt, Kamille, are you surprised?"

"I know and I'm sorry, but am I wrong to wanna get to know him, maybe learn a little about my biological mother? Please don't be mad. Hey, if he screws up," she laughed, "we'll have Malik put his ass back in jail."

"You're right, maybe I'm being selfish."

"And a little paranoid. I mean haven't you ever been curious about your biological parents?"

"Nope, they didn't want me then, so why would I waste my time? Anyway, how's this father-daughter relationship coming along?" I asked, genuinely interested to see if there was another side to Haney.

"I'm still tentative about it, but I really do believe he's sincere. I mean what could he possibly have to gain but a family? He lost everything."

By now I'd pulled up in front of my house, but I didn't want to get out of the car until I finished our conversation.

"You know he gave me a check for fifty thousand dollars, don't you find that a little strange?"

"It was from the law firm and you needed it, right?"

"That's not the point."

"Sis, chill out. Your husband is the mayor; anybody would be a fool to mess with you."

"Guess I'm being overprotective."

"Of me or yourself?"

"Both of us."

"I like it when you protect me, but I think on this one, I'm good. Plus you know Brandon isn't going for any crap when it comes to the boys and me. More importantly, don't you do anything stupid."

"I promise you, I won

Chapter 4

Woodloch

A week later, I was glad to be behind the wheel of my own car, heading out the Northeast extension on a three-hour drive to Hawley, PA. I planned to use the time to sort out all the questions in my head, having also promised Malik that I'd give serious consideration to us having another child. I did want another child, but getting married, having Nylah, and then Malik running for mayor all within a few years had been overwhelming. Our plan had been to have at least three children and with Nylah now being almost five years old, it was time to get started. But having Haney to contend with somehow changed things.

There were so many unanswered questions, like why hadn't my sister or husband bothered to warn me? And what were his plans, now that he was home? I knew his being in that elevator had not been a coincidence. But more importantly, I wondered what, if any, revenge he was seeking on my husband for orchestrating his downfall. It was almost as if once Haney was tried and convicted, Malik began to make quick haste up the political ladder. Not many could be lauded as bringing down one of Philadelphia's top political powerhouses.

I wasn't sure how I was going to get those questions answered, but I also didn't want to wait for him to make the next move.

Rather than dwell on Haney, I called Janae to begin working from the car.

"Morning, Janae."

"Mrs. Skinner, good morning. You ready for your rundown?"

"Yup."

"I finally booked the conference call with the VP at Akine Entertainment to discuss them coming on board as a patron donor. A Mrs. Christine Walker phoned and said you promised you'd attend a meeting with the Women at the Well Ministry at their church in Mt. Airy."

"I forgot about her. Did she give you some idea of their agenda?"

"They're looking for you to speak at their Spring tea, which means they'd like you to bring along some sponsors."

"For a tea?"

"That's what she said. Oh also, Michael wants you to call him and your call with Judge Renwick is in about 10 minutes. Would you like me to connect you?"

"Sounds good. Tell Christine I'll attend the tea, but if she wants a conference call, only give her a fifteen minute block of time because you know those church ladies have a tendency to go on forever. I mean really, how do they expect me to raise money for them, and the Wellness Center?"

"One more thing, Mrs. Wayns, your brother's property manager needs to speak with you."

"Thanks, Janae. You can put me through to the Judge."

Judge Renwick, President Judge of the Court of Common Pleas, was one of BBWC's board members and had been responsible for ensuring all our zoning issues were pushed through, among other things that my husband wasn't able to do for us.

"Tiffany, my dear, how are you?"

"Hello, Judge, I'm well. How's the New Year treating you so far?"

"Not bad, spent the holidays with my wife's family in Colorado, skiing."

"Never been, but I hear it's beautiful."

"Tiffany dear, I have to get into court, but I wanted to invite you to lunch next week. I have somebody I'd like you to meet."

"Somebody?"

"Yes, could be money for the center, a friend of mine, he's in from DC. Tuesday, 12:30; Restaurant 1862 at the Union League. Will that work for you?"

"Of course," I answered, having no idea who somebody was, and obviously he wasn't ready to tell me.

"I look forward to seeing you, my dear."

I'd barely hung up from the Judge when the phone beeped with a call from Michael Reeves, a publicist from Platinum Images, the PR firm where I'd last worked prior to becoming First Lady. The firm was organizing the BBWC Gala and Ribbon Cutting in June and had been instrumental in helping me navigate the waters of prospective donors, versus those merely giving us kiss-off gifts.

"Tiffany, I know you're on the road, but as soon as you get back, and I mean soon, I need to schedule a dinner with you, the Mayor and Sye Richardson, who's now the new President of Philly Pride. They have deep pockets, but their donation is contingent on dining with you and the Mayor."

Even as busy as my schedule was, it still revolved around Malik, with an overburdening number of social gatherings, all politically motivated, either for him, or in support of others. However, over the last year he'd had to attend those same gatherings with me on behalf of Blessed Babies, leaving us with a small window of personal time.

With both our families being relatively small, our best times though were the holidays. Thanksgiving was spent at my parents' and Christmas at my sister's. For me, it was just my parents, Kamille, Brandon, my three nephews, and my brother, Julian. Malik's side was slightly larger, consisting of Nanny, his 79-year-old grandmother who'd raised him, Aunt Mot and Uncle Karl, who came in from Beaufort, South Carolina, and a few cousins who Malik had placed in city jobs.

As special as the holidays were, it was those nights at

home when it was me, Malik, and Nylah that I cherished the most.

"Now Michael, you know I can't confirm my husband's availability for anything, but I'll give him a heads up," I responded, reminding him of Malik's demanding and quite systematic schedule that he couldn't bear to break away from.

"I'm already on it. I'm working with his scheduler and Janae to make it happen."

"Thanks, Michael."

When the line beeped again, it was Huli's property manager, Mrs. Wayns. This one I let go to voicemail, assuming it was a progress report on his new condo property, Hamilton Square. This now brought his total properties to 22.

Glancing at the clock on the dashboard, I knew who'd be calling next. I was right when in the next few minutes Malik's voice filled the car.

"Hey, woman."

"I miss you," I told him over top Siri instructing me to turn onto I-80 toward Stroudsburg.

"Good. How's your drive going?"

"Actually it's quite scenic," I responded while glancing ahead at a powder blue sky that stretched for miles over the distant mountains.

"See, you already sound relaxed."

"Whatever, Malik. How'd you make out with Wesley?"

"I'm not sure. He had no reaction, he accepted what I told him and asked what he needed to do before reporting to his new position. He also apologized if his behavior had caused my reputation any harm."

"I hope you told him that was exactly what you were trying to avoid."

"He knows how I am, but what surprised me is that he didn't have any reaction at all. Hopefully, he'll be the same when we announce the changes at the press conference this afternoon."

"That doesn't sound like him. Did he even ask why or for any details?"

"No, he thanked me, shook my hand and left the office."

"Maybe somebody told him it was coming, somebody on your staff?"

"I kept the circle tight, me, Deputy Mayor O'Hare, and Chief of Staff Constance and Wu."

"So then you could've come with me," I teased.

"Don't start it, woman. I'm buried in here preparing for the budget address to city council next week. Now let a man get back to work. I'll call you tonight to tuck you in."

"All right, I love you."

It was close to one o'clock when I turned onto River Birch Lane and stepped out of my car into the crisp air of Hawley, Pennsylvania. The online photo gallery didn't give justice to the scenic beauty of what was truly a quaint resort.

I'd only brought one bag for my two-night stay and the staff who welcomed me into The Lodge at Woodloch were as gracious as any four-star hotel. The lobby itself held a cozy fireplace situated in front of a wall of windows that brought the outdoors inside. The seating area that faced the fireplace looked like a great place to curl up with a glass of wine to finish reading, *Freud's Mistress,* the novel I'd started a month ago.

After checking in, I was given a quick tour of the property, but my room proved to be an even better retreat. The fragrance of orchids, roses, and pussy willows overflowed from a vase on the coffee table, nestled between two overstuffed chairs with a view of the veranda, complete with a rocking chair. A king size bed took up the rest of the space, across from which was the dresser and a flat screen television that I vowed not to even turn on.

The best part of the room was when I opened the doors to the veranda, bringing with it a panoramic view of Pennsylvania's snow-capped mountains. Stepping out into the cold but fresh air, I noticed that to my left, a short distance from the lodge, there was steam rising from an outdoor hot tub. Now I knew the meaning of postcard perfect.

My first treatment, a lavender body polish, followed by a caviar facial was scheduled for four o'clock. Happy I had time to spare, I changed into a pair of corduroys, a sweater, and down vest, to check out the property.

Using the map I'd been given, I set out on the walking trail lined with colorful winter shrubbery that was full of lush evergreens, sprinkled with brilliant reds and dotted with gold, bringing back memories of the year Malik and I cut down our own Christmas tree. I stopped to take a picture with my phone.

Initially as I approached the lake, it appeared frozen; but as I got closer I could see that it was simply the way the sun laid slanted against the slow moving water. Taking a seat on a bench made out of tree bark, my eyes couldn't seem to adjust to so much of Mother Nature; my senses were on overload.

There were several bikers leisurely rounding the lake when suddenly I noticed a woman barreling toward me about to take a tumble, possibly into the lake. I held out my arms hoping to catch her.

"Damn it!" the woman bemused, while toppling to the ground at my feet.

I bent down to help her up. "Are you all right?"

"Yeah, thanks, I'm fine." She laughed. "I must be crazy to think I can still do this."

Her gloved hands brushed the dirt off her pants.

"Here, let me help you with the bike."

"Leave it. I'm done," she said, still down on one knee.

"I'm Tiffany."

She gathered her footing. "Hi Tiffany, Max Welker. I see you're the smart one, you're on foot."

"It's been a while since I rode a bike that actually went anywhere."

"First time here?"

"How could you tell?"

"You have that awestruck look, like how could a place be this beautiful."

I laughed. She was right.

Max stood her bike upright and said, "Well I'm a regular, twice a year for the past three years."

"So you came by yourself, too?" I asked, hopeful.

"Always," she said.

"Would you like to meet up for dinner later, unless you prefer to hang out by yourself?"

Max's eyes brightened when she responded with, "Dinner would be great. I hate eating alone. I do that enough at home. How's seven?"

"Perfect. Well, I'm going to head back. I'll see you later."

"Okay, Tiffany, see you tonight and thanks again for helping me off my ass."

I waved goodbye and headed back down to the lodge.

Chapter 5

Make New Friends,
but Keep the Old

I arrived to TREE restaurant at 7:15 p.m. The room was tastefully designed, with red and green suede chairs surrounding square tables, and fortunately, not overwrought with ornate décor. I'm sure the wall of windows lent for a beautiful view during the day, but this evening the fireplace substituted as a great focal point.

"My apologies for being late. I made the mistake of laying down after that incredible massage," I explained to Max as the waiter pulled out my chair.

"Not a problem. But hey, I didn't realize earlier that you were Mrs. Skinner! I saw you on television right before I came down here. Wow!"

"No need for formalities. Please, call me Tiffany and promise me, no political debates over dinner."

"You won't get that from me, but you did once own a nightclub, correct?"

"Yes, Teaz."

"That was a real upscale place; I used to go there sometimes."

Her compliment made me smile. "Thank you," I said noticing she was probably my age, but simply dressed and her hair a mass of beautiful locs.

"What happened to it?" she asked.

"The climate in the city changed."

"Good evening, ladies, my name is Tim. Welcome to TREE. Is this your first time?" the waiter asked me, after giving Max a familiar smile.

"Yes, it is."

Handing up menus, he continued, "If you allow me, I'll share our specials with you for the evening."

Tim went through the list and Max suggested we have the steamed sugar snap peas and watermelon feta salad to start.

"Might I suggest a bottle of the 2011 Caymus, Cabernet Sauvignon to accompany your appetizer?"

"Sounds delicious. Will that work for you, Max?"

"If it's alcohol, it works."

Once the waiter stepped away, I said, "So tell me, do you live in Philadelphia?"

"We live in Wyncote, right outside. What about you, you're somewhere in South Philly right?

"We're in Girard Estates, but I'd love to move to the suburbs, maybe Jersey where I'm from. You know, a better school district, but don't tell anyone I said that."

She giggled like we had a secret, then crossed her hands over her chest.

"What's good here?" I asked perusing the menu for an entrée.

"I assure you, whatever you chose it'll be orgasmic," she replied.

I put down the menu. "What line of work are you in? Wait, I can't believe I'm asking that question. It's such a bad habit. I'm sorry."

"It's okay. I teach 11th grade math at Haverford High School. What about you? I guess you don't work, or is that being presumptuous?"

"I don't have a traditional job, but being the Mayor's wife comes with a host of responsibilities, along with my foundation and being a mother."

"Sounds like a job to me. Wait, I donated to your charity, Blessed Babies, right? A few weeks back, you had the television event. I missed it, but I donated through your crowdfunding page."

Hearing Max say that was nice because it gave me a chance to put a face to crowdfunding rather than it being donors who you never imagine meeting.

"Thanks, Max," I said, touching her hand, hoping not to come off as patronizing. "I really do appreciate it. You should come to the gala in June."

"If I can make it, I'll do that. But I have to ask you, how'd you wind up spearheading such a difficult project?"

As sad as the story was I never tired of telling it because it had a positive ending and I could see she was genuinely interested.

"That's always the question. What happened was, I was in labor with my daughter at University of Penn, and this young girl in the room next to me was having an extremely difficult labor. When I asked the nurse what was wrong, they shared with me that the mother was a crack-addict suffering from withdrawal and subsequently when her baby was born it would suffer as well. To make it worse, they told me that they'd have to administer morphine to taper the baby off the drugs. It was so sad."

"Well so much for HIPPA laws."

"Yeah, you're right; I never thought of that."

"Did she leave him there? The mother?"

"No, but after he was born, I could hear him violently screaming his poor heart out, so I asked the nurses if there was anything I could do. That night for an hour and the next night, I sat in a rocking chair in the nursery cuddling and soothing little Tej."

"Now that's a check writing story."

"Not as much as you'd think. People don't want to identify with it. 'It's not their problem'."

"I'm sure having your husband as Mayor helps raise funds."

"He tries to help, but he can only go so far without it becoming unethical. It costs so much to not only care for these children, but the hospitals aren't equipped, and the nurses don't have time to sit and rock every baby. So that's how I came up with the idea of a center for them, though I didn't quite realize what I was getting myself into."

"How costly is all that?"

"We're short about twenty-five million, which we need to be solvent and run as a non-profit for the next 10 years."

"Damn."

"The biggest challenge though is giving the babies the warmth of a body holding and cuddling them through those awful tremors. It's hard to get people to commit to that."

Tim interrupted us, and placed bread on the table. Then, displaying the bottle of wine to us, he said, "Ladies, may I?" and poured for us both.

Max held her glass up to mine and offered a toast, "To Blessed Babies."

"Yes, Blessed Babies."

"Are you ladies ready to order?"

We placed our orders; Chilean sea bass for me, and Max ordered marinated lamb.

"What about you Max, husband? Children?" I asked, already noticing the beautiful diamond ring she was wearing.

"My husband travels a lot; he's a tractor trailer driver, which keeps Lynn on the road all the time. It also means there's no time to make babies. But I'd love to be one of your cuddlers and I might be able to get some of my girlfriends to commit, you know, like a cuddling committee."

"That would be incredible."

"Hey, I don't have my own baby so I might as well cuddle someone else's," she said, her downcast eyes giving away that she wasn't happy about it, which made me feel bad that I'd been rambling on about children.

Tim returned to our table, placing our appetizers and refilling our wine glasses.

"They look delicious," I said.

"Let's say grace."

We held hands while Max prayed over our food.

As we ate, I shared, "I'll tell you Max, the Mayor might as well be on the road for as much time as he spends at City Hall."

Resting her chin in the palm of her hand, she said, "Okay, I have to ask. Does he really do his own tweeting because I'm one of his followers?"

"I think all 1.5 million Philadelphians follow him, but to answer your question yes, he does. He loves that stuff. Me, I haven't tweeted or posted on Facebook in months."

"The kids I teach are social media junkies. They could run an entire business on Instagram alone."

Enjoying her upbeat personality, I smiled at her statement and asked, "How long have you been teaching?"

"Long enough to think about retiring. But I can't complain because I love my job and it allows me to live a comfortable life."

Max and I continued to talk and I had to admit, it was refreshing spending the evening with her. She was smart, quick-witted, funny and easily shared stories about her privileged students and their air of entitlement. I, in turn, told her about the pretentious and flirty women I met when attending events with Malik. The more we talked, the more we drank, and the more we laughed.

Tim returned to our table and said, "Ladies, the Chef sent this over."

"Wow, nice, what is it?" Max asked him.

"It's from the Blackmore Farm. It's their Garden Vegetable Ratatouille."

We both looked toward the kitchen at a smiling Chef.

The other diners looked on at us, which made me realize we may have been getting a little loud but tonight I didn't care. There were a group of women on a weekend bridal shower retreat, but mostly there were couples, which made me feel glad I'd met Max.

"Okay, another question, I mean actually it's an observance."

"Go on, what else would you like to know about the Honorable Mayor Skinner?"

"Actually it's you, on TV, and in interviews you look so uptight, always wearing that bun on top of your head. I mean, I remember you from the club and you definitely *matured,* I guess."

I patted the bun neatly centered on my head. "You mean more like I'm reserved and boring? I guess I've conformed to the honorable role of First Lady. But hey, am I boring you tonight?"

"Not at all, I'm loving hanging out with you, Tiff. But be warned, I don't care much for conformity, being a teacher is enough," she said, shaking her head, her locs swinging back and forth.

"Let's toast," I suggested.

We held our glasses out, and Max said, "To new friends."

"Yes, new friends."

By the time our entrees arrived, we were halfway through our second bottle of wine and finished our ratatouille.

Lowering my voice, I leaned in. "You know what, Max? It might be a shame to say this, but I'm glad to be away from my family, the city, and all the pretentious bullshit going on."

"Let it out, girl, 'cause guess what?"

"What's that?"

"I'm glad to be away from them bad ass students," she said, offering up another toast.

We clicked glasses.

"Are they really that bad?"

"They're bad in a different kind of way than the city kids. They think they're smarter than you. A few years ago, I taught at West Philly High, and they're actually the smarter ones because they work harder. The only real difference is the kids in the city carry guns, and the kids in the suburbs build bombs. And don't tell nobody I said that."

We were laughing so hard that I almost didn't feel my mobile vibrating with a call. I glanced at my watch and said to Max, "Girl, you can set your clock by my husband."

"Okay, I'm going to the bathroom," Max said, giving me privacy.

"Hi, Honey."

"Oh, you go away and I'm honey, I like that. You in your room?"

"Not yet, is it that late? I'm having dinner with a friend."

"A friend, up there?"

"Well, she's a woman I met and we're having dinner. How'd the press conference go?"

"It was fine. Wesley stood there all stiff, then said what Cyndi wrote for him, you know the standard. 'I'm looking forward to getting closer to the community on a daily basis. . . appreciate the opportunity.' Then Jason spoke and that was it. It lasted 13 minutes."

"Do you think you and Wesley will be all right?"

"Time will tell. But look, woman, I'm headed home. Enjoy your dinner."

It was close to eleven o'clock when Max and I left the empty restaurant and headed to our rooms with a slight stagger. We'd laughed until the point of soreness and I could honestly say I'd enjoyed dining with her. The plan was for us to meet for yoga at seven and then have breakfast before our Moroccan Oil manicure and pedicure.

Entering my room, I noticed the hotel had given me turndown service. A thick bathrobe laid across the bed, along with a few devilish chocolate treats. I stepped out of my clothes and laughed while I undid my ridiculous bun, wondering if perhaps it did make me look older than my 36 years.

Standing in front of the mirror naked, I noticed that since having Nylah not much about my body had changed. I had retained a few pounds that rounded out my ass and hips and there were two barely noticeable stretch marks on either side of my stomach. Either way Malik never complained.

Feeling reckless, I turned out all the lights, opened the veranda doors, and stepped out into the freezing night air, for all of two minutes. I could've never tried anything like that at home on our backyard deck.

Back in the room, I was getting into my robe when I heard a light tapping on the door. I ignored it, but then it came again. Figuring it was Max, without looking through the peephole, I turned the knob and flung the door open.

"Evening, First Lady," his voice crooned.

"Haney, what. . . how. . . " was all I managed to say before taking too many steps backward, tripping over the table, sending the vase of flowers crashing to the floor with water spilling onto *Freud's Mistress.*

"H-How'd you get here?" I stammered, all while glancing over to where my mobile sat charging on the nightstand.

"You need to make a call?" he asked, before stepping inside the room, and closing the door behind him.

"How'd you get here?" I inquired again, noting that his black leather jacket and dark blue jeans, made him look much younger. Unfortunately, what I also noticed was his erection.

"You see something you want?" he asked, his tongue peeping between his lips, indicating what I recalled him being so very good at.

I was trying to think fast, but my thoughts were muddled from the wine, and my knees weak from the shock of seeing him. Tightening the belt on my robe, then pointing to the door I told him, "Get out of here right now, Mr., ah, Mr. Haney."

"Sounds like somebody had too much to drink," he retorted, with that ridiculing laugh that had haunted me for months after he'd gone away.

"I'm fine. Now get outta here before I call security."

He closed the distance between us. "I needed to see you, Tiffany," he pulled the belt from my robe, "like this."

My breathing hastened but my words were stuck. "I won't, I swear I won't let you do this to me again."

"I never did anything you didn't want me to do, or should I say, beg me to do."

Immediately the scenario of our threesome at my summer house in Montauk, New York entered my mind -- the way he'd forced me to take that other woman, the unforgettable sweet and salty taste of her orgasm in my mouth, and the way we'd both rode him. I became flushed.

"Oh you remember," he said, probably seeing the carnal look on my face that I tried to hide.

"Fuck you!"

"As much as I'd like to," his hands reached under my robe, pulling it from my shoulders, "I'm not going to do that, at least not yet. Believe me First Lady, if I thought that man was fucking you well, I wouldn't be here. But I could tell by the way you tasted in that elevator, that well, you know, how do they say it, he's not making it rain."

"Things are different, you can't do this. I'm not that girl anymore," I said, hating that I was pleading, attempting to cover myself with my robe.

He bent over, picked a pussy willow branch from the floor, and tapped it on my chin.

"Now tell me how are things different?" he asked, his voice condescending.

Using the pussy willow stem, he circled one breast, then the other, hardening my nipples until they pulsated.

"Please don't do this, I'm begging you." I pleaded, frozen in fear. Not of him hurting me, but simply put, of him fucking me.

He only smiled and moved closer.

The anxiety of his closeness was making me dizzy, so I grabbed onto the drapes for support, but fell backward into the chair.

Bending over me, he forcibly gripped my breasts, one in each hand, and he said, "These are heavier than I remembered. From the baby, from Nylah?"

"Don't mention my daughter," I said, squirming to regain my footing, but he had me blocked.

"Your daughter? She could've been mine."

Pushing myself up, I moved around him. "You're insane and you need to leave right now, or I'm calling security."

He turned me around, pinning my arms at my side, my back against his chest, and my behind against what I knew was his overgenerous hardness. I had to get away from him. I had to get out of that room.

A breathless silence lay between us, waiting to see who would make the next move, say the next word. Why didn't he just throw me on the bed and get it over with?

Loosening his grip on me, he didn't let go, but his body relaxed while mine was peaked with anxieties.

His tongue touched my earlobe with every word he spoke as he said, "You're right. I've stayed too long. But the reason I've come is to offer my assistance."

"I don't need you, for anything! Now get out! Please get out. . . " I begged, wrestling myself loose to turn around and face him.

His face grew serious. "You will need me, because need I remind you that this game of elected official your husband is trying to play, I invented it. I own it and not only will you need my assistance, but your husband will need it as well, trust me."

"What are you talking about?" I asked, assured now that I'd been right, he was up to more than just seducing me.

"You'll see." He paused, taking another look at me. Again, he lowered his voice. "Let me ask you this, does the Mayor make you cum like I did?"

I didn't answer.

"Like I thought."

"If you don't leave now, I'm calling. . ."

"Nobody," he said, and then in an unexpected move, his right hand gripped my throat. "This, all of this," he paused to peer down at my body and through gritted teeth added, "all this belongs to me, and you remember that when you lay in bed with the Mayor."

Chapter 6

Homeward Bound

I never met Max for yoga on Saturday morning and it was past eleven a.m. when I made it down to TREE. I was stirring sugar into my second cup of coffee when she plopped down in the seat across from me.

"Hey girl, I see you decided to sleep in."

I kept my head down and nodded.

"You don't look too well rested, though. Maybe we drank too much."

The waiter came over and asked, "Coffee for you, Mrs. Welker?"

"No, I'm good, but you might need to keep it coming for Mrs. Skinner."

"Huh?" I mumbled while cutting my eyes behind her, over to the entrance, and across the restaurant to see if Mr. Haney was still lurking.

Max's eyes followed my gaze and she turned to look behind her. "Are you expecting someone?" she asked,

"No! Who would I be expecting? Why would you ask me that?"

"Whoa, hold up. Why are you so jumpy? Is everything okay back home?"

"What's with all the damn personal questions?"

She stood up. "Listen, it sounds like you need to be alone. I'll catch up with you later."

I put my hand over hers. "Max, wait I'm sorry."

My mobile rang, it was Malik's number. When I hadn't accepted his call at eight-thirty this morning, I knew he'd be calling back.

"Hello."

Cautiously, Max backed into her seat.

"Hi Mommy, when you coming home?" Nylah's perky voice asked when I answered.

I held eyes with Max. "Tomorrow, sweetie. You being a good girl?"

"Daddy, am I being a good girl?" she asked her father, who I could hear in the background.

"Daddy says yes. Mommy?"

"Yes?" I responded, with not only tears choking my throat, but thoughts of Haney throwing suspicion about the parentage of Nylah. We'd never used condoms and I hadn't been on birth control, but I was so stoned out my mind half the time when I was with him that anything was possible.

"Daddy wants to know if *you're* being a good girl."

Tears fell from my eyes that I couldn't restrain. I could see concern etched into Max's face. I took a sip of coffee.

"Mommy loves you, baby."

"I love you, too. Here, Mommy, Daddy wants you."

"Hey, woman."

"Malik, hi. I missed your call, I was at yoga this morning," I lied, wiping my tears with the back of my hand.

Max's eyebrows went up.

"Good, now aren't you glad you listened to me?"

The waiter came to take our order and Max flagged him away.

"Honey, I have to go. I have a massage. I'll talk to you this evening, okay?"

"Sure, I love you."

"Malik, everything okay back there?"

"Everything is perfect, now enjoy yourself. See you tomorrow." And with that, I disconnected the call, barely waiting for him to say goodbye.

"Okay, what's really going on?"

"I didn't mean for you to hear that, that lie. That's not who I am."

"It's okay, but what the hell happened?"

"I can't talk about it, but I've gotten myself into a terrible situation."

With a smile, she said, "Fine, you don't have to talk to me, I mean, you don't even really know me. But while you figure this out, let's go for our treatments."

During the course of the day, Max didn't push me to talk while we sat side-by-side for our mani and pedi, which made me appreciate her presence even more. Afterward, without asking, she'd booked us for body firming detox treatments, followed by a healing water bath, then we were off to a cooking demonstration. If nothing else, Max knew

Woodloch and she knew what treatments would not only feel good, but also which would take my mind off the predicament I was in.

The sun was barely cresting the mountains when I left Woodloch on Sunday morning, without even having said goodbye to Max. The crystal blue sky I'd watched on the way up had now turned a dismal gray and with each mile I drove toward home, my body grew tense with the anxiety of having to face my husband.

No matter how many times I replayed Haney's visit to my room, I couldn't figure out a way to tell Malik. There'd be too many questions of why he was even there in the first place. He'd want to know why I hadn't called hotel security, called him? But what could Malik have done? Press charges? For what, stalking me? The real question was, how had Haney known where to find me?

But telling Malik and bringing about any kind of legal charges would also bring the media. We would be ruined if it became public knowledge that not only had I been in a relationship with the son, but the father as well. I didn't want to imagine how those headlines would read, nor what it would do to my family, as it would certainly damage the relationship I had with my sister, since she believed that I was over him. I had to deal with this on my own.

Not until I saw the headlights behind me, and heard the siren, did I realize I was driving as fast as my thoughts, reaching speeds of 85 mph. The result was a $150 ticket from a state trooper that I wasn't able to sweet talk.

It was almost noon when I pulled into our driveway, waving to Keenan, who sat watch outside our house. Inside, I found Malik in the kitchen reading the newspaper and watching the pre-Super Bowl Game activities, pitting the Steelers against the Cardinals.

"Look who's home already, my beautiful wife. C'mon over here."

"Where's Nylah?" I asked, setting my suitcase at the bottom of the stairs.

"She's at Nanny's but what about me? I'm here. I don't get a kiss, an I miss you, nothing?"

"I'm sorry."

I walked over, put my arms around him and kissed my husband deeply. I pulled back and kissed him again, this time easing my hand down into his sweatpants.

"Now that's more like it. I'm taking you upstairs."

"No right here, take me right here," I begged in his ear, needing to prove to myself, and Haney, that Malik satisfied me.

"You're serious, aren't you?"

"We're alone, c'mon let's have some fun," I said, all while pushing him back against the kitchen counter and subsequently pulling down his sweatpants, along with his boxers.

"We. . . got. . . dinner at Nanny's. . . the guys coming over for the game and. . . "

While he mumbled, I took his hardness in my hand and was on my knees, about to take him in my mouth when his mobile rang.

"Hold up. Let me take this," he said, guiding me up by my chin. "I'll meet you upstairs."

Upstairs in our room, I undressed and waited for him, naked across the bed. I had to get thoughts of Haney flushed from my head and making love to my husband was the only way to do that.

"Hope you didn't change your mind," he said, panting as if he'd taken the steps two at a time.

Turning on my back, I spread my legs open and said, "Come here. Make love to me."

Kicking off his sneakers, he responded, "I'm gonna do that."

"I love you, Malik."

"Show me," he said before he laid on top of me.

Two hours later, Malik was still in the shower when I went downstairs to check my emails on the kitchen laptop, that's when I noticed the article he'd been reading in the *Philadelphia Inquirer*, "*Seniors Getting The Boot.*" As social media savvy as my husband claimed to be, I thought he and his grandmother were the last two Philadelphians who still read the actual newspaper.

Before I could see what it was about, I heard the doorbell ringing and music begin to play. I peeked out the curtains, but nobody was there except Keenan, still sitting in the Tahoe. I heard the ringing again and this time I could clearly hear Elle Varner singing, "*I only wanna give it to you.*" It definitely wasn't the house phone, which lay next to the paper, and it wasn't my mobile or Malik's which was upstairs. That's when I realized the music was coming from another room.

I searched for the origin of the sound and found it in the family room. Surprisingly, I discovered a Galaxy phone stuffed behind the cushions of the couch. I answered. "Hello?"

"Oh hello, Mrs. Skinner, I hate to bother you. It's Cyndi Kilrain, the mayor's press secretary. I was calling to see if I'd left my cell phone there."

I pulled the phone away from my ear to see the caller ID and said, "I'm answering so obviously you did."

At the same time, Malik peered into the room and asked, "You ready?"

I simply handed him the phone.

"Hello. Sure Cyndi. I'll bring it to the office tomorrow. Not a problem."

Standing with my feet firmly planted in front of him, and my arms crossed, I said, "Malik, what are you doing?"

"Before you say anything, yes she was here and so was my Chief of Staff, Constance, and Deputy Mayor O'Hare; we had a meeting, she left her phone."

It was no secret that women were attracted to my husband, and Cyndi was clearly one of those women, with her unruly dirty blond hair, tight skirts that rose way above the knee, and her knack of anticipating his needs before he could even speak.

"Do you think you could've told me you had people here?" I asked, possibly projecting my own guilt onto him.

"I didn't know I had to ask? Now stop, let's go. I already called Nanny and told her we were running late for dinner," he kissed me, "because you were insatiable."

"Very funny."

"I have the fellas coming over later to watch the game," he said, as I trailed him into the kitchen.

"Who's coming?"

"Since I have to tell you who's coming over these days, it's your brother-in-law, Commissioner Outlaw, and O'Hare. Is that okay with you, woman?"

"Stop playing, Malik. I hope I don't have to do any entertaining."

"Nope, fellas only and they're bringing the food, so you don't have to do anything," he said, picking up two six packs of beer from the floor and putting them in the refrigerator.

"Any word from Wesley?" I asked, hopeful, since he'd always been a part of Malik's game day crew.

"I sent him a text, no response. Now tell me about this spa weekend I paid for."

I'd forgotten Malik was going to want a full recap of my weekend and maybe this was my chance to be honest.

"It was nice. I met a friend, a woman from Philly, a schoolteacher."

"I hope she's a Democrat."

"Malik, stop. We didn't talk politics."

"What else? How about your spa? Were you able to sleep without me?"

"I slept, but Malik. . . "

Distracted by an incoming text message he said, "It's always about politics."

"Anyway, what else has been going on in your town?" I asked, changing the subject from my spa trip, while I pulled our coats from the hall closet.

You'll be happy to know your husband has been working on readjusting his schedule. I plan to be home with my family on Sundays, and maybe earlier during the week, you know, before Nylah goes to bed."

"Why are you doing that?"

"So we can do more of what we just did. I mean we are building a family, aren't we?"

"I guess."

A quizzical look covered his face when he said, "You guess? I thought we were on the same page with having another baby. You said you'd think about it."

"I did."

Holding onto my shoulders, he asked, "Well, birth control or not? Talk to me, Tiffany, tell me that upstairs, wasn't only because you missed me, but because you want the same thing I want."

"Of course, Malik, of course I want to have another baby," I lied. "Now tell me what's been going on in your city and why you're having private meetings at my house?" I asked, trying to change the topic of babies and my spa trip.

"This right here is what's happening in Philly," he said, tapping his finger against the newspaper headline. He read aloud, "Resident's homes in the crime-infested neighborhood of Point Breeze, known for its home invasions and drug wars have been put under eminent domain. . . Wallus, Spevak & Rule, and their representative, former DA Mr. Gregory Haney, II met with the Mayor and the City Redevelopment Authority last week to discuss alternatives.'"

He slipped into his coat, helped me with mine, then continued. "They want to build luxury townhomes, an upscale restaurant, fitness center, you know the drill, it's all for the millennials," he stated, then added, "I hope it's not one of your brother's ventures, because it's Nanny's neighborhood they're talking about."

"The article says you met with Haney, is that true?" I asked more concerned about his meeting with Haney than his grandmother's neighborhood being obliterated for condos.

"Can you get my iPad over there?" he asked, pointing to the shelf over the television.

"Your meeting, Malik?" I asked again before handing over the iPad.

"Yes, it was Friday morning at my office, Haney, Ron Spevak, Wallace Pitts and Jason Wu."

"Why would you do that?" I asked, leaning back against the sink for support.

"Do what?"

"Meet with that man; I don't understand how you could be comfortable with him."

"Tiffany, he's not a threat to me. C'mon it's time to go," he said, checking his watch.

Recalling the comment Haney had made about Malik needing his assistance, I kept asking questions as we headed down the hall toward the front door.

"What did he want? I mean what can he do for you?"

"The law firm is representing the neighborhood and he's the liaison. They're hoping to slow things down until I can speak to city council. It was no big deal."

"Don't you make the final decision on eminent domains?"

"It's complicated like everything else in this city. But listen, if he wants to represent the neighborhood through the law firm, then that'll make their case stronger."

"You should've told me you were meeting with him," I said, while standing behind him as he set the house alarm.

"We're back to that, you wanting to know who I meet with? I'd say you're being a little irrational."

"Malik, he isn't any ole body."

"You're right, but it was added to my schedule on Thursday and I didn't want to bother you. It's no big deal. We met, discussed the situation, and that was it."

Little did my husband know, that wasn't it.

Chapter 7

Soul Food Sunday

Malik's grandmother resided in a typical three-bedroom row home, and regardless of the deteriorating condition of her neighborhood or the increase in crime, she wasn't moving. A highly respected member of her Point Breeze community, you could often find Nanny gossiping with neighbors, scolding children, and doling out unsolicited parental advice, all from her front porch, which barely held two chairs and a fly swatter.

Politics, of course, was her favorite topic and she let everyone know that God wasn't taking her from this earth until Malik reached the White House. It took her six months to stop bragging when Malik and I attended the White House State Dinner during his first year as Mayor.

Refusing to learn anything about computers or the Internet, she retired after 37 years with the Department of Recreation. However she stayed active by visiting the senior center for an exercise group, church on Sunday and Bible Study on Wednesday.

To my husband, Nanny meant everything. She'd been given the responsibility of raising her newborn grandson, when Malik's parents died in a tragic car accident. And even though she herself was legally blind, she never wavered in caring for him nor did she listen to naysayers who said she couldn't do it.

Nanny was a big woman, more by personality than size, so it was easy to see why Malik never gave her any trouble.

Arriving on Latona Street, there were a few guys hanging out who acknowledged Malik as we got out the car. He barely had his key in his grandmother's door, when I heard Nylah screaming.

"Mommy's home! Mommy's home!" my little girl yelled, running toward me and wrapping herself around my legs.

I scooped her up in my arms and nuzzled her neck. "Mommy missed her baby."

"Did you bring me a present?" she screamed over the loud volume of the living room television.

Unfortunately, after Haney's shocking visit, I'd forgotten all about bringing something back for my daughter. "No, but Mommy has something special planned for us, okay?"

"Come on in, dinner's on the dining room table," Nanny yelled from the kitchen, confident that she could time her meals to Malik's exact arrival.

It wasn't easy moving around in her house, as it was filled with mementos of Malik at every stage in his life: from elementary school, high school, college, law school, and his political accomplishments. The largest picture (poster size) in her dining room was of Malik when he took his oath of office.

The top of her china cabinet held Malik's trophies, while across the room on her server were photos of his parents and his diploma from both Clemson and Harvard Law. She'd even framed his Magna Cum Laude certificate.

As much as I teased her, I could imagine doing the exact same thing for Nylah.

"Daddy, I helped cook, and I set the table, right Nanny?" Nylah proudly told us when I noticed they were both wearing aprons.

"Yes, you did, baby."

"And Daddy can't wait to eat."

Before Malik came to the table, he went into the kitchen to take a call and to peek inside the refrigerator, as was his habit anytime he came in her house.

The dining room table was still covered with a Christmas tablecloth, and set for four, with Nanny's treasured Dresden china, which included solid gold silverware and matching bowls of various sizes and patterns.

This afternoon, they were filled with cabbage, candied yams, and a fully dressed ham, complete with pineapples and cherries. And as she did every Sunday, Malik's beverage of choice, cherry Kool-Aid, overloaded with sugar and sliced lemons, sitting in its original Kool-Aid pitcher she'd had since he was a kid. I had no idea how he drank that syrup.

"I see you put out the good china again," I told her.

"What I'm saving them for? All this gonna be yours anyway so you better make some room."

I kissed her plump cheek and said, "I love you, Nanny."

"Tiffany, sit down," she told me, never one for too much affection.

"You need me to do anything."

"Nothing, chile. Sit down before this food gets cold," she scolded.

Not having had a grandmother on either side of my family made it easy for me to love Nanny, but she'd initially been cautious of my relationship with her grandson, that is until she met my parents. When Nylah was born, I'd been skeptical about having her babysit, but Malik reassured and reminded me that she'd raised him since birth with those same eyes.

Coming into the dining room, Malik went over to Nanny and gave her a bear hug. "Nanny, sweetie, what you got for me?"

"Get off me boy, c'mon and eat. I know you wanna get back home to the game."

After taking his place at the head of the table, Nylah jumped in her father's lap to steal one more kiss. Watching the two of them, I told myself there was no way she could be Haney's child. My daughter was long and lean, and her complexion a unique blend of me, and Malik, coloring her a toasty brown.

"What's this I hear about you went away to get a massage or something? Ain't that what husbands are for?" Nanny asked, while spooning potato salad onto Malik's plate.

"Your grandson insisted. It was all his idea."

"Malik, honey, slice that ham up," she said to him before she turned back to me. "My grandson is a good man, that's why you married him, right? Now bless the food, Malik."

"I wanna do it," Nylah offered, and then rushed through, "God is good, God is great and we thank Him for our food, Amen."

Malik pulled her to him and kissed the top of her head. "Good girl."

"She knows how to use that computer you left here, had me playing games with her."

"I taught Nanny how to play ABC Mouse hunt," Nylah proudly announced.

"See Nanny, it's not that bad. You might get used to it," Malik reassured her.

"I ain't got time."

"Did you get to the doctor's last week?" he asked her since she always had an excuse not to go.

"You just won't let me be. I been to every doctor you sent me to. You see I'm wearing these big ole ugly glasses, don't make no sense to be worried about cataracts, can't see anyway."

"If you want, Nanny, I could get one of my guys to bring you a few joints, it's legal now."

Smacking him with a serving spoon, she said, "Boy stop talking like that, you the mayor."

"Nanny ain't gonna beat you, Daddy, don't be scared."

"Nylah, what did I tell you about the word, ain't," I said.

Together, her and Malik responded, "It ain't a word."

Nanny's house was always busy with neighbors and extended family, so it was no surprise when the doorbell chimed. Before anyone could get up to answer, it opened.

"What's up, y'all?" said Tootie, Malik's childhood friend who lived three doors away.

"C'mon in here, Tootie, Malik's here. Get a plate," Nanny told her, all the while getting up to fix her a plate.

Playfully punching Malik on the shoulder, she asked, "What's up, Mr. Mayor?"

"Tootie, you just getting off?" I asked, since as always, she was wearing her Septa Railroad uniform, with its belt pulled tight around the waist of her blue pants and a white shirt whose buttons were begging to be set free against her large breasts.

"Yeah, Tiff, Happy New Year," she answered, kissing me on the cheek before taking a seat next to Nylah.

"Hi, Nylah girl."

"Toot! Toot!" Nylah exclaimed, while pulling on an imaginary horn with her hands.

"Where's Sheema?" Nanny asked, referring to Tootie's four-year-old daughter, a constant playmate for Nylah when she visited.

"Baby Daddy. He's bringing her home today. So, Mr. Mayor, I saw your tweet last night about the Mental Health Urgent Care place. You think City Council gonna pass that?"

Nanny responded before Malik had a chance. "They need to, 'cause these crazy people killing folk. If they'd had somewhere to go besides the emergency room, it might save a few lives. Might've helped that couple who killed themselves New Year's."

"I agree with you, Nanny," I added.

"Tiffany, how's that place of yours coming along?" Tootie inquired, while using her finger to stir the lemon in her Kool-Aid. I didn't say anything when I watched Nylah do the same.

"Still a few months before we open, but it looks good for us."

"Count me in to hug some babies."

"You got plenty to hug with," Nanny murmured.

"Tootie, any word from Wesley?" Malik asked, while cutting up Nylah's ham.

"I told you when you were here New Year's that he ain't been responding to my texts."

"You were here New Years?" I asked, wondering how with a murder-suicide in Germantown, he'd managed to come to South Philly. My husband never knew when to call it a night.

Tootie's eye cut to Malik, then me, like she'd spilled the beans.

"I was out on patrol, so we stopped by here to check on Nanny and the neighborhood," Malik explained.

"I keep telling you, I don't need checking on. I got my 45 under my mattress," Nanny told us.

"Well, I was glad you came by," Tootie said. "Them niggas was acting crazy for real. Shooting for no reason."

I could see Malik getting agitated. Tootie was his friend, but she was rough around the edges. He put up with it because they'd grown up together and she was one of the people who looked after Nanny, along with some of his other shady friends from Point Breeze. Me, I rather enjoyed Tootie's antics.

"No New Year's party for you?" I asked her.

"I had to run them trains for the Mummers Parade in the morning."

"You should've come to the Mayor's party," I teased.

"Not my thing. Too bougie, but I saw you all dressed up on the news, real niggas in Paris."

Nanny and I chuckled, but Malik didn't find it funny.

"Anyway I can't stay, my baby daddy on his way. See y'all later," she said, taking the two plates Nanny had wrapped in foil.

After dinner, while Malik and Nylah were in the basement rummaging through his old stuff for more junk to bring home, I helped Nanny clear the table.

"You know the old DA, he's doing a decent job around here cleaning up the neighborhood. The boys aren't hanging on the corners as much. He's got patrols and everything. Says he's gonna look into all these delis popping up, selling beer and who knows what else."

"You mean Mr. Haney?" I asked, surprised at yet another revelation of his involvement. "How's he planning to do that?"

"He's living not too far from here so he's been coming to our town watch meetings. Told us he plans to save Point Breeze from City Hall. Might run for ward leader."

Before I could ask another question, Malik and Nylah came up the steps.

"All right ladies, time to pack up; it's almost game time."

"I know, I know. Here, I packed up some food for y'all and there's some lemon pound cake sliced up," Nanny said, handing Malik a shopping bag full of containers that probably included all of her leftovers.

By the time we said our goodbyes, it had begun snowing, hopefully without much accumulation because that would mean a day home from school for Nylah and I had too much to do after being away.

Once we were settled in the back seat of the SUV, I couldn't help but ask if Malik knew what Nanny had told me.

"Nanny says Haney is doing a lot more than working on the eminent domain stuff."

He nodded, while being totally engulfed with checking emails, and I'm sure tweeting about the Super Bowl.

"Do you really think he can be that instrumental without any real power?"

"As long as he doesn't break any laws, he can do whatever he wants," he said, still without looking at me.

"She said he wants to run for ward leader. Can he do that with a record?"

"Like I said, he can do what he wants as long as it's not illegal."

"I don't like it."

With Nylah bouncing up and down in the seat between us, she blurted out, "Mommy, Daddy says we're going to have a little brother."

"Nylah, your father and I are talking right now. Malik, are you really okay with Mr. Haney in your grandmother's neighborhood?"

"But Daddy said. . ."

"Nylah, be quiet!"

Malik's jaws tightened and he spat out, "Why are you snapping at her?"

"She knows to say 'excuse me' when someone is talking."

Wrapping his arm around her, as she whimpered out of pure manipulation, Malik said, "Nylah, Mommy's sorry."

Laying his iPad on the seat, he added, "Listen Tiffany, I'm tired of hearing about Haney from you. I don't understand why you feel so threatened."

"I'm looking out for you."

"Is that what you're doing? Well, I can look out for myself," he exclaimed then returned to his iPad.

Chapter 8

Happy Birthday

It snowed for two days, enough to be a nuisance, but not enough to close schools. Malik had been up earlier than usual preparing for his speech to City Council, facing a battle with Council President Evelyn Gillman, who was blocking council approval on the minimum wage hike.

My morning had been busy, there'd been a breakfast meeting with Mark Carter, the CEO of Carter Crafted, who'd agreed to become a sponsor by donating their services to the landscaping of BBWC property, including erecting a children's garden. Next up, I needed to go home and pack for our trip to New York, a birthday present from Malik.

If anybody could slow the pace of my hectic day, it was my brother, Julian, better known as Huli, who was home for a visit prior to Spring Training; he was a short stop for the Los Angeles Angels. Huli was 100 percent Dominican and played right into it by learning the language from his teammates, dabbing in the culture and cuisine and most recently having purchased a beachfront condo in Puerto Plata.

Huli was never shy about being a momma's boy and often spoke about his gratitude for having been adopted. At the end of his first year in the league, he'd received the Rookie of the Year award at the ESPY's. He'd dedicated the trophy to our parents with a speech that brought the audience to tears as he spoke on how blessed he was to have been chosen as their son.

All of us benefited from Huli's success. Last Christmas, he'd surprised our parents with a customized RV for them to travel at their leisure, and that was only because they wouldn't let him buy them a house in some expensive Florida retirement community. For Kamille and me, there was a monthly stipend that even Malik wasn't aware of, and for his niece and nephews there was always an abundance of gifts and overpriced toys, but he'd also established a family college fund, naming it, *In Johnson We Trust.*

Today, the three of us were meeting for lunch at Halfway House Café. I'd dropped off my car with the parking valet and was walking down Walnut Street when I saw Huli's long legs climbing out of a very expensive Mercedes SUV. Before I had the chance to call out to him, a man, probably on his lunch break, approached him for an autograph. It only took that one fan and within minutes there were ten people, men and women wanting to take pictures, get autographs and, of course, women trying to seduce him. I thought it was hilarious that my little brother, who I'd had to force to take a bath, was now one of the world's most recognized athletes and eligible bachelors.

I tapped him on the shoulder. "If I don't get you inside, there's gonna be a riot."

He stepped away from the crowd, his face breaking into a big smile.

"Big sis, what's up?" he asked, pulling me in for a hug. My brother had the best arms for making a sister feel safe. "Where's Kamille?"

"Inside, I hope. C'mon, it's freezing out here."

"Sis, this is Jose," he said introducing his bodyguard. "This is my big sister, Tiffany, married to big time Mayor Skinner."

"Shut up, Huli. Hi Jose, nice to meet you."

"I'm gonna go for a walk, if it's all right with you, boss."

"Go 'head, man, do some shopping, pick up some ladies while you're at it. I'll hit you when I'm ready."

Kamille came to the door and yelled, "Git your butt in here, the food is getting cold."

And not to disappoint his fans, he threw them his signature kiss, and we headed inside the restaurant. Before sitting down, he took pictures with Chef Haak and the cleaning staff, passing out tips to everybody, which made me wonder exactly how much money he carried with him. All of this, I was sure, would make its way onto social media.

With the restaurant closed for the day, Kamille had a table set up for us and a lunch spread of my brother's choosing that included lasagna, fried whiting, Spanish cabbage, candied yams and banana pudding for dessert.

"All this for me?" he said, regarding the spread my sister had prepared.

"You're the one that called the meeting," Kamille reminded him.

"C'mon, let's sit down," I suggested, with Kamille and I on one side of the booth and Huli on the other.

"Season about to start soon. Had to see my family," my brother said, before snapping a picture of the food and posting it to Instagram.

"We know, just make sure we have tickets for Phillies, Yankees, and the Nationals," Kamille told him.

"I got you covered, just let me know how many. What's up with my big head nephews anyway? When you gon' let them come out for a few days?" he asked Kamille, while I fixed everybody's plate.

"Right, and who's gonna watch them? I don't want them little tricks you run around with molesting my sons," she told him, since his relationships were duly noted on TMZ and YBF.

"Don't worry, they'll have fun. I'll hire a nanny. C'mon sis, you know I wanna show them off."

"Let me talk to Brandon. And by the way, they love those Monster headphones you sent," she said, pressing her face against mine to take another selfie. Meanwhile, Huli stole a chicken wing from her plate and she snapped a picture of him taking a bite.

"You two are crazy," I added as they took more pictures and posted them to Instagram.

"Seriously though, I flew out here 'cause I need to talk family business. I know you heard I'm about to sign a new contract."

"Of course we heard. It's all over the news," my sister acknowledged since she kept up with my brother's every move through her sons and husband.

"I'm talking quarter of a billion, if I stay healthy and out of trouble."

"Why would you be in trouble?" I asked, always concerned about his lifestyle.

"I'm not, but you know they have a clause for everything. Why you think I'm so damn careful?" he said before stuffing a huge forkful of lasagna in his mouth.

"What's your agent saying? Is it going to happen?" my sister asked, as she poured ice tea in our glasses.

"Next week. Signing bonus is going to be crazy. Accountant says I need to spend some money and Mom won't let me buy them anything."

As good as he was on the baseball diamond, my parents made certain that Huli wasn't another dumb jock. All throughout high school, they instilled in him that he needed a plan post baseball and for that he was currently working on his Masters Degree in Business Management.

"Well you can buy me a house," Kamille told him.

"If I thought you were serious, I would. Damn this food is good."

"Like Brandon would let you do that?" I asked, wondering if she were indeed serious.

"Uh, my husband is not insecure; if his brother-in-law wants to buy us a house, he'll be all for it."

"What about you, Tiff?"

"You already know what I have going on, BBWC."

Releasing his fork long enough to slide an envelope out the front pocket of his backpack, he said, "That's why I got this for you."

Having already discussed his contribution to Blessed Babies, I didn't expect to be surprised when I opened it. However as always, my brother went over the top. The check was for twenty-five thousand dollars.

"Huli, we talked about this, but not this much. I said ten-thousand."

"You wanna give it back?"

"Hell no! Thank you so much! I'm going to name a room after you," I exclaimed, moving from my side of the booth to his and happily kissing him all over his adorable face.

"You're my big sister, anything for you. You hear me? *Anything.*"

"Now what's going on with you, Kamille; you really want a house or you still considering expanding your business?"

"Brandon and I have been talking about it, but I haven't made up my mind yet. He's letting me decide."

"You should check out some spots, you know, out by Villanova or maybe Delaware. Those college kids be hung over and hungry."

Eventually I knew anything to do with real estate would fall into my lap so I added, "Why don't I talk to Mrs. Wayns and see what she suggests. By the way Huli, did you have a chance to see the new property?"

"Yeah, I need another one of those down in Ole City; what you think?"

"Slow down, little brother. Let's give this one a few more months. We're only at seventy-percent occupancy right now."

My brother didn't only make money on his physical talents, but he'd heavily invested in Philadelphia real estate, going as far as establishing Johnson Properties. Under this umbrella, he purchased, sold, and flipped properties that ranged from abandoned houses to luxury homes all across Philly and its suburbs. His goal was to leave no house abandoned, and ensuring that the majority of them were not only affordable, but offered jobs and training for the unemployed.

His latest venture, *UNAbandon Philly* was in its early stages. This project was being prepared by his real estate attorney for presentation to the city, as well as the Sheriff's Office, on how best to abolish the city's blight.

"What's this I heard about you and Nikki Minaj getting tight?" Kamille teased.

"That's all bullshit. You'll know when it's the real thing. But seriously, I did hook up with somebody nice before I left Cali. A little reserved, but real nice. I need y'all to give me some suggestions on what to give her for Valentine's Day."

"Please don't give her jewelry; that's such a cliché," I told him.

"I did hear about this spot in the South Pacific, some private island, yup that's it," he said, having answered his own question.

"We know where that's going," my sister commented, with both of us knowing he'd never had a relationship to last more than six months.

"How old is she? What is she, black, white, other?" I asked.

"Older and yes, she's a sister, you happy?"

I chided him with, "Does she know your reputation?"

"Thanks to social media, everybody knows my reputation. But that's the thing, we've spent a little time together but she won't go out with me in public."

"All right, who is the little trick?"

"I'm gonna keep that a secret for now."

While we teased our brother on his love adventures, to my surprise the kitchen staff came out of the kitchen carrying a cake and singing Happy Birthday to me.

"You two are full of surprises. Thank you," I said, kissing one, then the other. To me and I'm sure to them as well, when we were together it always felt like we were kids again.

"I have a little something for you," my brother said.

"Really? You know I love presents," I said rubbing my hands together in anticipation of whatever little treat my brother had in his backpack.

Placing a white envelope on the table, he rocked back in his chair. "Open it."

Like a kid, I tore open the envelope and when I saw the contents my mouth dropped open. "You're kidding, right?"

"Nope, seven days, in France, all expenses paid; first class air, hotel, chauffeur driven Benz, and a little something else when you get there. You and Malik don't have to put out a red cent, so you can tell those watchdogs to kiss your ass."

"Huli, I don't know what to say. I love you, little brother. Thank you," I told him, excitedly waving the envelope in the air.

"Here, this one is from me," my sister said, holding out a large square box, wrapped in Happy Birthday paper that I wasted no time in ripping open. It's contents held a beautiful Saint Laurent tote bag in a rich shade of Bordeaux.

"Kamille, this is beautiful, and soooo expensive. Where am I supposed to carry it?" I exclaimed, while massaging the supple leather with my hands.

"If you don't stop that. It's a gift, stop worrying about what people think."

"What you waiting for, carry it now," my brother exclaimed, as Kamille began dumping the contents from my Michael Kors bag into my new one.

"I love it! Thank you," I said, then gave my sister a hug and kiss.

"Enough with the mushy. So Kamille, what's this I hear that the Feds let your Pop out?" my brother asked, who like me hadn't been interested in searching for his biological parents. However once he hit the major leagues, his biological mother contacted him and instead of giving her the cold shoulder, mostly because our mother told him not to, he saw her twice a year, and sent her a monthly stipend.

"Don't you start, Huli. Tiffany is already on my back. And so you know, Haney's okay. He's been coming over to the house quite often, hanging out with me, and the boys.

I kept out of that conversation by slicing up the cake because I certainly wasn't going to discourage Kamille from building a relationship with that man, as long as it didn't include me.

"I'm making sure I don't have to send anybody to check his ass. What about you? You cool with him?" Huli asked, his eyes now focused on me.

"Right now I could care less about Haney cause I have a trip to Paris and a Saint Laurent bag."

By the time Malik came home that evening, I'd finished packing for our trip to New York, with Nylah having begged to stay up and wait for him. All she'd been talking about was spending the weekend with my sister's boys. Not only was I praying they didn't lose my daughter in Kamille's big Victorian house, but I was also hoping she wouldn't have to be around Haney.

Luckily for Nylah, it was an early night. Malik was home by seven and she was able to sit downstairs and talk to him while he ate. He also had the luxury of reading her a story and tucking her in bed. So far, his plan of coming home early was working.

"How was your day?" I asked, when he came into our room.

"I got word that Wesley's talking trash," he said before taking a seat in his chair.

"What do you mean?"

"I heard from Tootie that he was at the barber shop talking about I don't ride with him. I mean really, Tiff, he knows he messed up. If anything I saved him."

"He doesn't see it like that."

"I don't know what he expects me to do."

Perching myself on his lap, I whined, "I know what I'd like you to do."

"Anything you want," he told me, tapping me on my thigh with his mobile phone.

"I'd like it to be just me and you this weekend, no security detail trailing behind us in New York. What do you think, I mean, really Malik, nobody is going to know you're the mayor."

"You know I can't do that. Plus you won't even know they're around."

As inconspicuous as they tried to be, sometimes it was a nuisance with them on our heels, bringing more attention and less privacy.

"Please, just this one time?"

He patted my stomach and said, "I plan to put something in here this weekend so we might not make it outside to need security."

"I guess that means we're actually going to have sex," I joked.

Putting his hand up under my blouse he unsnapped my bra. "You get them clothes off the bed and we'll start making that baby right now."

Popping up from his lap, I stated, "You'll have to wait, I'm busy."

He smacked me on the butt and teased, "Birthday booty."

A few minutes later, I was coming up from the basement and initially ignored the consistent ringing of Malik's mobile, figuring he would answer it. But when he didn't, I realized he was in the shower. When I reached our bedroom and it was still ringing, I peeped at the caller ID; it was Police Commissioner Outlaw and he'd called three times.

Walking into the bathroom, I handed Malik the phone and a towel. I'd barely made it out the room when the doorbell rang. On my way downstairs to answer it, I heard Malik say, "Jesus!"

That told me our trip was cancelled.

Chief of Staff Constance stood on my doorstep. This wasn't good.

"Good evening, Mrs. Skinner, is the Mayor. . ."

"Hi Constance, he's on the phone with Outlaw. What happened?"

"Cop's been shot and he's not going to make it."

"Where? What happened? Please, come in," I said, moving aside for her to enter into the house.

"Broad and Girard in North Philly. Details are still sketchy, but he was pulling out of the McDonald's drive thru when someone walked up to his window and ambushed him."

"Oh my God, that's horrible. Did they catch him?"

"Unfortunately, no, and the scene is getting processed, so it's chaotic right now."

When Malik came downstairs he was back in a suit and tie and talking on his phone.

"Constance, give me a minute."

"I'll be outside. Goodnight, Mrs. Skinner."

He turned to me, his hands on my shoulders, "Tiff, I gotta go. I'll make it up to you. I promise."

"I love you. Go and please be safe," I said, helping him into his coat.

He began walking toward the door and looking back over his shoulder, he added, "By the way, I peeked at the envelope from your brother. Tell him I love him, too."

Back upstairs, Nylah had already sensed her father had left the house and she'd crept out of her room and into our bed. I left the television on for updates, but as I drifted in and out of sleep, I caught a glimpse of the officer's family members being escorted into Hahnemann hospital, and watched as the media set up for a news conference. The first one to speak was Commissioner Outlaw.

"Tonight we are sad to report that one of our own, Officer Leonard Campbell, a seven-year veteran of the force, was fatally shot and killed with no warning or provocation." He paused, cleared his throat and continued. "Officer Campbell passed away with his wife, Georgina and three children by his side."

"Details are sketchy, but a manhunt is underway throughout North Philadelphia and the city at large. Officers are going door-to-door canvasing the neighborhood, which has been locked down for a 40-block radius. We will collect and analyze all video surveillance in the area. It's still an active crime scene and will be for quite some time. Unfortunately, Officer Campbell was murdered simply because he was in uniform. . . now the Mayor would like to say a few words."

Malik stepped in front of the cadre of microphones. "This is a sad night for the Philadelphia Police Department and for our city. Our officers face danger every time they come on duty, often sacrificing their own lives. Officer Campbell was not given a chance to defend himself. . . and to you who committed this heinous act, we will find you and hunt you down for the coward you are. . . I'm asking, all of us up here tonight are asking, for the collective strength of the community in supporting Officer

Campbell's family and the officers who will descend upon these streets to find those responsible. Philly, we can certainly do better than this."

I lay there stroking Nylah's hair and thinking about Malik. This was the first time an officer had been murdered since he'd taken office. Officers had been shot, hit by cars during police chases, but never murdered in cold blood. It had been scary enough once, when Malik had been threatened by some anti-government group, who'd been adverse to his economical platform. I couldn't imagine losing him to such a sudden and violent act.

I'd managed to nod back off to sleep when the vibrating of my mobile awakened me.

Reaching for it in the dark, I answered, "Hello?"

"Did I wake you?"

"Malik?"

Silence.

Then, "You know who this is."

"How'd you get my number?" I asked. This was the first time I'd heard from Haney since he'd arrived to my room at Woodloch.

Pulling the phone from my ear, I took note of the unfamiliar number. I imagined the smirk smeared on his face.

"Why are you calling here?"

"Actually I'm about to give you what you want."

I could only imagine to what he was referring.

"You see, I have a friend, a very wealthy friend, who's interested in making a sizable donation to your little charity."

"I'm not interested."

"Don't be a fool, Tiffany. You'd turn down a million dollars?"

I muted the television, sat up in bed and replied, "If it means being indebted to you, then yes."

"And what about your poor babies and their crack head parents?"

"Fuck you." I disconnected the call, turned off the television and got out of bed.

At that point it was 7:30 a.m. and I wasn't going back to sleep, so I went downstairs to make coffee. Pondering what Haney was up to besides the obvious, I turned on the kitchen television and took a seat at the counter. He must be crazy to think I'd accept money from anyone he knew. Personally, I was sure it was some kind of trick, maybe he was trying to set up a money trail or maybe he was trying to get me alone somewhere again. Whatever it was, he couldn't be trusted.

In the past, I would've called my sister for advice, but she was now his ally. Instead, I returned a call to Max, who'd left me two messages since our weekend at Woodloch, but I'd been too embarrassed to return her call.

"Hi Max, I'm surprised you picked up. I thought you'd be in class."

"Tiffany, hey how are you?"

"Please accept my apologies for not getting back to you, but that weekend. I didn't know what to say."

"No apology necessary. You're a busy woman and judging from this morning's news, your husband looks pretty busy, too."

"Yeah, it's bad."

"Do they have any idea who did it?"

"Don't know yet."

"That's right. I'm asking too many damn questions," she said, mocking me by imitating my voice, referring to my outburst at breakfast.

"No, seriously, I really don't know, but it's scary. This is a first since he took office."

"Are you okay?"

"Yeah, I'm here with my daughter. Malik and I were supposed to travel to New York this morning, but that's cancelled. By the way how are your students?"

"Who knows? I'm off today. You want to grab lunch?"

"Actually I was thinking of keeping Nylah home, maybe taking her over to the Camden Aquarium."

"Mind if I tag along?" she asked in her cheery voice, reminding me of how much I'd enjoyed her company.

"Really, you'd go with us?" I said, surprised that since she didn't have children she'd want to come along.

"Would love to."

"I should warn you that we'll have a security detail, you know, with us," I told her, while keeping an ear out for Nylah as she stirred around upstairs.

"Will he need to search me?"

"No, but he is good looking so you might enjoy it," I joked, referring to Phinn, who'd been sitting outside since Malik left.

"By the way, before I forget, I wanted to invite you and your husband to a small dinner party I'm having. I'll understand if you can't make it, but it would be nice. They'll be three other couples, and I can give you their names beforehand if you need to have them vetted or something."

"Will you stop it? Malik's not the president."

"And Tiff, it's casual. I mean really casual, it's a house party, not a cocktail party."

"I get it. I won't wear a bun."

My mobile vibrated with an incoming text.

GDH3: I need to see you. It's important.

I stared at the screen until I heard Max ask, "Hey, you still there?"

"I'm here."

"Well if you can make it, that would be great. What time shall we meet at the aquarium?"

"How's eleven thirty?"

"See you at the hippos."

Chapter 9

Million Dollar Baby

I waited three days before I responded to Haney's text. Having been intrigued, I agreed to a ten a.m. meeting at Halfway House. I figured at that time, for a weekday, the restaurant would be empty and even though Kamille wouldn't be there, I made her aware of the meeting.

I didn't bother to tell Malik; he had enough on his plate, as he'd left early that morning to attend the funeral of Officer Campbell. The sad part was they had yet to arrest anyone, which I understood they typically tried to do before laying an officer to rest. The reward amount leading to an arrest had reached seventy-five thousand and was steadily growing with monies coming in from the Citizens Crime Commission, Pennsylvania Crime Stoppers, and the Fraternal Order of Police, as well as contributions from private citizens.

The surveillance video they'd pieced together from various cameras, showed a person of average height dressed in all black, including a hoodie, with a scarf tied around his face, leaving his race and age indistinguishable. Unfortunately, this was now standard dress code for all perpetrators. Subsequently, that footage had now been sent to the FBI for a forensic review.

That morning after dropping Nylah off at school, I'd stopped by to see my mom, who'd been dealing with a bout of the flu. She was also concerned about Malik's safety and wanted to know all the details of the case.

It was exactly ten o'clock when I arrived to my sister's restaurant, which meant Haney was late. To pass the time, I ordered coffee and began scrolling through emails, but that's when I noticed not only had Haney entered the restaurant carrying a briefcase, but directly behind him was Wesley, picking up a take-out order.

I'd dressed casually in lightweight wool pants and a cashmere sweater and had chosen Royal Exclusive by Creed for my scent of the day. As First Lady, every time I stepped out of the house it gave the general public as well as the media an opportunity to pass judgment. Malik reminded me of that often so even when I took Nylah to school, I made sure I was dressed camera ready.

My initial reaction at seeing Wesley was to conjure up an excuse as to why I was meeting with Haney. But not wanting to appear suspicious, I pretended it was any other business meeting, because in my reality it was.

"Tiffany Skinner, I'm surprised to see you in here this morning," he said, bending down to kiss me on the cheek, ignoring Haney.

"Business meeting. How've you been?" I asked, hoping to sound casual, which was no match for the question on his face.

"Doing my job, whatever that is."

I knew he was referring to his role as community liaison, but I wasn't going to allow myself to get into that. So I ignored what he said and referring to his fiancé and their four children, I asked, "How's Curtiss and the kids?"

"Everyone's cool. They miss coming over to the house, though," he said, while rocking back and forth on his heels.

He was right; our occasional get together at each other's homes had come to an end once Malik had gotten wind of Wesley's double-dealings.

"We'll have to set up a play date for the kids."

"Yeah, I'll be sure to tell Curtiss, I'm sure she'll be happy you sent a message."

"Thanks, take care," I told him, trying my best not to be dismissive, yet picking up the menu as if I were about to place an order.

Swiping a look at Hancy, then turning his attention to me, he said, "You should be careful with whom you do business."

Haney didn't respond to Wesley at first; instead he kept his eyes on his mobile phone, presumably reading emails or text messages. But then, he said, "Excuse me, Wesley, but shouldn't you be focused on your new assignment, rather than my personal affairs?"

"I thought you said it was a business meeting?" he asked, turning back to me.

"Either way, it's none of your concern," I answered, annoyed that he was questioning me.

Fixing his gaze on me, he lifted his shoulders in a shrug. "I guess that's my cue to roll out."

"You're tougher than I thought," Haney said, once Wesley was out of earshot.

"Never mind that, now why am I here?"

"Like I told you on the phone, I have someone you need to meet."

"Who and where are they? I need to get on with my day," I told him, displeased with myself in how I'd spoken to Wesley and wondering if he would tell Malik he'd seen me before I could.

"Raquel Turner-Cosby."

I couldn't hide my surprise; this woman's rumored estimated worth was $8 billion. Her title was simply, philanthropist.

"I don't believe you."

He paused, then tapped his phone until a recording played, "Good morning Mr. Haney, this is Gwendolyn Ranier from the office of Mrs. Raquel Turner-Cosby, please let me know when you've confirmed her appointment with Mrs. Skinner."

"Why are you involved?" I asked, knowing the price of being indebted to him.

He laughed, then said, "As I told you on the phone, she has disposable income. I don't need to tell you what a woman of that caliber can do for your charity."

"And when will this meeting supposedly take place?"

"Today, two p.m., her office."

"What's your connection? I'm sure she could've called me herself."

"Let's say I brokered the introduction."

This time I laughed. "I hope you're not expecting anything in return."

"Nothing you don't want to give me willingly," he sneered, over the rustle of the kitchen staff cleaning up.

Contemplating if this were a good idea, I said, "You can confirm that I'll be there. Thank you."

I'd pushed back my chair and was ready to go when he placed his hand over mine, his thumb stroking the inside of my wrist. "I heard it was your birthday."

Snatching back my hand, I began to ask, "How did you—" but then realized my sister must've mentioned it. I had to talk to Kamille and tell her not to tell this man anything about me, or my daily routine.

"I have something I wanted to give you," he said, reaching into his briefcase. He removed a flat box, tied with a single bright pink ribbon.

"What are you doing?" I asked, nervously glancing around the empty restaurant.

"It's for you."

I'd never recalled him giving me a gift because what we had wasn't based on any of that. But my curiosity got the best of me. What could he possibly have thought to get me?

Untying the ribbon, I lifted the box top and was completely taken aback to see a coffee table book titled,

Parfums Rare by Chabbert and Férat. I knew the book, it was a study in old and new world perfumes, an absolute treat for a perfume enthusiast like myself. I ran my hand over its black and fuchsia cover. How had he known?

"Why would you do this? You know I can't accept it."

"It's my understanding that you're a women who loves everything French."

"That might be true, but a gift from you is inappropriate," I said, sliding the box back toward him.

His hand covered mine. "There's one more thing," he said, this time placing a purple oblong box on the table.

I furrowed my brows, looking around the restaurant at who might be watching. Chef Haak pretended not to notice, but I knew better.

"Here, try this. I thought it might delight your senses. I understand it's hard to get," he said, opening the box and setting it down on the table.

Before me sat the most exquisite 20th century apothecary styled bottle of Farmesiana Caron perfume, a work of art in itself.

"I. . . what. . . why would you do this?"

He paused, relishing, I'm sure, in practically taking my breath away.

"At least open it."

I opened the bottle and drew in the fragrance of vanilla, jasmine, and heliotrope. It captured me; there was no way I could go home without it.

He pushed the book across the table back toward me.

"Nobody will ever know they were from me."

"We can't have secrets."

"We won't, except this. Take it Tiffany, please?"

I hesitated, knowing this was a bad idea, but picked up the gift bag and said, "Thank you," then clumsily hurried out the restaurant.

I had two hours to prepare for the meeting with Mrs. Cosby, and to see what details I could ascertain about her philanthropy efforts. I didn't doubt she knew every detail about BBWC down to each penny we'd raised and what we still needed.

Once in the house, my first call was to Janae. I needed her to reschedule my calendar for that afternoon. The only thing she couldn't reschedule was the conference call I needed to take with the organizers of the Philadelphia branch of The First Ladies Literacy Program, that I'd take on my way to see Mrs. Cosby. Janae also informed me that I'd been invited to host a workshop at the Pennsylvania Women's Conference in October, which I told her to confirm because this was an event hosted by the governor's wife.

While I searched through my closet for something to wear, I phoned Craig to give him a heads up. "Craig, I hope you're not busy."

"I was about to call you, we need to—"

I cut him off mid-sentence and said, "Wait, this is more important. I'm about to sit down with Raquel Turner-Cosby."

"You're not serious? Wait, you are serious. What do you need to know? I'm pulling her up right now on my computer."

"Tell me everything that you find on her," I said, putting the phone on speaker so I could multi-task.

"Wealth dates back to early 1900's, family discovered and patented some kinda parts for helicopters, then years later, sold it to some Italian company, which as an only child, gave her a fat inheritance. She married twice, very young, like 19 the first time, both times I might add to not very attractive men, yet very wealthy. First husband owned a tech company; the other was in multi-media. No pre-nups, divorced, created her own empire, the privately held RTC Holdings. Oh yeah, no kids to share the money with either and some even say she's a lesbian. Either way, she's a good person to be bed in with, well not literally, but you know what I mean, for BBWC."

I pulled a suit from the closet and scampered through boxes for the right shoes, telling him, "Thanks. Listen, let's not send word to the board until I get her confirmation, but expect a call from me at three p.m. Oh yeah, call Michael and give him a heads up as well."

"You're going to make me crazy waiting. There's so much going on right now. I'm going to burst before our board meeting."

"If this meeting ends with a check, we'll be celebrating, so keep your phone handy."

I didn't take Malik's noon call because he would've been too distracting with all his questions and advice about Mrs. Cosby. He had his own set of problems trying to balance the city's budget and searching for a cop killer.

The first order of business, though, before I even met with Raquel was what to do with the gifts from Haney. If I hid them and Malik discovered them, he might get suspicious. The best thing to do was hide them in plain sight, so I placed the book on the living room coffee table, and the beautiful perfume bottle, I sat on my vanity among the others.

Then before getting in the shower, I did a quick Google search on Raquel Turner-Cosby to see what else I could find out. It appeared she was on the *Forbes* list with the likes of Oprah, Christy Walton, Mary Dorrance, and Meg Whitman. There were even rumors of her belonging to a secret society of women, which sounded about as absurd as Beyoncé and Jay Z belonging to the Illuminati, but those same sites also mentioned her being gay.

She was definitely a Republican and had given heavily to various politicians. Her family's past in Philadelphia dated back as far as prohibition, however it was interesting to note that in addition to her being an avid baseball fan; her first husband had previously owned the Atlanta Braves.

Her main residence was the entire 52nd floor at the Four Seasons, now located inside the Comcast Innovation and Technology Center, which also included the offices of RTC Holdings. Additional properties included a five-bedroom home in St. David's, PA, a country house in France, villa and winery in Tuscany, and there were grainy aerial photos of a private island she owned off the coast of Jamaica. Craig was right, I needed to be in bed with her.

I arrived to the Comcast Center at one-thirty and was whisked into a private elevator that carried me to the 52nd floor. From there, Tristan, a very young and handsome man, who could've very well been a Calvin Klein model, greeted me.

He seated me in the reception area, where I met the receptionist, Gwendolyn Rainier, who appeared to have been plucked from Victoria's Secret's runway. Gay or not, it was easy to see that Raquel liked being surrounded by beautiful and young people.

Other than that, the furnishings of RTC Holdings were conservative and nondescript. Then at exactly two p.m. the double doors to the right of the reception area swung open and there she stood.

"Good afternoon, Mrs. Skinner. I'm so glad you could make it," said Mrs. Cosby, appearing in an herbal green wrap dress, with her golden brown hair swept behind her ears, all of which reflected well off the sun streaming from behind her.

Extending my hand, I made notice that if she really were 50 years old, she could easily pass for 40. "Good afternoon, Mrs. Cosby," I replied,

"Please, come in," she offered, ushering me into what I initially thought was a conference room, but once inside I saw that it was connected to her oversized office. It had floor to ceiling glass panels giving a panoramic view of the city that led to a furnished wraparound deck, which at 52 floors in the air, I had no interest in seeing.

The enormous space was warmer than the reception area, decorated in hues of plum and gray, with abstract artwork and baseball memorabilia bringing it together. The personal space at the far end of the room held an oversized L-shaped mahogany desk, on which sat two MacBook computers, two mobile phones, and a seating area equivalent to a living room, which included a wet bar, flat screen television, and a full bathroom.

Taking in my surroundings, I whispered to myself, "So this is what a billion can buy."

"Please, here, put your things down," she said, offering me a chair onto which I sat my purse.

"Thank you."

"What can I offer you?" she asked, while moving about the room as if she controlled the world.

"Everything looks delicious."

On the server, there were silver trimmed dishes, heavy silverware, and beautifully shaped water glasses. Nanny would've loved this set up. The afternoon's refreshments included delicately cut fruit, tea sandwiches, cookies, mini salads, beverages, and a chilling bottle of Krug Clos d'Ambonnay, a brand of champagne that was new to me, but which also indicated there may be a reason to celebrate.

"You have a beautiful space," I said, in an effort to make small talk, while adding bite size fruit slices to my plate. While standing so close to her, I also tried to take in her scent, which usually told me a lot about a person. But she obviously was a woman who didn't wear perfume, which to me meant she didn't want to be remembered.

"Thank you. I still think it could use some more artwork. What do you think?"

I had no idea why she was asking my opinion because I hadn't even gotten my bearings yet. "I. . . I think your space is amazing," I stuttered. "Is this really an original by Zelda Fitzgerald," I asked, admiring the *Times Square* piece that hung above the server.

"Yes, I picked it up at Christies. *Who Stole the Tarts*, should be arriving next week. Very clean suit you're wearing. Theory?" she asked.

"Why yes, thank you," I responded, surprised she'd even noticed my two-piece tweed suit that had been delivered on Saturday.

We moved to the conference table and instead of sitting across from me or at the head of the table, she sat two seats down, leaving a chair between us. Folding our napkins across our laps we both began to pick at our food.

"Gregory has spoken very highly of you," she said, her eyes crinkling to get a better look at me. I wondered if she wore glasses. "But I've been noticing you're not one to seek the limelight."

"My husband's the politician. I'm simply his wife."

"My research tells me you're more than that. It's my understanding that you set the direction for Blessed Babies, framed the tough issues that faced your organization, and it's you who weighs all the decisions to ensure they're right for the actual mission. I'd say your leadership skills are far more than average and you shouldn't consider yourself as *simply* anything."

"The way you put it, it does sound like I actually know what I'm doing. Thank you, I'll have to use your characterization the next time I'm asked for my bio."

"You're a smart woman, Mrs. Skinner, not as reserved as one would think. Which makes me wonder why you haven't taken more of a role in your husband's administration," she said, making me feel uneasy in the way her eyes took me in.

"I'm quite comfortable in my current role."

We both pause to eat, she bites of her tea sandwich and I relish in the sweet taste of the fruit.

"I must admit I was slightly surprised at the platform you'd chosen. It's certainly different than standard charities in which I'm asked to contribute, and there are many."

"I will admit, it hasn't been easy and we still have a ways to go."

"Well not one request came in to RTC Holdings from your organization. Needless to say, I took it personally," she joked, all while insinuating it had been a slight.

"Our board members, Elise Nielsen and Gretchen Hockstein, offered to reach out to you personally."

"They didn't do a good job, I barely know who they are. I did hear from a Deacon Brown requesting a donation for your church."

I almost laughed aloud knowing how pissed Elise and Gretchen would be to hear they hadn't made it into her circle of main line socialites. Yet surprised that Deacon Brown had.

"Yes, Deacon Brown is a member of our church, Shiloh Baptist. He serves as chairman of the deacon board and he also chairs the building committee. I wouldn't have anything to do with that."

"No, it's fine; that's what I do, give money to the less fortunate and this year they faired pretty well from RTC Holdings," she said, her crinkling eyes drifting past me.

I wasn't sure I appreciated her reference to our church being less fortunate, as I'm sure she was aware that some of Philadelphia's wealthiest African-Americans attended Shiloh.

Becoming somewhat impatient with her version of small talk, I was ready to get to the real purpose of her calling this meeting, so I queried her with, "Is there anything I can tell you about Blessed Babies?"

"I have to ask, do women really volunteer to hold babies?" she asked, the question in her eyes as well.

"Yes ma'am, women, as well as men. It makes a big difference to a newborn.'"

"Funny, you know not having children, I can't even remember the last time I held a baby."

"We'd welcome you to BBWC on any day."

She pushed her chair back, removed our plates from the table and walked back to the server. Casually poised, keeping steady eye contact with me, without blinking she stated, "I'd like to be a patron donor, five million over the next five years."

Stunned at what she'd offered, I assumed my brain had short-circuited and when I opened my mouth to speak, only an embarrassing low squeal escaped. I swallowed hard, but my throat was dry so my words came out raspy and barely audible.

"Excuse me, you want to donate five million over the next five years?" I asked just to be certain I was hearing correctly because by now my legs were beginning to shake. If this woman were honestly giving us that kind of money, I wasn't sure how much longer I could contain myself.

"No, five million a year, totaling twenty-five million dollars, over the next five years."

My instincts were to jump up and dance on her conference room table, instead I took a sip of the very expensive, Veen bottled water and before saying thank you, I asked, "Why?"

"My dear, you are different. I've never had anyone ask why," she said, covering her mouth as she laughed. "However to answer your question, I believe a woman of your stature deserves the support of someone like myself. And if my research is correct, you need about forty-million to make you solid for the next ten years?"

As I'd suspected, Raquel Turner-Cosby had thoroughly done her homework but I never expected her to donate at this level. Someone was definitely watching over me. Had this been Haney's doing?

"Forty-million yes, but I don't know what to say, how to thank you. Believe me I'm truly grateful, but thank you just doesn't seem to be enough. I mean it's so much more than I expected or could've imagined. Thank you."

Bringing over the selection of mini desserts, she returned to her seat and facing me said, "You're very welcome, it's what I do when I believe in a project, but I do have one request."

My stomach flipped. It was coming -- she was gay, and I was going to have to sleep with her to get the money, and for twenty-five million, I just might do it.

"I'm hoping you'd consider an invitation to High Tea with a group of my friends. We meet a few times a year at each other's homes to discuss things that I'm sure would be of interest to you. We call ourselves High Skirts."

Even before responding, I couldn't help but laugh at the name. "High Skirts, isn't that kind of sexist?"

Her French manicured fingernails gracefully swept away the strands of hair that had fallen across her eyes.

"Exactly, so who'd expect it to be us?"

I sat back, crossed my legs, ready to receive whatever else she had to offer. "Mrs. Cosby, I'd be happy to attend your tea."

In that instant, a broad smile filled her face and I realized that in all the pictures I'd seen of her online, this face hadn't been one of them.

"Great, because we're the women behind the men who *think* they run this damn city. Now listen up, this is how it'll play out. First we'll have champagne, then Gwendolyn will email you an itinerary detailing tomorrow's brief press conference. The necessary paperwork for us both to sign off on as a patron donor will be messengered to your Craig Ernst. I'm giving you my personal cell so if you have any concerns please call me, I'll do my best to make myself available. Are we clear?"

"Mrs. Cosby, yes we're clear; I don't know how to thank you, but thank you." I said, unable to imagine how this would change things for Blessed Babies.

"Good, now let's have champagne."

That night at home, I was too excited to cook, especially after six bottles of Grand Krug Cuvee champagne were delivered with a note from Mrs. Cosby stating that we were on our way to bigger things. This woman had class and I planned to be in her company for a long time.

My night was busy, filled with not only tending to my daughter, but there were also phone calls to be made, emails to be sent, and I had to thank Mr. Haney. But more importantly, there was Malik to contend with. Not so much about Mrs. Cosby, but about how I'd gotten to her. To test his mood I sent him a text.

Tiffany: Nylah wants to wait up

Malik·   10:30

Tiffany: Chinese?

Malik: Works for me

Malik arrived home at exactly ten-thirty and even though I was excited to tell him about my meeting with Mrs. Cosby, I'd yet to figure out the best way to tell him about Haney being the catalyst.

"What's up? Nylah sleep?" he asked, walking into the kitchen.

"Yes, I checked on her a few minutes ago. I hope you're still hungry?"

"Starving."

As was our routine while he ate, I listened to him recap his day at City Hall, filling me in on the search for Officer Campbell's killer and the ongoing issue of whether or not to decriminalize marijuana.

"I landed another patron donor today," I casually offered when he finished.

"Nice," he said, paying more attention to Sports Center and the beer I'd sat down in front of him, than to what I was saying.

"Raquel Turner-Cosby is donating $25 million to Blessed Babies. We have a press conference tomorrow."

Chopsticks down, television muted. "Woman, are you serious or you trying to distract me?"

"I'm serious, I met with her this afternoon and we're holding a press conference tomorrow. Mr. Haney connected the two of us."

"For someone who was so paranoid, look who's friends with Haney now. But seriously, how the hell did he, or did you, do that?"

Either Malik wasn't surprised or maybe my being involved with Haney wasn't a big deal; it was simply business.

"She sent word through him that she wanted to meet. I guess they're friends."

"Turner-Cosby doesn't have friends, only puppets that do her bidding. What's next?" he asked, returning to his iPad, presumably tweeting.

"What do you mean?"

"Is she taking over your center?"

"Of course not, why would you ask that?"

He finished off his beer before saying, "She's a power hungry woman who takes what she wants, that's why."

His comment was deflating because instead of being happy for BBWC, and me, he was distrustful.

"Thanks, Malik, I'm glad you're happy for me," I said, turning my back to begin loading the dishwasher.

"It's not that, I am happy. Usually though, when people throw that kind of money at you, they want something in return. I'm sorry."

Changing the subject, I told him, "I saw Wesley today."

"He's been trying to meet with me and I haven't had time."

"What does he want?"

"I don't know, but I don't have time for his whining about what's wrong in the community. He needs to take that to Wu What time is this press conference tomorrow and where's it being held?" Malik asked, turning the conversation back to Mrs. Cosby.

"It'll be at noon, in time for the news and it's being held at the Wellness Center."

"You know she's a Republican, right?"

"Does it matter?"

"Would be nice if she'd consider tossing some money into my re-election campaign."

"She doesn't appear to be the type of woman you'd ask to toss anything."

"Good, I'm happy for you. Any more Chinese?"

"Sure, here, give me your bowl."

"I'm going to stay down here and watch the game, you going to bed?"

"I wasn't, but if you'd rather be alone. . . "

"No, it's not that, I just have some documents to read and a few calls to make, so I won't be much company and I know you have a big day tomorrow."

I realized then that my husband was dismissing me. If it was for work, then fine, but it felt more like a slight because of my meeting with Mrs. Cosby. But like it or not, I was not turning down what she had to offer.

Chapter 10

Maxed Out

To make up for my cancelled birthday trip to New York, Malik agreed to attend Max and Lynn's dinner party. I was a bit nervous because rarely did Malik and I attend social gatherings that weren't politically motivated. However, my husband assured me that the night would not turn into a debate.

Following Max's instructions on the party being casual, I dressed in a knee length smoke gray pencil skirt with exposed buttons down the back, a sheer pink blouse on top, matching silk teddy underneath, and a pair of killer three-inch heels that I knew would be off by the end of the night. Then, for the first time, I dabbed on *his* perfume, Farmesiana in all my special places. And to show Max I wasn't boring, I took my hair out of its bun, flat ironed it straight, and wore it down over my left shoulder with a side part. Even I was surprised at how sexy I not only looked, but felt. This, I told myself, was going to be a good night.

To ensure we wouldn't be the first to arrive, I'd purposely lied to Malik, telling him that the party started 45 minutes later than it did. He was picking me up after having attended an earlier cocktail reception at the Union League, which worked out well because Phinn rang the bell at exactly eight-fifteen.

Sliding into the backseat, before Malik even spoke to me, he gently took my face in his hands, bringing me to him for a kiss. He pulled back and then kissed me again before nuzzling my neck. With a smile dangling at the corner of his mouth, he said, "Stop the car, Phinn, I think you picked up the wrong woman."

"Maybe you should take me out more often, to more than those stodgy political functions," I teased, pushing back from him.

He moved my hair from my shoulder and playfully bit my neck. "Seriously turn this car around, we're going home."

Phinn bought the car to a halt. "Yes, sir."

"Malik, stop playing, you're going to make us late and you're messing up my hair."

"You smell so good, what do you have on?" he asked.

I smoothed my hair back into place while he stared at the sexy woman he'd forgotten was his wife, never though answering his question about my fragrance. "Phinn, please don't listen to him," I said, tapping on the seat in front of us.

"Sir?"

"Phinn, it's whatever Mrs. Skinner wants tonight, how's that?"

"If it's whatever I want, then I want your undivided attention all night, beginning right now and that means no calls, no texting and no social media."

"And that you shall have," he said, before putting away his mobile and closing the cover to his iPad.

With his attention now focused on me, he asked about Blessed Babies, the Philly schools I'd been researching for Nylah, and when I thought would be the best time to travel to Paris. He even asked if the new housekeeper was working out. I relished in all his adoration.

The drive to Wyncote took about 25 minutes and after turning off Church Lane, we veered into what seemed to be a park, until we came to Serpentine Lane. There were only five houses on the tree-lined street, and at the end of the cul-de-sac there was a circular driveway leading to Max's two-story colonial.

When the double doors opened, a bubbly Max, outfitted in a candy apple red maxi dress, with her locs pulled up in a loose bun, greeted us.

"Tiffany, oh my God, I'm so glad you made it," she exclaimed over the music of John Legend singing, *"Tonight"* in the background. Pulling me in for a hug like we'd been friends for years, she said, "And you smell wonderful!"

"Thanks, Max, and I see who's wearing the bun tonight," I teased, bringing girly laughter from the both of us.

"Mr. Mayor, I'm sorry; good evening, it's nice to finally meet you," Max said, a bit more reserved, yet opening her arms to hug Malik as well.

"Tiffany, Mayor Skinner, this is my husband, Lynn," she said of the thick and handsome man who came to stand next to her.

Taking my hand and kissing it, Lynn said, "First Lady, it's a pleasure to meet the woman my wife keeps talking about."

Liking him already, I responded, "We're happy to be here."

Extending a hearty handshake and chest bump to Malik, he said, "Welcome to my castle, brother."

Max gave him a disapproving look as if he'd been disrespectful.

Sounding like every bit the politician, Malik told them, "I've been looking forward to meeting the both of you, and attending tonight's event."

I wanted to say, it's not an event, Malik, it's a party; but instead I turned my attention to Max, handing her a gift bag that included a bottle of Gran Krug champagne and a money tree plant. "Here, these are for you."

"First stop is the bar. You drink Bourbon, right Mayor?"

"Lynn, on that you'd be correct."

We followed Max and Lynn around the open staircase that separated the formal living room on the right and dining room on the left. Behind the staircase was the family room, centered with a curvaceous beige leather sofa that was across from a brick fireplace. Above the fireplace hung a 60-inch flat screen television.

"Everyone's outside," Max said, gesturing toward open French doors that led to a terrace where I could see the sparks from an open pit. "Tiff, before you go out, I have something for you. Now I know you like your red wine, see if you like this."

"I'm sure I will," I said, following her to the makeshift bar in the dining room.

"Zen Zin, a red Zinfandel? You ever have it? If you don't like it, I also picked up a bottle of Jordan Cabernet Sauvignon 2010, how about that?" she asked, pouring it into a sexy long stemmed goblet.

"What did you do? Become a wine enthusiast overnight?" I asked while swishing and breathing in the wine before taking a sip. "This is good."

"C'mon, we're well stocked," she said, leading me out to the terrace.

The three other couples had already arrived, and we were introduced to Chris, a professor of English at Temple, and his wife Christy, an administrator at Haverford High and Renee, a PwC accountant, and her husband, Thomas, who owned a string of daycares throughout the suburbs. Lastly there was Peterman, Lynn's fleet manager and his wife Sonia, a stay-at-home mom to three children.

Everyone was quite friendly and welcoming with backgrounds that made for a diverse conversation. It was a bit uncomfortable though, having everyone in such a personal setting keep referring to Malik as either Mr. Mayor or Mayor Skinner.

Fortunately, it wasn't a sit down dinner, but the appetizers were heavy and plentiful, both being passed and set on the high top tables in the house. Servers offered seared scallops and lollipop lamb chops and there were endless dishes of seafood guacamole, honey chicken, sushi, overstuffed potatoes, and riblets. I wanted to taste everything.

"How'd you come up with such a variety of food?" I asked Max.

"Girl, I've had so many of these gatherings over the years that I started keeping a list of my friends' favorite things. Thus the theme for tonight! C'mon with me in the kitchen."

If I thought Max's home was beautiful, her kitchen was a chef's dream. Besides all the food that was being replenished by the servers, there was a glass front Jenn Air refrigerator, gleaming copper pots suspended from an overhead rack and frosted glass front cabinets. And underneath the stone kitchen island was a built-in Electrolux wine cooler that was fully stocked.

By no means was my semi-detached home in Girard Estates shabby, as I'd taken great care in selecting furniture, paint colors, art, and window treatments. But the Welker's home was straight off the pages of *Architectural Digest*. It made me want to immediately go home and redecorate.

"What the hell kind of stove is this?" I asked, admiring the grill and range hood that extended to the ceiling.

"It's a Wolf; they said it was damaged, but it's like new to me."

"I get it, it fell off a truck?"

"You didn't hear it from me."

"Max, your house is beautiful," I said, wandering through to the dining room with its high back leather chairs and a table that seated twelve.

From the doorway, she said, "I know you're wondering about all this on a teacher and trucker's salary."

"I am not counting your money."

Twisting her lips, she chided, "Yeah, right."

"Maybe a little."

"When I told you Lynn was a truck driver, actually he owns the company, Welker Trucking, six trucks, drivers, staff and an office over on Stenton Avenue."

"Really?"

"His clients are interior designers, very high end, like Carmen, she'll be here later."

My eyes were wide in disbelief. Talk about making an impression and I thought their home would be average because he was a truck driver and she a teacher. I couldn't have been more wrong.

"Don't look so shocked, his insurance premiums are ridiculous. I mean we're talking transportation for like thirty-thousand dollar couches and million dollar chandeliers."

"Then I can't wait to see the rest of house," I exclaimed.

Max was about to take me on a tour when I heard Malik in the other room getting loud with excitement. I peeped into the family room to see what the noise was all about.

"Tiffany, woman come here; I have somebody for you to meet."

Putting his arm around me, Malik proudly said, "This here is Coach Marshall Dillon, of Gwynedd Mercy College and his wife, Carmen, designer to the stars."

"Nice to meet you, Carmen and Marshall," I said, extending my hand to shake, but instead they took turns greeting me with a hug, while my husband stood there grinning.

Looking from Lynn to Malik, Marshall asked, "How the hell do you two know each other?"

"Our wives met at the spa," Malik told him.

Hugging Malik again, Marshall exclaimed, "This is great! Man, I haven't seen you since you took office."

Carmen chimed in as well, "Is Tootie still down in South Philly? How's Nanny? I stopped in to see her around the holidays."

"Everybody's good. Wow, this is great!" he replied, honestly happy to see old friends.

"What about Blu Eyes? I hear that crazy-ass Negro's a cop; how'd that happen? I know for sure he got a record," Coach Dillon joked.

"Don't we all got a record, at least a juvenile one?" Malik surprisingly responded.

"Point Breeze for life!" they all said together.

I had to laugh because I'd never seen Malik like this, among real friends, with the exception of the time we spent with Tootie and Wesley. It was also a surprise that he'd never mentioned these two.

By now everyone was back in the family room, joining in on the Point Breeze reunion.

"Mr. Mayor, looks like it's old home day for you," said Peterman.

"C'mon man, call me Skinner, we're among friends," responded my husband who was pouring himself another drink.

"So tell me, man, what's happening down the old way? I'm all the way up in Lower Merion now."

Malik lowered his voice, making me wonder what he was about to say.

"Here's one for you, that dude, Tootie's daughter's father, well she found out around Christmas that he was pitching for the other team."

"Get the hell outta here. What she do, beat the brother down?" Carmen asked, now standing in between her husband and mine.

"She wanted to, I had to talk to her, she was pretty messed up about it," Malik told them.

I was a little taken aback that Malik had never told me that story. I'd have to follow up to get the details because I was sure Tootie put on a show hearing that news.

"Man, what's up with your boy?" Coach asked.

"Yeah, Wesley seems to have an unapologetic zest for trouble, always did," offered Carmen.

"I did my best by him, but it wasn't enough," Malik told them.

"You know he was always jealous of your moves," Coach added.

Shifting her attention to me, Carmen asked, "Tiffany, didn't I see you on television recently? You're working with that Turner-Cosby woman. That's a big deal."

"Actually, she donated to our Wellness Center."

"Right, the cuddle campaign," said Christy.

"Hey, Skinner, let's cuddle now and post some videos on your Twitter page," Carmen suggested, her eyes on me as she loosely put her arm through Malik's.

I practically spit out my drink at the audacity of this woman, old friend or not, she was flirting with Malik right in front of me, and her husband. I knew women vied for his attention, but they usually had more respect than to do it when I was around. I'd have to keep my eyes on this Carmen.

"It might look a little risqué if we all start hugging up in here, you know like one big orgy," Coach joked, causing everyone to break out in laughter, yet his eyes were on me, making me wonder if that might be something him and his wife were into.

Max must've sensed my uneasiness when she told them, "You're supposed to cuddle babies, and I don't see no babies around."

"How much money will it take? Here take this," Chris said, putting ten twenty-dollar bills on top of the fireplace mantel.

"The campaign is closed," I shared, hoping they weren't trying to impress my husband.

"But the money don't stop," Peterman said, as he too dug into his pocket.

"Yeah, woman, let them unlock them wallets," said Malik, who I noticed was on his third drink, told the group.

Stepping away to the bar to refill his drink, Lynn offered, "I ain't hugging a bunch of men, but I'll put up some cash."

"Seriously, how can we help with your baby project?" Sonia asked.

"Let's cuddle, c'mon y'all, let's take some selfies," Carmen said, now having become obnoxious.

"Carmen, I don't know if that's a good idea, we've been drinking," Max told her.

"Anything to support my beautiful wife, c'mon," Malik responded.

"At least take that drink out your hand," I told him before reaching over to take his glass.

"This is great, I'm going to post to Twitter and let my city know that the Mayor knows how to have a good time, for the right cause, right, woman?" he asked, winking at me, this time to make sure I was okay with it.

"Go on, Malik, enjoy yourself."

With the exception of me, who was taking the picture, the entire group gathered in the living room to take what turned into several pictures, from everyone's individual cell phone.

"All right folks, pictures posted, now give up the money!" demanded Lynn, peeling bills from under his money clip.

"We're turning up tonight!" said Carmen, who was now trying to get Malik to dance to *"Blurred Lines."* Luckily, he declined, as Malik wasn't the least bit naïve.

"This calls for champagne. The Skinners brought Grand Krug Cuvee," Lynn told everyone, as he held up the bottle.

"That's the good shit, open it up," said Renee, whose husband couldn't keep his hands off her and was grinding on her butt the entire time *"Happy"* played.

Once we toasted, before I knew it, we were all dancing to Frankie Beverly belting out *"Before I Let Go."* I couldn't recall the last time I'd seen Malik dance like he was at an old school basement party. This was good because so far, there'd been no knock on the door from Phinn saying the Mayor was needed and I'd only caught Malik checking his watch twice. The last time, I put my hand over his wrist, kissed him and said, "Not tonight."

"You having a good time?" I asked him in between him trying to feed me fondue-dipped strawberries and kiss me at the same time.

"Woman, this is the best. I love you," he whispered.

It was Carmen though, who I couldn't seem to warm up to. Her eyes caught mine every time I turned her way. I'd have to ask Malik if she'd been one of his childhood sweethearts. Instead of being jealous, after a few drinks I thought it was comical the way she kept checking me out.

Maybe she, too, realized that I wasn't as boring as my public persona.

I was the one though, who was envious of Max and Lynn for having a normal life and being able to entertain without pretense. Who could I possibly invite to my house that would create this type of atmosphere?

By one in the morning, things had begun to wind down and everyone had left except me and Malik, Carmen, and Coach, who were on the terrace smoking the Cuban cigars that Lynn had passed out. They were seated around the fire pit so deep in conversation about South Philly that I lost interest. Even Lynn had stepped away to his office to check on the next day's logistics.

Max suggested a tour of the house since we'd never gotten around to doing that. She grabbed a bottle of wine and we headed upstairs. The front room was an enormous master suite, complete with a seating area overlooking the driveway. Connecting to their bedroom, was a large bathroom, with an extra large Jacuzzi, a rainforest shower stall and a private toilet area. On the other side of the bathroom was another door that led to a walk-in closet. Down the hall from their room were two smaller bedrooms that had been converted into Lynn's office. Finally at the back of the house was a cozy sitting room with a view of the park, and a winding staircase that led down to the kitchen.

"Max, your house is amazing."

"Thanks, girl. I can't tell you how happy I am you're here. Lynn bet me that the Mayor," she laughed, "that Skinner wasn't going to show."

"We really needed this. I don't think I've ever seen Malik enjoy himself so much," I shared with her, as we stood looking out the large window at the pit flames flickering in the dark below.

"Good. Now tell me, since you and I haven't really had a chance to talk all night, how've you been?"

"Honestly, Max, there's so much going on, if I wanted to tell you I wouldn't know how," I said.

"I was worried about you."

I decided to take a chance, a big one and turning to face her, I asked, "Can I tell you something in the strictest of confidence?"

"I would never break your confidence, but are you sure you wanna tell me?"

Lowering my voice, I said, "It's the former DA, Greg Haney, he showed up in my room that night."

Her eyes flew open in astonishment. "What night? At Woodloch?" she exclaimed a little too loudly, causing me to cover her mouth with my hand.

"For what? Do you know him like that? I mean why would he come to your room, unless. Wait, no wonder you were acting all paranoid at breakfast. Tiffany, what's going on?"

I kicked my shoes off and slowed, pacing the space, pretending to be admiring her artwork, then said, "It's a long story, from a long time ago, but it's not like that now.

I probably shouldn't even be telling you this, but I have no one to talk to about it."

Max had come to stand so close behind me that it stopped me from moving.

"What about your husband, does he know? Did you tell him? I'm so confused."

"No, I can't, Malik would kill him if he found out. Hell, he might kill me. You don't understand, it's complicated."

She refilled our glasses, then stated, "I need you to help me understand why that man would come to your hotel room, three hours away from Philadelphia."

My eyes told her what I couldn't say.

"Wait, you're not saying that you and him are. . ."

"No, no, we didn't, I swear, but a long time ago before he went to prison."

"You were in a relationship with him, the District Attorney? Wasn't he married to some white woman?" she asked, pulling me down onto the futon.

"He was and I was seeing his son at first and then things got out of control."

"Wait a minute, it's all coming back to me. When you had that club you used to date his corny ass son, G-Dog; he went to jail for selling drugs or something and oh my God, so did his father, it was a big scandal. And he's your sister's father too, right? That was all in the paper, I remember. This is crazy and your husband doesn't know."

"Like I said, it's more complicated than I can say."

"Girl oh girl, your husband was the one who uncovered their mess. I remember that was all over the news. He moved right up the political ladder and after that, he was like a hero. I mean, he brought down the district attorney."

We were quiet, if only for a minute, before Max figured it out. "Wait, girl are you telling me you were doing both of them, father and son?"

I bowed my head in embarrassment before saying, "I'm begging you, Max, don't tell anyone, you can't even share it with Lynn. I need to know I can trust you."

"Never! But I gotta say, you're a bad bitch, Mrs. Skinner," she teased, throwing up a high five.

"Not the bitch I need to be. I'm trying so hard to keep my distance from him."

"Don't sound like that's working too well for you."

"It's not. I mean I haven't had sex with him yet, but he does have this way of getting to me. I can't stop thinking about how it was then," I said without realizing I was biting my lip.

"You poor thing, I feel for you 'cause I've been there. I had a man like that once, and girl, not only was he loaded, but he knew how to make me. . . damn."

Simultaneously, we both took a big gulp of our drinks. Lost in our memories, neither of us spoke for a few seconds.

"Then you totally understand. Max, I swear in the last few months, I've come to realize that as women, we're programmed from little girls to you know, get a college education, and then in the end, it's get married, have kids, that's it. But nobody tells you to look for passion, real sexual passion."

"You're getting deep on me, but you're right. Once a man has touched that core, that spot that even you didn't know existed, well you're screwed, literally and figuratively."

Max moved to the edge of the futon, then turned to me and said, "Now it's my turn to tell you something in confidence."

"I'm listening."

"A long time ago, while Lynn and I were dating, I got involved in something that almost caused me to chose the wrong man."

"You cheated on Lynn?"

"No, well not initially. Initially, I was only dancing, but then came the private dances."

"Huh?"

"Dancer, stripper, you know on a pole. C'mon Tiff, you know what I'm talking about."

Holding my mouth to keep from laughing too loud, I said, "You can't be serious. You're a teacher."

"Actually, I'm dead serious. It started out innocent, plain curiosity. Well anyway, it happened and I made a ton of cash. How do you think I got this house? It was all good until I met a man like him, like Haney. Someone who knew no limits when it came to making love to a woman."

"Girl, Haney doesn't make love," I lowered my voice and whispered, through a smile, "He fucks."

"Exactly."

With Max's eyes holding a gleam of deviltry, she continued, "This man elevated me sexually to places a woman shouldn't be taken. It was like he'd studied me, making me feel him even when he wasn't there. But when he discovered I wasn't another broke stripper, everything changed and to make it worse, right before I moved here, Lynn found out and my life imploded."

"What happened? What did you do?"

She waved her hand, "Believe me it wasn't easy, but Lynn finally sat down and listened to me. Really Tiffany, I told him the truth, how it had originally been a dare while I was on this boring vacation and strangely enough, I became so good that it turned into a lucrative second job. What I didn't tell him was about that one man who turned me out. I'll admit though sometimes, every now and then, I second-guess myself. You know when I want to be reckless, to do that nasty stuff you can't ask your husband to do. It just ain't fair."

We both grew quiet, caught up again in memories that we shouldn't have been remembering, until I said, "Max, I'll keep your secret if you do me one favor."

"And what's that?"

"Teach me how to dance."

Chapter 11

BBWC

It had been two month's since Officer Campbell's murder and no matter how many persons of interest they'd marched into homicide; all leads had proven to be dead ends, mostly people trying to cash in on the reward money.

Commissioner Outlaw and the homicide division were catching hell from the public, and so was Malik for not having kept his promise of keeping the city safe. Sometimes I wondered if people expected him to don a uniform, holster a gun, and literally fight crime himself. When I said these things to him, he would tell me I didn't understand how the city worked.

There was some good news though, for my husband, and the city. Vetri Construction & Engineering, a 70-year-old firm, had agreed to relocate their headquarters from Conshohocken to the Cira Center in Philadelphia, along with expanding their operations division to the Naval Yard. Both would be adding approximately 200 jobs, some union employees, others would be welfare to work and ex-offenders, all of which gave Vetri a huge tax break. For that, the city patted Malik on the back with the hopes that other businesses outside the city might follow.

In addition, the city's Office of Sustainability had been the winner of a White House competition on solar energy that Malik had fought Council President Gillman to approve. That news conference, held earlier in the week, lauded Malik as moving Philadelphia into the future. Malik and the program's developer were now waiting for a date to attend a White House reception to formerly accept the award from President Obama.

For me, Spring was definitely in the air and this morning I was happy to be on my way to the BBWC Executive Board meeting, being held in the Lincoln Room on the second floor of the Union League. Even though Malik and I weren't members, we were often at the League and this morning it was on Judge Renwick's account.

Our board consisted of ten members, all well-respected movers and shakers in the city. Members had either been selected or volunteered, knowing we had an uphill battle with the platform we'd chosen. One of the by-laws for being on our board was that each member was required to donate $10,000 of their own money, with a pledge to bring in at least one-million each, all of which we'd surpassed.

Since the beginning of the year, there'd only been subcommittee meetings and a litany of emails between us, causing some members to feel alienated since we hadn't met prior to the press conference with Mrs. Cosby. That was all about posturing from certain members and I knew exactly who they were.

Gretchen Hockstein, VP of Operations at PGW, and Elise Nelson, CEO of Nelson Broadcasting were always the first to arrive, and this morning was no different. Gretchen resided in St. David's, PA with her husband Bill, a highly regarded Wall Street Banker. Elise, on the other hand lived at the Ritz Carlton residences with her wife, an actress who spent most of her time in California.

At every opportunity, the two of them bragged about the money they'd pulled in, and the circles in which they traveled. Needless to say, they were the ones most shocked about my signing on RTC Holdings.

It wasn't so much my position as the mayor's wife, but they expected me to have an Ivy League background, rather than a bachelor's degree from Temple University. Perhaps having worked in corporate America would've given me more credibility with these ladies. But now I had something they didn't, Raquel Turner-Cosby.

It didn't matter to me if I measured up to people's expectations so long as those people they called friends contributed their old money or their new millennial money to BBWC. For that, it was worth listening to all the places they traveled and the persons to whom they entertained because I wasn't in the least bit envious of their superficial lives.

"Good morning, Gretchen, Elise," I said, greeting them when I entered the conference room.

"First Lady, how are you?" asked Gretchen, keeping her back to me and pouring orange juice.

"I'm doing great, looks like this should be a good meeting for us."

"We're all waiting to hear about your new cohort, the mysterious Raquel Turner-Cosby," said Elise, eagerly standing in my personal space.

"I'm not sure I'd call her a cohort; she's a supporter like everyone else. She's just one of the wealthiest."

Standing off in the corner was Judge Renwick, who was on the phone probably with some defense attorney, threatening to put his client back in jail. He nodded hello, then returned to his rant.

On the other side of the room, Craig was busy organizing his handouts to deliver his financial report. Ever since the contribution from Turner-Cosby, we'd begun to receive commitments from other deep-pocketed donors. Today, we'd see the breakdown and tally on where our finances stood.

I attempted to get around them and put my things down, but they had me hostage.

"Well I'm sure that woman's on for more than she's told you," echoed Gretchen.

"You're reading way too much into this, Mrs. Cosby simply wants to support BBWC."

"How'd you get to her anyway? We sit on the board of Trustees at Drexel with her and when we mentioned meeting with her to discuss Blessed Babies she blew me off," said a perplexed Elise.

I turned to see Janae slipping into the room with her clipboard and iPad in tow, scurrying for a coffee and croissant. I knew little about my assistant's personal life, except she was a tall and fashionable 23-year-old, no children and she lived in a studio apartment at 2100 Chestnut. I didn't generate enough work to employ her full time, and I no idea what else she did to generate enough income to live in such a ritzy building. But when listening to her, nothing else mattered except shopping and living in the city. The one thing I did know over the last three years was that she had a good sense of anticipating my needs.

"Good morning, everyone," said Deacon Brown when he entered the room. "Tiffany, I need to speak with you before the meeting starts," he said, his hand on my elbow.

"Of course. Is everything all right?" I asked, unable to imagine what could possibly be so urgent that it couldn't wait for our meeting to begin. I dropped my things on my chair and followed him.

"I could use your help," he told me once were outside the room.

"What is it? What's wrong?"

"How much do you know about Raquel Turner-Cosby?"

"Probably as much as anybody else, why?"

"All I'm asking is if you get the opportunity, can you tell her that Deacon Brown would like a few minutes of her time."

"I'm not sure what that'll mean coming from me."

"In your position, it'll mean a lot. Trust me."

"I don't know what position you think I'm in, but she simply signed on as a patron for donor. I can't go to her and ask for favors."

"You don't get it, do you?"

"Obviously I don't," I said, not wanting to admit she'd told me about the donation to Shiloh's building committee.

Luckily before I broke that confidence, we were interrupted by the arrival of my favorite board member, Brother Ahmeen Sadiq who I knew from my days as a nightclub owner. For our board and the city, Brother Sadiq represented the Philadelphia's Muslim community and was often called upon to diffuse volatile situations.

Recently Commissioner Outlaw had sought out his advice as they searched for and profiled the cop killer. His full time job though, was working out of DA Leander's office as a member of the Gun Violence Task Force.

Brother Sadiq was every bit the ladies man, with intense dark brown eyes, a smooth bald head and a meticulously groomed Lihyah beard. A devout Muslim, he made Salah five times a day, stayed away from pork, attended Jummah Prayers on Friday, and maintained two wives and several children.

I always joked with Brother Sadiq that if Malik and I ever broke up, I'd be his third wife, albeit without the hijab and khimar. However, what I liked best about Brother Sadiq was that he always smelled good, the kind of scent that made a woman want to get underneath a man. I didn't know if it were Muslim oils or if his cologne was from the counter at Saks.

"Greetings, Sister Skinner," he said, pulling me in for a hug so warm that I didn't want to let go.

"Assalamu Alaikum, Brother Sadiq. How are you this morning?"

"I'm blessed to be here for you," he said to me before turning to Deacon Brown. "Greetings, Deacon Brown."

"Mr. Sadiq, good morning."

Before I could swoon anymore, Janae peeked her head out the door and said they were ready to start.

Judge Renwick called the meeting to order and we began moving through the morning's agenda; Jim Molk, our secretary, who was also a restaurateur and head of the Molk Restaurant Organization, began with the minutes from our previous teleconference. Judge Renwick gave the executive report on our selection of a CEO to head up the Wellness Center, followed by a report from Gretchen on rounding out the staffing requirements.

Michael, although not a board member, was there to provide an update on how things were shaping up for the Gala, ribbon-cutting ceremony, and our overall public relations campaign.

"What's the crowdfunding page look like?" I asked.

"Final count was seventy-five thousand as of this morning and we'll be uploading the photos and videos to the BBWC website by end of the week. It did more than we expected and even though the campaign has ended, people won't stop hugging and posting. Have any of you visited our Facebook page recently?"

"It's received over 13,000 hits this week," Janae added.

"Let me also add that to date, we've sold 214 tickets for the gala, bringing in $53,500, but you'll see that in Craig's report."

"That's good work," I told Michael, offering him a round of applause.

"Craig, let's hear the financial report. You know that's what everyone's waiting on," said Judge Renwick.

"Yes sir, I'm ready, here we go!"

While Janae distributed his handouts, Craig had us focus on the screen, where he showed slides from his laptop.

"Our goal was to raise $40 million to cover operating costs for ten years. As of January 2, we were at $15 million. By March, we'd received $220 thousand in donations, and then, last week the big one hit, taking us over the top, twenty-five million dollars from the phenomenal Raquel Turner-Cosby, all of course thanks to our First Lady!"

Everyone clapped, but he wasn't finished, "And let's not forget that cute little donation from her brother Julian 'Huli' Johnson for twenty-five thousand."

"So what you're saying is, if we don't raise another penny, we're solid for ten years?"

"Yes Judge, yes, yes, yes!"

"Craig, I picked up a check yesterday from the PO Box," offered Janae.

Rubbing his hands together in anticipation, he asked, "Tell me quick Janae, how much?"

"It's a cashier's check for $5 thousand from The Friends of Tiffany Johnson-Skinner."

"From who?" asked Deacon Brown.

"The accompanying letter says it's from your friends at the Welker's party. It's signed by several people," Craig said, waving the letter in the air.

"Are you running for office, Tiffany?" asked Gretchen.

"Let me see that," I told Craig, holding out my hand for the letter, and wondering how those few twenties on Max's mantel had turned into five thousand dollars. "I barely know them," I said, more to myself than the group.

Ralph Dovi, our Vice Chair and the VP of Player Relations for the Philadelphia Flyers, began to clap, the others followed suit.

"Whoever they are, I think it's pretty damn nice to have friends like that," Ralph commented in his deep and distinct voice.

"Excuse me, but I'd like to take a minute to discuss Raquel Turner-Cosby," Gretchen said. "Are you expecting any of *her friends* to donate?"

"I don't know her friends," I said, not mentioning I had a date for High Tea and giving Janae the eye not to mention it either, then continued with, "I believe a few of her business acquaintances have made donations. I'm sure it's in Craig's report."

"She'll want to take over, that's what she does," commented Deacon Brown, making me wonder why he, who was ever the optimist, was now being so pessimistic. I couldn't wait to speak to Malik about it, maybe something was wrong.

Judge Renwick chimed in and said, "Folks, seeing that we've surpassed our financial goal, might I suggest we put some of that money in a reserve account and perhaps start a foundation connected to BBWC so there are no questions about how our finances are being used. I mean, if that's okay with you, Craig."

"Judge, I'm all over it," Craig told him, as he fervently tapped notes into his laptop.

I stood up, poured myself another cup of coffee and leaned against the back of my chair waiting for them to finish.

"Tiffany, has she asked to sit on our board? Is her contribution contingent on anything? I mean, have any promises been made?" asked Elise, who didn't seem to want to let this go.

"Who cares what she wants, we got what we wanted, didn't we?" said Ralph, sounding every bit annoyed.

"Let me be clear, nobody is controlling this board, or the Blessed Babies Wellness Center. And honestly, I'm really confused as to why everyone is so suspicious of this woman giving us twenty-five million dollars. Would you like me to give it back? She signed the same agreement as our other patron donors, so if I'm missing something, please tell me what the problem is."

Judge Renwick's powerful, but soft voice garnered everyone's attention as if he were on the bench. "You folks are losing focus, worried about some woman who's only trying to help us. Now listen up, because I don't have all morning. Six years ago, there were three of us at this same table, Craig, Tiffany and myself, with thirty-thousand dollars and now we're ten members looking at over forty-million. I'd say that's not only significant, but a credit to all of us. Now what the hell are you complaining about?"

Brother Sadiq's sexy voice spoke up, "I agree with the Judge; we've done more than we set out to do and we should be celebrating."

"I'm with you, Brother Sadiq," Craig told him, as he began to gather his things.

"Damn it then, let's celebrate," said Judge Renwick before going into the hall and requesting that the server bring us two bottles of Dom Perignon.

"It's 8:30 in the morning," complained Dr. Marie Ennis, a cardiologist at St. Christopher's Hospital for Children.

"Then we'll mix it with orange juice," commented Jim Molk.

Once the champagne was poured, everyone stood, their glasses held high in the middle of the table.

The smile that washed across my face was evident for everyone when I said, "Judge, will you please do the honors?"

He nodded and began, "May we *all* have the hindsight to know where we've been, the foresight to know where we're going, and the insight to know when we've gone too far."

After hailing a toast, everyone began to scatter, but as I was packing up to leave, Dr. Ennis sat down in the chair beside me. "The old DA came to my office the other day."

I steeled my body and asked as casually as I could, "Really, does he have a sick child?"

"No, not at all. Actually, he's quite a charmer and he's interested in sitting on our board; what do you think?" she said, while tapping her fingers on the table.

Knowing Mr. Haney's motives, but unsure of hers, I replied, "Our board only holds ten."

"We could make an exception since we don't have a lawyer and we've been wanting one. He is a results oriented man, which is clearly evident by the work he's been doing around the city," she said trying to defend him while hiding behind a coquettish grin, which led me to ponder if their relationship was more than platonic.

"I believe he was disbarred when he went to federal prison," I answered.

"What about as a legal consultant to review contracts and the like? I mean, your husband certainly seems set on giving him a second chance."

She was really pushing for him and I'm sure he'd put her up to this without her even realizing it, that's how Haney was, he'd ingratiate himself to you and you'd find yourself his cheerleader and clearly Dr. Ennis had fallen for his antics.

My mobile vibrated with a call, but before answering, I said, "My husband is only Mayor of this city, and does not sit at the head of this board. Now if you'll excuse me, I need to take this call."

"Think about it, he could make a difference."

Chapter 12

Happy Mother's Day

It was the Wednesday prior to Mother's Day and Malik was packing for New Orleans, where he was attending the Black Mayor's Conference. Usually we took this opportunity to sneak in a mini vacation, extending it by a day or two, but this year I couldn't make it. Nylah had come down with a fever, and leaving her with Nanny or my parents wasn't an option because when my daughter was sick, the only person she wanted was her mother.

With so much needing to be done prior to the BBWC gala and opening, I wasn't as disappointed as I'd led Malik to believe. His being away would give me the opportunity to personally wrap up a lot of loose ends and hold a meeting with Janae, Craig, and Michael at my house.

The other reason I was glad to be home was that Haney had managed to get himself on the agenda. For someone who couldn't practice law, he'd made quite a name for himself since January.

Along with his legal consulting, and spearheading the absolution of eminent domain, he'd also developed a platform on prison reform, re-entry, and recidivism. By all accounts, he'd become the ideal reformed inmate and the face of second chances.

What I wasn't ready for was the request Malik made while packing up to leave. It seemed Cyndi was trying to catapult her experience as press secretary into a television job.

"Cyndi would like to interview you for a series she's writing for the *Huffington Post* on the wives of inner city mayors," he stated, in the process of zipping up his garment bag.

"You mean she's not going with you to New Orleans? I can't believe she passed up that opportunity," I said, handing him his toiletries.

He stopped his packing and took a seat on the bed. "Tiffany, you're not being fair. That woman has done nothing but help me."

"Why do you always take up for her? You know she wants you," I teased, managing to wedge myself between his open legs.

"Maybe because even if she were interested, I'm not. " He kissed me and said, "Tiffany Johnson-Skinner is all the woman I need."

"Oh please. Well you better make sure she doesn't leave anything else at my house when you have your 'meetings'."

He squeezed my butt cheeks, causing us both to fall backward on the bed. "Okay, what's it going to cost me for you to do the interview? C'mon, she belongs to some liberal woman's group who has a big online presence. Might get you additional funding, unless you don't need money anymore since you're friends with Turner-Cosby."

"That's not it. She's just not my favorite person."

"It'll give you a chance to get to know her a little better, then you can see she's not my type."

"Whatever the Mayor wants, the Mayor gets. When's the interview?"

"See, that's why I love you. It's tomorrow."

That evening after Malik left and Nylah finally fell asleep, I sat in bed with my laptop, scrolling through dresses on Net-a-Porter, while simultaneously watching Huli's game against the Astros. It always made me proud to hear sportscasters talking about my brother, his skills, and of course, his new contract. They also joked about him having been photographed in Miami with Tika Sumpter, making me wonder if that was the woman he'd mentioned at lunch. I sent a group text to Kamille and Huli.

Tiff: Is Tika your new chick?

Kamille: Is she coming for Thanksgiving?

Tiff: Probably dumped her already. LOL

We wouldn't hear back from Huli until after the game, but I was sure he'd get a kick out of that.

Perusing online also gave me the idea to login into Haney's website and watch one of his presentations. As soon as I clicked on GDH3.com, it opened to a video of him speaking as part of a panel discussion.

"Oftentimes the cycle can be broken. You simply can't say to an ex-offender 'get a job'. There has to be a vehicle for training and development that leads to solid employment. On the back end, analytics need to be put in place to not only track who's going back to jail, but if the proper skills are put in place to decrease the recidivism. . . we've paid our debt. . . no man wants to be unemployed. . . we want to be responsible. . . we want to vote, we want to make more than $7.50 an hour."

Studying Haney made me wonder what his life had really been like. Not only had he been disbarred and stripped of his position, but also his wife had divorced him and his son was still in jail. My question was, where was the rest of his family and if they weren't around, maybe that's why he'd reached out to Kamille.

My sister had nothing but good things to say, and even though she hadn't told me, according to my parents they'd recently gone to dinner with him and my sister's family. Malik certainly didn't have a problem with him. So then why was I still hesitant about accepting this supposedly changed man? One reason could be that each time I'd seen him, I'd responded to him in ways that I shouldn't and even now sitting here, I imagined what it might be like to be with him again.

Between Haney and Malik there was a vast difference in their lovemaking techniques. My husband had always been passionate, showing me he loved me in how he handled my body. Haney on the other hand showed no mercy and would force me to do things I'd only imagined, always telling me he was giving me what I wanted. He'd also become the first and only man with whom I'd ever had anal sex. All of this reminded me of the danger I faced getting too close to him.

The next afternoon while I prepared for my interview, my mother came over to watch Nylah. At exactly two p.m. Cyndi Kilrain and Lou Mendels showed up to the house. Restricting them to two rooms, Lou began taking pictures before we even started the interview.

I'd prepared a small spread of refreshments set out in the living room and once we finished the preliminaries we were set to begin. The objective, as Cyndi put it, was for the public to see me in my everyday environment - see me as a *regular* person, whatever that meant.

Since this was supposed to be a casual interview, I wore pale blue linen pants and a matching pale blue linen button down shirt, with my hair in a low bun.

Sitting across from me in Malik's favorite chair, Cyndi was dressed in a pair of white jeans, a black long sleeve t-shirt and white sandals, all of which were unflattering. If anything, I should've been offering her some fashion tips. Perhaps Malik had been right, Cyndi certainly was not his type.

"Are you ready?" she asked, having turned on her recorder, pen and notebook in her lap.

"I am."

"So Mrs. Skinner, what was your initial reaction when your husband told you he wanted to run for office?"

"Actually it was kind of romantic, he simply asked me if

I was interested in becoming his First Lady."

"How would you define your role?" she asked, her smile insincere.

"I think each First Lady brings her own definition to the role based on how she'd like to be perceived. I'm no different than any other woman who supports her husband. I'm here to 'have his back'," I said, mimicking a poster I'd seen of the President and Michelle Obama.

"Is it hard to 'have his back' as you say, when sometimes you might not agree with his choices or decisions?"

"My husband, as you know, is very good at deciding what's right for this city, but when I offer or am asked for my opinion, I give it honestly."

"It's public knowledge that you and your siblings are adopted. Have you taken a particular interest in any of the organizations that foster adoptions?"

Lou was now taking pictures of our pictures, and pretty soon I feared he might sneak upstairs to get pictures of where we slept.

"With BBWC having been my focus, I have not. However, if these children aren't cared for initially, they too will become part of the foster system, so to answer your question, yes I'm involved on the preventive level."

"I know your sister discovered years back that former DA Gregory Haney was her biological father, and your brother has found his mother. What about you?"

The mention of his name caught me off guard. Had she done that on purpose? Did she know something? What was her angle?

"I've never had the slightest bit of interest in searching for someone who for whatever reason, didn't want me, however I understand and support Kamille and Julian's decisions."

"I see," she responded, while looking down at her notes.

"Your daughter, Nylah, she attends kindergarten in New Jersey, Crème de la Crème? That's a very prestigious and expensive school, isn't it?"

"Is that a question or some sort of accusation?"

"I'm sorry. What I was meaning to ask is will she be attending a Philadelphia public school in September?"

"That would be the plan," I said, when actually that had been a point of contention with Malik and me. I wanted Nylah to attend private school and as Mayor, he needed Nylah to be in our neighborhood public school. That battle was far from over.

"The Mayor is known for being meticulous about his time, particularly his daily schedule. I understand it's been a personal habit of his since college. How does that fit into his home life?"

I thought to myself, does this woman think she knows my husband better than I do?

"We've been living on a schedule for so long, I'm not sure I'd know how not to, so yes, it translates into our home life."

"Recently, the Mayor of St. Louis was caught cheating, and his wife, as in most of these cases, stood by him.

Would you do the same for Mayor Skinner?"

Was she really asking me that question? Did she know I'd been suspicious of her sleeping with my husband?

"I highly doubt Mayor Skinner would ever put himself in that position, but if by chance it did happen, well my husband knows the answer to that."

"Interesting," she whispered as she once again wrote in her notebook, then sipped her diet coke. I sipped my water.

"And lastly, Blessed Babies, we understand your friendship with Mrs. Raquel Turner-Cosby played a big part in getting you out of the red."

"We are extremely grateful to everyone who's contributed to BBWC, however it goes without saying that Mrs. Cosby's contribution was a welcome and much needed surprise. Are there any more questions?" I asked, now glancing at my watch.

'No, I think that's it. But if you wouldn't mind, I'd like to get a photo with you, you know to put on Instagram. I have a lot of followers."

As awkward as her request was, I said yes, and posed for the ridiculous selfie as if we were friends.

"Thanks for doing this, Mrs. Skinner, I really admire you."

"When will this run?"

"I'm going to edit in on the plane, then when I get back from New Orleans I should be able to wrap it up in time for your gala."

Trying to keep my composure. I wasn't sure I'd heard correctly. Had she said she was going to New Orleans?

Once the shock began to melt away, I walked around the coffee table to regain myself.

With my mind buzzing and an uptick in my heartbeat, I bit down on my lip and asked, "You're headed to New Orleans?"

"Yes, I got called down there this morning."

If I could've gotten on a plane, I would've followed her down there. I'd been to New Orleans, I knew that the sexually charged culture of that city could make men and women do strange things. Searing with jealousy, I needed this woman to get out of my house so I could call my husband and tell him he was a liar. But after taking a moment to consider all things, glancing down at my gift from Haney I plotted out a better plan.

I stood up and moved probably a little too close to her as she packed up her things and when she looked up at me, I said, "I'm sure my husband must need you for some reason."

"I do my best, Mrs. Skinner, to anticipate his needs, but sometimes even I don't get them right."

I sent a text.

Tiffany: I need to see you

Haney: You will

Malik returned home early Sunday morning in enough time to shower and change to attend church, which he never missed on Mother's Day. I had yet to mention Cyndi's sudden trip to New Orleans and he never even asked about the interview.

Last year, Mother's Day had been extra special because

both of our families had dined at Prime. But this year it would just be me, Nylah, Malik and Nanny and she wanted to have dinner at Red Lobster.

My parents, along with Kamille, Brandon and the boys had all driven down to Baltimore to Huli's game, including a weekend stay at the National Harbor.

When I went downstairs that morning, the dining room table was filled with presents from Nylah and Malik and before leaving for church, Nylah pestered me to open all of them.

My first gift was a shopping bag filled with all my favorite things from L'Occitane, then of course there was the standard Tiffany's bag, which held a gold-heart necklace, encased with Malik's photo on one side and Nylah's on the other. In addition, there were numerous gifts and cards that Nylah had made for me at school. Needless to say, I played a happy mother.

Shiloh Baptist Church in Overbrook was where we'd begun attending when Malik took office and where Reverend Shoulders presided. He usually insisted that Malik say a few words at service and most times he did, but this morning, Malik declined, saying he wanted to sit with his ladies for Mother's Day.

After walking around for the offering, upon returning to our pew, I realized Malik wasn't behind me. I assumed he'd either gone to the men's room or someone had rudely pulled him aside for a trivial conversation.

However, when twenty minutes had gone by and he still hadn't returned to his seat, I began to wonder where was my husband. A few seconds later, I felt my mobile vibrating in my purse. Nanny gave me the side eye, but I ignored her.

It was a text from Malik.

Malik: Bad news, cop shot, gotta go, leaving the car and driver for you.

Without being obvious I glanced toward the narthex, but he was already gone. Instead, there sat Phinn two rows behind us.

At the end of service, it was obvious everyone had heard the news and were huddled in and outside the church discussing this latest tragedy. As we departed the church Nylah, sensing something was amiss, held tightly to my hand as I did my best to make small talk with members without responding to anyone's questions. I'd learned when Malik took office not to engage in matters of City Hall with the general public, less my opinion be misconstrued as having come directly from the Mayor. Nanny, on the other hand, didn't hold back from giving her opinion on anything that related to headlines or her grandson.

"Tell me what happened?" I asked Phinn, when we finally made it to the Tahoe where I took a seat in the front so we could talk out of Nylah's earshot.

"A rookie cop was gunned down outside a deli in the Northeast," he said, his voice filled with angst as he weaved around cars in the church lot.

"The Northeast, isn't that where the academy is?"

"Yes ma'am, a few blocks away on State Road."

"That's so awful. What the hell is going on? Did he have a family?" I asked, always wondering who'd been left behind to endure the pain of such a senseless and untimely death.

"It was a woman, Officer Christine Fanelli; she was engaged to another cop. They had a little girl."

Gasping, I asked, "That's horrible. How does something like that happen again?"

"They say she was sitting in her car in a parking lot off Rhawn and Torresdale. There were no cameras, and like before, he walked up to her window and ambushed her."

I was silent for a few minutes trying to take it all in, knowing the affect this would have on my husband, the police department, and the city.

"Who's with Malik?" I asked, since Phinn had driven us to church.

"Blu Eyes picked him up," he grumbled, which told me he wasn't happy that he'd been replaced on Malik's direct detail.

I rarely saw Blu Eyes, so it came as a surprise that he'd been called into Malik's detail. "Where's my husband now?"

"They're headed to the Northeast, then he's meeting the Police Chief and DA Leander at City Hall."

In light of the news, I was relieved when Nanny suggested we cancel our dinner reservations. Phinn dropped her at home first and her parting words to him were, "Young man, don't you let nothing happen to my grandson."

My intuitive daughter began whining on the way home about wanting a Happy Meal and without me asking, Phinn pulled into the drive-thru of McDonald's.

I wasn't hungry, but figured I'd cook anyway, just to ease my own anxieties. Pulling up in front of the house, I almost wanted to ask Phinn to come inside because the idea of these police officers being randomly shot, left me with an eerie feeling. But instead I began to prepare one of Malik's favorite meals, red salmon cakes, home fries, and baked beans. It wasn't balanced and full of carbs, but in times like these, I wanted to give him what he liked.

After dinner, Nylah was so antsy that I took her around the block a few times to ride her bike, then we rode to Rita's for water ice. Phinn, of course, followed behind us on foot, while another officer sat outside the house.

Later that night after having fallen asleep in Nylah's bed, I heard the alarm beep, and when I glanced at the cable box, it was eleven-thirty.

I began making my way down the hall toward the front steps, but stopped when I heard Malik talking with someone; it was Wesley. Initially I thought it was a good thing, that maybe these tragedies had brought them back together, but the more I listened, the worse it sounded.

"Your man, Wu, that you put in office, knows these cop killings are gang related. Ask him, Malik."

"C'mon man, I appreciate the information, but you can't put this on Wu simply because he took over your position. That was my decision."

"I'm not putting it on him, but we both know why you gave him that job, his people fattened your pockets."

"I didn't pocket anything, that money went into my campaign."

"But I was your man, remember? Point Breeze."

"Wes man, let's not revisit that, your financial situation hasn't changed, has it? You're still good, aren't you? Just tell me what you heard about this gang."

"It's an Asian girl gang, Ho Ching Girls. It's a rite of passage, the bigger the kill, the higher you move up."

"That doesn't make any damn sense. Plus, we already checked into the gang theory. We have a gang Czar, remember? You helped me pick him."

"Check social media; it's there. You just gotta know what to look for."

"Who told you this? Where'd you get it from?"

"I still got people in the street, remember?"

"It doesn't make any sense, girls killing cops."

"I know that, that's why I'm coming to you. You need to check Wu, I bet he knows what's going on."

"You want me to investigate the man I already put in office 'cause you think he's involved with girls killing cops? What is it you really want?"

"You think I want something from you? I don't want nothing; I'm trying to help you out, but you know what? Screw you, Skinner."

When I heard the door shut, I slipped back into bed. Malik had enough on his mind without me drilling him with questions. I wondered though, could Wesley have been right? Were Asian girls killing cops? And what had he meant about Malik pocketing money?

The house was quiet and I could hear him on the phone, but not understanding what he was saying. I could also hear him dropping ice in a glass and pouring over it what I was sure was Pappy Van Winkle. I checked the clock on the cable box, it was 1:42 a.m. and I wondered if I should go to him, but fearing a possible argument I stayed in bed.

Later that morning when he collapsed onto his side of the bed, the stench of liquor mixed with a cigar was heavy on his breath. I was about to turn over and ask if he was okay, but then, using his last bit of strength, he threw back the covers, and climbing on top of me, he let me know that now wasn't the time for talking.

Chapter 13

Under the Sea

My interview captioned, *She's Every Woman* ran in the *Huffington Post* and was linked to other social media sites. That ending up bringing in additional funds for BBWC. But in Philadelphia, it unfortunately ran alongside the stories of the police murders, which didn't sit too well with the public, or Malik.

Tonight though, wasn't about Malik or me. Tonight was the Blessed Babies Gala and to the delight of the board and all involved, it had become a highly anticipated event on Philadelphia's social calendar. My guess was the city had become so weighted down struggling to deal with the murders of two officers and no solid suspects, that we all needed something positive to focus on.

The gala was being held at the Hyatt at the Bellevue and with so many rooms reserved by guests, they'd offered me a two-night complimentary suite, which I'd stayed in alone last night. But Malik would be staying with me after the gala.

For us, I'd scheduled a romantic midnight couples' massage, complete with champagne, strawberries and warm chocolate. I also planned to take this opportunity to give him an early Father's Day gift. At my brother's suggestion, I'd gone overboard with the purchase of a Cartier Santos 100 watch and a bottle of Malik's favorite and rare bourbon, Pappy Van Winkle's.

Under the Sea was our theme for the evening and when Michael and I entered the ballroom for a walk-through, I fell in love with it. It certainly fared better than the overused Nights in Vegas or The Great Gatsby themes.

The ballroom had been swathed in varying hues of Caribbean blues and greens, bringing the nautical theme to life. In place of flowers, tall glass vases filled with water that held swimming goldfish, sat as centerpieces for the tables. Large fish tanks ran the length of the three bars, filled with multicolored fish of varying sizes, along with blue and silver balloons that lined the ceiling. Party favors for the evening were a set of glass coasters etched with the BBWC logo.

The evening was set to begin with cocktails and a silent auction at six p.m., followed by dinner, a live auction and dancing to music from UGO with a performance by Jazmine Sullivan. Our menu included eight different appetizers, with dinner entrees of filet mignon and lobster tail. Our emcees for the evening were Mike Jerrick and Alex Holley from *Good Day Philly*.

As board members, we'd decided not to all sit together so we might reach as many guests as possible. Each member had purchased a table, and joining me at the

Johnson Properties table would be Malik if he made it, Max, Lynn, Brandon, Kamille, Tootie, Nanny, and Huli, who was bringing his mystery woman.

From where we stood at the front of the room, donor representation was everywhere: RTC Holdings, CHOP, PECO, Verizon, Mitchell and Ness, Carter Crafted, and the City of Philadelphia had purchased two tables.

"Is there anybody that didn't purchase a table?" I asked Michael.

"Does that mean we did good?"

"I'm honestly overwhelmed, thank you and everyone at Platinum Images," I said, before kissing him on both cheeks.

"I knew you'd love it. It's fun, yet white jacket formal. We have 600 guests confirmed and I'm sure they'll be stragglers wanting to pay at the door."

"Are we set up to do that?"

"Yes ma'am, no money will be walking out this door."

"Well then, let's get ready!"

Three hours later after primping and pampering courtesy of Salon Tenshi, and the $1,300 Carmen Valvo dress that I'd let my sister talk me into, I was officially glamorous. Since Malik was en route from a meeting in Harrisburg with the governor, I wasn't sure what time he'd make it to the party, or if he'd make it at all. Fortunately for me, I had to settle on being escorted by Brother Sadiq, who showed up to my suite in a white tuxedo, topped with a black and white bowtie.

"Brother Sadiq, I'm surprised to have you as an escort tonight."

"Why would you be surprised, you said the Mayor might not make it and there's no way we'd let a beautiful woman be unescorted," he said looking at me with eyes that confirmed my primping was all worth it.

"But your wife, I mean wives, didn't they want to attend?"

"They understand, I'm working tonight."

As we headed to the elevator, the front desk manager, who was delivering a small black gift bag to me from Jay Roberts, stopped us. Anxious to see what it held, I opened it right away and inside laid a beautiful diamond hair clip in the shape of a dolphin. Malik had done well.

Upon exiting the elevator and making our way down the freshly laid red carpet, I felt like we were celebrities. The media, now turned paparazzi, snapped pictures and asked for sound bites, while guests complimented me on the *Huffington Post* article and the spectacular evening. Brother Sadiq and I stopped to take selfies with guests and pictures with Lou Mendels, who I knew would be hounding me for photos all night. *Philadelphia Style* and *Entertainment Tonight* (who were there because of my brother and other expected celebrities) were interviewing people as they arrived. This would definitely be a night I'd never forget.

Having entered the ballroom, my eyes landed on Raquel Turner-Cosby and her guest, the managing partner of the law firm, Mitchell & Ness, Cynthia Cunningham, another powerful woman in the city, who was infamous for her work with the LGBT community. Which made me wonder if they were business partners or lovers.

What also made this evening different was instead of the typical boring fashion show, we had pop-up boutiques from 4Sisters Designs, Boyd's of Philadelphia, WXYZ, and Tory Burch, just to name the few that I could see from where we were standing.

As Brother Sadiq and I stood talking with the School Board CEO, Dr. Hite and his wife, I noticed the noise level building and people flocking to the foyer.

My brother had arrived, and was throwing his signature kiss my way. He was wearing a custom fitted black and white tux and on his arm was R&B singer Ciara, dressed in a stunning emerald green cocktail dress.

Here it was my young brother, who'd been seen out with the likes of Nikki Minaj, Tika Sumpter, La La Anthony, and photographed out with Victoria Secret model, Jada, now shows up with Ciara. Now I understood why his new love interest hadn't wanted to be flaunted, she'd been through that parade already. I couldn't wait to talk to my sister.

As he made his way to our table, paparazzi followed, along with guests taking pictures with their camera phones, all of which would have social media in a frenzy. Jose, his bodyguard was with him and didn't interfere because he knew my brother enjoyed the attention.

"Ciara, this here is my family," he said introducing me, Kamille and Brandon, all of whom tried to act cool.

"Good evening, Ciara, welcome to Philadelphia," I said, greeting the beautiful young woman.

"Thank you, your brother talks about the two of you all the time."

"Really, and we thought he only talked about himself," teased my sister.

I whispered to him, "I didn't think you were really coming. Don't you have a game tomorrow?"

"Private jet got me here and will get me back. Stop worrying," he whispered. "Aren't my sisters beautiful?" he said, kissing me, then Kamille.

"Yes they are, and your event," she looked around, "very classy and for a good cause."

Without realizing it, Mrs. Cosby had sidled up next to me for an introduction.

"Huli, Ciara, I'd like you to meet Mrs. Raquel Turner-Cosby of RTC Holdings."

Once that was done, she took over the conversation, giving me a chance to move around the room to greet others.

Surveying the silent auction items that lined the sides of the room, there were awesome items up for bid that included, an all-inclusive 10-day Mediterranean cruise, a five-piece art collection by E. Brown, one-year wine supply from the Jordan Vineyard and Winery in California, and three nights at The Lodge at Woodloch.

Jason Wu and his wife were seated at the City table alongside Wesley and Curtiss, who didn't look too happy to be there. As I began to maneuver through the crowd toward Curtiss, Council President Evelyn Gillman stopped me, and complimented me on the evening's turnout, which was surprising because she hardly acknowledged me.

As hard as I tried, I couldn't make it to the other side of the ballroom to personally greet my former boss from Platinum Images, Sasha Borianni and her husband, New Jersey State Senator, Trent Russell. The best we could do was wave to each other, as her husband was flocked by reporters, who all had questions on his possible run for Congress.

I did, though, stop and chat with Janae who, dressed in a form fitting black dress, wanted to introduce me to two dates, Eagles players Conner Barwin and Miles Austin. I could certainly see why she liked the freedom of her lifestyle. That's when I noticed Nanny had arrived and was giving Jason Wu an earful. Standing beside Nanny was a voluptuous Tootie, who I rarely saw outside of her Septa uniform, in a black gown that fit all her curves; she was stunning.

Back at my table with Max and Lynn, we engaged in conversation with Marshall and Carmen Dillon and were later joined by Max's other friends, Chris and Christy, where I thanked them profusely for their donation and for coming to the gala. Max, of course, teased me, by inquiring about Brother Sadiq.

I was about to take my seat when I felt her nudging me, saying, "Here comes your man."

Assuming it was Malik, I turned around, but instead it was Mr. Haney and he wasn't alone.

"Good evening, everyone," he said to my group, with his arm around the waist of a striking Asian woman, wearing a sweeping gray silk gown.

"Mr. Haney," I said.

Taking my hand and kissing the underside of my wrist, he said, "First Lady you are breathtaking this evening."

Shaking my hand free, I introduced Brother Sadiq, Max, Lynn, and their friends.

"I'm sorry, allow me to introduce the lovely, Sato," he said, motioning toward the woman whose dress was cut deep enough in the front to reveal a small dragon tattoo on each of her swelling breasts. "She's the new President of the Asian Arts Initiative."

"An honor to meet you, Mrs. Skinner. Gregory says you're a woman on the rise and one to be admired."

"Thank you. I think it's time to take our seats," I told everyone, however when they walked away from me, I noticed a dolphin shaped diamond barrette holding back her slicked black hair. I was outraged because it now meant Haney had sent me the diamond clip and not my husband. In a panic that someone else might notice we were wearing matching barrettes, my hand went straight to my hair to remove, it but it was tucked in too deep.

Much didn't get past Max, as she asked, "Wait a minute, are you and Haney's trollop wearing matching diamond clips? Somebody's been naughty."

"No, I haven't. I thought it was from Malik. What am I going to do?"

"Nothing."

The lights began to flicker, signaling time for the official part of the evening to begin so we took our seats. Alex and Mike took to the stage greeting everyone and opening the live auction. There was a photo shoot with Erskine Isaac; 10-piece wardrobe outfitted by the design house of FNO; golf outing for two at the exclusive Pine Valley Golf Club, a weekend with my brother at an LA Angels game, and a movie walk-on role for the film, *The Velvet Rope*.

Haney's table was in my direct line of sight, so I couldn't help but notice the attention he paid to Sato, affectionately touching her, smoothing back her hair and intermittently kissing her bare shoulder. And she reciprocated, laughing at his jokes, her hand under the table, presumably between his legs. Their antics made my imagination soar with thoughts of what they were doing in the bedroom and it also ignited a memory, a voracious memory. After having been with him one night, he called me to his office on the pretense of wanting to talk about his son, as he was concerned with rumors he'd heard about G-dog selling drugs. It was certainly something we needed to discuss because he was doing it in my club. When I arrived there was lunch set up on his credenza, but we never got to eat or talk. Mr. Haney, the most powerful man in the city took advantage of that closed door and after binding my wrists with his necktie, he'd pushed me onto my knees, filling my mouth with him until I gagged from his release. The mere thought of his capabilities made me excuse myself to the ladies room.

They'd begun to clear the dinner dishes and were preparing for dessert when Michael alerted me that it was time to make my way to the stage. According to Michael, there were at least 500 people in the packed ballroom, making me realize that I'd never spoken in front of so many people. It was one thing being at Malik's side, but totally different having the spotlight on me. I was nervous as hell.

My heart galloped when I stood up, smoothed out my dress, and took one last sip of water. I dried my clammy hands on my napkin and tried to think of every anecdote I'd ever heard about public speaking and decided to go with imagining everyone naked. My brother waited and then began the escort to the podium. I whispered to Huli, "Are they clapping for me or you?"

"It's all about you tonight, sis, kill it."

As I stood behind Mike Jerrick, he announced, "Ladies and Gentlemen, I give you the woman whose dream of helping the helpless, the woman who sits besides the man in charge of this city, the creator of the Blessed Babies Wellness Center, our First Lady, the extraordinary Mrs. Tiffany Johnson-Skinner!"

I hugged Mike and took my place in front of the microphone and while waiting for the applause to die down, I realized imagining a naked audience might not be a good idea.

"Good evening everyone, what a beautiful night with a room full of beautiful people, for a great cause. Distinguished guests, there are not enough words to. . . this accomplishment we're celebrating is a result of ours, and your combined -"

I hesitated in my speech, noticing guests being distracted by a disturbance outside the ballroom. I glanced at Michael for some indication as to what was going on, but he nodded for me to keep talking. At my table I saw Brandon and Brother Sadiq get up from their seats and head toward the foyer.

". . . as a result of your donations, support, hugs. . . we'll begin accepting babies on Tuesday morning, and I invite all of you to tour the facility and more importantly, to come spend time with our babies."

Then I saw Curtiss rush into the ballroom, retrieve her purse, and head back out.

". . . We the board of the Blessed Babies Wellness Center thank you. Please continue to enjoy yourselves and take advantage of the fabulous auction items."

From where I stood, I could see Malik being pulled away from Wesley and then the ballroom doors closed.

". . . and with that I turn the evening over to our hosts to get this party started. . . entertainment by the beautiful and talented Jazmine Sullivan."

The audience clapped when I finished speaking, but it was obvious they were more interested in whatever had transacted between my husband and Wesley.

With Michael escorting me from the podium, I asked him, "What happened?"

"An altercation with your husband and his friend."

"They were arguing here? Malik and Wesley?" I asked, heading directly to the lobby without stopping at my table. I couldn't imagine what could've caused them to argue here at my event.

"Tiffany, wait!"

When I reached the lobby, Phinn, Blu Eyes, and Keenan were surrounding Malik to keep the media at bay.

Moving in between them, I asked, "What happened?" But flanked by his security he'd already begun walking away from me. "Malik, where are you going?"

Turning back to me, he said, "It's best if I leave, I'm sorry about all this."

"I'm leaving with you."

"You don't have to do that, it's your event."

"Malik, you are not leaving me behind."

His security detail escorted us out of the lobby, where the Tahoe sat idling at the curb.

While Blu Eyes drove, Malik sat next to me in the backseat, texting on his mobile. No one said a word until we were about to get out of the car. Then, Blu Eyes turned to him and said, "I'll talk to him."

"Don't bother."

"Malik, that wasn't right, he disrespected you in public. I don't care what you say. I'm gonna talk to that nigga."

After a moment, Malik said, "Do what you want."

Inside the house, Malik went into the kitchen, where he poured from a half empty bottle of Le Reviseur that sat on the kitchen table. There was also an ice bucket and glasses on the counter.

"Malik, you need to tell me what happened," I begged, still not knowing any details and refusing to be shut out.

He took a long swallow from his glass, then said, "I told him I'd have someone investigate the gang theory, but now he comes to your event, accusing me of giving the job to Wu for kickbacks. Says I didn't have his back, that I broke the code. I don't know even know what he's talking about, but if he keeps it up, he's going to lose his job altogether. I'm not going to let him humiliate me in public. Blu could've hurt him in there." He downed his drink, poured another, then stated, "I may be his friend, but damn it, I'm the Mayor!"

"What was wrong, was he drunk?"

"I don't know, but somebody's filling his head up with a bunch of bullshit."

"C'mon sit down," I said, guiding him into the family room. "Malik, I don't care about the gala. I'm worried about what this is doing to you."

"It's getting out of hand. I gotta fix this," he said, from where he stood in the middle of the room.

"You can't fix it tonight baby, okay? So I want you to calm down some," I said, gently pushing him to take a seat on the couch.

"Tiffany, you don't understand what I'm saying. He's accusing me of taking kickbacks, if that mess gets out. . ."

"Shhhh, didn't Blu Eyes say he would talk to him?"

His eyes searched mine for whatever reassurance I could give him.

"We can deal with it tomorrow. There's nothing you

can do about it tonight."

Taking a seat on his lap, I began massaging circles from his temples to the nape of his neck. Tilting his head against the back of the couch, he moaned. "I don't know what to do."

I kissed both of his closed eyelids, and in turn, he brought his arms around me, pressing the cold glass against my warm back. He said, "I love you, Tiffany."

"And one of the reasons why I love you is because you're a brilliant man, who always knows what to do."

In an effort to unbuckle his pants, I began to straddle him, that is until my foot became tangled around something between the cushions. Shaking loose what was probably one of Nylah's toys, the object fell to the floor. Reaching down to pick it up, I noticed it was a red lanyard from which hung an ID badge, bearing the picture and name of Cyndi Kilrain.

"Malik, what is this?" I asked calmly, not wanting to jump to conclusions too soon.

"What?" he mumbled, his eyes still closed, eager for me to continue undressing him.

With the badge swinging from its lanyard, I exploded from his lap, waving it in front of him. "Open your eyes Malik. What is this doing here?"

"Uh, what is that?" he asked, yanking the badge from my hand.

"I'm not stupid. It's obvious she was here!"

He sat up straight, with his creased brows showing the strain of the night and now my accusation on his face.

"I was in Harrisburg last night, you know that."

"You're lying! Did you screw her in my house?"

"You sound foolish. Please don't start that again."

"Then why every time I'm gone, I come home to find her stuff? Next it'll be her panties."

"Why do you have to have such a nasty mouth?"

"And why do you have to act like every other stereotypical nigga, with a white mistress," I said, slamming my feet back into my shoes.

He drowned the remainder of his drink and slammed the glass back on the end table. "I don't believe this, do you know how ridiculous you sound?"

"Do I? And you want me to have another baby? Now that's what's ridiculous."

He stood up and we were now face-to-face, closer than we'd ever been while arguing. Yet when I thought about it, this was the worst argument we'd ever had since getting married. To know things had gotten this bad scared me, but I wasn't about to back down, not when it came to his sleeping with another woman.

"Is that why you haven't gotten pregnant? Because you think I'm sleeping with Cyndi or are you still taking them pills?"

I hadn't mentioned it to Malik, I'd stopped using birth control when I came home from Woodloch. But I wasn't going to tell him that now. I stayed silent.

He said, "Why don't *you* be honest? You're the one who's been walking around here like you're the damn Mayor, ever since you started with that Turner-Cosby woman. Everybody's talking about you and her, so you tell me who the hell do you think you are?"

Now I was really confused. How had this argument become about me, and Raquel Turner-Cosby? I'd never bragged to him or anyone about my meeting her or the donation, but I guess everyone else had put me on top of a pedestal without my asking to be there.

"What are you talking about? Nobody's changed, you need to stop listening to those bitches in your office. But wait, maybe you're jealous 'cause I landed the big fish for my little non-profit, when you couldn't get a dime outta her for your damn campaign."

"Why would I be jealous of you? You're my wife. That's not what I meant, so stop acting crazy. I've had enough crazy for one night," he said, turning his back on me, heading into the kitchen.

"And why'd you lie about New Orleans? You had that all planned, her interviewing me, then coming down there to meet you. I swear, when this comes out, I will not be one of those dumb bitches standing by your side. NEVER!"

"Nothing's coming out, 'cause I'm not doing anything. Now let's go to bed," he demanded, grabbing me by the arm and pushing me toward the stairs.

"Just like that, you think you can dismiss me? I'm leaving," I told him, shaking myself loose from him and then heading toward the garage.

Dumbfounded that I would actually leave, he stood watching me grab my purse and keys.

Following directly behind me, he yelled, "Tiffany, don't you leave this house!"

Before opening the car door, I took another glance back at him, wondering if maybe I was making a mistake, but his cheating had become way too obvious. "Goodbye, Malik!"

"Tiffany! Tiffany!" he pleaded, from where he stood in the open garage as I drove off in my car.

Normally Sundays were my favorite days because time moved slower, you lay in bed longer. However this Sunday morning, I was waking up alone in a hotel room, suffering from a terrible headache.

Obviously my idea of a romantic night had been wasted as I looked over at the massage tables, folded in the corner, candles situated throughout the room, and an overturned bottle of champagne sitting in a puddle of water. All remnants of an evening gone horribly wrong because I'd discovered my husband was having an affair. Last night I'd been angry, but this morning I was heartbroken.

It was almost ten a.m. when I checked my mobile, noticing there had been numerous voicemails and text messages. I'm sure everyone wanted to recap the event. There were three missed calls from Malik and one text message.

Malik: @ Nanny's

I couldn't believe that was all he had to say. He should've been desperate to convince me that he wasn't having an affair. He should've followed me back to the Hyatt. As much as we'd joked about politicians having affairs, I guess I never thought he'd risk it all for a piece of white trash. Needless to say, I was in unfamiliar territory.

Lying there, I wondered who I could talk to about how to handle my current situation. I tried Kamille, but she was too busy to talk due to an electrical problem at the restaurant. Max was next, but she didn't answer so I assumed she was enjoying her Sunday morning with Lynn. Against my better judgment, instead of responding to my husband, I sent a text.

Tiffany: Let's meet

GDH3:   12:30 Zodiac @ NM

Driving out to King of Prussia to meet Haney probably wasn't the best idea, but my excuse was that maybe he might be able to use his connections to find out if Malik were indeed having an affair. I valet parked outside of Neiman's and took the elevator up to Zodiac.

Inside the restaurant, I found Haney seated near the windows, already sipping on a mimosa.

He stood up to greet me, this time with a hug, which I didn't resist.

"My, my, now don't you look like sunshine dipped in chocolate this morning," he said, referring to the yellow linen dress I was wearing.

"Thanks for meeting me," I responded, pushing my sunglasses on top of my head and taking his offered seat.

"Must say I was surprised to hear from you."

Too quickly I responded with, "Did I interrupt you and what's her name? Sato?"

"You could've joined us."

Ignoring his comment, I said, "I needed to talk to you."

The waiter came over. "She'll take one of these," he said, lifting his glass.

"Why'd you send that gift to my room?"

"Ohhh, the little diamond dolphin. I thought you'd like that, you know, to go with your nautical theme."

"And you thought your girlfriend would like it as well, or do you simply like all your women to have something in common?"

"Ahhhh, so you *are* still my woman. Good to know."

I hadn't expected to be nervous. Haney looked good in a navy blue linen jacket, pants, and a white collared shirt. This wasn't a good idea. I was going to need more than one drink.

"That's not what I meant. Anyway, how are things with my sister?"

"Your sister, my daughter, is an amazing woman, full of energy and she definitely knows that restaurant business. Those boys, you know, they call me Pops."

I sipped my mimosa. "Nice."

"What's going on, Tiffany? I know you didn't call me out here to talk about your sister 'cause I'm the last person you want to spend your Sunday with."

While trying to figure out the best way to ask my ex-lover if my husband had a mistress, I finished my drink, then held up my glass for a refill. "What do you know about Cyndi Kilrain?"

"Is she screwing your husband?" he asked, then smiled in an attempt to soften his blunt question.

"Do you know anything or not?"

"What would you like to know?"

"What kind of woman is she? Does she have a husband, boyfriend, is she gay? You know, what's her background? And you're right, I want to know if she and my husband are having affair. Can you find that out for me?" I asked more terse than I wanted to.

"I don't know her very well, nice body, but trashy isn't my thing. I like my women refined," he said, his eyes sweeping over me.

"Is that what Sato is, refined?"

"She is that, and so many other things," he said, while probably recalling some deviant sexual tryst.

"I'm happy you've found someone that satisfies your sexual appetite."

His face grew serious, etched with everything he was capable of, then his hand reached across the table, jerking mine to his before saying, "No woman will ever satisfy me – nobody, you are the best at what you give."

"Mr. Haney, I didn't come here for this."

"Yes you did, you don't want to admit it. But hey, for you, my chocolate truffle, I'll see what I can find out," he said, relaxing and releasing my hand.

"Thank you."

"So what do you think? Me, you, and Sato?"

"You're sickening. Is it always about sex with you?" I asked, a playful smile on my lips.

"I can't help myself, it's what you do to me. But you know what they say?"

"What's that, Mr. Haney?"

"Men never crave what they already have and you, Tiffany Johnson-Skinner, I will always crave you."

He drew a deep breath and was momentarily silent, which made my mind wander to places it shouldn't, until he said, "It seems we've gotten off track. Now tell me, how're things with Turner-Cosby? What does she have in store for you?"

"Nothing, she's a patron donor, as you said she would be, and I appreciate you making that happen."

"You know she has a thing for beautiful women."

"Is this another gay story? If so, I'm not interested."

"Turner-Cosby likes to control everyone around her. She gets off on luring people in under the pretense of support, then making them her puppets."

"Is that what you are? Her puppet."

"You, of all people, know I'm better at being the puppeteer. But seriously, with all the money you've raised and her in your pocket, you have more leverage than most people in this city."

I thought to myself, is this what Malik was talking about, me having some kind of influence with Turner-Cosby?

"You could get people to sign on for anything and so the question is what is your next project?"

"If you're right, maybe I'll take advantage of that with my brother's new project, UNAbandon Philly," I told him, finally giving into the man that I could no longer resist because I'd finally realized that he had something more to offer me than sex.

"Tell me about it."

Haney and I talked for another hour, with him offering solid advice on how to move forward on working with City Hall to rid the city's blight. His suggestion was instead of Huli purchasing one property at a time from the Sheriff's Department, we could bundle it by purchasing blocks of property at a time. He was also able to tell me who to contact at City Hall, and Licenses and Inspections, to bypass the red tape. It seemed even with his having been away for six years, he still had his grip on City Hall.

Leaving the restaurant, I wasn't ready to go home yet, and decided that since I was at the mall, I'd take a chance at shopping. For the next three hours, I shopped, buying shoes and a suit from Neiman's, dresses for me and Nylah from Nordstrom, a clutch from Louis Vuitton, and two suits from Theory. I couldn't dare leave the mall without a new fragrance, Tobacco Vanille by Tom Ford. I even picked up a sweat suit, and fresh Nike's from Lady Footlocker. And to prove to my sister that I'd actually been shopping in a brick and mortar, I purchased her a Hermes sport scarf.

Loaded down with bags, when I reached the valet, I heard someone from behind me ask, "Can I help you with those?"

I turned around. "Phinn, what are you doing here?" I asked, shocked to have run into him.

"I've been with you since last night when you left the house."

"Why? What? You followed me?" My words were jumbled because if he'd been with me since I left the hotel, then he'd seen me with Haney.

"It's my job."

"Yes, but you don't— It wasn't. . . " I fumbled with my bags, while focusing my eyes on the valet who extended his hand for my ticket.

"It's okay."

"But you saw me with Mr. Haney."

"Ma'am, I only see what you want me to see."

"It's not what you think."

"I'm not here to draw any conclusions, just to keep you safe," he said, giving me a half-smile like we had a secret, which for now we did.

Chapter 14

The Ribbon Cutting

June

I'd been checking the weather for two weeks prior to the gala and today's BBWC ribbon cutting ceremony, and it was projected to be warm and sunny. In addition to a gorgeous day, the media had been filled with rave reviews and photos from the gala on Saturday. But for every positive write-up, there was a mention of Malik and Wesley's confrontation. No one had been able to get close enough to hear it, but from the photos that had been snapped, it was clear that they'd been tussling.

Also overshadowing my day was the affair Malik was having with Cyndi. When he came home on Sunday night with Nylah, I ignored him by giving my attention to our daughter, reading her a story, and putting her to bed. Then, I stayed downstairs until I knew he was asleep. I wasn't ready to discuss his affair simply because I didn't know how to handle it and I couldn't afford to come unglued before tomorrow's ceremony. In the meantime, I'd wait to see what Haney was able to uncover.

For the ribbon cutting, I'd dressed in one of my new purchases, a mint green Zac Posen skirt suit, with a white orchid on my lapel. For any insecurities I might have been feeling (that I wasn't trashy enough for my husband, nor an Asian seductress, which seemed to be Haney's preference) my confidence was restored when Phinn picked me up, complimenting me several times, even glancing back at me in the rearview mirror.

The ceremony was due to start at eleven a.m., and when we arrived, there were about 100 people crowded into the beautifully landscaped courtyard. Pink and blue balloons were tied around the perimeter with ribbon roped between two stanchions in the front of the building. A podium was set up where the other board members and I would stand for the short ceremony.

While the friendly center staff was distributing brochures, I stopped to speak to ward leaders, city council members, and parents who'd already benefited from our services. I noticed the board members were all present and there were more media crews and police than I would've expected. I'm sure it was partially because my husband was due to arrive at 11:20 before heading to Splash Down, the official opening of the city pools at one p.m.

My eyes, though, sought out the most important guest of all, Tej, who'd been the catalyst to the start of BBWC. He and his mother were sitting on a bench in the children's garden.

"Ana, hello."

"Mrs. Skinner, oh my gosh. There're so many people," she exclaimed, standing up to give me a hug.

"You'll be okay. Hi, Tej," I said, bending down to kiss the handsome five-year-old who, once born to crack-cocaine, was now a physically and emotionally healthy little boy.

"Godmom, is this my party?" he asked, jumping off the bench into my arms.

"Yes Tej, all of this is because of you, so c'mon it's time to get started," I told him when I saw Craig and Michael ushering everyone to the front of the building.

At exactly eleven, Craig gave a brief welcome, introduced the board members, including our new CEO, Dr. Shayn Tolliver. Then it was my turn.

"Good afternoon, everyone. Wow what a beautiful day to celebrate. I am humbled to stand before you this morning. . . to know that our collective hard work and sometimes relentless pestering of donors over the past six years has resulted in the Blessed Babies Wellness Center. We can now be proud in knowing that newborn children who suffer from Neonatal Drug Syndrome will receive not only the medical attention they require, but also round-the-clock care that will help them survive. It truly is amazing what a hug can do, it can save a life..."

As I spoke, my eyes surveyed the crowd, where I saw Mrs. Cosby, along with my parents and Nylah, who sat high on my father's shoulders, waving at me.

"Six years ago, as a new mother myself, I wondered what I could do to possibly help another child survive. My thoughts…what happens when they leave here, where do they go? What happens when parents and caregivers get frustrated, how do they get support? Today, because of our supporters, the board, my friends, and donations from across the country, as well as right here at home, this has all been made possible."

"I'd be remiss if I didn't thank our Mayor, Malik Skinner, and my family who pushed me to spearhead this project, and my daughter for being born on that special day."

I turned to the board members and said, "To my fabulous board members who never gave up, despite all of the challenges we faced, thank you.

"Everyone always asks who or what was my inspiration for this center. Well right here beside me is that inspiration, Tej and his mother, Ana Cavuto. "…Tej, would you do us the honors please…"

While the audience applauded, Tej and I took the scissors in both our hands and cut the ribbon.

Once the crowd settled down, we began moving inside for refreshments and a tour. That's when the media turned its attention to the arriving black SUV. The moment Malik disembarked from the SUV, microphones were pushed in front of him with a litany of questions.

Malik was being his usual debonair self, putting the focus on me, saying how proud he was of my work and what it meant to Philadelphia, but then I could see him getting frustrated with all the questions about Wesley.

"Can you tell us more about the argument between you and Mr. Lawson? Are you still friends?"

"Will Mr. Lawson be reprimanded?"

"We understand he's given you a lead in the cop killings?"

Having exited the other side of the SUV, Cyndi took over. "Today isn't about Mayor Skinner, it's about Mrs. Skinner and what she's accomplished for the children of this city by establishing this Center. I do hope you'll have a presence this afternoon at the Splash Down when we open the pools at Whitehall Recreation Center in the Frankford section of the city at two p.m. Thank you."

By now Malik had made his way to me and we both smiled for the cameras as he hugged and kissed me, until I whispered, "Why would you bring her?"

"I only caught the end of your speech, but you were great up there. I better watch it and make sure you don't run for office," he joked.

Not wanting to but knowing I had to play the game, I asked, "Didn't I ever tell you I hate politicians?"

Others who were standing close by laughed at our antics, including Lou Mendels who was still taking pictures.

Holding onto my arm, Malik guided me away from the crowd, before saying, "Tiff, I'm really sorry about all that stuff with Cyndi, but I swear to you I'm not sleeping with her."

"Not here, Malik."

"Do you think I would've brought her here, with me today, to your event? I'll fire her if you want me to, but c'mon Tiff, she's not even my type."

"I don't believe you," I told him, trying to gently move around him without others noticing.

"Tonight, I'll be home early, we'll talk about everything, I promise," he said, and with that he kissed me and headed back across the courtyard.

After another hour of small talk and promises, I was ready to go and Phinn was, too, because I could see him getting restless. I took a moment to use the ladies room and called Max.

"Where are you?" I asked, slightly disappointed that she'd been unable to make it.

"Hey girl, congrats. Are you free yet?"

"Trying to get outta here now," I told her while fiddling with my hair in the mirror.

"Do you think you could come over? I need to talk to you," she said.

"What's wrong?"

"Nothing I need to talk to my friend, okay, can you come?"

"I'm on my way," I told her, already headed back to the lobby.

Within the hour, Phinn and I were crawling through rush hour traffic on East River Drive toward Wyncote. It was also when I received a text from Haney.

GDH3:   Congratulations

Tiffany: Thanks. Did you find out anything?

GDH3:   Talk to you soon

"Ugh," I mumbled, but obviously loud enough for Phinn to hear.

"You okay, Mrs. Skinner?"

"Exhausted, but I'm fine," I told him, while I tried to decipher Haney's response.

"Ready for another trip to the spa?"

"That would certainly be nice right about now."

"If that's what you'd like, I'll keep straight out the turnpike," he kidded.

"Phinn, you're the best."

"Doing my job, Mrs. Skinner."

By the time we arrived to Serpentine Lane, I'd nodded off. Phinn had to call my name to wake me.

Stepping onto Max's porch, I could smell the aroma of charcoal mingled with the sight of smoke coming from the grill behind the house.

"It took you long enough! C'mon in," she said, when she opened the door and then called out to Phinn, "You hungry? Food's almost done."

"Yes, ma'am," he said.

"Okay, I'll let you know when it's ready. Medium or well done?"

"Well, Mrs. Welker. Thanks!"

"Is he always so damn formal?" she asked, closing the door behind us and hurrying back into the cool air inside the house.

"I know. He can't help it."

"Yeah, but he is easy on the eyes, in a Channing Tatum kinda way."

"Who?"

"You know the movie, '*White House Down*,' the sexy white guy with Jamie Foxx?"

"Yes, I've seen it, now what are you cooking?" I asked, in response to my growling stomach, which made me realize that lately, I hadn't made the time to sit down and actually enjoy a meal.

"We got filets on the grill, grilled veggies, corn on the cob and a Caesar salad."

"Great, cause your girlfriend's starving, and if I have to eat another damn appetizer, I'm going to puke."

While Max was in the kitchen fixing Phinn a plate, I came out of my shoes and jacket, and then called my parents to check on Nylah. The five o'clock news was on, covering the pool opening, showing Malik in swim trunks, jumping in with the kids. This of course, was overlapped with the earlier deluge of questions from reporters at the ribbon cutting. The comparisons never ended.

"You mind if I turn this off? I'm not in the mood to hear my husband's bullshit speeches."

"I saw those reporters grilling him about his friend and those cop killings."

Max handed me a glass of wine and said, "Let me take this to your driver, be right back."

When she came back in the room, I simply blurted out, "He's having an affair."

"Who, Malik? Stop playing. You can't be serious."

"Cyndi Kilrain, his press secretary."

"The one that interviewed you? No way, she's not his type – too trashy," she said, setting down trays of food in front of us on the family room coffee table.

The food looked good, butter oozing off the corn, heat rising from the steak and veggies charred to perfection. I picked up and bit into the crunchy asparagus.

"Some men like that, they think it's sexy. But never mind him and his tramps, what did you want to talk about?" I asked, after downing my glass of wine and pouring another.

"I'm pregnant."

She said it so matter-of-factly, that I didn't catch it at first. "What did you say?"

"Pregnant!! Having a baby, bun in oven, with child!"

"Max! Oh my, God, Max!" I screamed, while leaping from my side of the couch over to hers, practically knocking over our food trays.

Laughing, she said, "Slow down, I found out last week. I'm two months, due January 25th."

Wrapping my arms around her, I started crying.

"What's wrong?"

"I'm sorry, it's just been an emotional few days, but this, you pregnant, this is such a blessing. I'm so happy for you. Lynn must be so excited."

After taking a sip of her juice, she laughed and said, "That man is crazy, he's worse than me. He wants me to quit work."

"Is everything okay? I mean, you know," I asked, nodding vigorously while she spoke.

"You mean 'cause my ass is almost 40? Doctor says he doesn't foresee any problems."

"Boy or girl, what are you having?"

"We want to be surprised, but Tiff, there's something I need to ask you."

"What, anything? Can they call me Auntie Tiff?" I asked, anticipating decorating the nursery, or hosting one of many baby showers.

"Would you be my child's Godmother?"

Placing my hand across my heart, I asked, "Max, really, are you sure?"

"Of course, I'm sure. What are you talking about? I know we haven't known each other long, but you're my best friend," she said, with a sparkle in her eyes and a glow on her face that only pregnant women could carry.

My eyes filled again with tears as I said, 'I love you Max, thank you."

"Are you okay?"

"What do you mean?"

"Well you just drank a half bottle of wine in minutes and you haven't really eaten anything."

"I'm fine, it's just all this stuff with Malik."

"And Haney, what about him?"

"Nothing, I've done nothing yet."

I moved over to sit closer to my friend, hugged her tight, then asked, "Forget about me, now tell me, how'd you find out?"

"You know, it was weird. Every morning I kept getting this tingling sensation in my breasts. My nipples were so sensitive I couldn't stand for Lynn to touch them. Then one afternoon at work, I got sick, cramping, vomiting and everything. I thought I had food poisoning or worse, a damn kidney stone or something. It never entered my mind to take a pregnancy test. I simply went to the doctor and boom!"

"We have to celebrate," I said, before skipping into the kitchen and removing a chilled bottle of Santa Marghertia from the wine cooler. For Max though, I poured a glass of orange juice for us to toast to our friendship, and Baby Welker.

"C'mon, let's put some music on," I said, waltzing across the floor to the bar.

"I thought you were hungry," Max said, her face quizzing my now upbeat mood.

"Not anymore, I'm *Happy*, where's that song at?" I asked, while thinking I wanted to be happy for so many reasons that I didn't want to talk about with Max while we were celebrating her good news.

"Wait, I think I owe you something," she said before going behind the bar to open the closet where the AV equipment was stored. It only took a minute for music to fill up the room. "I promised to teach you how to dance, you ready?"

"You sure it's okay for you to do this?"

"We're only dancing, ain't nobody climbing poles. Slow or upbeat, how do you like it?"

"I don't know. I've never been a stripper before. Are you sure this is a good idea?"

"Tiffany please stop, you're acting like Lynn. Here, let's put in my housecleaning music, it'll be easy."

"I'm surely about to make a fool of myself."

"First you have to come out of that suit."

I removed my shirt, down to my teddy and pencil skirt, but put my heels back on. Then I watched Max dance to Rihanna's *"Rude Boy"* with me trying to follow along. It wasn't as if I didn't have rhythm, but this was different. I was moving too fast and spinning too loosely.

We fell out in uproarious laughter. This definitely wasn't something I was good at, but I gave it another try.

"You're killing me right now, it's not a party. Here, just watch me first. You have to slow it down, like you're making love to Malik. Here wait, try this," she said when Beyoncé began with her sensual lyrics of *"Drunk in Love."*

With my eyes glued to her, Max started dancing, her svelte body gyrating in ways that I couldn't imagine doing, her hands moving through her locs. It was so damn sexy that not only was I fascinated, but I also felt seduced. Her body glided like it was made for the music. She was in sync with every beat, her hips, her hands, it all moved. Even her facial expression was sensuous. I'd never seen anything like it.

Fanning my hand across my face, I said, "Whew, girl, you turning me on."

"That's the point. Man or woman, you gotta stay focused. You must keep your eyes on the mark, make Malik think he's the only one in the room. Then, when you have him, you start to undress, to the beat of the music, and not the first beat, but the one you feel pulsating deep in here," she teased, grabbing hold of her vagina.

I took a big sip of wine and said, "Start it over, let me try again."

Dancing to Kelly Rowland's, "*Motivation*," I tried my best to emulate her, but it wasn't working. So, I closed my eyes and allowed the wine to carouse through my body. Then it came. The memories of Mr. Haney touching me, pushing me down on my knees, bending me over, entering me over and over again. Handling me anyway he chose, simply because he could.

I unzipped my skirt, pushing it down slowly over my hips until the sound pulsated where Max said it would.

As one song ended and another began, I kept my eyes on my mark, my mark was Phinn. He stood watching me from the patio.

Chapter 15

Devil in the House

Dinner at Nanny's proved to be uncomfortable for Malik because all Nanny could talk about was the situation with him and Wesley and she felt he should reach out to him. My husband, although frustrated, would never disrespect Nanny and instead just listened and told her he would take care of it.

Malik and I had never got the chance to talk about the Cyndi situation, and I believed he was avoiding the subject. In turn, I carried on as usual, waiting to hear from Haney to see if he could confirm their affair. Nylah though, was the only one excited because Sheema was spending the night at our house.

After they'd gone to bed, Malik and I tried to talk, with him attempting to convince me that he wasn't having an affair with Cyndi, but all he did was dig himself in deeper. It then escalated to me giving him excuses as to why I hadn't gotten pregnant. Finally, tried of arguing, I went to bed, leaving him downstairs drinking Pappy.

When he finally did come to bed, instead of making love, he forcibly took what he wanted, using my body to take out all his frustrations; however his masochistic lovemaking became so painful that I had to beg him to stop.

Sometime during the night, I woke to hear the pounding of rain against the house. I checked the clock, it read 5:30 a.m., then my mobile vibrated with a text.

GDH3: Turn on the news

In the dark, I found the remote on the nightstand and powered on the television.

"Wesley Lawson, former friend to Mayor Skinner is claiming. . ."

"Malik, wake up," I said turning up the volume so he could hear.

"What?" he groaned.

"It's Wesley, on the news."

Without budging, he lay there and listened.

"Mr. Lawson is accusing the Mayor of taking kickbacks from Asian business men in exchange for. . . "

"My phone," he mumbled, feeling around the covers, disoriented from the argument, the drinking, and the sex.

"I'll get it."

Knowing he'd be leaving out soon, I climbed out of bed, turned on the shower for him, then went downstairs to find his phone. There'd been eleven missed calls and even more text messages throughout the night. I filled a glass with water and took that, and two aspirins upstairs to him.

"Wesley's out to get me. I have to go," he said, while sitting on the side of the bed, scrolling through his numbers before calling the Deputy Mayor.

While he took a shower, I checked on Nylah and Sheema, who were still sleeping. So, I closed her door and went downstairs to make a pot of coffee.

"My head is killing me," he complained, coming into the kitchen.

"Did you take the aspirins?"

He sipped his coffee, popped the aspirins in his mouth, then said, "I don't know when I'll be home."

I handed him his messenger bag, stuffing his iPad inside.

When I walked him to the door, there were two city cars at the curb. Blu Eyes strolled toward Malik, holding up a large black umbrella.

We stood on the porch for a moment, with the wind slapping the rain against our faces.

He began first, "About last night, I'm sorry if I. . ."

Knowing he was in for a bad day, I stopped him and said, "How about we forget it?"

He kissed me on the cheek. "Thank you, but Tiffany, I swear I'm not having an affair with Cyndi."

Taking the plastic-covered newspaper from the front step, Malik climbed into the back of one the Tahoes, the other backing up to block the driveway. When I saw it was Phinn, I waved him inside.

He jumped out of the car, making a quick gait to the porch. "Good morning, Mrs. Skinner, your husband asked that I sit on the house today."

"Is it really necessary?"

"I think so; a few reporters showed up, but they're gone now. They followed the Mayor out."

"Thanks, Phinn."

"Will you be going out later?"

Glancing up at the dreary sky, I answered, "I'm staying in."

"If you change your mind, let me know," he said, turning to go back to his vehicle.

"Why don't you come inside for a minute? Have you had coffee yet?"

He looked behind him, then said, "For a minute."

I went to the kitchen to retrieve my vibrating mobile and while doing so, I poured him a cup of coffee.

"Thanks, Mrs. Skinner," he said while moving toward the door with his coffee mug.

"How long have you been outside?" I asked, detaining him for my own selfish reasons.

"Since about two-thirty this morning."

"I was going to fix some breakfast. Why don't I make enough for you, too?"

"I had a few donuts."

We both laughed at the old cliché.

"Really, I'm okay. The coffee is plenty."

"Phinn, I insist. I mean it's not like you're not still guarding the house."

"You're the boss. Mind if I turn the television on?" he asked, nodding toward the 19-inch flat screen that hung on the kitchen wall.

Leaning across the counter to pass him the remote, I said, "Go ahead."

As soon as the television came on, *Good Day Philly* was tossing out teasers that they had breaking news on accusations being made against the Mayor.

"One of the mayor's former aides, Wesley Lawson, claims Mayor Skinner has taken kickbacks from an unnamed organization connected to the hiring of his Senior Director of Community Affairs, Jason Wu."

Included was a clip of Wesley sitting down with investigative reporter, Dave Schratwieser, who was infamous for uncovering dirt on politicians and in Wesley, he'd found the perfect candidate. My thought was why hadn't Cyndi seen this coming?

"Why do you think you were demoted, Mr. Lawson?"

"He got paid to do it, to put Wu in place to make good on campaign promises. It was all part of the plan, to which I was never consulted."

"You're saying the Mayor received financial contributions to his campaign as well as money in his own pocket?"

"Plenty. The Asians gave him plenty of money."

"And you say you have proof that Asian gangs are involved in the police murders?"

"I gave him a lead and I've yet to see any results."

I turned the volume down. I couldn't believe this was

the Wesley I knew. What had turned him against Malik? The broader question of course was, if my husband actually had taken pocket money. If he had, I certainly hadn't seen any significant bump in our accounts.

"Why is he doing this?" I said aloud, while staring at the man on the screen that my husband had called a friend.

"Ma'am, I can tell you any leads the Mayor's been given are being investigated. But I'm sure you already know that."

I didn't say it to him, but I didn't have any details on the investigation because Malik and I hadn't been talking, that is until this morning.

"Anyway, let's see what we have to eat this morning," I said, opening the refrigerator, removing a dozen eggs, sausage, and a sleeve of biscuits.

"Can I help you with anything, Mrs. Skinner?" Phinn asked, with a short pause, giving away the fact that his eyes were focused on my braless cleavage, making me realize I was still in my pajama shorts, a tank top, and my hair an absolute mess.

Asking him to keep an eye on the food, I went upstairs, took a quick shower, afterward slipping into a pair of cotton sweatpants and an Angels t-shirt, this time with a bra underneath. Then, I brushed my hair into a loose ponytail.

As I was coming back down the stairs, I overheard Phinn on the phone. "I can't. I have to work. I told you that. Why are you so damn selfish?"

When I walked back in the kitchen, he hung up and for the first time since I'd known him, Phinn looked tired. I couldn't imagine his life, always on call for a man to whom you couldn't say no, and to now be relegated to watching his wife. I presumed it didn't give him much of a personal life. It was also then when I realized that Max was right, he did resemble that actor.

From the cabinet, I pulled out a box of grits and poured some into the boiling water.

"So Phinn, tell me about yourself. How'd you wind up on the Mayor's detail?" I asked, my back to him.

"Usual route, corrections officer, cop, then I guess somebody was looking out for me," he said before taking another sip of his coffee.

"Is that a coveted position, being on the Mayor's detail?"

"Best job in the city."

"Somehow I don't believe you. But anyway, wife, children?"

"I have a set of twin girls by my first wife, and I'm mid-divorce from the second."

"Really? How old are your girls?"

"Hanna and Hailey are seven," he said, a proud smile on his face.

"I'm so embarrassed not knowing that," I stated, moving about the kitchen fixing breakfast as I made an attempt to get familiar with the man who'd become my personal security.

"It's all right, it's my job to know about you," he said shyly, causing me to wonder how much he really knew about me.

My mobile rang, interrupting us.

"Tiffany, chile," Nanny said the moment I answered my phone, "what's going on?"

"I'm not really sure, Nanny. Malik left for City Hall. I'm fixing breakfast for the girls," I said, hoping to block any additional questions.

"You let me know as soon as you hear from him."

"I will. Thanks for calling," I said, realizing that she probably had more details than I did.

While I was on the phone, Phinn had refilled our coffee mugs.

"This is going to be ringing all day. Sometimes I wish I could turn it off," I told him.

"I feel the same way some days."

"I bet, and I'm sure the last person you wanna hear from is me," I joked, turning my attention to the slow bubbling grits.

"Actually, Mrs. Skinner, I don't mind at all," he said, now having turned the television to ESPN.

I wanted to tell Phinn it was too early in the morning for all the formalities, but I knew he'd never call me Tiffany. "Can I ask you something?"

"Sure."

After scrambling the eggs and pouring them into the frying pan, I asked, "What do you know about Blu Eyes? He scares me. I mean really, what's up with him?"

"He's your husband's friend, and I hear he used to work in homicide until the Mayor pulled him into his detail."

Before I could ask him about Cyndi, the girls came racing downstairs and Nylah screamed out, "Hi, Mr. Phinn!"

"Morning Nylah, who's your friend?"

"My cousin, Sheema! She spent the night," she said, referring to Tootie's daughter.

"Good morning, Sheema, how old are you?"

She held up four fingers, then Nylah chimed in. "I'm older than her."

"Yes Nylah, we know you're a big girl. C'mon girls, you can eat in the family room, that way you can finish watching that Lego movie, how's that?"

"Here, let me help," Phinn offered, taking the trays from my hands and placing them on the coffee table in the family room.

"Hope you don't mind, I fixed your plate," I said when Phinn returned to find a hearty plate of food on the counter in front of him.

"Thanks, this looks so good," he said, while absentmindedly, stirring butter into his grits. "Mind if I ask you something, Mrs. Skinner?"

"Not at all, what is it?"

"Mr. Haney, what's up with him?"

I caught myself stuttering, "We. . . well. . . he's working with Malik and he helped me out on a few things for the center," I said, keeping my back to him.

"And you meeting him in King of Prussia, can I ask what that was about?"

The phone buzzed again, and this time I was glad for the interruption.

"Hey sis, you all right?" Kamille asked when I answered.

"Yeah, I'm good. I'm staying in," I reassured her, while watching Phinn as he ate.

"You want me to send some food over?" Then, there was a pause before she asked, "Who's that man talking? It doesn't sound like Malik," she said when she heard Phinn in the background talking to the girls who had just come into the kitchen.

"No silly, I do not have a man in my house. I mean, it is a man, it's Phinn."

"Oh." Then, my sister said, "What the hell is up with Wesley? I never thought he'd be a snitch."

"Lotta surprises these days. I'll call you later, okay?" I said, but before I could hang up a text came through from Max.

Max: Concerned about you. Call me when you can Luv Max.

Tiffany: No worries, will call later.

And if the calls and text messages weren't enough, the doorbell chimed.

Phinn and I both looked toward the vestibule because I certainly wasn't expecting anyone.

"If you don't mind, I'll get it," he said, already headed toward the door.

"Good morning, Mr. and Mrs. Johnson," I heard him say to my parents.

"Mom, Dad what are you doing here?" I asked when they walked into the kitchen, both looking at me, questioning me with their eyes about who the man was in my house. I introduced them to him. "This is Phinn, Malik's security, and mine."

My father shook Phinn's hand. "Good morning, son," he said, before kissing me on the cheek and asking, "Where's my granddaughter?"

I looked over my shoulder. That fast, the girls had darted out of the kitchen. "In there, she has company," I answered, nodding toward the family room.

My father went into the room and I heard Nylah squealing for her Pop-Pop.

"Anymore coffee?" my mother asked, still giving Phinn the evil eye.

"Sure Mom, let me get you a cup."

I was sure Phinn was feeling uncomfortable, especially when he said, "I'd better go, shifts will be changing soon. Thanks for breakfast, Mrs. Skinner."

Being confined to the house for the day proved to be beneficial. My parents took the girls to the zoo and I gave the housekeeper the day off. With things having slowed down for me, I realized I'd been neglecting my home. It was clean, but the cupboards were empty and I'd gotten so carried away with shopping lately that I hadn't done the wash in a month, which was the one thing Malik preferred that I do. I started with a load of clothes, then made a shopping list, and finally unpacked two boxes that had arrived from Net-A-Porter.

I worked on notes for the BBWC files, and paid some bills. In checking my emails, I'd been invited to Fairfax, VA and Canton, Ohio to speak about the Wellness Center, one being a panel discussion on infant mortality and the other on prenatal cocaine exposure. It was an honor to have been invited, but I needed to make sure these people understood that I wasn't an expert. I forwarded those requests to Janae for us to discuss.

The day at home also gave me time to think about Haney's question: what was I was considering for my next project. I'd always been busy volunteering and working on BBWC, never thinking it would lead to other cities wanting to develop our model. According to Michael, there was real money out there as a consultant, but I wasn't sure how that would affect my home life. However, the idea of receiving a paycheck did appeal to me.

The only thing was Nylah would be starting first grade in September, and before we married, we'd agreed that we'd have at least two children. In thinking of Malik's political career, it would be good optics for me to be pregnant when he began campaigning for re-election. Maybe that would keep him out of Cyndi's bed, though the more I thought about it, I began to believe that maybe he was telling the truth.

When we'd had our big breakup during the time I was seeing G-Dog and subsequently seeing Haney, the woman he'd taken up with was white and she'd been polished, degreed, and a lawyer like himself. That's what made me even more suspicious of Cyndi. However, if he wasn't willing to admit to an affair, and I didn't have confirmation, then I tended to believe my husband. He simply had too much to lose to take up with that woman.

Hoping Malik made it home at a decent hour, I pulled a bag of frozen shrimp from the freezer, tossing them with scallions and mushrooms over brown rice. For myself, I uncorked a bottle of Caymus, fixed a plate and took a seat in front of the television in time for the five o'clock news.

After a replay of Wesley's interview, they began showing the public's reaction to Wesley's accusations, which were pro and con as they related to Malik.

"I knew he was too good to be true. No mayor can be that popular."

"Let's stop beating the man up, he's done a lotta good for this city."

"Look, the brother is raising the minimum wage."

"He's no better than the politicians before him, there've always been back room deals. I mean really, isn't that the culture of politics in this town?"

"As an African-American he's made great strides for this city, better than any of his white predecessors. We're out of the red and I'd say that makes him a smart man."

Then came the political analysis from so-called experts and pundits.

"He built his campaign on social media, but I don't hear him talking about Mr. Lawson."

"How is it possible for two police officers to be killed and there be no arrests made?"

Finally, they were on to the next story or so I thought, but as I began to thumb through the *Parfum Rare* book from Haney, I suddenly heard his voice coming from the television. LeAnne Jones from NBC10 had a microphone in front of Mr. Haney, outside the Juvenile Detention Center in West Philadelphia.

"Mr. Haney, I know you and Mayor Skinner have had your differences in the past, but what's your opinion on these allegations of him taking a kickback for the hiring of Jason Wu?"

I held my breath waiting for his answer.

"Believe me, you don't get this far without a little dirt being slung; it builds character. Our mayor is a smart man, who right now is under attack and it's always those closest to you. As for the untimely deaths of Officer's Campbell and Fanelli, I believe the search for those responsible falls into the hands of Commissioner Outlaw."

I lay there on the couch thinking about this new Haney, the one with whom everyone seemed in awe. Certainly I'd given him a second chance, and so far besides the elevator and Woodloch incidents, he'd done nothing but help me. It wasn't his fault that I allowed him to excite me in places that he shouldn't. I'm sure had he really wanted me, he would've had his way with me by now, but if I were honest with myself, that's what made me want him even more. Maybe it was finally time for me to admit that Mr. Haney had changed, which prompted me to send a text to my husband.

Tiffany: I love you

Malik: Wait up for me.

When the girls returned home, I fixed them dinner and then, let them play outside. Later that evening, I read the girls a story, but left the television on for at least another hour until they fell asleep. Nylah didn't often have friends over, my sister's boys were older than her so with the exception of scheduled play dates with the children at her school, the only one who spent the night was Sheema.

I'd fallen asleep on the couch and didn't hear Malik come in until he was sitting beside me, bourbon in one hand and a cigar in the other. He only combined those two things when he was thinking through a problem, and he never smoked in the house.

"Hey," I said, nuzzling underneath him.

"Hey. Do you believe this is happening?" Malik pondered more out loud than to me directly.

"I cooked."

"I saw it, thanks."

Reaching across him for the remote, I turned the television off.

"I met with Leander and he knows it's bull, but the man has to do his job. We can't afford mistakes."

"Have you tried talking to Wesley?" I asked.

"He's only talking through his attorney, Aronowitz."

His tie was already hanging loosely around his shirt collar, so I pulled it through and tossed it around my own neck, hoping he'd see that I wanted to play.

"I didn't think he'd do this to me. I set him up with a nice job, kept his grade and salary. He was the one that blew it and now I can't even fire him."

"Shhhh," I told him, as his eyes closed and he wilted into the sofa.

I sat up and unbuttoned his shirt, laid his cigar in the ashtray, then I sipped his drink.

"Woman, what do I always tell you?"

"All you got is your reputation."

I kissed him, and took another sip from his drink before setting it down on the end table.

With his mobile vibrating on the couch beside us, I unbuckled his belt, wishing for once he didn't have to answer.

He looked at the caller id, sat up from his slouched position, and motioned for me to back off. "Skinner," he answered, enthusiasm lost from his voice.

He listened, sipped on his drink, then said, "Haney, man, I don't have a lot of time. We gotta find a way to kill this story."

I knew there wasn't much my husband wouldn't do to further his political career and preserve his image, but this, his discussing his problem with Haney was absurd.

He paused, then continued, "You're saying he agreed to meet with you? All right, why don't you come by the house," he looked at his watch, "tonight, and we can talk."

It was obvious my husband had slipped into another persona, one in which I wasn't familiar, if he thought I was going to allow that man in my home.

He'd barely disconnected the call when I asked, "Did you invite that man over here?"

"I need his help right now."

My mouth dropped open and I almost fell backward before I regained my composure and said, "Malik, that's not a good idea."

I was up now, poised in front of him, my hand on one hip. "For what? He can't help you, Wesley is *your* friend."

"I'm not so sure about that anymore," he said, having propped his feet on the coffee table, landing on top of *Parfum Rare.*

"Why not? You two might still be able to talk," I told him even though I honestly didn't believe that myself, but I continued. "What can Haney do? I mean, he's not a lawyer; he's been in trouble. How will that look?" But even while I spoke, I remembered Haney's words from Woodloch when he said Malik would need him. He'd already been right about me. "I hope you're not meeting with him alone."

"No, that's why I have you here; this situation affects both of us." He swirled his drink, then took a sip, adding, "He helped you get Turner-Cosby, didn't he?"

"Yes, but this is different," I said not realizing I was pacing the floor in front of him.

"How?"

"Fine, you're the mayor, it's your decision, but I don't like it."

So there I was at two o'clock in the morning, trying to talk my husband out of opening our home to the one man who was capable of making me behave like a reckless whore. And what was I doing when, minutes later, I was upstairs, foolishly trying to decide what to wear.

"This is ridiculous," I told myself, after I'd dabbed on the perfume Haney had given to me and applied a bit of sheer gloss to my lips before I pulled on a pair of jeans and a Clemson Tigers t-shirt.

When the doorbell rang, and I heard Malik welcome him into our home, I almost wished Malik would've known about our past. Then, maybe he wouldn't be inviting in the devil.

I waited until they were settled in the living room before I slowly descended the back steps -- but not before taking one final glance at myself in the mirror.

"Good evening, Mrs. Skinner," he said, standing up to shake my hand when I cautiously entered the living room.

"Hello."

"You have a beautiful home," he added, his eyes scanning our personal space.

"Thank you," I mumbled, trying to deny my arousal.

"Haney, I know it's late, but I appreciate you making time. What can I offer you to drink?" Malik asked him.

"Whatever you have is good."

"Tiffany, can you please?"

I went over to the cabinet and without even asking, I poured what I'd known Haney to drink, Old Grand Dad, fixed neat, Pappy for Malik and a fresh glass of Caymus for myself. I'd need to finish the bottle to get through this night.

Malik patted the sofa for me to join him, and across from us, Haney sat in my husband's favorite chair.

"It's late and I don't want to keep you long, but it

would help for you tell me a little about your friend," Haney asked, as I tried to keep my eyes off him.

Malik sipped his drink, then said, "We grew up together, looked out for each other. Then he took advantage of the position I put him in."

"Him and that other guy they call Blu Eyes, in Point Breeze, right?"

"Yeah, pretty much."

"I take it Wesley knows where your skeletons are buried. We all have them," he said, he eyes catching mine while I pretended to be absorbed in the process of watching the wine swirl in my glass.

"My closets are empty."

"Is there any truth to what he's saying?"

"You mean about me getting money for bringing on Jason? Not really."

"I'm taking *not really* to mean you were aware that putting Wu in office would secure the Asian vote for your re-election." Haney paused, then added, "And dump money into your campaign."

"That's normal."

Haney shrugged his shoulders, then asked, "How much does he know about your campaign?"

"Quite a bit."

"Married? Children? Illegal activities? A mistress maybe manipulating him?"

"He's engaged to a great woman, they have four small children, he's a solid brother. As for another woman, why would that matter?"

"It all matters in this game of politics, but if you prefer not to discuss that in front of your wife, I can understand."

Mr. Haney sounded like the intelligent and smooth politician that I'd known him to be when he was district attorney, a man who did things, who made bold, important moves, without asking permission. He was also a man who knew me intimately, in ways my husband didn't.

"It's not illegal for his people to put money in my coffers. . . but morally speaking, I guess you could argue. . . well, you get it," Malik said, trying to clean it up.

Haney cut his eye toward me and said, "It's called a favor."

"I don't know, I guess it's hard for me to believe Wesley's out to get me. I mean, was it my fault he couldn't handle the job I'd given him? Maybe I put too much on him."

"What can I say, a man without power, well, he's a desperate man."

"Maybe somebody's lining his pockets, using him to get to me. What do you think?"

"Could be? Maybe it's Councilwoman Gillman. I hear she wants to run for Mayor. It's clear she doesn't seem to favor you much. On the other hand, it could be someone you may have wronged. Sometimes revenge can run deep."

"Is it you?" I asked, my eyes now directly meeting his.

That silenced both of them, and then Malik, with disapproval all over his face, said, "Tiffany, c'mon don't start. He's trying to help me out here."

"No, it's okay, Mayor. It's a fair question, and actually how do you know it's not me?"

"Is it you?" I repeated.

"Regardless of my past with your husband, I love this city and if I can help the Mayor, then that's part of my restitution as well. Plus, there's no gain for me in this. *Power* is no longer my weakness, First Lady."

Now I pushed. "You went to jail behind my husband's investigation and you're telling me you don't have a grudge against him?"

"I did, and your husband certainly did benefit from my prosecution, but he was justified in what he did. I'm man enough to admit that."

I could practically see Malik's chest swell with pride and it pissed me off that he was allowing Haney to patronize him. Didn't he realize he was the one with power and Haney was neither a friend or an ally?

"I appreciate that Haney, but here's what I can tell you. The gang thing is real; Wesley was correct in that it's a group of Asian girls, Ho Ching Girls, they call themselves."

"Malik, you didn't tell me that."

He squeezed my thigh and said, "Wu brought in the East Coast Asian Gang Unit. Leander's certain there'll be an arrest in a few days."

"So my friend Sato has been helpful?"

"Yes, very much."

I refrained from asking, but was curious as to how Sato had factored into the politics of City Hall, and a murder investigation. But I also wondered how much my husband and Haney had been communicating.

"Tiffany, can you fix me another drink? Man, you want another one?"

Getting up to refill their drinks and mine, I could feel Haney's eyes following me, seducing me, and unfortunately, I was getting aroused. When I returned to my seat, I curled up next to Malik, my hand resting between his thighs. Haney's smirk told me he knew exactly what I was doing.

He cleared his throat, sipped his drink and said, "The other piece to this is making sure that Wu in no way is personally connected to these gangs, other than that, we can fix it."

"I don't have to tell you, these accusations could kill my re-election. I swear, Haney, I will not be a one-term Mayor."

"You don't have to be. You can make this work to your advantage," he said, with words so improbable I wasn't sure what he meant, but what I did know was that Haney was squirming at my small affectionate touches on Malik. "Let me talk to your friend. I think I might be able to persuade him to temper down."

"As long as whatever you do doesn't come back to bite me."

"Believe me, it won't, I'm good at what I do."

Between the wine and the dim lights of the living room, I found myself watching Haney's every move, the way his lips curled around his glass, the way he gesticulated with his hands when he spoke, and imagining those same hands and lips on parts of my body.

"We appreciate your help with this, don't we?" Malik said, placing his arm around my shoulder and me moving just enough for it to land on my breast.

Haney's eyes followed my husband's hands and my body reacted to the game we were playing; however, I also realized the game was dangerous. I needed to get out of that room and away from the two of them. Then he winked at me before landing his eyes on the *Parfum Rare* book.

Malik's phone buzzed, he looked at the caller ID and excused himself, leaving me alone in the room with Haney.

He crossed his legs, rubbed his beard and whispered with that smirk I'd come to know so well, "I like that." He motioned with his glass, and referred to my casual attire. "And I like the way you're teasing me, but be careful; you forget who you're messing with."

I took a sip of wine, letting it swirl inside my mouth, then closed my eyes and swallowed.

"Sorry, I needed to take that," Malik said, having come back into the room.

I squirmed in my seat, not knowing what to say. Haney, of course, knew how to transition well.

"Mr. Mayor, I was just asking your wife about her brother's new condo building, Hamilton Square. My daughter tells me I need a place to call home and I'd like to take a look at one of the units."

"I'll give you the realtor's number, her name is Mrs. Wayns, she handles Johnson Properties," I said.

"Can't you show him the place? He's gone out of his way tonight. Let's extend some personal courtesy," Malik said, returning to his seat next to me.

"I know you're busy, Mrs. Skinner, whenever you can make the time, I'll make myself available for you."

Malik kissed my hand, then said, "She's not that busy, right, woman?"

"I'll have to check my schedule."

"Haney, take my word, my wife will be happy to give you a personal tour."

The sad truth was, unknowingly, Malik had played me right into Haney's hands because now I saw what he'd been doing for the last few months, baiting me, preparing me, making me come to him, when he was ready, and now I was ready.

Chapter 16

Hotter than July

For three days I tried to reach Haney via phone calls and text messages, all to which he was unresponsive, but I knew our paths were going to very soon cross.

On this day at ten-thirty a.m., it was already a sweltering 85 degrees in the city with no relief in sight, and I had a full day ahead of me. I'd begun by dropping Nylah off at summer camp, then I had a breakfast meeting at BBWC, staying afterward to meet with the staff, then spend time cuddling newborn babies.

Next up, I was scheduled for a twelve-thirty lunch meeting with Mrs. Cosby, and would be wrapping up my evening with dinner at my sister's house in University City, where Haney and Sato would also be guests. Malik was in Detroit, due to return home that evening.

In between breakfast and lunch, I was pulling up in front of my house when the radio announced there was breaking news. I sat still wondering if this was Wesley recanting his accusations as Malik had told me he would.

"This morning at nine-fifteen a.m. Philadelphia law enforcement apprehended two women in connection with the murders of Officers Campbell and Fanelli.

"Tamako Liang and Yoshie Sun were taken into custody without a struggle, in a residence overtop a restaurant on Aramingo Avenue. They were arrested with the handcuffs of the deceased officers, and subsequently taken away in their respective patrol cars.

"Unnamed sources are reporting that they were indeed part of the Ho Ching Girls gang that has infiltrated Philadelphia. A local citizen is being hailed as having assisted the police in their capture. Right now, they're being held at Police Headquarters waiting to be arraigned and formerly charged with first-degree murder. A press conference is slated for five p.m. today."

This arrest, of course, meant that Wesley had been correct in pointing Malik toward the Asian girl gang, which made me ask myself if he'd been right in accusing Malik of taking kickbacks. With not much time to ponder, I left Malik a voicemail, made a quick dash in the house to use the bathroom and freshen up, then headed back out to Old City.

My lunch with Mrs. Cosby was at Prime Stache, a steakhouse owned by Philadelphia Eagles football player, Brent Celek, making it a popular spot for the business lunch crowd, though that was my guess. I'd only been there once with Malik for dinner, but I imagined that during lunch it would be equally as crowded. I'd arrived about 15 minutes early to find her already seated.

"Good afternoon, Tiffany, so glad you were able to make it," she exclaimed when the hostess showed me to her table.

"Hi, Mrs. Cosby, thanks for the invitation," I responded, as the waiter pulled out my chair.

"Oh, you can surely call me Raquel by now."

"Raquel, how are you holding up in this heat wave?"

"It's more than I can stand, but I'm glad we're lunching. Is champagne okay for you?" she asked, as the waiter stood patiently next to the champagne bucket.

"Are we celebrating something?"

"Of course, the capture of those awful girls, haven't you heard?"

"Then yes, champagne is good," I answered, resting my purse on the chair next to me.

"Your husband must be glad to have this weight off of him."

"Malik is traveling, so I haven't had a chance to speak with him yet, but I'm sure he is."

We waited until the waiter finished pouring, then she offered up her glass in a toast. "Cheers to the Philadelphia Police Department."

"Yes, cheers."

Licking her perfectly painted lips, she said, "Delicious. I so enjoy the taste of the bubbly. It has a way of tickling one's throat."

I smiled and wondered if champagne was all she drank and as good as this stuff tasted and cost, I could see why.

"I understand you were in Houston recently. How was your trip?" I asked, having heard, as everyone else had that she was interested in purchasing a MLB franchise.

She tossed her head back in laughter. "Nothing gets by you. I have a friend outside of Houston, Hal Stryker, you may have heard of him. He's a well-known horse breeder, we ride, go skeet shooting, do a little hunting."

I had not heard of Hal Stryker. "That's funny because it's hard to imagine you with a gun, shooting anything," I said, of the refined woman who sat across from me in a mint green double-breasted dress, her skin tanned, and hair highlighted from the Texas sun.

"I grew up around guns, hunting, horseback riding. You know we socialites have to be well-rounded. As a matter of fact, why don't you and your daughter come out to the estate in Spring City; it's only about 45 minutes from here."

"Thank you, I'm sure my family would love that," I said, clearly noticing that she hadn't invited Malik. Did she not like my husband or was it because she was a Republican? Regardless of her status, she needed to show some respect for him as Mayor of this city.

Briefly we were interrupted when the waiter sat down our salads and bread.

"Tell me, Tiffany, how's your center coming along?" she asked, half filling our almost empty champagne flutes.

"Excellent. I met with Dr. Tolliver this morning and was very pleased with the progress she's making. We have seven newborns in house right now."

With her eyes squinted, she said, "Then I'd say it's time for you to move on. Which brings me to my reason for lunch."

"I'll never move on from Blessed Babies, it's part of me," I told her, somewhat insulted that she thought I'd leave an organization that I'd birthed.

"Spearhead a new project, is what I meant to say. You're in a good position to make a difference in this city."

Having realized that it was best to let her do most of the talking, I ate a forkful of my salad, then simply asked, "How so?"

While drizzling dressing on her salad, she answered, "Let's say, you're in bed with the right people."

My eyebrows furrowed a question in response, wondering who she was referring to.

"Well, of course not literally. What I'm saying is, I could put you in a position that would not only pay you a lot of money, but it would also put your husband directly on the path to let's say, Washington, DC."

"I'd be interested in hearing more about that," I said, pushing my salad bowl away.

She sat up straight, crossed her legs and eagerly began to fill me in. "There are only a few people who run this city, this state, and this country, and fortunately for you, I'm one of them. The unfortunate thing is your husband isn't. And you, my dear, could be the catalyst to bring that together."

She must've seen the expression of befuddlement on my face. Why was she acting as if my husband was powerless? Before she continued, the waiter placed a select tray of appetizers on our table.

"The question though, is how bad does your husband want it? Or maybe better stated is what might he be willing to give up?"

"I'm confused. Why would he have to give up anything? There's a road to the White House and as far as I can see, he's on it. Not sure how I can get him there any faster."

We paused in conversation for her to greet and introduce, Ralph Muller, the CEO at Penn Medicine, as he walked by our table.

After he walked away, she picked up as if we hadn't been interrupted. "You see, it all has to line up. It's the natural, well maybe not natural order of things, but he has to have the right people behind him. And you, as his wife, as First Lady need to take more of a proactive role outside the home to complete that package. So when I say give up something, he'd be giving up you in that typical role that political wives are forced to play."

"I have no interest in being part of the political landscape. I know my role."

"My dear, you can be honest, you have to be terribly bored. The center is self-sufficient, your husband's engulfed in the business of the city and your beautiful daughter is at school all day. Certainly you don't want to be one of those women who takes up with her yoga instructor for excitement," she said, pausing for my reaction, to which I gave none and instead sipped my champagne.

"You see, what I'm saying is that non-profit CEO's can make a lot of money, especially on the national level. I have several ventures that are scattered and I'd prefer they be under one umbrella, headed up by someone like yourself who could focus on the Arts, Education and Humanities."

"Tell me, how does my working for you help my husband get to the White House?"

"The people I'm talking about, they'll give you the respect you deserve as CEO of one of, let's say, The RTC Foundation. And with my guidance you'd ingratiate yourself to them and the rest is easy. You see, whether Republicans or Democrats, when it's time to select a candidate, your husband would be the one. You work with me, Tiffany, and I can personally assure you I'll do everything I can to get him there."

This was a bit more than I expected, and my brain needed a minute to digest what she telling me, so I began to put pieces of the edamame ravioli and grilled octopus on my plate. She did the same.

After taking a few bites, I said, "It's been my impression that voters follow the party, not the candidate."

"Money follows whichever party or person has their best interest."

Before I could respond, Brian Roberts, CEO of Comcast, and Eagles Owner, Jeffrey Lurie stopped by our table for an extended conversation, complimenting me on my brother's talents and inviting me to their private Comcast suite at the next home game.

I realized lunching with Raquel was all about positioning me. Had I unknowingly become her protégé or was she trying to make me her puppet? Whatever it was, she was very strategic in selecting who she wanted on her team, I just didn't understand the reason she was choosing me.

"I don't have the experience of a CEO nor would I want that responsibility," I said when it was just the two of us again.

"Blessed Babies is evidence of what you can do."

"There's a lot going on in my life right now. Malik's re-election campaign, our plans to have another child, and my daughter starting school in September."

"Another baby? Well that sounds like what the Mayor wants. It'll make him look like a safe candidate, a family man, which is nice, but it's an amateur move."

"Why can't I want the same thing?" I asked, growing tired of playing her game and wanting her real purpose. I took a sip of my champagne, refilled our glasses and took a chance at baiting her. "Raquel, I appreciate Mr. Haney getting you to invest in Blessed Babies, but I'm not sure how I fit the profile of—."

Waving her hand in the air, she abruptly cut me off. "Nobody tells me where to put my money and Haney, he's a minor player in my game. That man is like a cow that gives a good pail of milk, then kicks it over. He never knows when to stop. But believe me, Haney has his weakness, we all do. You agree?"

Taking note that the mention of Haney's name shifted her attitude made me wonder the exact nature of their relationship. Certainly she was too powerful to be controlled by anyone, especially Mr. Haney and I seriously doubted he was sleeping with her.

"I agree, but I don't know anything about Mr. Haney. My question is why take a chance on me when you can hire someone with real experience to be your CEO?"

"That's not how it's done, or not how I do it. And believe me, it's about way more than fundraising. You wouldn't have to jump right into it, I'd groom you, you could have another baby, and by the time the Mayor begins his second term, you'd be ready."

I didn't interrupt, but she was really pouring it on, making me feel as if I'd overlooked my own self-worth. Had I given up too much to become a wife, mother and First Lady? Where *was* my career? And if my husband hadn't been so dismissive and envious of my new ally, then I could be discussing her offer with him.

"In this political arena, wives have to carve out their place, and when your husband is ready, you'll be holding both Democrats, as well as Republicans in your hand. Plus, we need a fresh face at my foundation. And let's say if you chose not to have another baby, he could skip the re-election and go straight to the Governor's mansion."

I had to admit her offer did sound intriguing, but was I really ready to make that big a commitment? If she was right and it did help Malik's political career, what could be wrong? She hadn't said exactly how much it would benefit us financially, but if it meant money in Malik's coffers and me with a personal salary of seven figures, then I was interested.

"Raquel, this is a lot to digest at lunch."

"The decision is in your hands to come up with a plan that works for you and your family. I promise you, my dear, you work with me and you'll be the woman on top of this city, right beside your husband, that is, unless you prefer to be one of those women sitting on the sidelines."

We didn't finish lunch, which included almost three bottles of champagne, until after three pm and needless to say I was mentally drained and a little tipsy. What was even funnier was that we'd never placed an order for lunch, but every time I looked up the waiter was setting down more food, which gave me even more to digest.

While waiting for the valet to bring my car, I received a text from my husband.

Malik: Home at 10:15

Tiffany: Can't wait

Instead of wasting time going home, I drove over the Ben Franklin Bridge and picked up Nylah from school. I phoned Kamille and asked if she wanted me to bring anything to dinner; she said no because she never wanted anyone to bring anything, but I grabbed up a fresh fruit tart from Wegmans anyway.

Haney arrived to Kamille's directly behind me, dressed in a pair of cargo shorts, polo shirt and sneakers.

Unfortunately, it seemed Sato had been unable to make it. After he said hello to Nylah and gave me a friendly peck on the cheek, we went inside.

My brother-in-law was in the backyard sweating over the grill, where he was cooking up barbecued ribs, chicken, corn on the cob, burgers, roasted potatoes and grilled asparagus. My sister was in the kitchen mixing potato salad and stuffing deviled eggs.

The kids were everywhere.

Since it was too hot to sit outside, the four of us sat in the kitchen around my sister's big country table, where I did more observing than talking.

I listened as Haney and Brandon talked sports, politics, and the overall security of the country. Of course, the discussion turned to the Ho Ching Girls and how they'd managed to evade police for the last few months. Haney even provided us with an insightful view of life inside Federal prison, which didn't seem to be the playground everyone painted it to be.

My nephews, Kareem, Raphael, and Anthony, had fun playing card games and taking pictures with him. Nylah seemed to fit right in with him, too. As I watched him, it was still hard for me to believe that this man was now part of my family. He interacted with everyone as if he'd always been here with us. Was I now to expect him to attend Thanksgiving and Christmas celebrations? Surprisingly though, instead of being nervous in his company, I was rather enjoying it, making me almost glad Malik and Sato weren't there, which of course would've changed the evening's dynamics.

"My apologies, First Lady, for not getting back you to about seeing the condo," he said, interrupting my thoughts of him. "I've been pretty busy, but I would like to see the place," he continued, displaying that disarming smile of his.

"Yeah, Sis, Pops already rented office space, but he needs to get out of that efficiency he's living in," Kamille said, standing next to him, her hand affectionately on his shoulder.

"A man like you won't get a woman living in South Philly," chimed in Brandon, as he poured Lemoncello for the four of us.

"I thought Sato was your. . . "

"Acquaintance," he said, winking at me before continuing, "Oh yeah, I looked into that situation for you and didn't find anything. So what do you think? Three bedrooms, nothing over the top, just a comfortable place for my grandsons to visit."

"I can have the realtor. . . " I began, but then Nylah interrupted me asking if she could spend the night with her cousins. I agreed because I was looking forward to spending time with Malik.

"Tiff, why don't you take Pops over there now. It's still early."

"I need to get home before Malik and fix him some dinner."

"There's plenty of leftovers. Plus I'm sure, knowing my brother-in-law, you have the exact time of his arrival. I mean, how long could it take? The place is empty."

It was only seven-thirty and Malik wasn't due home until ten-fifteen, so I did have some time to spare and our goal was for the place to be 100 percent occupied.

"I guess it'll be all right, but we'll need to make it quick."

"Thanks sis, you're the best," she said, then continued by whispering in my ear, "see he's not that bad."

Leaving my sister's, Haney followed behind me in a late model red Cadillac CTS. It took me less than 20 minutes to get from her house to 20th and Hamilton Streets.

We parked on the street, him pulling in right behind me, but he remained in his car on the phone, watching me while I crossed the street. That annoyed me because I needed to hurry up and get this over with.

Once he joined me inside the lobby, I gave him an overview of the building's amenities, its 24-hour doorman, on-site parking, fitness center, which included an Olympic sized pool, and chauffeured car service for residents. There was no need to sell him on the neighborhood, which was walking distance to Center City, The Barnes Museum, Museum of Art, and The Franklin Institute.

On the quick elevator ride to the 10th floor, Haney was preoccupied with texting, so in turn, I took to texting with Max on exactly where I was and with whom. After I unlocked the door to the unit, I searched for the light switches, but the only light was the kitchen, ceiling fan.

Then I became frustrated with not being able to locate the air conditioning panel. This was not going good.

"It's okay, we won't be long. I'll take your word that it has air," Haney joked, then proceeded to take a call that I presumed was from Sato as he made plans to meet her at Del Frisco's for drinks.

"I'm sorry about that," he said when he finally finished. "Let me hear your pitch."

Standing in the kitchen area, I said, "This particular unit, as you can see, faces Center City. The kitchen has granite counter tops, cherry wood cabinets and all the rooms have plenty of closet space with Brazilian hardwood flooring throughout."

"Very nice. Your brother hits all points, I see."

"As you requested, it has three bedrooms and two full bathrooms."

"Can I see the other rooms or are you just gonna tell me about them?"

We began walking the unit as I explained, "Back here, this is the smallest bedroom, and could be used for an office or dressing room. Across there is the guest bathroom connected to another larger bedroom for when my nephews visit. And back here facing Spring Garden Street is the master bedroom with a soaking tub in the bathroom, perfect for you and Sato."

"Be careful, First Lady, you're sounding jealous or are you frustrated?"

"I'm neither."

However, I was beginning to perspire from the lack of air conditioning and the fact that he was walking so close behind me into the master bathroom that I could feel him creeping into my skin.

"Is that good enough for you?" I asked, the walk-through now complete as I moved back toward the door.

"Can you show me the view again from the living room?"

Now I was agitated; there was nothing to see and the sun was beginning to set. He reached up and pulled the chain turning off the kitchen light and fan.

"I'd like to see the lights from the city."

Reluctantly, I walked back in the living room and stood next to the sliding glass doors that led to the balcony.

"Mr. Haney, I don't know what else you need to see. With this apartment, you have everything you asked for, and the rent is $3,500 a month. Can you afford that?"

"Have I done something to warrant your attitude? I thought we were okay."

"Why didn't you return my calls? Is that one of your tactics, ignoring me?"

"I was busy taking care of things for the Mayor," he replied, standing in front of me, close enough that I could smell his aftershave. I tried to move around him, but he blocked me by putting his hands on my shoulders.

"My husband doesn't need. . . "

"Be careful, First Lady," he said, not having to remind me that Malik had needed him and so had I.

"I have to go. Do you want the place or not?"

Ignoring my attempts to keep it business, he prodded, "You've been calling me so I know you wanted to see me."

"To show you this place, that's was all."

"Tell me, First Lady, how does it feel to have everything you want? You're the Mayor's wife and you have Raquel Turner Cosby as your ally, what more could you want?" he asked, his hand now caressing the exposed skin around my neckline, drawing my eyes upward toward his.

"I have to go and stop calling me that," I stammered, turning my back to him, all while anticipating his next move.

Taking my hand, he kissed the soft skin under my wrist. "You used to like me kissing you right here."

Feeling myself getting pulled into his spell, I snatched my hand from his and said, "Mr. Haney, I didn't come here for this."

"Nobody says my name like you, say it again for me."

With the back of my hand, I wiped at the sweat beading up on my nose then told him, "We're done, it's time to go."

"Stop fighting me, Tiffany. There's nothing wrong with knowing what you want," he told me, all while his hands slowly unbuttoned the back of my dress until it hung loosely on my shoulders.

Sweat gathered under my bra, which he unclasped, releasing my breasts into the palms of his hot hands. I attempted to gather up my dress until he forcibly stopped me by pinning my hands down at my sides, rendering me as helpless as I'd always been in his presence.

"Mr. Haney. . . " I began to say when he tilted my head to the side.

"Six years and you're all I thought about. You have no idea what it's like to want a woman like you," he said, his fingers now massaging the nape of my neck, until his hands reached up, undoing my bun, removing one hairpin at a time, until my hair slowly fell to my shoulders.

"Mr. Haney, I. . . "

"Shut up, Tiffany," he whispered in my hair, all while taking deep breaths of my essence.

"Please, I can't, please," I begged, not sure if was for him to stop or continue.

His beard brushed back and forth across the cheeks of my face, sending chills crashing through my body.

"You remember how good Mr. Haney used to fuck you? One time, that's all I want," he said.

He was right, I did remember and it was those memories that, if I were truthful, had brought me to this very spot with him pressed against me. But it was different this time; I was married and I couldn't use the excuse that he'd drugged me or I was drunk because this time it was what I wanted.

I turned my head just enough to offer him my lips and he took them, licking them, kissing them, sucking on my tongue, and gently with his teeth, he began biting my lips.

"Tell me what you want, First Lady," he said, his voice barely audible as his mouth still covered mine.

And that's when I forgot I was First Lady, married to the Mayor of Philadelphia because at that moment I was a reckless woman wanting to be satisfied by a man who knew me in ways my husband didn't. Malik had always been a good lover, but he never went outside certain boundaries and I never asked him to for fear he might think me too salacious. But Haney was right, I knew what I wanted.

By now, the only sound in the empty room was the slurping sound of his tongue licking me, making we want this man so bad that my body trembled as I stood there in my kitten heels.

"You sure you want what I have to give you?"

"Yes, yes," I cried, when I heard the unbuckling of his belt, which only made me beg even more. "Yes, Mr. Haney, please take me."

"That's what I wanted to hear; tell Mr. Haney what you want," he demanded, roughly pinning me against the glass, my arms stretched above my head. I held my breath waiting for it, but instead of plunging himself inside me, he teased me, swirling circles, round and round my pulsating lips. Not only was he driving me insane, but the walls inside me were contracting, trying to grab onto him, until I was so weak with desire that I literally began to cry. Then without warning, he pushed, he pushed hard until the strength of it took my breath away.

He didn't move and neither did I.

"Breathe, First Lady, it's okay. I know what you want," and with that, using the entire force of his body, he plunged himself so deep inside me that my body shuddered and my scream resonated throughout the room. I couldn't hold on,

I was sliding down the window and my orgasm was exploding, running down my legs.

Then in slow motion, holding onto my hips, he moved my body with his and it made me think of the dance Max had taught me. So I gyrated and moved with him, my eyes closed listening for a beat only I could hear. That's when he started moving harder, penetrating deeper, then pulling back and smacking me on my ass and each time the harder the sting, the harder my orgasm. Unable to control myself, I cried out to him, "Oh my God, Mr. Haney, oh my God."

I could hear him muttering words, but they weren't clear and just when I thought I might fall through the window, I began falling to my knees. But he held me by my waist and pulled back, easing himself from deep inside me. But I knew him, and he wasn't finished.

"Come with me," he said, before hoisting me onto the granite counter, where he tossed my purse aside, its contents spilling onto the kitchen floor.

I pulled at him, bringing him to me, biting his chest, grabbing him, wanting him in my mouth, but he stopped, making me scream, "What, what do you want?"

With his lips curled up in the corners and without breaking a smile, he proclaimed, "This is what I've been waiting for."

Two hours later, with the back of my dress half buttoned and my skin clammy with sweat, I gathered up my things, and hurried out of Hamilton Square to the safety of my car, far away from Mr. Haney. I snapped down the visor mirror to see that the reflection peering back at me wasn't the First Lady, it was that of the thirty-year-old Tiffany Johnson. But who had Haney been? In the past, he'd taken what he wanted, and now tonight, he'd been a combination of passion and aggression, at times it almost felt as if we were making love. It didn't make sense.

Using my fingers, I combed through my mussed hair since all my pins were gone. My lipstick was smeared, so I scrounged around in my purse for my handkerchief. My hand touched something foreign, an envelope, inside was his deposit, $10,000.

When I pulled into the driveway, the house was dark, so I knew Malik wasn't home yet. I sat there flushed, trying to organize my thoughts, all while savoring the taste of Mr. Haney in my mouth and his scent all over my clothes.

BEEP! BEEP!

The sound of the car horn startled me. Taking a look in the rearview mirror, I panicked. Oh my God, Malik was home.

Scrambling to get out of the car, Malik had opened my door before I could, then pursed his mouth to kiss my already swollen lips. I prayed he couldn't taste all the places that my mouth had been.

"Hey, woman, where you been? Where's my daughter?" he asked, peering into the back seat for Nylah.

With my heart furiously drumming against my chest, I said, "She spent the night at Kamille's."

"Perfect, because we're celebrating tonight," he told me as I wiggled to get out of his embrace.

What was he talking about? Had I forgotten our anniversary, his birthday? What cause did we possibly have to celebrate?

Seeing the puzzled expression on my face, he said, "The arrests? C'mon let's get inside, I don't want you to melt."

When we got inside the house, I rushed toward the stairs, but he grabbed my arm pulling me to a stop.

"Where you going so fast? Let's have a drink and order some food."

"Go 'head, I wanna take a shower first," I stammered, trying to hurry upstairs before he noticed my half buttoned dress.

"Hold up, I'm coming with you."

What was he doing? We hadn't showered together in months. I tried to think of a million excuses for him not to join me, and even considered bringing up Cyndi, but after what I'd just done, it didn't seem fair.

In our room, I stripped down, stuffing my damp clothes into the hamper and hurried into the shower stall. Luckily for me, Malik's mobile rang while he was undressing. Maybe it would be something urgent enough for him to leave the house. It wasn't, and before I knew it, he was standing naked in the shower behind me. I was all out of excuses.

"Turn around, woman, I haven't seen you in three days," he said, when I kept my back to him.

Finally I faced him, but was too ashamed to meet his eyes. He began lathering me with my new shower cream, Arlesienne, gently sponging away the scent of Mr. Haney.

The more he sponged me, the more I was filled with guilt, almost making me want to confess. What kind of woman was I to lay with another man and have my husband wash him away?

"Tiffany, baby, I missed you. I couldn't wait to get home," he said, his soapy hands cupping my breasts, with my nipples defying me by hardening in response.

The more Malik's hands massaged me, the more turned on I became. How could that be? Haney had given me numerous orgasms, and now here I was, staring into the eyes of my husband, young, hard, and soft in all the right places. I wanted him.

"It feels good, don't it?"

"Malik, I'm sorry."

"Be quiet, woman, and give me what I want; get down on them knees."

I did as he asked, taking all of him in my mouth, until he pushed down so hard that I began to gag from the mere length and width of him, and the water that rushed in between us. Reluctantly he set me back on my feet.

"I know I been loving you hard, but I can't help it. It's your fault, it's what you do to me," his stern voice told me, while slowly he began inserting one, then two fingers in what was already warm and waiting for him.

At that moment I couldn't wait for my husband to have me, yet I was so confused as to why when I'd just been with another man. But he didn't give me time to consider the reason why because in one swift move, his muscular arms lifted my body off the shower floor, and holding me up against the tiled wall, he pushed himself inside me while I held tightly onto his shoulders.

"Wait, Malik, I'm not ready," I screamed, at the force with which he took me.

"Shut up, Tiffany, shut up and take it," he demanded, while water streamed down between us, and my nails dug deep into his flesh.

I was taking it and I no longer felt guilty. I wanted Malik to have me because he was right, I did like the brute force of him, showing me who he really was and told him as much.

Then with the same quickness, he stopped, pulled out, set me on my feet and said, "You know what I want." And what he wanted was to go into that place deep inside me where he'd never been, my chocolate truffle.

"Malik, wait, n-o-o-o-o, don't," I begged, trying my best to get out of his grip, feeling like he was about to punish me for my earlier transgression.

"Shut up, you can handle it. I'm your husband, I'm the Mayor, now give me what I want," he demanded.

"I can't take anymore, please not like this."

He didn't listen and instead repeatedly smacked me with his hand across my face, once, twice, then kissed me deep, telling me, "This belongs to me, you hear me woman, this belongs to me," and with that he bent over, taking what was rightfully his, leaving me no choice physically or otherwise, but to submit all parts of my body to him.

Afterward, my body was so weak and limp, and cradling me in his arms, he carried me to bed, kissing my forehead, and then, tucking me under the covers.

The last thing I heard was my husband on the phone ordering a pizza.

Chapter 17

Disney World

While I was at home packing for our trip to Disney World, Malik entertained the Asian Affairs Commission, along with Jason Wu and Sato, at Citizens Bank Park where the Phillies were playing the Nationals.

As usual, Nanny traveled with us on vacation, and this time Sheema came, along with Phinn, who we'd convinced to bring his daughters, Hanna and Hailey. I'd extended the invite to my nephews, but they'd finally made it out to Los Angeles with Huli for a four game stretch. Mickey Mouse was no match for a baseball game.

It was Labor Day weekend and we'd rented two rooms and a suite at the Grand Floridian. Because of the holiday it was crowded, but it was our only opportunity to get away as a family. The lines were long for every ride and attraction, but that didn't bother the girls, as they willingly waited to get the most out of their days, then they fell fast asleep by eight-thirty at night.

In the evenings, Malik and I had drinks at the bar with Phinn, who then went off on his own adventures to Downtown Disney or some other retreat he'd found away from all of us.

On the second night we were there, we went to the ESPN Zone, where we watched Huli hit a home run with flashes of my nephews cheering on their uncle in the stands. The two of them were seated on either side of Rihanna, which meant Ciara was out of the picture. If that was his idea of a nanny for the boys, I'm sure my sister was going to be thrilled. I couldn't wait to call her.

It was day three of our vacation and to get a head start on the crowd and the heat, we'd made it to the park by nine a.m. Malik and Nanny were at the vending stand getting cronuts and coffee for everyone, while the girls circled and waved from the Mad Tea Cup ride. Phinn and I sat on a bench in the blazing sun waving back to the girls, and I didn't think much of it when his mobile rang or when his face turned a shade of red that didn't match his tan. I figured it was the twin's mother checking on them, as she'd phoned several times since we'd arrived.

But then I watched his body stiffen and he nodded more than he spoke. Without turning my way, he said, "Excuse me."

He wasn't walking fast or running, but his deliberate 20 paces to my husband let me know it hadn't been his children's mother. Something was wrong. I prayed another cop hadn't been killed.

Looking over my shoulder, I watched the interaction between him and Malik, but Phinn was intentionally blocking my view. I did see Malik toss our coffee in the trash. Nanny, walking away from them, made her way over to me.

"Something ain't right. My grandson is upset."

We hurried to get the girls. Luckily, Nanny had the tray with their cronuts, so we sat them on the bench.

"What's wrong?" I asked Malik and Phinn when they reached us.

"It's bad, real bad. I gotta go back," Malik told us, his face etched with something I couldn't read.

"Why, what happened?" I asked a little too loudly.

"Come on, let's go, so we can talk," he said to me.

"Where are we going?"

"Back to the hotel."

When I told the girls we had to return to the hotel, the scene turned chaotic. Nylah began whining because she didn't want to leave the park. Nanny offered to stay behind, but then Nylah started crying because we were leaving her. I took Sheema's hand, and Malik picked up Nylah, while Hailey and Hanna sidled up next to their father.

"Let's take the monorail, it's the fastest," Phinn suggested to Malik.

Nylah cried to her father, "Daddy you promised we could take the ferry, I wanna take the ferry."

"Next time, okay, sweetie," I told her.

Pulling on his arm, Nylah was insistent. "Daddy, I wanna take the ferry. Please Daddy, you promised."

"We will; c'mon, it's okay," Malik said to quiet her, and give himself more time to think about whatever had happened back at home.

"Malik, please tell me something," I said as we rushed to catch the ferry.

"I can't, not right now. Do me a favor don't answer your phones," he instructed me, as well as Nanny.

Now I was scared.

When we arrived at our suite, Phinn waited inside the door and Malik asked Nanny to take the girls into the adjoining room.

"Sit down," he told me.

"Is it my parents, my sister, Huli, what happened? What is it? You're scaring me."

He closed his eyes, slowly opened them, and blinking back tears, he said, "Wesley's gone."

"What do you mean he's gone? Gone where? What are you talking about, Malik?"

He lowered his head. "He was murdered, this morning."

Covering my mouth so as not to let out a scream, I shook my head back and forth. "No, that can't be right." He reached out to me, but I pulled away and sat further back.

"Do you understand what I'm saying? He was shot."

"No, Malik!" I screamed, looking from him to Phinn.

Nanny came rushing from the other room, closing the door behind her and said, "I already know. This is a bad thing, Malik, a bad thing," she told him making it obvious that she'd answered her phone.

Malik's expression was deadpan, the muscles in his face tightening to conceal his pain and anger that he was straining to hold back.

"Malik, why? I don't understand; who'd want to kill Wesley?"

He turned to Phinn and said, "Talk to them, tell them what you know. I need to make a call," he mumbled, and then went into the bathroom.

When we were alone, Phinn started, "It was last night or this morning, they're not sure of the exact time yet. But they said he was leaving City Hall through Dilworth Plaza and he was shot, a robbery it looks like."

"City Hall? City Hall?" Nanny repeated, unable to believe it.

"They couldn't ID him right away 'cause his wallet and everything was missing. It happened around five this morning; what he was doing there, I don't know. But the cameras I'm sure will give us all the leads we need," Phinn told us, his body rigid like a solider against the door.

"Oh my God, his family. This is awful. I can't believe it," I cried, and my body shook with sobs, putting Phinn in the awkward position of having to hug me.

"Mrs. Skinner, please Mrs. Skinner, don't cry."

"What we gonna do now?" Nanny mumbled from where she sat, rocking on the edge of the bed.

When Malik emerged from the bathroom, I could tell he'd been crying. "Did you call Curtiss?"

"I can't, not now, not yet."

Heading to the closet, I told him, "I'll get our stuff packed."

"No, stop, I need you to stay here," he said, holding onto both my arms.

"Stay here for what? Malik, I'm coming home with you. What are you talking about?"

"The media is going to be all over this, they'll be waiting for me at the airport and I'm not putting my family through that," he told me, his voice straining to hold back emotion.

"I don't care about that. I'm not letting you go home alone," I said, still crying and pulling our suitcases out of the closet. My anxieties continued to rise as all four of our phones continued to ring.

Malik took one call after the other, and Phinn did much of the same. I paced the room, too nervous to pack, while Nanny unnerved me with her comments.

"It don't make no damn sense! What time was it? Somebody had to see something. Malik, you gotta get out here, we need to talk, that man was your best friend."

"Excuse me, Mr. Mayor, it's Outlaw," Phinn said, knocking on the bathroom door and handing Malik his phone where we could hear him screaming and cursing at the Police Commissioner.

Meanwhile, there were text messages and calls going unanswered on my phone, coming in from my parents, my brother, sister, Max, Raquel and even Mr. Haney. I didn't know what to do with myself, my husband had just told me his best friend had been killed and that I couldn't go home with him. I stood outside the bathroom waiting.

"What's going to happen?" Nanny asked Phinn.

"Ma'am, I don't know, but the Mayor's right. They're going to be all over him."

"Wait, you're not saying they're going to accuse my grandson of having something to do with this?"

That hadn't even crossed my mind. Then I remembered Haney, and how he'd said he'd take care of things for Malik with Wesley, details to which I'd never been made privy.

But a few days after our meeting with Haney, Wesley released a statement, apologizing to the Mayor saying he'd been incorrect in accusations. His statement had barely made the news.

"No ma'am, no one is going to accuse the Mayor. They said the motive was robbery. Outlaw says his wallet, cell phone, iPad were all missing and they took his weapon."

"Well, I'm worried about what they gonna say about my grandson."

"Stop worrying about me, this isn't about me, and I don't care what they say," Malik cried, wiping his eyes, as he emerged from the bathroom.

"Grandson, are you okay? You gonna be able to handle this?" Nanny asked, standing up to face Malik.

He turned away from her and lied, "Yes ma'am, I'm okay. I have to get back, and I need all of you to stay here."

"Can't we get picked up on the tarmac; we've done that before," I suggested, as an alternative to being left behind.

"Tiffany, we can't cancel Nylah's vacation. We've only been down here three days," he said, leaving me confused as to why my husband would want me to stay behind. Rather than stress him even more, I took a seat on the bed.

"I'm going to let my girls know we have to go," Phinn interjected.

"No Phinn, I need you to stay here with my family," Malik ordered.

"What? I don't understand. Mr. Mayor, I need. . ."

"No Phinn, I need you here. I trust you with my family. If you get me to the airport, Blu Eyes will meet me on the other end."

"But Mr. Mayor. . . "

"Listen, the governor of Florida has offered his private jet. It'll be on the runway waiting to take me home. Have hotel security stay outside the room while you come with me to the airport. Once I get home, I'll have a second man come down and travel home with you."

"Yes sir," he mumbled in disappointment.

"I'll get your things together," I told Malik, still hopeful he might change his mind.

"I don't need anything. Bring it all with you when you come home."

He went over to Phinn, and put his arm on his shoulder. "I need you to take care of something for me."

"Yes, Mayor Skinner, anything."

"I need you to take my wife to dinner tonight."

I jumped up from the bed and standing between the two of them I asked, "Dinner, what dinner? I don't wanna go to dinner! I wanna go home with you!"

"You have to, it's all been arranged. Do it for me, please. I don't want you sitting in this room worrying about what's going on back home." Then, he turned to him and said, "Can you do me that favor?"

Phinn's face was tight, as I'm sure the last thing he wanted to do was take me to dinner when all the action was back in Philly.

"Whatever you say, Mayor," he answered.

Next, they both went into the adjoining room to talk to the girls and I could hear Nylah crying because her father was leaving.

"Daddy, but I don't want you to go."

By all accounts our vacation was over.

Coming back into the bedroom, Malik said, "Nanny, can you excuse us for a minute?"

Malik sat in the chair by the window and pulled me down onto his lap.

"Tiffany, listen to me, you only need to stay another day or two, but you gotta be ready for this."

"But you'll be by yourself, you'll be alone. I'm your wife, I want to be there with you," I cried.

"I know you do," he said, pulling me toward him and soothing me by rubbing my back. "I won't even be home. I'll be at City Hall day and night until you get back. I have to find out. . . " He began to choke up and for the first time ever I saw my husband cry.

My husband was in pain and I was hurting for him.

"It's okay," I told him, now rubbing his back.

"Tiff, I loved Wesley like a brother. It feels like it's my fault, like I let him down."

"What about Curtiss and the kids?" I asked, thinking of Wesley's family and his parents who were still alive, along with four siblings, one of whom worked in Malik's administration. They would be devastated.

"I'm going to see them first, then I'll head to City Hall."

"Will you be okay going there?"

"I'll be fine. I spoke to his father."

"I'm so sorry; I love you," I told him, planting a light kiss on his lips.

"I know. I love you, too."

"Malik, oh my God, what about Tootie? You have to call her," I said thinking of their Point Breeze foursome.

"I did, she can't even talk. Blu Eyes went to get her."

The hardest thing for me was to see my husband walk out that door knowing the burden of pain and guilt he was carrying. More than anything I wanted to be by his side.

After they left, Nanny and I ordered pizza for the girls, then came back into the bedroom and turned on the news. Every national network FOX, CNN, MSNBC, was running the story, and even the local Florida networks were reporting that while the Mayor was on vacation people were being killed on the doorstep of City Hall.

When I powered up my iPad, the local Philadelphia networks were showing more of the same. I had no idea how'd they'd gotten pictures of us in Disney World - we all looked so happy.

"Is someone sending a message to Mayor Skinner by killing his friend on the doorstep of City Hall? Did he and Mr. Lawson ever patch things up? Why did Mr. Lawson retract his statement? Is the Mayor back in the city yet?"

The sight of City Hall physically sickened me with the yellow police tape cordoning off Dilworth Plaza. In addition to the police covering the courtyard, there were homicide detectives, the crime scene unit and helicopters were flying overhead. The water sprinklers had been turned off, the café had been closed, and all entrances on the north, south, east and west were barricaded.

The media, and onlookers had been held back to the other side of 15th Street and there was no access to City Hall as it had been officially closed for the day. In addition to City Hall coverage, cameras covered Wesley's home, the hospital where they'd taken his body, and the Philadelphia International Airport as they awaited Malik's arrival.

I had no idea when I might talk to Malik again, but he was right, this would not have been a good scene for the children.

I'd never seen Nanny upset and this had truly shaken her. She sat on the edge of the bed rocking back and forth and wiping away her tears. Finally she got up from the bed, unlocked the mini bar and poured us both drinks. It was the best move she could've made.

To assure my family that I was all right, I returned their calls, that is everyone except Mr. Haney to whom I sent a text. Raquel graciously offered to have us flown by private jet back to Philadelphia, but I didn't think Malik would approve.

Then came the press conference headed up by Deputy Mayor O'Hare and Commissioner Outlaw outside of Hahnemann Hospital.

"This morning at approximately 5:13 a.m., Wesley Lawson was fatally shot. . . every cop and law enforcement agency in this city is here today. We will pull people from the academy to go door to door. Details are sketchy, but what we know is the shooter came out of the shadows wearing a black hoodie, black sweatpants, black backpack and a silver handgun. We will not stand for someone committing murder on our doorstep."

From there, reporters began firing a barrage of questions. I was actually glad Malik hadn't been there for this initial press conference because I doubted he would've been able to hold up. I was praying for my husband's strength and sanity.

Later that afternoon after we'd taken the girls to the pool, I tried my best to talk Phinn out of dinner, but he was adamant about following Malik's instructions.

Victoria & Albert's restaurant was located in the lobby of our hotel and we had an eight p.m. seating. The first thing we did was change our reservation from a romantic little alcove, to a communal table, where we were seated with two other couples.

With Phinn's hand placed on my back, he guided me to the table, wasting no time in ordering a double shot of

Kettle 1, while I kept it safe with a glass of Malbec. However, try as we might to talk between ourselves, the other couples kept drawing us into their conversation. I had no plans on telling them we were from Philadelphia, so to have some fun I came up with new identities for the both of us.

The other guests, seeing us huddled so close together, assumed we were a couple so upon introducing ourselves, I said, "We're Mr. and Mrs. . . ."

"Baker," Phinn added when I couldn't think of his last name, which drew a hearty laugh from the always-serious Phinn. But I also had to remind him that being Mrs. Baker meant he had to stop calling me Mrs. Skinner.

"I thought you were Channing Tatum, you know the actor," the Southern woman told us.

I whispered to Phinn, "So I wonder who they thought I was?"

"Where you from?" asked the woman who hailed from Louisiana.

"Manhattan," I said.

"That's a big city. What do y'all do up there?"

"I'm a dancer and my husband is a Navy Seal, but don't tell anyone."

I thought Phinn would fall out his chair laughing. He certainly spilled a little of his drink and this time he whispered in my ear, "You're a good liar, Mrs. Baker but we both know you can dance."

That's when I realized that even though he'd never mentioned it before, he hadn't forgotten my sultry dance in Max's family room.

"You folks on vacation?" asked the man from Corpus Christie.

"It's our honeymoon," Phinn told them.

This time we both broke down in laughter, which made everyone at the table laugh, too, none of them really knowing what was so funny.

"No wonder y'all look so in love."

We had another round of drinks, and while joining in the conversation with the others, I realized that I'd had no idea how interesting Phinn was or how infectious was his laughter.

"We'll leave y'all alone. But we gonna buy y'all a drink so we can toast the newlyweds, 'cause fella, you got a long night ahead with this beautiful woman," said Corpus Christie.

Phinn bent his head toward me and said, "So beautiful lady, do you make a man work hard?"

"You have no idea what it takes," I said, teasing him with a lingering kiss on his cheek.

Throughout dinner, Phinn continued to be gracious to our guests as well as accommodating to me. At one point, I rested my back against him and breathed in his cologne, which had the distinct aroma of Tom Ford. I also took the time to really look at Phinn; he was handsome, especially tonight in a navy blue linen blazer and white pants. For the first time, I wondered if he had a girlfriend.

"Hey now, I ordered some shots, I hope y'all city folk can handle it," said the other man who hadn't told us his name or where he was from.

"I can! Bring on the Don Julio!" I told them, already having surpassed my usual two-glass limit.

"You already had a shot, and two glasses of wine," Phinn said.

"Counting my drinks? I'm a big girl," I told him, feeling the effects of my drinking.

"Every time a woman says that, it gets her in trouble."

The shots came, but it was more like three shots as I was determined to keep up with everyone else.

For as much as we were having fun, the dark reality of what was happening in Philly still hung in the air between us, especially since neither of us had heard from Malik.

"I had no idea you could be this cool, Mrs. Baker. You're always so mysterious."

"Me mysterious? I'm an open book."

"I don't think so."

"Go 'head, ask me anything!" I told him, now turned in my chair so that I was facing him, with my legs between his.

"Here's what I know. You're close with your family; your only friend, from what I've seen is Max. You and the Mayor, well I can tell when you've had an argument."

"Really? How so?"

"His attitude is bad, he's short with everybody. And you, you try to cover it up with small talk and you know, other stuff to keep you busy."

I threw back another shot of Don Julio and boldly asked, "And how does he handle Cyndi?"

His shifting eyes gave away what I'd suspected. "Cyndi and the Mayor? I don't know anything about them and wouldn't want to. You're way more interesting. . . and sexy, Mrs. Baker," he said.

"Well, we already know you're the most handsome guy in the room," I told him, which gave way to a slow and sexy smile appearing on his face.

"The other thing I know. . . is that you always smell good when you get in my truck; it's like damn, I can smell you in the air all day. . . and while I'm at it, let me just say right now that I apologize for everything I've said tonight."

"You don't have to apologize, we're on a date, remember?"

When it was time for dessert, we declined, but the other guests at our table ordered a tasting of the entire dessert menu. Once it arrived, they convinced us to try the Hovnanian Kona Chocolate Soufflé, which I fed to Phinn by the spoonful. Licking his lips, he stated, "Best chocolate I ever tasted."

"Thanks for doing this, but I'll tell you, this is not the best," I whispered in his ear, my hand resting on the dark stubble of his beard.

Taking my hand in his, he said, "Let's get outta here."

Saying goodnight to our table guests, Phinn stayed close to me as I swayed walking toward the exit.

"Nightcap at the pool?" I suggested, once we were standing in the middle of the dimmed lighting of the lobby.

"Mrs. Skinner, we both. . . "

"Wow, you really know how to change up on a girl. I thought I was Mrs. Baker tonight."

He glanced around the lobby, settled his hands onto my hips and in a voice that I was sure was reserved for the women he dated, he asked, "Can you be Tiffany tonight, for me?"

"I can. . . I am. . . whatever. . . " I tried to say, but my words were slurred and rather than let me finish, he did what we'd both been anticipating, he kissed me.

After a few seconds of our tongues searching each other's mouths, he stepped back and averting my eyes, he said, "I'm sorry, damn, I'm sorry."

But then, I reached for him and kissed him, and he didn't resist as his hands made their way through my wildly curly hair.

I didn't care that it was wrong or who might be watching, all I knew was that he felt good, and I felt safe from all that was going on back home. My husband had left me in the care of this man and he was now protecting me.

"Mrs. . . . "

"Shhh, don't say it, don't stop."

He brought me to him again, his face buried in my hair, taking deep breaths of my natural scent, and there we stood in the lobby of the Grand Floridian, kissing like we were really on a date. But this was a date that had gone terribly wrong.

With his arousal rising against me, he backed off. "If I don't stop, I won't be able to and we'll regret it."

"Take me somewhere, Phinn. Now, I want you to taste my. . ."

He quieted me with one short peck on the lips, then taking me by the hand, he said, "Mrs. Skinner, I really think we should call it a night."

The next morning I threw up.

Chapter 18

FALL

If you couldn't be safe at City Hall, then where were you safe? For as much as the crime rate had gone down since Malik had taken office, the cop killings, even though solved and having no connection, and his best friend having been murdered on the grounds of City Hall overshadowed it all.

Across the city, there was a heavy police presence and even when we weren't home, a police vehicle was stationed outside our house. Blu Eyes and now, Meryl Pope detailed Malik, while either Phinn or Keenan was with me. All of this confirmed that Wesley's death had not been a random act of robbery.

Malik's days and many nights were spent at City Hall, where he tried to focus on running the city, but in reality, he was consumed with Wesley's murder. Every informant had been brought in and questioned and if the commissioner had allowed it, Malik would've donned a gun and walked the streets personally. They'd initially suspected the Ho Ching Girls, but that proved wrong because they'd had nothing to gain by killing an average citizen. However, even with the large reward money being posted for the mere capture and arrest of a suspect at $125,000, all leads went nowhere.

At night, I would hear Malik juggling calls between Commissioner Outlaw, DA Leander, Deputy Mayor O'Hare and even the district captains who'd been instructed to call him if they received any credible information. I was sure to them, he was micromanaging the case, but he couldn't help himself.

The media had no sympathy for my husband; he was scrutinized at every turn. His loyalty to Wesley was being questioned to the point that Jason Wu considered resigning. No one would dare come out and directly accuse Malik, but the implications were worse because he couldn't defend himself.

After all my husband had given to the Mayor's office and this city, I'd come to realize how news coverage could dramatically shift from a good thing to a bad thing and you never knew what side you were going to be on. As much as we both tried to ignore it, he was at their mercy.

Not only was Wesley's murder draining the city, it was draining our marriage and had taken away Nylah's father. When he was around, though, she was the only one who could make him smile. But he was barely home, so he rarely smiled.

As much as I tried to be supportive, Malik wasn't letting me in, and whenever I tried to talk to him, he kept telling me he was okay. He didn't seem to understand that I was hurting too, yet he refused to discuss his feelings or provide me with updates on the case. He had no interest in sex and when he did come home late, with the smell of liquor on his breath, I couldn't help but wonder if he was grieving with Cyndi. But I didn't dare bring her up, knowing my own transgressions.

With the spotlight on us, without discussing it, I enrolled Nylah in McDaniel Elementary School. There was no way we could bring attention to ourselves by enrolling her in a charter or private school now.

I'd visited Curtiss several times, taking trays of food and desserts and helping out at her crowded house where everyone was coming to offer their condolences. The pain in her face was indescribable. Every time I left her house, I'd sit in my car crying.

We had to wait two weeks for Wesley's funeral; there had to be an autopsy, family needed to travel from out of state, and special arrangements had to be made to accommodate for his fraternity and the Free Masons.

Wesley had taken out a million dollar insurance policy, ensuring that his family would be financially secure and that didn't include what he'd earned from the city. Without asking me, Malik had gone to Wells Fargo and set up a college fund for their children in which he'd personally deposited $5,000. His executive assistant, Nicole, set up a funding page to which money was pouring in for their college expenses. Not that I would've objected to our contribution, but it bothered me that Malik was making financial decisions under such emotional strain.

Two days before the funeral, Malik was preparing to travel to Washington, DC for a reception at the White House to finally accept an award for the solar energy competition. Initially, he'd been looking forward to it, but now it was just one more thing to get in the way of mourning for Wesley. I didn't doubt though, that the police department, and his staff, would be relieved to have him gone for a day since he'd entwined himself in their investigation. I actually thought it might be a good thing as well, until before walking out the door he asked me a favor.

"There's this scholarship dinner tonight at the University of the Arts. I kept meaning to tell you, I need you to attend."

"Tonight? The funeral is tomorrow, I was planning on going by to see Curtiss again tonight."

"I know, but I need you to do this for me."

"I don't have to speak, do I?"

"The speech is short and it's already written."

"But isn't that what Deputy O'Hare is for?"

"Please, do it for me. It starts at five-thirty and you can be out of there by seven-fifteen," he said, a slight beg in his voice.

Knowing the pressure he was under, how could I say no? "Not a problem, I'll be there. Whatever you need me to do."

"There's one drawback, well, not really a drawback. But Haney will be there, and I know he can get under your skin."

"I'm not worried about him, but why is he coming?" I asked, trying to remain indifferent, but also realizing Mr. Haney might be able to answer questions relevant to Wesley's murder.

"He pushed for one of the kids who's been living in a shelter to get a scholarship. The kid wants to study graphic design, he did Haney's website, or something. I don't really know."

"It wouldn't be Haney if he didn't have his hands in everything."

"I'll tell O'Hare you'll be there. Thanks."

My mother came to the house and picked up Nylah that afternoon since she would have her while I was at the funeral the next morning.

Phinn was driving me that evening, which made it a bit awkward after our intimate moment in Disney. We hadn't spoken of the incident, but both of us, I'm sure were embarrassed that we'd drunk too much and acted inappropriately.

"Phinn, how's my husband doing?" I asked, after settling into the backseat.

"Ma'am, we barely interact so I don't know. Blu Eyes has been put in charge of his personal detail."

"Did he go with Malik to DC?"

"Yes ma'am, he doesn't go anywhere without him."

"Where does that put you?"

"Protecting you, Mrs. Skinner."

"Have there been any real leads into Wesley's murder?"

"Nothing solid."

"Don't you think that's strange with there being such a big reward?"

"Actually I do, but then again what do I know?"

I wasn't sure if he was holding back information or if he really didn't know anything. Surely he had to know more than I did because Malik wasn't telling me anything. Then again, maybe he was trying to maintain his professionalism after our encounter.

I arrived to Dorrance Hamilton Hall at five-fifteen p.m. where about 60 people were gathered. The media had a low, but visible presence and I wound up chatting briefly with Lou Mendels, thanking him for the great photos from my interview and events. But then I was forced to hear his opinion on the climate of the city. For all it was worth, his travel throughout the city to both political and private events made him privy to a lot of conversations. It was just that sometimes he could be a bit lengthy.

Haney strolled in right before the program started, wearing a suit that was way more expensive than any my husband owned. O'Hare was seated on my right at the dais and after Haney greeted us, he took the seat to my left.

In reading over the short program, if all went as scheduled, I would be out of there by seven-thirty, early enough to drive out to see Curtiss. The Program Director, Ms. Bingham, took to the podium, welcomed everyone, described the awards, and then followed with my introduction.

As I listened, I pondered Raquel's offer to me to become CEO of her arts initiative. That really would be a good move for me, as she said I could prepare myself for it over the next two years. If it were my plan to design, I'd have another baby and then be ready to step into the role. This time though, I'd get a nanny and a bigger house. I doubted that Malik would complain if he got what he wanted.

"Thank you, Mrs. Bingham," I said as I began my speech. "The arts encompass a broad spectrum. . . develops the total human being. As artists, you will see the world through a different lens and offer that view to us. . . music, literature, art, drama and dance are part of our lives. . . the arts community. We need the arts, we need you to give us the arts, in all its forms. This is a great opportunity for all of you, so please be sure to live out your dreams."

Out the corner of my eye, I could see Haney, reared back in his seat, arms folded across his chest, appearing to be genuinely interested in what I was saying.

When I returned to my seat, my bare leg accidentally brushed his and when I went to cross my legs, his hand held onto my knee. Not being in a position to say anything or move it without O'Hare noticing our interaction, I left it there.

Next on the program was O'Hare, who assisted Ms. Bingham in handing out the scholarships.

With his voice barely audible under the applauding audience, Haney said, "Come see me."

Trying my best to ignore him and his roaming hand, which had now made its way between my thighs, I smiled and clapped on cue, and while Lou snapped pictures, I noticed Phinn on the back row, texting. This was when I realized that having a conversation with Mr. Haney would not be in my best interest.

"Let go of me," I said through lips that barely moved.

Glancing at the face of my watch, if the program were correct, then I had seventeen more minutes before this was over and I could get away from his sexual taunting.

"Please," he said, his breath too close to my ear, until finally Ms. Bingham called him to the stage.

After the official ceremony ended, we took group pictures, and each time Haney managed to tug me closer to him. I had no intentions on staying for refreshments.

"I want you, Tiffany," he told me, having now slipped his arm around my waist for a selfie with one of the students.

"I can't do that."

"You can do whatever you want. Isn't this your city?"

"But I'm riding with Phinn."

"He'll bring you. He owes me."

What did he mean by that? How could Phinn possibly owe him, and for what? I couldn't dare ask him to take me to Haney, could I?

On the way down Broad Street with City Hall looming in front of us, Phinn and I didn't talk because when I told him where to take me, I could sense his disappointment. Before I stepped out the SUV, I felt the need to explain.

"Phinn, this isn't what you think; we're just conducting business. Malik will. . . "

"No need to explain, you have my confidence. I'll be here when you're done."

I had Haney's confidence, too. So confident that I'd come, Haney had left the door slightly ajar. So I wandered inside, curious about the place he'd made his home. The rooms appeared to have been professionally staged for a showing, thereby lacking any genuine warmth. A flat screen television took up an entire wall of the living room, in front of which was a table, holding various remote controls. His furniture was a smoky gray leather couch and two matching chairs. The only evidence of him living there was an 11x15-framed photo of my nephews that sat on the sofa table and two flickering scented candles. The other free space held a tabletop humidor and a few pieces of Asian art sat against the wall, waiting to be hung.

I followed the light to his bedroom where he sat in a leather recliner, across from a king-sized iron bed that took up most of the room.

"I made you a drink," he said, offering me a glass of white wine.

"I hope there's nothing in it," I responded, still standing in the doorway.

"We're past that, but you do seem a bit nervous. Anything I can do to help you relax?"

"Isn't that why I'm here?"

"We could just talk."

"Funny thing is, I've never been in your personal space," I stated, realizing that all of our past encounters had been in every place and on every surface except a bed.

Getting up from the chair and motioning me to sit down, he said, "Come on, I've learned to be patient, relax."

"Relaxing, is that what I'm here for?" I asked, my voice tinged with attitude because I'd allowed myself to be manipulated into coming here. But had I really been manipulated?

"When did you get wound so tight?"

"These last few weeks have been very stressful for me and my husband," I said, now having taken a seat on the footstool.

"Can I assume the Mayor has his hands full with something other than his wife?" he asked, while removing my purse from my shoulder and setting it on the floor next to me. I pushed back, sinking into the warm leather of the chair, while he kneeled beside me, slipping off my shoes.

"Me coming here, it's not right."

"I wanted to see you. Make sure you were all right, that's all. We haven't really talked since the last time."

"I didn't think we needed to, we both got what we wanted."

"Tiffany, stop acting hard and enjoy this time," he told me, his hands now massaging my feet and up my calves until I began falling under his spell.

"You see, being in prison I've learned, the trick to good living is knowing when to relax and I'm here to help you do that."

I wanted to resist the warmth of his fingers, the pressure of his hands, but I was too tired and it felt too good. I repositioned myself in the chair to get more comfortable and he took advantage of that by kissing each of my toes, while caressing the back of my heels. Where had he learned to do this so well?

Taking a sip of the cool wine, I allowed myself to relax in the moment. It had been a long time since a man had massaged me, since I'd been given this kind of attention. The last time I recalled Malik and I making love was on vacation.

"Tell me what you want me to do. Tell me how you want it."

Reaching down, I fingered through his beard, then put my hand over his mouth and said, "Stop talking."

Three hours later, we lay there tangled in his sheets, exhausted, the bed soaked and now cold from my gushing orgasms.

"You okay?" he asked, his beard rubbing up against my behind, where his head had come to rest.

Releasing my fingers that had become entwined with his, I said, "I have to go."

Pulling himself up behind me, he whispered in my ear, "I love you, Tiffany."

Not that it mattered, but he'd never said those words to me, which meant I didn't have a response. Turning my head enough to meet his eyes, I said, "I have to go."

A shadow covered his face, disappointed that I hadn't reciprocated his love, but I couldn't because I didn't love him.

While gathering my clothes from the floor, there was an uncomfortable silence between us, until the tone of his voice brought forth the old Haney.

"So tell me First Lady, how is the Honorable Mayor Skinner doing anyway?"

"How do you think? His best friend's funeral is tomorrow and they haven't caught anyone."

"They won't."

With my back facing him while I slipped my dress over my head, I pondered his words. What did he mean by that? Did he know what happened to Wesley and if he'd orchestrated it, then he was right they might never get caught. I knew Haney was a calculating man, but the sad part was I couldn't even tell Malik what I suspected. I asked Haney, "Why not? What do *you* know?"

As he sat up against the enormous iron headboard, he said, "Wesley had more on your husband than he was willing to tell you. Actually, on a lot of people."

"What did you do?"

With his lips twisted in a sardonic smile, he said, "If you're asking the question, then you already know the answer."

Chapter 19

Philly, We Can Do Better...

Wesley's funeral was being held at Christian Compassion Church in South Philly. Blu Eyes was driving us that morning and when he arrived at the house, dressed in a black suit, white shirt and a black and white polka dot tie, it occurred to me that not only did I not know much about Blu Eyes, I didn't even know his real name.

"Good morning, Mrs. Skinner," he said, when I opened the door.

"Good morning, Blu Eyes," I responded, and since this was the first time that I'd seen him since Wesley's death, I added, "I'm so sorry about Wesley. How are you doing?"

His cold blue eyes seemed to warm for a moment when he said, "Thank you, it's been tough on all of us."

"Has Phinn picked up Nanny and Tootie yet?"

"Yes, they should be at the church already. How's Malik this morning?" he asked, not moving from the doorway.

"He's still upstairs, he got in late from DC."

"And what about yourself, Mrs. Skinner, are you okay?"

"I'm fine," I responded, slightly uncomfortable having a conversation with him.

"Glad to hear that. Malik needs you."

I wish he knew that, I thought to myself.

When we finally piled into the SUV, the mood in the Tahoe was very solemn. Malik stared out the window as he held my hand. For as handsome and powerful as my husband was, I could see that at this moment he felt powerless.

Staring at my husband made me think back to Haney and his words. As ruthless as he'd been as a DA, I couldn't imagine him being capable of murder. But if that were true, did it mean Malik was ultimately responsible because he'd asked for Haney's help?

I should've asked Mr. Haney more questions. Maybe he'd told me what he did because I hadn't returned his words of love. Whatever the reason, I wasn't able to share or confirm my suspicions with anyone.

We were three blocks from the church when Blu Eyes had to maneuver through the barricades where uniformed officers directed traffic, keeping the media and onlookers at a respectable distance. The media had been told Malik would not be giving interviews, nor did Curtiss want any cameras or photos to be taken inside the church.

When Blu Eyes brought the vehicle to a stop in front of the church, Malik took a deep breath before stepping out.

"You all right, my man?" Blu Eyes asked, as he held open my door.

"Yes, let's do this. Let's send our boy home."

Malik held my hand as we made our way through the large crowd and finally to the stairs of the church. There were so many people stopping him to give a hug, offer condolences, as well as encouragement, that it became overwhelming.

With Sato on his arm, Haney made it easy for me to notice him, especially with that smile on his face proving to be as sinister as he was. As Malik spoke with Leander, I moved ahead when I saw Tootie.

Over the past two weeks, I'd tried to reach her several times to offer my condolences, but had been unsuccessful. When I'd mentioned it to Malik, he'd told me that she'd become depressed and wasn't talking to anyone.

Upon seeing me, we both opened our arms to embrace. "I'm so sorry Tootie, how are you?" I asked, noticing that she was in a tight dark blue pantsuit, with a white tank top underneath. Black sunglasses trimmed in rhinestones covered her eyes.

"I don't know, this is tough. What about you?"

"Worried about him, that's all," I said as we both looked over to where Malik stood talking with Outlaw and Leander.

"They need to catch this mofo instead of standing around talking."

"I'm sure they will. Have you viewed yet?"

"Yeah, your family's inside, sitting with Nanny."

"Tootie, I'm here if you ever wanna come over, go to lunch, anything, okay?"

"Thanks, Tiff, we better get inside."

Christian Compassion was filled to capacity with the overflow of people standing along the aisles, and sitting in folding chairs along the back. Flowers filled the front of the church from one end to the other, with Wesley's casket at its center.

Moving down the aisle, Malik stopped to speak to no one and was focused only on getting to the front of the church. As with any funeral, there were those who came to sincerely pay their respects, but also those who just came to see and be seen.

On reaching the front row, we greeted Curtiss, Wesley's parents, siblings and children, then made our way to the casket as a hush went over the church.

Curtiss had dressed Wesley in a soft gray pin striped suit, white shirt and a paisley gray and blue tie, held down with a diamond tie clip and a Mason emblem on his lapel. He looked not only peaceful, but beautiful.

Malik's body was rigid as he gripped hold of my hand and started talking to Wesley in a hushed tone, while tears fell from his eyes. When his shoulders began to tremble and people in the sanctuary called out, telling him it was going to be all right, Blu Eyes and Tootie came to stand on either side of us. Finally, he kissed Wesley's forehead and we took our seats.

Glancing through the three-fold program, I took in the family photos, as well as all the pictures of Malik, Blu Eyes, and Tootie with Wesley from when they were toddlers to adults. They really were family.

Reading the obituary, I realized there was a personal side of Wesley I didn't even know. He'd sat on the board of three non-profits, held a degree in Criminal Psychology, as well as Criminal Law, and had once been the Worshipful Master of his Masonic Lodge. It was also obvious that his love of family and friends was paramount above all else, which told me anything he'd done was because he'd loved my husband.

After the singing, the prayers, Masonic funeral rites, and reflections from family and friends, it was time for Malik to give the eulogy. Malik had always been able to deliver a speech with ease, rarely did he need a script in front of him. But today his fingers tightly held the notes he'd written. After kissing my hand, he let go and I watched, like everyone else, as he took painstakingly slow strides to the front of the silent church.

"Good afternoon, Pastor Henry, clergy, dignitaries, family and friends, I stand before you today, not as your mayor, but as a man who has lost his best friend. . ."

With his lip quivering, he cleared his throat and continued. "Curtiss, my heart breaks for you. . . and the children. . . it will be the collective strength of the community that will help you to heal."

With Malik pausing so many times to quell his emotions, I feared he might not make it through the eulogy, but he didn't give up.

"There are so many stories I could tell about the four of us," he stopped to smile over at Tootie and Blu Eyes, ". . . the four of us have been together for a long time, riding pedal bikes through the streets of Point Breeze and getting in more trouble than I can talk about here. . ."

There was laughter and there were tears as he spoke.

"Losing Wesley has been an unimaginable loss, creating unspeakable pain. . . he lived an amazing and full life. . . his family, Curtiss and the children were all that mattered to him. . . whatever Wesley did, if you didn't like it, then it meant it was for your own good, even if you didn't realize it at the time.

"I encourage all of us to hold onto my brother's legacy and remember what Wesley meant to you, and be thankful you knew him because, Wesley. . . I will never forget you."

The church exploded with applause as Malik took his seat; I'd never been prouder.

Besides the emotional strain, they say funerals make you hungry and horny and I was both. I thought Malik would be feeling the same way, but instead, on the way home, I could see how Wesley's funeral clung to him. Needless to say, I was a bit surprised when pulling up in front of the house, he invited Blu Eyes inside because I'd rarely seen them socialize together, but today he needed his friend. Once inside, Malik went straight to the cabinet to get glasses, to the refrigerator for ice, then into the family room to the liquor cabinet.

Assuming they wanted to be left alone, I went upstairs to change into something comfortable. A few minutes later when I stepped out the shower, and then into the hallway to see if I could hear if Malik and Blu Eyes were still downstairs, the whisper of their voices piqued my curiosity.

Wrapping the towel around me, I crept halfway down the steps, and realized they were standing by the front door.

"There's gotta be a way for you to get him legally," I heard Blu Eyes tell my husband.

"I've tried everything, he's clean. I need you to handle it, Blu."

"You don't want me to do that; that's not your style."

"It's Wesley, man; he killed Wesley. We put our boy in the ground today. Somebody's gotta pay."

"You don't even know for sure if Haney had anything to do with it."

"I don't care, get it done."

When I heard the front door close, I returned to my bedroom and slipped into a tank top and panties. After hearing their exchange I was too afraid to go downstairs and instead prayed that they weren't planning to actually kill anyone and if Haney was responsible for Wesley's death, then he should go back to prison.

In was some time later that night when I felt Malik's body collapse onto the bed and reaching for him, I hoped that maybe he'd respond. He did, but not in the way I'd hoped. It turned out to be another one of his overly aggressive acts of lovemaking and rather than complain, I let him have his way.

Afterward, we lay there in the dark of our bedroom, his breathing heavy, with me curled underneath him.

"It's gonna be okay, Malik."

"That's bullshit. I look like a fool. I'm the damn Mayor and we can't even catch my brother's killer. I can't let this be my legacy. I need this case closed."

His tone was a bit frightening, so rather than respond, I pulled him closer to me.

"Curtiss and the kids are counting on me."

"Is that why you asked Blu Eyes to handle it for you?"

He fell silent and for a moment I thought he may have fallen asleep. Then, he said, "You need to go to sleep," before pushing me from underneath him and climbing out of bed.

Over the next few weeks, Malik began to unwind and in turn, I made every effort to be a supportive wife.

Without complaining, I willingly attended all the functions to which we were invited, and there were plenty, including the Whiskey and Fine Spirits Festival, Liberty Medal Awards Ceremony, and the Marian Anderson Awards. He even had me looking forward to the year-end Pennsylvania Society event being held in New York. However it was business as usual at each event, we smiled and made nice with guests who vied for his attention. No one dared to mention Wesley's murder.

One night, we attended a dinner with Dan and Lindsay Katz, the CEO of Katz Pharmaceuticals, another company considering moving from Lawrenceville, New Jersey to the old IRS facility on Roosevelt Boulevard. I'd suggested we take them to Citron + Rose in Bala Cynwyd, and according to Malik, I sealed the deal by offering to let his wife manage a volunteer campaign for BBWC.

Malik responded to my support by coming home early, bringing me flowers, and cooking dinner when he could.

Nylah relished in the new home life we provided. In the mornings, he'd often take her to school on his way to City Hall, and some days he even picked her up. We didn't discuss having another child, but it was there every time we made love, which was often these days.

Each day I could tell my husband was less stressed and I attributed that to his unloading the responsibility of finding Wesley's killer onto Blu Eyes. But I knew he was still haunted by Wesley's death because some nights, he'd sit quietly in the living room with a glass of bourbon in his hand, staring off into space. And on those nights, I left him alone.

As for me personally, with the exception of intermittent texts from Mr. Haney, which I ignored, all else was as it should be. Max and I were planning her baby shower for what I now knew would be my Godson. Kamille was working with Mrs. Wayns on a second location for Halfway House Café, and my brother was clearly on his way to becoming Mr. October, as the Angels were entering into the World Series. To show their support, my parents made plans to break-in their RV, by traveling to California.

We rarely discussed the goings-on at City Hall because Malik wanted time away from the city when he was at home. However, he did inform me that Cyndi had landed a new job and she was moving to Hartford, Connecticut in January to co-anchor a mid-day news program.

Raquel had called me twice seeking my decision on heading up her charity division. However, for as good as a seven-figure salary sounded, and the benefit it might have for Malik's campaign, now was not the time. My focus was on being a wife, mother, and First Lady of this city.

Chapter 20

Selfies

I loved autumn in Philadelphia, the gold and browns of the trees, leaves falling, and crunching underfoot, made this my favorite time of year. Between planning for Nylah's birthday party and decorating for Halloween, my house was in a frenzy. Personally, I'd been contemplating trying to convince Malik to join me for a weekend getaway to The Lodge at Woodloch, where I imagined it would be beautiful right now.

This day, busy as always found me traveling back across the Ben Franklin Bridge, having had breakfast with my parents before they left for California, then onto the Wellness Center for my weekly volunteer work as a cuddler. I was also scheduled to have lunch with my sister, who'd been pressuring me to get involved with an adoption agency, Children's Choice, who in the process of revamping their program. Huli had already signed on, which meant I had no choice but to participate.

While on speakerphone with Michael reviewing my upcoming workshop at the Pennsylvania Conference of Women, my phone signaled a text message coming in. When I picked the phone up to peek at the sender, the screen displayed only a six-digit number. Keeping an eye on the road, I clicked on the message, but instead of a message with text, there was a photo. Being a proponent of not texting and driving, I told Michael I'd call him later.

Once I pulled to the light at the base of the bridge, I tapped once again on the screen. A horn beeped behind me, but I was still staring at the photo. The horn beeped again, and I jolted forward, making a hard left turn, swerving into a spot at 4th and Wood Streets. Using my two fingers I stretched the photo wider, until it filled the screen.

"Nooooo, this can't be! God no, not now!"

I couldn't believe what I was seeing; my face on an angle, my eyes closed, lips parted, with my arms stretched over my head, pressed against the window of Haney's condo.

"Please don't. No, no, no," I screamed, beating on the dashboard, the phone still in my hand.

I looked at it again, was it really me? It wasn't grainy, and the cityscape made for a perfect backdrop as it glittered with lights, but it was clearly me because I remembered that exact moment.

My mind raced with questions. How had he done it? There'd been no phone in his hand, at least I didn't think there'd been. Had someone else been there? Who else had this photo been sent to? Was this a joke or was Haney trying to blackmail me?

I steadied the phone in my hands and stared down at the numbers, there weren't enough digits to make it an actual phone number. Who was doing this to me? It had to be Haney.

There was no time to text. I pressed the home button on my phone and shouted, "Siri, call that asshole, Haney, call him now!"

Siri answered back, "I don't see an asshole Haney in your contacts."

I screamed again, "Please Siri, call Mr. Haney!"

"Calling Mr. Haney."

The phone rang once, twice, then was sent to voicemail.

"God, what am I going to do?"

For the third time, I examined the photo, turning it horizontal, then vertical to see if I could tell if it had been a selfie, or taken from inside the condo. Had there been cameras? Had someone else been there? I started to cry slowly at first, but when my heart and pulse began to pound, the tears poured from me. Unable to breathe, I unbuckled my seat belt to prevent myself from hyperventilating.

I had to get to Malik before anyone else did. Not realizing that I hadn't put the car in park, when I stepped on the gas, I rammed the car in front of me. Shifting the car into reverse, I hit the gas and the car jerked backward. Ignoring the occupants beeping horn, I pulled out and barreled down 4th street.

Once onto Market Street, blinded by my tears, I didn't stop for yellow lights and barely stopped for the red ones. I had to talk to Malik.

I swerved around cars, buses and taxicabs and even when I heard the siren and saw the flashing blue lights of a police cruiser in my rearview mirror, I didn't slow down. There was no time for me to pull over; I had to reach Malik before the picture did.

Rounding City Hall, I beeped the horn repeatedly at pedestrians, then jumping the curb, I drove onto the wide sidewalk on the north side of the building, screeching my car to a halt. The police officer followed suit, jumping the curb, his door swinging open as he jumped from his vehicle, with his hand on his gun, trying to stop a presumed maniac from storming City Hall.

"Ma'am please, move away from your car, now!" he shouted, until he realized who I was, which made it worse for him.

"What? What?" I yelled, daring him to stop me, as I ran toward the lobby doors.

"Mrs. Skinner, I didn't know it was. . . " he said, and then backed up a few steps, easing his gun back into its holster, but staying close enough behind me to keep up with my frantic pace.

I made my way through the entrance, not even stopping to greet the security personnel; they knew who I was. With no patience to wait for the elevator, I took the wide rounding staircase to Malik's second floor office, with the patrol officer still on my heels.

I probably should've had more control, showed some poise and restraint in handling this, or maybe called Malik or perhaps waited until he'd gotten home that evening, but I didn't do any of that.

Outside Malik's office, there were four uniformed officers, casually standing around talking and drinking coffee.

"Good morning, Mrs. Skinner."

"Morning, Mrs. . . ."

No time for greetings. I ignored them, pushing through the glass doors to the Mayor's suite.

"Where's my husband?" I demanded of Rasheeda, Malik's receptionist.

She stood up, blocking the city crest on the wall behind her, and said, "He's in a meeting, Mrs. Skinner, would you. . ."

I didn't wait for her to finish; instead I burst through his double office doors, and blurted out, "Malik, I need. . ." but I stopped short. Sitting around his conference table were Deputy O'Hare, Chief of Staff Barnes and Mr. Haney. Utter shock was on everyone's face, but the confusion and concern on Haney's face, matched that of my husband's.

However, now that I was there in front of Malik, Haney, and some of his senior staff, I didn't know what to say. My eyes darted around the paneled office, searching for something to focus on, to regain my balance and to formulate words that made sense.

The red, white and blue flag stood off in the corner of the room, Malik's scarred oak desk was in the middle, there was a couch stacked with files, and two chairs, a coffee table, end tables with lamps.

Malik sprang from his seat asking, "Tiffany, what's wrong? Where's Nylah?"

With everyone staring at me, I realized I'd come here without a plan and it was obvious he hadn't seen the photo, at least not yet. I couldn't tell him, not here at work.

I swallowed hard and said, "Malik. . . I. . . I have to talk to you please, right away."

"My apologies everyone, can you excuse us?" he told the group.

They didn't bother to gather up their papers, files, iPads or phones; they just all scurried out the office, as if they too were afraid of what I had to say. All except Mr. Haney, who kept turning back to look at me. Did he not realize what he'd done?

Malik brought me to him and pleaded, "What's wrong, baby? What happened? Talk to me."

The lies came quickly.

"I almost had an accident. I did have an accident."

"Where? Are you hurt? Is anybody hurt?"

He pulled away, his hands on my shoulders, his eyes searching to see where I'd been injured.

"I hit a car, I was texting, and a cop followed me. I'm so sorry."

"Here, sit down," he offered, bringing me to the couch beside him. I glanced around me at all that was important to him. This office was a symbol of everything he believed in about justice, the law, and his character, now, because of me, it was about to crumble.

"Is anybody hurt? Where were you?"

"I was parked and I pulled out and hit the back of the car, the front, I don't know, the car was empty. . . I think. . . I don't know. . . I panicked."

He began to laugh. "Slow down, all right, stop crying."

"Malik, you don't understand," I cried, burying my head in my hands.

"So you're telling me that my wife, who campaigned to end texting and driving, hit a parked car while texting and driving?"

"Malik, it's not that, it's more. I mean, it's bad."

He stroked my hair. "Woman, nobody knows you were texting. It won't be in the papers, relax. I thought something happened. I'll take care of it."

"I've ruined everything."

"No, it's okay, stop crying, you haven't ruined anything," he told me, then wiped my eyes, giving me a tissue to blow my nose.

"I love you, Malik, I swear I do. I would never do anything to hurt you." I looked around, probably for the last time and said, "I'd never do anything to take away this."

"I know, baby, hold on."

He hit the intercom on the end table. "Rasheeda, can you send Phinn in, please." Then he turned to me and asked, "Who were you texting?"

I gripped the phone in my hand, paranoid that the

photo was still on the screen. Luckily, Phinn entered the office before I conjured up another lie. Malik explained the situation to him.

"I'll take care of it, sir."

"Tiffany, let Phinn drive you home and I'll be there later."

"What about Nylah? I have to get her from school. . . my car is here."

"I'll take care of it, go home, relax and have a glass of wine, okay."

"Malik, I love you, no matter what, I love you. I'm sorry."

He laughed, whispered in my ear and teasingly said, "How about I punish you when I get home?"

Before following Phinn through a side exit, I kissed Malik, certain it would be our last.

In the backseat of the Tahoe, I thought about who I could call, who could help me. Who could stop the hell that was about to reign down on not only me, but also my husband, my family, and the city?

I couldn't call Kamille, she'd say it was my fault and she was right since I'd willingly been with Haney twice. I tried calling Max, but when she didn't pick up, I decided against leaving a frantic message; she didn't need my drama while she was pregnant. I had to find a way to fix this myself.

"Mrs. Skinner, are you going to be all right?" Phinn asked, gazing at me through the rearview mirror.

"No, I'm not."

"Is there anything I can do for you?"

"Greg Haney, I need to see him – in private. Can you do that?"

"Yes, ma'am."

Once inside the house, I needed something to relax me, calm me down so I could think clearly and figure this out before Malik came home. I scrounged around in the kitchen cabinets and found a bottle of expired Xanax. I took one, chasing it with a half bottle of flat champagne that had been left in the refrigerator.

I tried calling Haney again, two, three times, thinking I could talk him out of exposing the photo to Malik, and to the media. Whatever he wanted, I'd give him. I just didn't want to ruin my husband.

However his unanswered calls just heightened my anxieties, so I took one more Xanax, this time opening a bottle of wine.

Somehow with my mobile still in my hand, I'd fallen asleep. I was laying across the bed when I heard the alarm chime. Malik was home. The clock on the cable box read, four a.m. He knew.

My head was in a fog from the Xanax, and so slowly I made my way to the top of the staircase and called down to him. "Malik."

He didn't answer. I went halfway down the stairs and tried again. "Malik."

I continued down the stairs until I was standing at the entrance to the kitchen. The lights were out, but the blue light from his mobile sat blinking on the counter.

"Why, Tiffany? Why the fuck did you do this to me?" he asked, not even turning around when I entered the kitchen.

I mumbled, "Nylah, did you get her?"

"You didn't think I'd bring her here, did you? She's with your parents."

"I didn't mean to do it, Malik. Give me a chance to explain."

"That's funny 'cause I think this picture is explanation enough." He held up his phone, the photo staring back at me. "What do you think?"

Turning my eyes away, I tried to talk. "It's not that. . ."

"Stop, don't even try to lie. I know everything."

"What do you mean?" I asked, realizing that if he really did know everything, then only one person could've told him.

"You fed me all that bullshit when he came home about being worried about *me*. When here, I'd married Haney's whore," he said, his statement ringing with disgust.

In all the years we'd been together, Malik had never called me a derogatory name, and now I was everything evil and bad that had happened to him in the last ten months since Haney had come home.

"Malik, I'm not a whore. Please hear me out. It wasn't like that. I made a mistake."

"What is there to hear? You ruined my reputation," he retorted, and then took a drink from the bottle of Pappy he was holding down on the counter.

I reached out, my hand on his arm, but he shook it off and moved to the other side of the counter. Pleading, I said, "Malik, we can fix this."

"Really and who's gonna fix it, Olivia fuckin' Pope? Or, let's see, maybe your lover, Haney? Yeah, he can fix it, like he fixed things with Wesley?"

My words constricted my throat, but I had to ask. "Does the media know yet?"

"Not yet, but they'll be here."

"There's still time, Malik. We can figure it out. You can say it was photo shopped."

"You sound ridiculous. I'm not getting caught up in that lie. Do you think when someone sees that photo, they won't know that it's really you? And what would that change? Even if we fooled everyone else, I'd still know that you're a whore. Shit!" he said, slamming his glass onto the counter, breaking it into shards that crashed to the floor.

I moved to the opposite side of the counter, facing him, but he kept turning away. Was he afraid of hitting me, and if he did, what would I do?

"You have to listen, give me a chance, please, I'm begging you."

"Go 'head, Tiffany, tell me how you were fucking that man and his son, how you videotaped your threesome with your girlfriend. Yeah, that's right, I know it all."

Backing up away from him, I stepped on glass, but that pain wasn't important. Using my hands, I covered my ears from his awful words and yelled, "Stop! Stop! Let me talk, I can explain. I was trying to help you."

"It's funny now, but I knew there was more to you wanting to bring him down. I was so blinded by you, by the power taking him down gave me, and now look, I'm the one that's powerless. It's always a woman, always, Nanny told me that a long time ago."

By now Malik's mobile had begun ringing with calls and vibrating with text messages. I felt myself fading away, probably from the pills and alcohol, but I had to hold on, to my thoughts, and to my husband.

"What? No! I'm home," he screamed at someone on the phone.

"Who was it?" I asked, assuming it was Cyndi warning him that the pictures were about to hit the press.

His head snapped up. "Are you really asking me that? Oh that's right, I'm screwing Cyndi. I guess that's mute now. You have nothing to say. You know what, Tiffany, why don't you get out?" he demanded, while his hands gripped the sides of the counter. I'd never seen my husband filled with so much anger.

"I am not leaving!"

"Why not? You've disgraced the one thing I believe in, my family. You had that man in my home. Ain't I the fool?"

"No! You had him here! You wanted him to fix things with Wesley. It's your fault Wesley's dead!"

As soon as the words were out, darkness covered his face. I knew I'd gone too far. He headed toward the door. I followed after him.

"Malik, wait, I'm sorry, I didn't mean to say that, please don't leave me," I begged, holding onto his arm.

Tossing me aside, he said, "You whore, get the fuck away from me!"

Chapter 21

Platinum Images

I don't know how long I slept, but the constant ringing of the house phone, coupled with the vibrating of my mobile, might've been the only thing that saved me.

Awkwardly sprawled across the bed, still in my skirt and bra, I attempted to sit up, causing the room to spin. I crawled to the bathroom, vomiting before I reached the toilet. Lying on the cold tiles of the bathroom floor eased my throbbing head, until I began replaying how things had unfolded. The photo, City Hall, arguing with Malik, the drinking, the Xanax, and now, more vomit.

The jarring light against the frosted bathroom window told me it was daytime, but the house was dark and cold. My panic came when I wondered where Nylah was, had she seen me like this? Where was Malik, had he taken her from me?

Using the sink, I pulled myself up, cranked open the window and even though I was blinded by the sun, I saw

Phinn. There he sat, protecting me from the throng of reporters gathered on my front lawn.

Back in the bedroom, tangled up in the comforter I found my mobile, filled with numerous missed calls, and text messages, the most recent one from my mother.

Mom: We have taken Nylah on the road with us to California.

There was also an earlier text from Haney.

Haney: It wasn't me. Let's talk.

It was too late, they knew, everybody knew. Rather than talk to anyone, I unplugged the bedroom phone. I was about to turn off my mobile when it rang, displaying a number and name that I couldn't ignore, and didn't want to. I pushed the accept button.

"I hear you could use a friend."

"Sasha," I cried to my former boss.

"Are you able to get to my office?"

I was crying too hard to answer.

"Never mind, stay there, I'm sending Michael."

I prayed that if nothing else, maybe Sasha could help me get out of town. I could go to my house in Montauk, figure things out until my parents returned.

An hour later when I opened the front door for Michael, who was carrying coffee and bagels, he hadn't come alone. Falling into Max's arms, her swollen belly was comfort until Lynn had to steady me down into a chair at the kitchen table.

"Here," Max said, holding a cup of coffee to my lips, "drink this, please."

I could tell my friend had been crying and instead of glowing in her pregnancy, Max was drawn and worried because of me. I hadn't been a good friend.

"Max, I'm sorry."

"Shhhh here, take a bite," she said, offering me pieces of a bagel.

Michael chimed in, "First thing she needs is a shower. Lynn, can you get her upstairs?"

"Sure thing," he said, before lifting me into his arms and carrying me like a baby upstairs to my bathroom. With Max's assistance, I undressed and stepped under the hot spray of water.

"I'll find her something to wear," Michael said, from now inside my closet.

"You're going to be okay, we'll get through this," Max assured me.

"I'll clean up," Lynn told them, having seen the vomit on my bedroom and bathroom floors.

The shower was helping to clear up some of the fog in my head, but my stomach was in knots. Max stayed right there with me, while I showered, washed my knotted hair, and brushed my teeth.

Once I was dressed, the next step was getting me out of the house, past the reporters and up to Manayunk. Phinn, and Lynn had the uniformed officers push the media all the way back to the street, making a path for Lynn's truck to back out. Then with Max and Phinn in front, and Michael and Lynn beside me, they hurried me outside through the swarm of reporters, shouting questions and cameras in our faces, all of which turned into one big blur behind my sunglasses.

Thirty-five minutes later, we arrived at Platinum Images. It had been remodeled in the seven years since I'd been gone, but there were still some friendly faces who smiled when we came through the reception area.

Sasha stood waiting at the bottom of the stairs to greet me with a reassuring hug, then ushered me upstairs to her old office, now occupied by Michael, who'd recently been promoted to President.

"How are you?" she asked, once we'd taken a seat on the couch.

"Worst time of my life," I told her, managing a weak smile.

"You're still among the living, so that's a plus."

"Sasha, you don't have to do this. All I need is to get outta Philly and up to my place in Montauk. I can sort it out there."

"Really, all by yourself? Because from what I've heard, your sorting it out consisted of Xanax and champagne. Odd combination."

"How bad is it?"

"I won't lie, it's ugly. The good news is, it broke over the weekend. But before we get to that, you have to call your family."

"Haney did this to me, didn't he?"

"We're still sorting through it, but Michael will lay all of that out for you in the conference room. Here, call your family, you're going to need them."

My first call was to my parents.

"Mom, it's me, Tiffany," I said, my voice trembling.

"Are you okay?"

"Yes. Mom, I'm sorry, I'm so sorry. Where's Nylah?"

"Your father and Nylah are up at the rest stop."

"Is she okay? What about school?"

"Malik had them send her homework, she'll be fine. But Tiffany, I'm telling you, you need to get yourself together."

Next, I tried Kamille, who I could tell, sent my call to voicemail. There was no need in leaving her a message because I already knew she wouldn't talk to me. I was sure she thought this was my fault, that somehow, I'd seduced Haney and maybe she was right, maybe everything was my fault.

I tried Huli's phone, it went directly to voicemail, but I did leave him a message. "Huli, it's me. I know you heard what happened and I'm so sorry for embarrassing you. I'm gonna fix it, I promise. I love you, little brother."

Next, Sasha led the way into the conference room where they were planning whatever strategy they thought might work. I wasn't worried about me, I wanted to fix things for Malik and my family, in hopes of saving them from any further pain.

Walking into the conference room, I was surprised at some of the faces sitting around the table. In addition to Max, Lynn, Michael, and Phinn, there was Janae, Craig, Judge Renwick, Brother Sadiq, and even Gretchen Hockstein. Did they all really care that much about me?

Burdened with self-pity, I cried, "I'm sorry, I'm so sorry."

"Here, take a seat," said Brother Sadiq, pulling out the chair next to him.

Janae sat across from me, her eyes sad, as she typed on her iPad. I'd disappointed her as well. What kind of role model had I been?

"We wanted to be here for you. Now what do we need to do, young man?" Judge Renwick asked of Michael.

Michael was about to launch into his plan, when the conference room door opened to someone that shouldn't have been there, Cyndi Kilrain.

"What! What the hell are you doing here, haven't you done enough damage?" I yelled in her direction as if it were her fault I'd slept with Haney.

"Tiffany, relax. I'm not so sure of that," commented Sasha, who stood at the back of the room."

"She's Malik's mistress, don't you understand?"

"Cyndi was one of the first people to call me," said Sasha.

Hesitating in the doorway, Cyndi said, "I know what you're thinking, but the Mayor and I have never had anything but a business relationship."

"That's a lie! Your stuff, I kept finding it at my house. Your badge, cell phone."

"It was pure coincidence, everyone knows I'm a klutz. I leave stuff everywhere and I'm sorry, but we really did meet there, all of us; it was never just me."

"I don't believe you," I said, looking around the table

for someone to agree with me.

"I swear, Mrs. Skinner, I'm not lying and to be perfectly honest, it wasn't me the Mayor was interested in."

That's when I recognized something different about Cyndi, her hair had been cut and colored, her clothes fresh and tailored to fit her body and her makeup was flawless.

"Wait a minute, so what are you saying? There was somebody else?" I asked, still not totally convinced it wasn't her.

Along with me, everyone around the table stared toward Cyndi waiting for a reply.

Cautiously, this time she looked around the table, I'm sure, hoping someone would believe her when she said, "The affair your husband is having, Mrs. Skinner, wasn't with me; it's his friend, Tootie."

I jumped up from my seat. Brother Sadiq held onto my arm, trying to pull me back down. Pointing my finger at her, I yelled, "You lying slut! I know it was you! Malik would never sleep with Tootie, that's his friend!"

Remaining calm, her face stoic, Cyndi said, "I'm sorry, but it's true, ask Phinn."

I whipped around toward Phinn who was seated at the end of the table. Lowering his head so I couldn't see his eyes, he nodded, cosigning what she'd said, but adding fuel to that fire by saying, "Blu Eyes has been having you followed."

"Why? This doesn't make any sense. You were with me all the time. Did Malik tell him to do that?"

"I don't think the Mayor knew, but Blu Eyes didn't trust you or me."

"Why would he do that? Why would he have an affair with Tootie? She's not even his type," I lamented in defeat, falling back into my chair because it felt as if I'd been paralyzed by what they were telling me. Gretchen quickly went to the server and brought me a bottle of water.

Cyndi began to talk, "Ma'am, I can't answer—" but Phinn cut her off.

"It started before you were married. They've been together, I mean, seeing each other for a long time."

"Where, when? I wanna know everything. Tell me Phinn, please?"

Sasha spoke up, "It doesn't matter, you need to put things in perspective right now, we all do. The priority is cleaning up the present dilemma."

"But the picture, who did that? Who sent that picture?" I asked of Cyndi and Phinn since they seemed to be the ones with all the information.

Cyndi took over, "Blu Eyes paid Mendels for the photo and well, Tootie. . ."

"Tootie?"

"Yeah, we think she got hold of it and sent it out to hurt you, of course," Phinn added.

This was crazy. I'd come here to save Malik from shame and hopefully to save my marriage as well, only to discover those Point Breeze friends of his were the ones who'd done the dirty work.

"Tiffany, I know this is a lot to process, but I need you to listen to me. You cannot mention to anyone about the affair or your being followed. That will be your ace in the hole, which means you can't let your husband know until it's in your favor," Sasha told me.

Gretchen added, "If you ask me, your husband's a damn fool. He should be asking for your forgiveness right now."

"I don't get it, why would he want *her*?" I asked, my head now flooded with every imaginable scenario. "One thing at a time," said Gretchen.

"Are you saying Haney didn't have anything to do with all this? He did send me a text saying it wasn't him."

Slamming his fist onto the conference room table, Phinn said, "Fuck Haney, he's a piece of shit!"

"I can get him taken care of," offered Lynn.

"I'd prefer to handle that," said Brother Sadiq.

Clearing his throat, Judge Renwick told them, "They'll be no talk of handling anyone, at least not while I'm in the room."

Michael stood up to take charge of the meeting. "There're a lot of moving pieces here, but we need to get back on track. Tiffany, we've scheduled a press conference for this Monday at eleven a.m.. It'll be held at RTC Holdings."

"Michael, are you crazy? I'm not doing that. I need time to figure all this out. It doesn't even make sense. What am I supposed to say? I'm sorry, for what? Malik is no better than me. And why would Raquel get involved anyway?"

"She was the *first* person to call me," Sasha interjected.

"This is your only option, people are waiting to hear from you," Craig said.

"What can I say, I can't deny it; the evidence is there," I told the group.

"Evidence of what?" asked Cyndi.

"Of me with Haney," I told her, still unable to absorb the change in her or what she'd told me about Malik and Tootie.

"The photo's gone viral and the Mayor had to shut down his Twitter account. Your name is trending on Facebook, Twitter, and Instagram and in the world of social media that means you broke the Internet," Janae offered.

"Well that counts for something, not everybody gets to trend," said Craig, his uneasy laughter breaking through my heartache.

It was bad enough that I'd gotten caught, but Malik and Tootie, I couldn't even fathom. I could hear them all talking, but my head was elsewhere.

"Janae, you need to clear her schedule for the next week," Michael said.

"The women's conference, too?"

"Hold off on that until after the press conference," Sasha added.

"You're really making me do this?"

Brother Sadiq responded with, "First Lady, when you get boxed into a corner, as you've done, speaking out about it takes away people's power to keep you there. You have to own it."

"You won't be alone, we'll all be right there with you, you can call us hashtag Team Tiffany," said Janae who was now fully engaged.

But I didn't want a team. I wanted my questions answered. I wanted to talk to Mr. Haney. I wanted to confront Tootie and what I really wanted at that moment was to kill my husband.

Chapter 22

Eye of the Storm

I woke up Monday morning to the smell of coffee brewing and bacon frying and even though I hadn't heard from Kamille, I was hopeful she might've been downstairs.

"Good morning, it smells good," I said, greeting Max in the kitchen.

"You've been sleeping all weekend. I thought I was going to have to force you to wake up," she responded, having insisted on staying with me for the weekend, after we'd left Platinum Images.

I could hear Michael in the dining room talking with someone, and asked, "Who's in there with Michael?"

"Hair and makeup, courtesy of Salon Tenshi."

"For what?"

"My friend, have you looked at yourself?" She laughed, then added, "There's someone else in there, too."

Maybe it really was Kamille, but to my ultimate surprise, it was my brother.

"Huli, what are you doing here?"

"You're my sister, where else would I be? Come here, give me some love," he said. For which I wasted no time falling into his open arms.

"I'm so happy you're here, but wait, you've got a game, you're in the World Series. Mom and Dad are out there with Nylah. Are they back?"

"Calm down, it's cool. Raquel Cosby-Turner flew me here."

That surprised me. "Are you sure, you're not going to get in trouble? I'm so sorry you had to come."

"We're flying back out after your press conference. C'mon big sis, you know better. So what? You messed up. I still love you, we still family."

I teared up. "What about Kamille? Does she hate me for all this?"

"She'll come around. Kamille's out there with the boys; she'll be back in a few days."

Michael interrupted us. "There will be no crying this morning. We cannot have your eyes all red and swollen. It's time to eat."

I was starved and having breakfast with Huli, Max, Jose, Michael and Lizzie, the stylist made it all better.

By ten a.m., we were traveling down JFK Boulevard to the Comcast Center with Phinn driving the Tahoe with me, Max and Michael; and following behind us in his Benz were Huli, Lizzie, and Jose. Bypassing the news trucks and bystanders, we pulled into the underground garage, where I held my brother's hand until we arrived to the 52nd floor of Raquel's office.

Once inside, Gwendolyn, who immediately caught my brother's eye, whisked us into a small conference room. Greeting us inside the room were Sasha, Gretchen, Janae, Judge Renwick and Brother Sadiq. I greeted everyone and was especially glad when Sasha told me that Michael would open the press conference, then I would speak and there'd be no questions. She said the entire press conference should be over in less than seven minutes.

"Have you heard from Malik?" I asked, hoping she had because neither Malik nor my sister had responded to my several calls and text messages. However, I refused to give up.

"I hear he's conveniently gone to Little Rock, Arkansas, a solar energy panel or something. But wherever the Mayor is, you can believe he'll be watching."

"What about Haney? Have you heard from him?"

"Not important. Now here's what I need you to do. I don't want you giving the sullen, poor me face. But you can't be too powerful either. You have to land somewhere in between. The purpose of this is for you to own your mistake, ask for forgiveness, and move on. You understand?"

I laughed and said, "Well what if I give them the finger?"

"Not funny, but you do look great," she commented, taking notice of the brown and cream boucle St. John's suit that Michael had chosen for me to wear.

Twenty minutes later, Michael walked out to the table set with microphones and waited until the reporters settled down. He spoke briefly, then nodded for me to take a seat with my brother taking a seat beside me, but not before Brother Sadiq whispered in my ear, "First Lady, you go out there and show them that you're still the woman on top of this city."

Having always stood at Malik's side, I never knew what it felt like to have those microphones waiting for your voice, and today there were too many to count. I wanted to pretend I was someone strong and resilient, but staring into the audience of reporters whose job it was to decipher not only my words, but my body language as well, made it rather difficult. I took note of what was around me, two bottles of water, a note pad and pen, and the script Sasha had written, which I'd already memorized over the weekend.

However, knowing that somewhere both Malik and Haney were watching, and my brother was beside me, I was suddenly ready, if for no other reason than to get it over with.

While Michael gave them the purpose and parameters of the press conference, reiterating that there would be no questions, I clasped my shaking hands together in front of me. Silently I said the Lord's Prayer, and tried to find someone on whom I could focus. Then I saw Lou Mendels, ruthlessly smiling my way.

"Good morning and thank you for coming here today. I sit before you to offer my sincere apologies for my recent irresponsible behavior that has hurt my husband, my family, and the City of Philadelphia. For this grave mistake,

I take full responsibility. The transgression that I committed has surely let my city down, but in no way does it reflect the man and leader that my husband has become for Philadelphia. My inappropriate behavior as First Lady and lack of judgment is neither a reflection on my commitment to this city or that of my husband in his efforts to continue moving this city forward. I love my husband, your Mayor, Malik Skinner and would ask that you give our family the privacy we need to heal. Thank you."

It was over, I'd done it. I'd asked for the public's forgiveness and hopefully, I could move on, which also might mean some sort of reconciliation with my sister, and my husband.

Raquel was gracious to receive us afterward with a catered reception on her wraparound deck, complete with a wait staff serving her signature champagne, and expensive Veen bottled water. Although I was hungry, I was too nervous to eat, choosing to sip on ginger ale. All I really wanted to do was go home and pray for Malik to call.

Everyone was pleased with my delivery, but at the same time the afternoon was chaotic with all the phones ringing and vibrating. Michael and Janae were reporting that I was again trending on social media, and that in addition to a fan page, I even had my own hash tag, #FLOP, First Lady of Philadelphia. Then Janae informed us that the organizers of The Pennsylvania Conference of Women no longer wanted me to host a workshop, they now wanted me as keynote speaker for their luncheon.

After individually thanking everyone, especially Sasha for coming to my rescue, I had to find words to thank Raquel for her support. However, I wasn't sure if I could break her away from my brother. It was funny seeing her enamored by someone other than herself, and even harder to determine if she wanted to adopt Huli or sleep with him.

Finally, he broke loose from her clutches so that he could head back to California, but little did Raquel know that flying in her private jet with him would be Lizzie, my new stylist.

"Your brother is a smart man, he could do a lot of things when his baseball career is over," she said, coming to stand at the elevator with me after we'd said our goodbyes.

"Hopefully that won't be for a long time. I really appreciate you flying him out here for this. Your support means a lot to me, I'm not sure how I would've done all this without you."

"The pleasure was mine, especially flying with your brother; it gave me a chance to get to know Julian personally."

"You were on the plane with him out here?"

"Actually it was he who insisted. Julian is quite the ladies' man," she said, with a teasing smile.

"Yes, that would be my brother," I replied, praying that Huli hadn't had sex of any kind with this woman. "Raquel, you are an amazing woman. You have the ability to touch everything and know everything."

"My dear, when it's important enough, I take care of things myself," she said, sliding her arm through mine as we made it out to the deck. "We women have to stick together, you know?"

"It might not mean much, but if I can ever be of any assistance to *you*, please don't ever hesitate to ask. Even though I have no idea what I could do to possibly match all you've done for me. You make a great mentor."

"Tiffany, I hope by now you'd consider us friends, and that eventually you might reconsider my offer," she said, closing her hands around mine, her eyes squinting, like always, giving the hint of something else impossible to read.

"I'd like that, us being friends," I said, feeling a little lightheaded as we were now standing directly against the half glass wall that surrounded her deck.

"Before you go, I want to let you know that if this fight with your husband gets dirty, I mean divorce, custody or anything, you call me first. I have the best attorneys and we can keep everything confidential."

"Thanks, but I'm praying that won't be necessary."

"It's my understanding the Mayor needs some forgiving as well," she said, letting me know she knew about his relationship with Tootie.

"We've both made mistakes; unfortunately mine became national news."

"You do realize that this press conference is going to change the course of your life forever."

I gave a little laugh and said, "That one photo has already changed the course of my life. Right now, all I want is to be normal, back with my daughter and husband."

"Trust me, you're bigger than your husband."

Chapter 23

#FLOP ~ She's Sorry

Splashed across the headlines, "*#FLOP She's Sorry*," made me easy fodder for daytime talk shows, as well as great monologues for Kimmel, Fallon and Bill Maher, and without even being a celebrity, a hot topic on *Wendy Williams*.

I refused to watch the news, read the papers, or fall prey to the comments on social media. I let Janae and Michael keep me updated on anything that was relevant, including the fact that my press conference had been viewed and downloaded on YouTube over 80 thousand times. Each morning, I didn't know whom the press would focus on -- my husband or me. And of course there was always some great news about Haney and his rising star as a community activist. As much as I wanted to, I still hadn't had the chance to speak with him and I doubted I ever would. Surprisingly, he hadn't taken advantage of the photo; even when given the opportunity for a sound bite, he was gracious.

"The taking, and the releasing of that photo was an unfortunate incident to which I did not take part. I admire Mrs. Skinner's courage and resilience, and only have the highest respect for her."

Phinn was still driving me and even more so, with my newfound popularity. He was protecting me from those religious groups and Republican women's organizations that shunned and labeled me a Jezebel. Democrats, of course, believed that if the Mayor couldn't watch over his wife, then how could he be trusted to watch over the city? Even with a situation so personal, there were not only critics, but also experts and pundits. I was even being criticized by some about my expensive wardrobe. Raquel had been right, I'd become a martyr for some women and a Jezebel for others.

My family life was not much better. Malik and I communicated via text messages and voicemails and we shuffled Nylah between home, my parents and Nanny, which is where he was staying. Needless to say, our daughter had questions as to why Daddy wasn't home with us, and my response was that Nanny needed his help, but my defenses were withering. I at least wanted to know where all this was going to end up.

Nevertheless, here I was at the Pennsylvania Convention Center about to be introduced by the First Lady of Pennsylvania, Frances Wolf, to 8,000 women eager to hear me speak. There hadn't been much time for preparation. The press conference had been on Monday and here it was Thursday, and I was running on pure adrenaline, made up of caffeine and sugar. I knew that if I didn't rest soon, I was going to collapse.

Wearing a cobalt blue dress, flared at the bottom, with silver buttons down the back, my hair, which had grown three inches, was swept to one side, since I'd promised Max I wouldn't wear a bun.

Michael and Sasha had written a twenty-minute speech, not to divert attention from the affair, but to make it about all women who'd been scorned because of transgressions beyond our control. It was about taking our power back, which I hadn't even begun to do, yet here I was.

Sasha greeted me backstage, excited that I had this opportunity. "These women are going to love you!" she exclaimed.

"Sasha, I wanna thank you for all of this. I don't know what I would've done had you not called."

"I believe I recall you wanted to run away to Montauk, but not even a week later, look at you now."

Anxiously, Michael and I stood at the side of the stage until we heard Mrs. Wolf say, ". . . and with that I give you the First Lady of Philadelphia, Tiffany Johnson-Skinner."

Not only was there applause when I walked out onto the stage and hugged Mrs. Wolf, but these women were on their feet.

"Good afternoon. . . it is very humbling and might I say overwhelming to stand before such an esteemed body of women today. . . and might I add a little confusing. I'm sure you'll agree that we all have to own our successes, as well as our failures. Recently my failure, might I call it a misstep, was epic and because of that lapse in judgment, I almost allowed myself to be shamed into silence. . . "

The audience shouted, "No! No! No!"

"We, as women, are to be commended. I am proud of being a wife, a mother, a daughter, a sister and still the First Lady of this city. But I could not be any of those things without first being a woman of substance and value. Did I fall short? Yes. Did I put myself in a compromising position? Yes, but it's not who I am. That one moment in my life doesn't define Tiffany Johnson-Skinner. We all live praiseworthy and admirable lives, even when we make a mistake. . . see walls that aren't there. . . recognize our self-worth. . . empower all of us. . . what affects one, affects us all. . .

"Who would've thought that because of my transgressions that I'd become the popular 'girl'. . . who is now known on social media with the hash tag FLOP, with 141,000 followers. . . WOW!"

The audience gave me another encouraging round of applause while I momentarily imagined telling this audience that my husband wasn't without blame as he was in a longstanding relationship with a woman whom I thought was only his childhood friend. These women had no idea the insecurities his affair had now given me, especially with the woman he'd chosen. What sickened me the most though was wondering if he was Sheema's father?

"The challenges we face in business and in our personal lives. . . differ from men. A few months ago, I spearheaded a project. . . my dream of helping our children, turned into the Blessed Babies Wellness Center. . . today it's about all of us as a collective body. . . of resilient, persevering, and powerful women, we can't give up and we can't let those dreams die. . . "

The applause drowned me out as they rose to their feet chanting, "FLOP, FLOP, FLOP!"

". . . In the words of Alice Walker, 'The most common way people, 'women' give up their power, is by thinking they don't have any.' As women, we have the power and *we can do better*. Thank you!'"

I couldn't have imagined the applause of 8,000 women, it was deafening. With Mrs. Wolf, Raquel Turner-Cosby, and other notable women coming to stand beside me, I wiped away tears as we held hands high in the air for everyone to see. I was no martyr and didn't want to be the spokesperson for all women. And for as strong as they'd made me feel on that stage, I wanted to be home with my family.

When I walked backstage to where Michael, Janae, and Sasha were waiting, the first thing Janae said was, "I think you just became a rock star."

It took more than an hour to get out of there, with the throngs of women wanting to personally meet me, shake my hand, and give me hugs. Business cards and phone numbers were handed to Michael and Janae with requests for interviews and speaking engagements. Thankfully, Phinn provided space between me and the reporters, who followed us to the curb taking pictures and hoping for a sound bite.

Afterward, the four of us headed to a private room at the Capital Grille, where I insisted that Phinn come inside and join us. I couldn't think of a better way to thank them than by treating them to lunch.

During that time, I took a moment to tell Janae that she was getting a raise, and for Michael, he'd now been officially hired as my publicist, at least until all this popularity blew over. As much as I wanted to do something special for Phinn, he refused to accept anything I offered. Sasha, who'd come to my rescue, all she wanted was for me to take advantage of the full plate I was being offered.

If I thought I'd received invitations before the press conference, the days that followed my speech were unbelievable. Everyone wanted my time and they were willing to pay. However, I had no desire to fill the role because it had been a week since the photo and I still hadn't heard from Kamille or Malik. I could learn to live without Malik, but not without my sister. However, having had a brief conversation with Brandon, he'd explained to me that Kamille was mad at both Mr. Haney and me.

On the other hand, Malik wasn't faring too well with his female constituents. There'd been no statement from him, his Tweets were all about the business of the City, and he refused to respond to reporters' questions about the status of our marriage. The public was ridiculing him for not standing by me – holding my hand like so many wives had done for their politician husbands. He was being crucified on daytime talk shows and even *Saturday Night Live* had done a parody on the First Family of Philadelphia.

But finally after two weeks, the call came. Malik wanted to meet, but what was odd was that he hadn't called me; he'd reached out to Sasha. This made me realize that whatever he had planned had more to do with this image than our marriage.

Making certain to get to Platinum Images before Malik, with Phinn at the wheel, we drove out to Manayunk, both lost in our own thoughts.

I arrived at nine forty-five a.m. Standing beside my open car door, Phinn asked, "You gonna be all right in there?"

"How bad could it be? He's my husband," I joked.

"I'm here if you need me. . . Mrs. Baker."

We both laughed, then I hugged him. "Thanks, Mr. Baker."

Not having seen Malik since that awful night, I had no idea how we would interact with each other. But I knew there'd be tension for both of us. I prayed for the best. Malik arrived twenty minutes late, appearing less than polished, in jeans and a button down white shirt.

Greeting him, Sasha said, "Good morning, Mayor Skinner, please have a seat. Can I get you anything?"

"No, let's just get this over with," he said, taking the seat closest to the door and the furthest from me.

What did he want to get over with? A divorce? A custody discussion? In that case, I would need a lawyer.

"I'm sure you're here because you've seen your wife's press conference and heard the feedback. My question is, what are your plans for handling it?"

"I'm running the city, that's how I'm handling it."

"Which means you'll be seeking re-election and you can't do that without Mrs. Skinner."

Shrugging his shoulders, he said, "I can't have a wife like her, she's a -"

"Please no name calling and could you not refer to your wife in the third person."

"I came here to hear what you had to say, not to make amends with my wife."

Glaring at him, I wanted to let loose my own rage by telling him I knew about his relationship with Tootie, and about Blu having me followed, but Sasha's cutting eye warned me not to because so far, Malik had no idea that Tootie was behind the photo.

"In that case, your wife can leave now, but you'll be kissing your election goodbye. Is that what you want?"

His face was shrouded in defeat. Silently, Malik drummed his fingers against the table, while I cringed, anticipating what he might say.

"Don't be a coward, Mayor Skinner. No one will judge you for taking your wife back, and what do you care if they do, so long as you get re-elected?"

"Excuse me, but I stand on very high morals and they don't include photos of my wife having sex with another man."

"Malik, I'm sorry. . ." But I stopped short when he wouldn't even look at me.

"Right now, morals, photos or whatever, your wife owns these votes. It's women who carry your election. They have the influence, and right now they're standing behind Mrs. Skinner."

Finally acknowledging me by casting a hateful glance my way, he said, "The state of my re-election does not depend on her."

"Then why'd *you* call this meeting?"

"I need this cleaned up and you said you could help," Malik told her.

"Then let's proceed. Your next step after the Mayor's office is in one of two directions, Senator or Governor. Once you get re-elected, you can do what you want. But right now, you need to publicly forgive your wife, and tell your voters that the two of you are working it out. Had this been in the reverse. . ."

"She wouldn't have stood by me."

I couldn't respond to that because he was right.

"I'm not doing that," he said. "I'm not working it out."

"Like it or not, you're both public figures now, with hard choices to make. And if you don't choose your wife, you won't have a political career. Certain people can make sure of that. I believe it's referred to as political suicide and you're already standing on the ledge."

I wondered if Sasha was referring to Raquel.

"Are you threatening me?"

"No, just being honest, Mr. Mayor. Listen, all you have to do is release a statement to the media. There will be no press conference. It'll be seamless and in a few days it'll be old news."

He mumbled something neither of us could hear, then rubbing his hands across his forehead in frustration, he asked, "Where's the statement?"

Just a few hours after that meeting, Malik released his statement.

"Recently, my wife committed an indiscretion by breaking our marriage vows. She has had the courage to stand before you, as she has done with our family, offering her sincere apologies and asking forgiveness for her transgression. I will admit, we are going through a very difficult time, but this is clearly a personal and private matter for our family, and contrary to false rumors being spread online, and across our city, I unequivocally love my wife and forgive her. As mayor of this city, I say to Philadelphia, in speaking for my wife and myself, we will do better."

Late that night, he showed up with his things.

Chapter 24

My Little Princess

Even with Malik home, I wasn't sleeping too well and there were no more Xanax at my disposal. During the day, no matter how much coffee or energy drinks I ingested, I was still sluggish. I'd scheduled a doctor's appointment to be checked for anemia, diabetes and possibly depression. With me nearing forty, my plan was to change to a healthier diet, start taking vitamins, sign up with a personal trainer, maybe even cut off my hair. But more than anything, I desperately needed him to prescribe me some sleeping pills.

Malik had come home, but it was more of an arrangement than a marriage, and for right now, I was okay with that. As expected, we were sleeping in separate rooms, with him staying in the family room until after Nylah was asleep, then retiring to the spare bedroom. He did keep more normal hours, there were no late nights, no excessive drinking, and absolutely no sex between us. I still hadn't mentioned what I knew about Tootie and Blu Eyes because I wanted him to forgive me without guilting him into it. I was still concerned though, wondering if he had fathered Sheema.

The only thing that forced us to communicate was Nylah and her upcoming birthday party. We were both looking forward to having some life and laughter back in the house, even if it was only for the day.

For the first time, Malik didn't gripe about the cost, as we'd gone overboard on decorations, party favors, a magic show, and catering for the children, as well as the adults. The biggest expense, of course, was when I surprised Nylah with a beautiful pink and white princess dress, complete with acrylic slippers. Her hair was in a bun, fixed around a glittering tiara. Malik didn't even object to her wearing a little sheer lip-gloss. Now I understood why couples stayed together for their children.

Nylah's happiness and excitement forced us to take family pictures of the three of us while hanging decorations and making up the gifts bags. Malik didn't even complain about having to ride out to Holmesburg Bakery to pick up the cake. All of this, of course, was to compensate for our broken marriage.

The hardest part of the day though, would be my having to face not only Tootie, but also Nanny. I didn't doubt she'd known about her grandson's affair, and since I hadn't heard from her, I knew she'd be treating me with disdain because of mine.

The party promptly began at two with five of Nylah's classmates and their parents being the first to arrive. Directly behind them was Curtiss with her youngest son, WJ, named after Wesley. I knew Malik would be happy to see them.

Max and Lynn were the next to arrive, but only stayed long enough to wish Nylah a happy birthday and drop off their gifts. My visibly tired friend, with her swollen legs, had been ordered by her doctor to stay off her feet, which meant she had stopped working.

Tej and Ana had also been invited and I was always so glad to see the mother and the son who sparked Blessed Babies. And to my delight, Ana brought with her a new healthy six-month-old baby girl, and Christian, her fiancé.

It didn't take much to ignore Blu Eyes, who'd slipped in without being noticed, because we'd never had much dialogue anyway. Of course I had no idea he had a three year-old son, with the same creepy blue eyes as his father.

As I thought over what had happened, I assumed Blu Eyes never intended to cause Malik harm, but Tootie wanted to destroy me, so she could have my husband.

However, I was glad to see Phinn when he arrived with his twins in their adorable matching outfits. And even though my sister hadn't responded to my invitation, my mom and dad brought my nephews.

Finally during the frenzy of the afternoon with Malik and I taking turns to greet guests, Nanny, Tootie, and Sheema arrived.

"Tiffany," Nanny said, her face drawn and her voice stern, when I opened the door for them.

Tootie stood beside her, hiding behind those same black sunglasses trimmed with rhinestones that she'd worn to Wesley's funeral.

I'd thought that I'd want to lash out at her, but instead, I felt sorry for her and was even curious as to what had been the basis of their relationship. In some ways she wasn't much different than me, having found herself lusting after the wrong man. It didn't bother me so much that Malik had slept with someone outside of our marriage, what bothered me was that it had gone on for years with a woman who he'd presented as a friend. I just couldn't understand the attraction.

"Good afternoon, Nanny. Sheema, the kids are in the back, c'mon," I said, with Sheema running past me toward the family room. Tootie stood talking on her cell phone.

"Tiffany, I wanna talk to you before I leave here today."

"Nanny, it's your granddaughter's birthday, I don't think today is good for that conversation," I told her, not wanting to sound disrespectful.

I heard Tootie snicker and I doubted it had anything to do with her phone call.

"Fine, but listen here, what you did, embarrassing my grandson with that man, well you are no longer welcome in my home for Sunday dinners, or ever!"

"Nanny, I'm not the only one guilty in all. . . "

Walking up behind me, Malik interrupted, I'm sure knowing that Nanny would be gunning for me. "Hey, Tootie. Nanny, come on in, let me get your coats," he said, greeting them. Then simply for show, he put his arm around my shoulders, making it the first time he'd touched me since returning home.

Finally Tootie spoke, "Hi Tiffany, Malik, what's up?"

Swallowing my pride and my anger, I left them at the door and went in the kitchen to check on the caterer.

Having calmed the kids down enough to gather to get ready to sing Happy Birthday, my Dad went to answer a knock at the door. I wasn't sure who it could be because everyone who'd been invited was already there. To my surprise, it was my sister, appearing distraught. I prayed she hadn't come here to cause a scene.

Instead she came and stood next to me, grabbing hold of my hand while we sang Happy Birthday.

"Are you all right?" I asked, once Nylah blew out her candles.

"Not now."

"What's wrong?"

"Later," she mumbled.

As the caterer began to serve cake, I'd gone into the kitchen to get more dessert plates, and there was Tootie, her back to me, talking and laughing with someone on her mobile, probably making me the brunt of their joke.

Standing in the doorway, I watched her tapping her foot to the music that played in the other room. She was slightly taller than me, and clearly had thicker curves that overflowed from being stuffed into a pair of black jeans. Malik had been the one always complaining about how crass and unpolished she was. I'd thought she was free-spirited, and a 'take no tea for the fever' kind of woman. Yet, she was the woman he'd chosen to service his needs, which obviously he didn't think I was capable of.

"Oh sorry, Tiffany, you need help with something?" she asked, half-turning, with her cleavage bouncing and bubbling over the V-neck of her sweater.

"Yeah, I do. I need you to stop screwing my husband," I told her, not having planned to have those words come out of my mouth.

"What did you say?" she asked, placing her hand on her big hip.

"You heard me, I said stop screwing my husband."

"Seriously? You gotta lotta nerve with what you did to him," she said, while rolling her eyes as if I were bothering her.

"Do you seriously think you're better than me?"

After telling someone on the phone she'd call them back, she responded with, "He wouldn't still be fucking me after all these years, if I wasn't *better*. What do you think?"

"You've been warned," I said, more forcefully, yet still not raising my voice.

She picked her sunglasses off the counter and put them on top of her headful of silky weave. "You know I ain't got time for your trick ass, Tiffany. You have no idea who I am."

"You know what, you're right 'cause I don't even know your name. So why don't you tell me, who are you, Tootie?" I asked, now placing both hands on my hips.

She poked out her chest, reared her shoulders back, then began counting off on her fingers. "First off, I'm the one *your husband* sipped champagne with on New Year's. I'm the one *your husband* came to when Wesley was killed. Oh that's right, he left your dumb ass in Disney World. And you wanna know what else? When your nasty ass picture got plastered all over the Internet, whose bed do you think *your husband* was laid up in?"

"And how'd that happen Tootie? How'd that picture get leaked?" I asked, now having moved further into the kitchen.

Twisting her lips, she said, "Don't know. Why don't you ask that ol' ass man that had you pinned up against the window. But don't worry about what me and *your husband* are doing, what we've been doing for a long time."

"Malik doesn't want you," I said, with my voice cracking under the weight of her hurtful words.

"Girl, you have no idea how your husband likes lying between all this," she proudly exclaimed, smiling and smacking her thighs for emphasis.

I couldn't believe this was happening. I tried to speak calmly, but I felt the bile rising in my throat. "Your obese ass is only good for one thing. You'll never be in my shoes or have any of this. You'll never be First Lady," I stated louder than the ringing in my ears.

Like a prizefighter, Tootie moved from her corner, her attitude smug, and she was now up in my face, where I could smell the grape soda on her breath, mingling with her cheap Victoria's Secret lotion.

"You bougie bitch, yeah, you got a degree and you the pretty girl with the perfect body, but I'm the one that makes your man holla. The only reason I'm not here, in this house, in your place, is because I didn't want to turn into you! So if you want that ol' ass Haney, go right ahead 'cause *your husband*, Mayor Skinner, likes all this jiggling fat ass in his face," she exclaimed, further humiliating me by jabbing her finger in my chest.

I'm not sure if it was from the taunting of her words or her finger, when it stabbed my chest, but the next thing I knew, I'd punched Tootie dead in the face and was literally on top of her on the kitchen floor, punching, screaming and crying. Having taken her and myself by surprise, Tootie was no match for me, as she relentlessly flailed her arms in an effort to free herself from my aggression. The only thing that stopped me was Malik wrapping his arms around my waist, lifting me in one full swoop to my feet. That's when I realized we were no longer alone.

"Tiffany! What the hell is wrong with you?" Malik yelled.

"Get off me, let me go, I'm gonna kill this bitch," I yelled still kicking at her.

Phinn stood in the doorway barring anyone from coming in as our guests clamored to see what the commotion was about. For her sake, Blu had now come to Tootie's rescue.

"Stop, calm down! You're gonna hurt her," Malik said, still holding onto me and obviously more concerned about Tootie getting hurt than he was about me.

"Get her, Malik before I fuck her up!" Tootie stammered, as she gasped for air with Blu standing over her.

"Tiffany, what are you doing? You're ruining Nylah's party!" my husband yelled, his eyes darting from me to Tootie.

"Look at you, your fat ass can't even breathe," I sneered at her, while Blu, struggling to get Tootie back on her feet, crushed the contents of the children's gift bags that had spilled to the floor.

"Tiffany, stop it! Right now!"

Violently, I whipped around ready to pounce on him as well. "How long, Malik? How long have you been screwing this tramp? Why didn't you just marry her?"

Wrinkles of surprise appeared on his forehead, and when his mouth opened, no words came out.

"No, you listen, I want her, and him," I pointed to Blu, "the fuck outta my house, NOW!"

Phinn had managed to push everyone back through the doorway into the family room; among them I noticed was Nanny.

"I can't believe this is happening," Malik said, looking from me to Tootie.

"Yeah right, well Malik, you need to get your wife in check before she get hurt," Tootie told him as Blu gathered up her shattered cell phone and broken sunglasses.

This time I laughed and said, "I don't think so; now why don't you get your fat ass outta my house."

"Bitch, you got lucky. C'mon, Blu."

As she passed by me, I told her, "Oh yeah, and as you can see, you ain't the only bitch from the streets."

Alone now in the kitchen with Malik, I demanded to know, "Is Sheema your daughter? Tell me the truth, no more lies, Malik."

"No, no I swear to you she's not, but we have to talk."

"You're a lying bastard."

"I'm not lying, we did a DNA test, she's not mine. Quiet down, please. You're embarrassing us. It's our daughter's birthday."

"Well guess what? I don't care. I've known about you and that troll for weeks, now get the hell outta my way!"

Passing through the family room, parents scrambled out of my way after probably already having texted and posted to social media about the drama unfolding at the mayor's house, but I no longer cared. Fortunately, the magician had the attention of the kids with a live magic show, but on the couch, there sat Nanny. She pretended to be oblivious to what she'd witnessed, however I didn't doubt she was a part of Malik and Tootie's dirty secret.

Positioning myself directly in front of her, I said, "I hope you're satisfied, because guess what, you're not welcome in my house either!"

Next, I went looking for my sister. I needed to know what was wrong with her. I found Kamille sitting alone in the dining room. "Come with me," I said, grabbing her up from the chair and pulling her into the laundry room.

When we were alone, I asked, "What's wrong, what did he do to you?" already assuming Haney was the cause of her distress.

"Tiffany, I messed up real bad. I'm sorry," she said, after taking a seat on the stepladder, while I stood in front of her.

"Stop with all this apologizing and tell me what's wrong."

"Malik. When he got the picture, he came to me asking if I knew. He was so hurt, I'd never seen him like that. He was crying and I was so angry with you for sleeping with Haney, for ruining your marriage, our family, so I told him everything. I told Malik about before."

Her words stunned me. I understood her hurt, but not her betrayal. "This just will not get any better," I groaned. "Is that why you haven't taken my calls?"

She nodded and then, hanging her head, she said, "I read his journal."

"Whose journal?"

"My address was listed at the prison, and this morning a box arrived addressed to me, so I opened it. I'm sorry."

"Kamille, please I can't take hearing the word sorry anymore. That's all I've been saying and hearing for the past month."

Before she could go on, the laundry room door opened and Malik appeared, asking, "Can you please let me explain?"

My frosted look told him more than my words. "Not now, leave us alone," I said to him before turning to Kamille and saying, "Go on."

"Tiffany, please?"

"What the hell? I said leave us alone." I slammed the door shut.

Turning back to my sister, she said, "There were letters he'd received, pictures I'd sent him, and his journal. He planned it all, Tiff. Drawing me in, luring you, and getting Malik to trust him. . . "

It was hard to understand what Kamille was saying in between her crying and sniffling.

"What do you mean?" I asked, feeling as if I'd been stuck with a pin, the air quickly deflating from my body.

"It was you he felt was responsible for bringing him down. He blames you and that's why all of this is going on. He's obsessed with you."

Her words made my head spin. "Have you talked to him? Does he know you read it?"

She shook her head. "All of this is my fault. I wanted you to accept him so bad. I don't even know why. And Mommy and Daddy, I love them. I'm so sorry."

I brought her to me, consoling her and telling her, "It's not your fault. It's gonna be all right. Have you told Brandon?"

She nodded and said, "He was home with me when I opened it. He's going to see him."

Knowing that Haney had hurt my sister had me seething. "I promise you, Kamille, he won't get away with this."

"No, Tiff, don't get involved. Please let Brandon handle him."

"It's too late, he's gone too far."

If anybody was going to talk to Haney, it would be me and there was only one person I could rely on to make that happen.

I found Phinn on the front porch, flirting with one of the mothers from Nylah's school.

"Excuse me, Phinn, can I speak with you?" I asked, then waited until the woman went inside.

"What is it, Mrs. Skinner?"

"Can you set up a meeting with Mr. . . ."

Before I could finish, his eyes turned away from me, out toward the driveway filled with cars, "I don't think that's a good idea. He's caused a lot of trouble for you and the Mayor."

"Phinn, please, I'm begging you to do this one last thing for me."

After a moment, he said, "I'll see what I can do."

Chapter 25

Trick or Treat

Now that I knew his secret, Malik was the one apologizing and asking to talk so we could work things out. I didn't even bother to have a conversation with him, I simply didn't have the energy. So instead, for Nylah, we kept up with our charade of being in a real marriage, especially now that she was excited for Halloween.

Phinn had done as I asked, and set up a meeting with Haney and me for Halloween night at ten p.m. My plan was to ask him what it would take to get him out of our lives. I had money, and within reason I could pay. The only thing I had to figure out was an excuse to get of the house at that time of night.

In the meantime, that morning I had an appointment for a physical at Jefferson Hospital with Dr. Goldstein. I hadn't realize that my last doctor's visit had been two years ago, so before I could even see the doctor, I had to update my paperwork and answer a battery of questions. Stepping onto the scale, it was clear that I'd lost considerable weight, my blood pressure reading was below normal and the nurse was barely able to draw blood from my shallow veins.

When I was finally able to sit across the desk from Dr. Goldstein, the concern on his face let me know that whatever my condition, it was serious.

"Mrs. Skinner, I don't have to tell you that you're running on empty. Your blood work shows an extremely low iron count, which doesn't surprise me and your urine sample reveals that you're borderline diabetic, which also doesn't surprise me in your condition, especially with all the recent stress."

"Dr. Goldstein, I don't understand, what specific condition are you referring to?"

"Oh I'm sorry, you're pregnant. I'd say you're about six to eight weeks pregnant, but we'll know better once we do an ultrasound," he stated, as if he'd just told me I had the flu.

Dr. Goldstein's words stunned me into silence. Being pregnant was the last thing I'd expected to hear. I began hyperventilating, the room grew hot, I unbuttoned my shirt, but still I felt myself slipping away. Before I could stop the spinning, I'd slipped from the chair onto the floor and fainted.

"Mrs. Skinner! Mrs. Skinner, would you like me to call your husband?" I heard a voice asking from somewhere in the distance.

"No, no don't. I'm all right," I responded to the nurse who was standing on one side of me. Dr. Goldstein was on the other side.

"Here, let me help you up," he said, as he and the nurse sat me up on the floor.

I drank from the bottle of water she offered, while attempting again to register what he'd told me. They settled me into the chair. The nurse exited the room.

"Dr. Goldstein, are you sure, I'm pregnant? Could there be a mistake? I mean, I haven't been sick," I began to tell him, but then I remembered I *had* been sick, vomiting several times, and I hadn't kept track of my period since I'd stopped using birth control. And then, of course, there'd been no protection with Haney.

"I don't usually get these things wrong, but you should follow up with your Ob-Gyn. I could do an ultrasound today, unless you'd prefer waiting for when the Mayor can be with you to see what your exact due date is."

I shook my head. "You don't understand, this isn't good news, not right now," I told him, when what I really wanted to ask was how soon could a DNA test be performed?

Sensing my distress, Dr. Goldstein removed his glasses and rubbed his eyes, recalling, I'm sure, the racy photo and press coverage of my affair.

"I see. If you'd like to speak with someone about your options, I can arrange that," he said, his voice having gone from concern to conspiratorial.

Grabbing my purse and steadying myself on my feet, I said, "No, I'll be fine, I just need to get some air. Thank you, and Dr. Goldstein, please don't tell anyone, not even my husband."

With my mind reeling, it was crucial now that I meet with Haney. There had to be a way to make him go away. I had no idea how I'd face Malik, but as of right now, neither of them could know I was pregnant.

That evening, Malik took the initiative to get Nylah dressed in her princess costume, taking her first to his old neighborhood in Point Breeze and then returning to trick or treat in ours.

Once they were out of the house, on my iPhone I made several attempts to Google the DNA testing process, and I also checked my calendar to figure out the exact days that I'd been with Haney, but I kept getting interrupted by the constant ringing of my doorbell with trick or treaters.

I realized that if I didn't want to take the chance of having another man's baby, there was only one person who could help me resolve this situation.

Tiffany: need your help with a very private matter

RTC: how soon can you come to my office

Tiffany: tomorrow

It was after eight-thirty p.m. when Malik and Nylah returned home from trick or treating. Malik was in a good mood and Nylah was exhausted, and he had to carry her into the house. Taking that opportunity, I casually mentioned that Dr. Goldstein had called in a prescription for me that I needed to pick up that night.

"How'd it go for you at the doctor's anyway? Everything okay?" he asked as we began to sort through her candy.

"I'm fine, just some B-12 and iron pills, he wants to boost my immune system. But I have to get that prescription tonight," I said, mixing lies with the truth.

"Did we have a lot of kids come by?"

"Yes, but we still have candy. I'm going to get Nylah ready for bed," I told him, before turning to Nylah and saying, "Go upstairs, sweetie, and get undressed. I'll be up in a minute."

"You want me to pick up your prescription," he asked.

"No, I'm going to run out to Walgreens later," I repeated trying to keep the desperation from my voice and face.

"Tiffany, I wanted to ask you a question," he said as his eyes brightened with a smile.

Standing on the bottom step, trying to get away from him, impatiently I asked, "What, Malik? What is it?"

"Later tonight, after you get back, do you think we could sit down and talk?" he asked, his voice hopeful.

What did he want to talk about? Had Dr. Goldstein called him? Did he know I was pregnant or was it possible he was ready to reconcile our broken marriage? My delay in responding made him ask me again.

"Uhm, sure, okay," I said, confused as to what he wanted to talk about.

"I'm serious, this has gone on too long. We can't keep ignoring it."

"I'd like that, but right now I'm going to give Nylah a bath so I can go out for that prescription before it gets too late. Can it wait until I get back?"

"Sure, but Tiffany. . ."

"Yes," I asked, annoyed that he was beleaguering the subject.

He kissed me lightly on the lips and said, "Thank you."

By nine-thirty, I'd given Nylah a bath, read her a book and she'd fallen asleep. I couldn't wait any longer, so I went into our bedroom where Malik was watching Monday Night Football and told him I was going to Walgreens. My plan was to meet Haney at ten p.m. and be back home by eleven. If Malik became suspicious, I'd tell him that the prescription hadn't been ready.

Making sure I had my set of keys to Halfway House, I hurried out the house, waving to Phinn behind the tinted glass of the Tahoe, then slipped into my Lacrosse, and headed to Center City.

The restaurants along 18th Street were relatively quiet. A few people were out walking their dogs around Rittenhouse Square, mixed with drunken Batmans, Elsas and Jokers who were heading home from Halloween parties.

Approaching Walnut Street, I slowed down to make the left turn onto Hope Alley behind my sister's restaurant, but was unable to because a black SUV was already there. Rolling down my window to peer around it, I could see the flashing taillights of Haney's red Cadillac parked in front of it.

Impatiently, I circled the block, passing the front of the restaurant to see if perhaps someone was inside, even though they were closed. Haney couldn't have been inside because according to my sister, he didn't have a key.

The second time I approached the narrow alley wasn't any better because now the SUV had backed up enough to block me from entering or seeing down the street. I did take note though of its municipal tags, which made me wonder who else Haney might've been meeting. I wanted to beep the horn, but I couldn't afford to be recognized. For a moment, I considered getting out of my car for a closer look, but thought better of it because whoever was in that city vehicle would question my being there and I couldn't risk getting caught up in another scandal. I checked the time, it was ten-fifteen and I still had to stop at Walgreens. I called Haney's mobile, but it rang until voicemail picked up. I sent him a text, no response. I couldn't wait any longer.

Heading back home to Girard Estates, I kept pressing redial, but he wouldn't pick up and my senses told me either something was wrong or his plan had been to make me look like a fool.

Walking in the house, I'd forgotten Malik wanted to talk, that is, until I saw the glow of candles coming from the living room. How could I possibly talk to him tonight, knowing I was pregnant, possibly with another man's baby? This talk with Malik had to wait until I'd at least taken care of things.

"Get what you needed?" Malik asked, who was now freshly showered, shaven, and wearing a pair of thin cotton sweats and a South Philly Rec t-shirt.

"What's all this?" I asked, noticing the bottle of very expensive Petrus wine and glasses he'd set out. It wasn't like my husband to throw away that kind of money on wine, especially not with his collection of bourbons, which meant this was a night he'd been planning.

"I thought we could relax, slow things down, and talk. I miss you, woman," he said, with a bit of apprehension in his voice, as he uncorked the bottle of wine.

Taking a seat on the bottom step, I said, "Malik, I don't wanna rehash Tootie and Haney, and all that mess, not tonight. I don't have the energy. I mean, can't we just leave it that we both fucked up?"

I waited for him to admonish me for cursing, but instead he drew in a deep breath and told me, "I'm fine with that, but I wanna make sure I haven't lost you. What I'm saying is, I love you, Tiffany, and I know we can do better."

We both laughed at his slogan reference, but he quickly cleaned it up by saying, "I'm sorry I didn't mean it like that."

"It's okay, I still love you," I told him, this time with all sincerity because I did love my husband, I just didn't understand how we'd gotten to this place.

"Good, 'cause I have a little present for you."

"A present?" I asked, not seeing his typical Tiffany's blue box.

"Here sit down on the step," he said, holding out his closed fist. "This is for you, a mere token of what you mean to me."

Unfurling his hand, I couldn't believe what I was seeing, a diamond band, filled with three rows of dazzling diamonds set in platinum. I had no idea how many diamonds or what the karats were, but the brilliance of the colors they reflected was hypnotizing. If this didn't tell me my husband was serious about our marriage, then his next move did.

Getting down on both knees in front of me, he said, "I know you don't want to hear this, but I am so very sorry for everything that has happened. I love you, Tiffany and I'm willing to do whatever it takes."

Before I could respond, the tears started sliding down my cheeks. I wanted so badly for this baby to belong to him and this would no doubt have been the perfect time to tell him. Instead, I said nothing and just allowed myself to cry.

"Don't cry. I'm sorry, I didn't mean to make you cry."

I touched my husband's face; he was so handsome, and his scent of mint, sweet grapefruit, and leather meant he was finally wearing the 1 Million-Paco Rabanne cologne I'd gotten for him. Holding his face with my hands, I sank my lips into his, kissing him, and showing him how much I'd missed him. This was right. I could make it right.

"Here," he said, slipping the perfectly sized ring onto my finger.

Finally, I wiped my tears and spoke up by asking, "Does this mean you're coming back to our bedroom tonight?"

"Tonight and every night."

Eagerly our lips met for another kiss, before I said, "Then why don't you bring that bottle upstairs?"

I didn't hear it, but at five a.m. Malik's mobile rang.

"Tiffany, wake up," he whispered.

"What is it?" I groaned, half awake, my arm around him, in a room filled with the scent of what had been the best night in all our years of lovemaking.

"Haney's dead."

I squeezed my eyes shut, while a tightness that began in my chest, crept up to my throat. I needed to vomit, but I knew if I did Malik might get suspicious, so instead I swallowed it back.

Reaching for the remote, Malik turned on the television. Neither of us said anything as we listened to the news report, live from the scene, an occurrence that had become too familiar over the last year.

I could hear Ukee Washington's' voice saying, "We have breaking news this morning. . . as scandal and murder continues to plague Philly's highest office. Former district attorney, Gregory D. Haney, II was found dead this morning on Hope Alley, a narrow street behind the Halfway House Café, at 18th and Walnut Streets, a restaurant owned by Haney's daughter, Kamille Alexander, sister of the Mayor's wife, Tiffany Johnson-Skinner. Mrs. Skinner was recently in the news when a photo of her and Haney was leaked to -"

"Turn if off," I said.

Malik slid back under the covers, enveloping me safely in his arms, but not tight enough to quell all my fears. Both of our mobile phones rang and vibrated several times before either of us spoke.

"If anybody asks, you never left the house last night."

"Malik, I -"

"Don't explain, you were home, here with me."

"I love you, Malik."

"I love you, too, now try to go back to sleep."

Climbing out of bed, Malik had no plans of going to City Hall, where there was sure to be a media circus. Instead, at 5:17 a.m. he left out for a private meeting with DA Leander, at his home.

There was no way I was going back to sleep. Sitting up in bed, I turned on the light, grabbed my phone off the nightstand and checked to see if there were any messages from Haney; there were none. I had so many reasons to panic. All those calls I'd left and text messages I'd sent to Haney's phone, my car circling that block and everyone knew cameras were everywhere. I had to tell Malik everything, especially since we'd both vowed that there'd no longer be any secrets between us.

Next, I phoned my sister.

"Brandon, what happened? Where's my sister?" I asked, when he answered her mobile.

"I'm down at the restaurant. She was pretty distraught, so I sent her back home. Your mom and dad are there with her, and I have one of my Homeland guys sitting outside the house."

"What happened? Do they know who did it?"

"I can't get into the details, but Chef Haak was riding by from a night out and saw Halfway Hal flagging down cars. He pulled over, along with an off duty cop, and they found Haney laying face down beside his car in the alley."

"Somebody had to see something. Cameras?"

"The one camera that covers the alley was broken, it was scheduled to be fixed on Wednesday. Homicide is checking all that out. But there's plenty of cameras in the surrounding area."

"What's gonna happen now? How soon will you know something? When will they have the footage?" I asked, pummeling him with questions.

"Tiffany, slow down, I need to ask you a question and I want you to be honest; it's just me, okay?" He paused before he asked, "I need to know if you and Malik were home all night."

Brandon was my brother-in-law, but he was still law enforcement, so I did as my husband had instructed me and said, "Of course, it was Halloween, we were trick or treating with Nylah."

"Where's Malik now?"

"He just left for the DA's house," I said, just as the phone vibrated with an incoming text.

RTC: Urgent that we speak, soon.

Chapter 26

Lies & Alibis

The days that followed were filled with speculation and sensationalism from the media. Not only were they questioning Haney's death, they were also replaying Wesley's murder and the fact that his killer had not been apprehended. But even worse, they were trying to draw a connection. That only put more pressure on my husband and subsequently, our already fragile marriage.

The only thing I knew for certain was that I hadn't killed Haney. I hadn't even had the chance to talk to him and the only person who knew I'd gone to meet him was Phinn. I was pretty sure Malik hadn't personally killed him either, but there was the possibility of Blu Eyes having done it on Malik's orders. With Haney, the suspects, known and unknown, were limitless.

Then I thought about Brandon, who according to Kamille was supposed to go see Haney the night of Nylah's birthday party. Maybe those weren't municipal tags I saw on that Tahoe; maybe they'd been government tags. If only I would've taken note of the license plate.

In the days that followed, Malik barely wanted me to leave the house for fear someone might ask me a question about that night, especially a reporter. Once again, I refrained from reading the papers and watching the news because every time they mentioned Haney, they showed that awful picture from his condo.

There was no autopsy, or public funeral for Haney. Brandon took care of all the arrangements, and without even a viewing, they had him cremated. Barring his son who was in prison, my sister was his next of kin.

Kamille had been named as his beneficiary to a $100,000 insurance policy, that including his personal items and cash totaled to almost $300,000, which she deposited into the Johnson Family Trust. Once that was done my bro-in-law took her to Puerto Rico for a few days, leaving the boys with my parents.

I wasn't sure what Kamille had told my nephews; we hadn't discussed it in depth because our phone calls and text messages weren't quite enough to figure everything out. It was almost as if Brandon and Malik were keeping us apart.

Malik had become very good at pretending we were okay. He'd been keeping a tight schedule, out of the house by seven a.m., two phone calls and one text during the day, with him usually home by seven forty-five p.m. It felt good to have him close by, but it barely lasted two weeks before his pattern changed. He began coming home late, and missing his afternoon calls until finally one night, he actually attempted to sneak in the house at two in the morning.

"Malik, what's going on?" I asked, meeting him downstairs in the kitchen where he was checking his mobile in the dark.

"Hey, I thought you'd be sleep."

"I've been waiting up for you."

"Why? I'm all right."

"I'm letting you know I'm going to see my sister when she gets back home."

"You two don't need to be seen conspiring, give it some time. The media is still snooping around, you know that."

"What are you talking about? I don't care about the media, that's my sister!"

"She was Haney's daughter and you were his lover, so why don't you let me and Brandon handle this?" he said, paying more attention to his mobile than to what I had to say.

His words literally made the hairs on the back of my next rise. "Malik, where were you tonight?" I asked, sensing more than I wanted to.

He stopped what he was doing and asked, "Why don't you tell me where you were when Haney was killed?"

"What are you talking about? You know I went to Walgreens to get my prescription that night."

Tapping on the face of his watch, he said, "You left here at 9:35 p.m. and didn't get back in till 10:38 p.m., so where were you all that time? I'm not stupid enough to think it took you that long to pick up a prescription."

"It wasn't ready, I had to wait," I said, dragging the words out because I really didn't want to lie.

"That's funny, 'cause I thought we were done with the lies. Oh and by the way, you came home empty handed," he said, his voice more nonchalant than accusatory.

I turned away from him because it was time to tell the truth.

"You're right, I'm sorry, Malik. I went there that night, but I never saw him. I wanted to reason with him to stay away from my sister. I swear; that was it."

"You saw him every chance you got, didn't you?"

"No, I hadn't seen him since. . . wait," I stopped defending myself, not liking the tone of his voice or the air of his attitude, and instead I posed the question to him, "Where were you tonight? You were with Tootie, weren't you?"

Walking away from me and toward the refrigerator, he said, "I was at the Union League, there was a reception for somebody."

With the light of the refrigerator door shining on his face, I could clearly see that my husband had the look of leftover sex. I not only knew what it looked like, but also how it tasted because I'd seen that reflection in my own mirror. I got up close to him, so close he pushed back away from me and if his being drunk wasn't enough, then it was the scent of Tootie's cheap perfume on his clothes that confirmed it. And for that, I slapped him.

"Tiffany, what the hell is wrong with you?" he asked, grabbing his face.

"You're lying, you were with her. I smell that fat bitch all

over you."

When his shoulders slumped, I knew I'd been right. "Why Malik? I've been here every day for you. You said you wanted this."

"I do, but ever since the party she's been calling me, texting me, wanting to talk and I felt I owed her that much. I swear, I went there to talk, tell her it was over but. . . I'm sorry."

"You're sorry for what? That you slept with her! Maybe you're the one that needs to be honest. Tell me the truth, you knew it was her who leaked that picture."

"Tiffany, all of this can be explained. She was hurt, she wanted me to leave you, but I told her it was over, and she wanted to get back at me, to hurt us both. But I didn't know, I swear, I didn't know it was her until tonight. I'm never going to see her again, okay? You hear me, never."

"No, you need to hear me out – I'M PREGNANT!"

He backed up, falling over the kitchen stool, landing on the floor, with his stupid expression still on his face. I reacted simply by stepping over him and heading upstairs.

A few minutes later is when I heard him leave out the front door.

I was done. I no longer cared about his political office or his reputation. I was getting rid of this baby, accepting Raquel's job offer and anything else that allowed me to be on top and in charge of my damn life. Then came a text.

Phinn: Need a friend?

Tiffany: Yes

I wasn't sure all that I needed, but I did want to let Phinn know that I hadn't met Haney that night. I checked that Nylah hadn't woken up from all the noise, then slipped on my robe
and unlocked the front door.

"I didn't kill him," I told Phinn before he'd even crossed the threshold.

"You don't have to tell me that. I know you didn't kill Haney."

"I never saw him that night."

"Is it all right if I come in?"

"Sure," I said stepping aside, to let him in.

"You okay? I saw the Mayor leave."

"Please tell me you didn't have anything to do with it. That night when you took me to his place, Haney said you owed him."

"I owed for helping me get my girls into Germantown Friends. I paid my debt when I brought you to him that night."

"I'm sorry about that. But Phinn, do you think it was Blu Eyes? Did he do it for Malik?"

"Mrs. Skinner, you don't understand, this thing is bigger than that."

"What are you saying, how big? Was it my husband? Please tell me what you know," I begged, grabbing onto the lapels of his coat in the dark hallway.

"Mrs. Skinner. . . " He paused.

"What is it?"

"If you would've asked me, I would've taken care of him; but it wasn't me."

"I'd never ask you to do anything like that, but you do know something. Tell me what you know, please?"

"What I am gonna tell you is that regardless of what you

did, I should've told you the Mayor was cheating on you; he hurt you and so did that Haney. Neither one of them appreciated you. I mean, I just don't get it with black men; they're always hunting for something better and quite frankly, you're the best either one of them could've ever had." He paused, then added, "Listen, I don't know what's gonna happen when it all comes out, but I have to tell you this first."

I waited, instinctively knowing as a woman what was next. He reached out and lay his hand on my cheek, ensuring he had my full attention.

"I love you, Mrs. Baker."

What the hell was wrong with him? We'd had one stupid kiss and now he wanted to confess his love? I didn't know how to respond, but I had seen Phinn looking at me. I'd seen it in his eyes many times, but I never knew that he'd actually loved me. And if he did, this wasn't the time and I certainly wasn't the woman for him. He was one of the good guys, and didn't deserve to be mixed up my complex life. But also, there was nothing weaker than a man who wanted a woman he couldn't have. Phinn had become one of them.

"You don't love me, Phinn, you have no idea what kind of woman I am."

"I don't expect you to feel the same way, but after tomorrow I might not get this opportunity again."

"Why? What do you mean? What's going to happen tomorrow, Phinn? Please tell me what you know!"

My vibrating mobile interrupted us, signaling a text.

Malik: on my way home.

"It's Malik, he's on his way. You should go, but we have to talk, Phinn. I need to know who killed Haney."

Chapter 27

Thanksgiving

Malik was in no condition to talk when he came back in the house and I was emotionally exhausted from racking my brain about what Phinn hadn't told me about Haney's murder.

In the morning, Malik took Nylah to school, while I waited for Phinn to take me to see Raquel. In addition to needing a doctor to terminate my pregnancy, I was also planning to tell her that I was accepting her offer. Afterward, I was heading over to our church to volunteer at the Holiday Food Drive, and lastly, I'd be meeting my sister for a late lunch.

As soon as I climbed into the Tahoe I was ready to question Phinn, but it seemed like he purposely remained on a call with his Captain until we pulled up in front of the Comcast Tower.

Staring at me through the rearview mirror, he said, "Mrs. Skinner, you said you wanted to know everything and I need to tell you this before you go up there."

"What is it?" I asked, hoping it wasn't more of him expressing his feelings.

"It was her," he stated, cutting his eyes toward the Comcast Tower.

"Her who, Raquel? What about her?"

"It was Raquel Turner-Cosby, she was there. I saw her kill him."

I shook my head from shock and disbelief. "You can't be serious. C'mon Phinn, that woman isn't killing anybody. I mean, why would she do that?" I asked, gathering up my things to get out the Tahoe.

"Ma'am, I know what I saw and that night, it wasn't me outside your house. I had Keenan cover for me because I knew you were going to meet Haney and I wanted to protect you."

"It was you blocking the alley?"

"Yes, ma'am, I didn't want you to get involved."

A sinking feeling came over me and in a tone I'd never used, I said to him, "Turn around, look at me and tell me what you think you saw."

He didn't turn around, but he began, "I parked on the other end of Hope Alley, where I'd be able to watch you, then I saw this figure coming around from Walnut Street. She was pretty covered up, but the funny thing is she was dressed in all black, like any other late night street crawler, and I thought maybe it was one of the Ho Ching Girls, maybe they were back."

"Do you know how bizarre this sounds?"

"You want me to finish?" he asked, still not having turned to face me.

"I'm listening."

"For a second, she turned to look behind her before going down the alley and that's when I saw her face. I knew dressed like that, she was up to something."

As he talked, I remembered Raquel's words, "If it's important, I take care of it myself." But that couldn't have meant killing Haney and for what reason?

"When she turned down the alley, to get a good look, I got out my truck and followed her. I heard them arguing, but couldn't make out what they were saying because Haney's car was still running. Then I saw the glint of her silver revolver, she was waving it at him. Then the gun went off; she shot him several times."

I fell back against the seat, as far away from Phinn and as far away as I could get from what he was trying to tell me. "Oh my, God, this is insane. What the hell could Haney have done to her?"

Phinn waited for what he was telling me to sink in, then he continued. "When she came back toward me, I crouched in the doorway of the 4Sisters boutique until I was sure she was gone. Then I crept down the alley and saw Haney on the ground with Halfway Hal kneeling beside him, cleaning out his pockets."

"You didn't call the cops? You might've saved his life."

He didn't let a moment pass before he said, "He got what he deserved."

My mind was reeling with questions for Phinn and certainly for Raquel. Did I even dare approach her with Phinn's story? Would she think I was crazy?

"How do you know she didn't see you? Didn't she even think about getting caught, I mean, cameras are everywhere?"

"Criminals aren't smart, even if they are rich."

"Have you told Malik any of this?"

"I wanted to tell you first."

I got out of the car without another word. Riding the private elevator to the 52nd floor didn't allow me much time to process all of what Phinn had told me, but he had to be wrong. What had been their relationship and if she had wanted him dead, then why hadn't she hired someone to do it? For as smart and savvy as she was, she'd certainly committed the dumbest crime ever. My legs barely moved when it was time for me to get off the elevator. I had no idea how I would face her.

"Raquel," I yelped, startled, to see her waiting for me when the elevator doors opened.

"Tiffany, I'm glad you came, I have someone for you to meet."

I was silent as I followed her into the conference room. I still couldn't come to grips with the idea of a powerful businesswoman and socialite, like Raquel Turner-Cosby, being guilty of murder. White-collar crime, tax evasion, stock manipulation, yes, but creeping down a dark alley and pulling a gun was pretty unimaginable, yet according to

Phinn, possible. I'd never loved Haney, but I didn't want to see him dead either.

Inside the conference room stood two men, one I knew, the other I didn't.

"This is my estate lawyer, Evan Hughes, and you already know Deacon Brown."

Evan reached out to shake my hand. "An honor to meet you, First Lady. You are more stunning in person than the media has ever portrayed you."

I shook his hand, but was not in the mood for ass kissing because if Phinn were right, Raquel needed a criminal lawyer. But why was Deacon Brown there? Was she looking for spiritual advisement?

"Why'd you do it? What did he have on you?" I asked her, ignoring their presence.

She gave me a long stare before she said, "Evan, Deacon Brown, can you give us the room?" She waited until we were alone before she said, "Who told you?"

"It doesn't matter. I just want to know why? What did he have on you that was so bad you had to kill him?"

She walked across the room, her head held high as if at any moment the police *wouldn't* be coming to question her. Pouring herself a glass of champagne, she asked, "Join me?"

"I don't think so," I said, realizing from the half empty bottle that it wasn't her first drink of the day.

Then squinting those eyes at me, she said, "It was you; he was ruining your life and it was the only way to stop him. I wanted to protect you."

"From what? Malik and I are fine, we're back together and now you've made it worse. You've made us look like suspects," I told her, even though Malik and I were a long way from fine.

"No, I've made it better, everything is going to be better for you."

As she talked, my mobile began vibrating with calls from Malik, Judge Renwick and Phinn. I turned it off because I didn't want to talk to anyone until I understood what Raquel was saying.

"Raquel, you didn't do that for me. I never asked you to get involved. Have you even begun to comprehend what you did? You killed Mr. Haney. You're going to jail for the rest of your life."

An uneasy laughter spilled from her mouth before saying, "Maybe for a little bit, but I have too many secrets on the right people."

"Now I know Mr. Haney was right, you do want to control everyone around you. Well, I won't be a part of any of it. I'm sorry, but this friendship, or whatever it was, it's over," I said, and began walking out the conference room.

"I had to, he was. . . I had to, there are things you don't understand."

"I originally came here to seek your help and to take you up on that job. What a fool I was, you're a sick woman."

She moved to stand in front of me, blocking my path, then blurted out the most ridiculous thing I'd ever heard, "I'm your mother."

I stopped short, almost stumbling over my own feet and said, "No. You're crazy."

"I'm your mother, your father was Firoz Alleyne. He was West Indian."

Pushing her aside, I said, "Please get out of my way."

"Tiffany, listen to me, I was sixteen and we were in love. When my parents found out, they sent me away to live with my aunt in Maine. You have his eyes."

"Let me outta here."

"Firoz and I tried to keep in touch, he even took the bus up there to see me, but it was hard, we were kids."

An uncontrollable laugh escaped from my throat, making me sound crazy. It scared me, but as I listened to the urgency in her voice, I also noticed her eyes, Raquel's eyes were swimming with tears.

She stepped in too close, reaching out to touch me, and I shrank back from her. "Please listen, I swear I'm your mother. You have to believe me. I'm begging you. I have evidence that I gave birth to you."

Raquel Turner-Cosby wasn't the type of woman who begged, which scared me even more, but then again I didn't think she'd been capable of murder.

"Only my aunt was there when I had you and I begged her to let me see you just once before they took you away. I wanted one picture to always remember you. And when I held you that first night, I swore I'd never forget your smooth skin and your beautiful almond shaped eyes, just like your father."

I backed up against the wall, staring at her in disbelief. I swallowed hard to keep the bile that was rising to the back of my throat.

She touched my face and tears spilled from her eyes. "That box over there holds the only memories I have of your father and the one picture I had of you," she said, pointing to a small leather box that sat on the conference room table. I never meant for you to find out who I was and certainly not like this."

"Why are you telling me this? I never wanted you, never looked for you. I'm not like my sister."

"Haney was obsessed with you, so I paid him to help me get close to you. Then I saw how he was ruining your life and
my plans for you. I wanted to save you."

"That's why you killed him?"

"For years, only two people have ever known, my estate attorney and Deacon Brown. But then somehow Haney found out, and he threatened to tell you. I couldn't have that. I couldn't let anyone hurt you again."

"Deacon Brown knew? Wait that's why you gave money to the church or were you paying him off?"

"He knew my family, had worked for my parents a long time ago. Deacon Brown warned me never to tell you, even though I wanted to help you with Blessed Babies. He told me to give to your charity anonymously, but I had to meet you up close, in person, at least once; you're my daughter and when he wouldn't make the introduction between us, I turned to Haney."

"But. . . but. . . I. . ."

"I know it's a lot, but I love you Tiffany. I've always loved you, more than I love myself or any of this."

For as much as this was bizarre, I found myself following her back into the conference room. Here it was, I'd come seeking her help as a confidant in arranging an abortion and now I was faced with this woman telling me she was my mother. I was the one who'd never searched or even cared about my biological parents, and now to find out by default that my mother was the omnipotent, Raquel Turner-Cosby.

With her hands shaking, she poured herself another glass of champagne, then said, "I've sold a few of my business interests and liquidated some properties, all of which should be enough to handle my legal fees.

"However, money has been put in a trust for you and your daughter, which will be controlled by my attorney, but under your name. You're the heir to everything that's mine. The board of trustees will oversee RTC Holdings, but you will have a silent vote in every decision that's made. The papers are drawn up, all you have to do is sign. I've set you up with a monthly stipend of $10,000."

My tone wasn't strong, but my words were. "I don't want your money, I don't want anything from you."

"Tiffany, don't be foolish, you are the heir to everything that's mine. At this moment, you have more power and money than anyone in the city. All you have to do is accept what's rightfully yours."

I felt myself getting sick. I looked at Raquel, closer than I ever had. We had nothing in common, we shared no physical similarities, but what would she have to gain by lying? I thought back to our conversations, how supportive she'd been. My eyes drifted to the leather box on her desk. Did I even want to look inside?

"It's all up to you."

There was a knock at the door, then Gwendolyn's voice, saying there were several calls waiting on her. It was time to go.

"I don't understand."

Tucking the leather box under my arm, she said, "Understand this my dear, you are my daughter, my flesh and blood, and if I have to spend the rest of my life in prison, it'll be a small price to pay for giving you up, because my dear, the worst thing a mother can do, is to allow her child to be taken away."

Epilogue
Tiffany

On this beautiful afternoon, Nylah and I sit riding in the back of a chauffer driven Maybach, past lavender fields and olive groves, headed to the countryside of Provence, where we'll spend a few days at my newly inherited vineyard. I can honestly say Paris has given me way more than I imagined, with its elegance, culture, fine cuisine, and shopping...well that's taken on a whole new meaning in this romantic City of Lights.

So much has changed in my life. In just the last year, I've gone from simply being the Mayor's wife, to the daughter of a billionaire. Having been convinced by Kamille and Huli, the only ones to know of my new status, I'd accepted Raquel's offer to become Executive Director of what I'd renamed The TJS Foundation, and according to the ever present media, I really was the woman on top.

It's unfortunate I never had the chance to talk with Mr. Haney that night because I'd like to believe that at times he really did have my best interest at heart. And even if he didn't, it was because of him that I found myself in this new role. So for that, my relationship with him, and subsequently his death had all been worth it.

In all likelihood, I'll return to Malik because this time it was about my image and it wasn't as if we both didn't have our secrets. However more importantly, I needed to ensure that my children had a father that was powerful and present.

As for Raquel Turner-Cosby, eventually I plan to visit the woman who now calls herself my mother.

Malik

"You promise to come back to me?" were my parting words to my wife when her and Nylah left for Paris. I'd decided it was time for me to leave the confines of city politics, so having been convinced by a powerful group of socialites, I'd announced I wouldn't be running for re-election. Instead I tossed my hat into the Governor's race. This time, I'm running a clean race with no favors for friends and no kickbacks from contributors.

There is one thing that keeps me from sleeping at night, the fact that we'd never captured the person who murdered my friend, Wesley. However my gut tells me that the person who ordered his murder, is, in fact, himself dead.

The other thing I had to clean up was Tootie. She'd packed up and moved to Newark, Delaware, landing a job with Amtrak as a Station Manager. It wasn't easy ending our 10-year relationship, but I couldn't take the chance of her ruining my future or me not giving her one.

As for Raquel Turner-Cosby, I've hired a private investigator to dig into her background because there are two things that still don't add up for me. What had made her so smitten with my wife that she'd offered her such a high level job, with such a lucrative salary? The other thing was Haney. I mean, what kind of vendetta did she have against that man? There was no doubt he was ruthless and from what I'd learned about his relationship with my wife, if I could've killed him myself I would've. But for Raquel to have pulled the trigger, well that was personal.

Unfortunately, I still don't know if I'm the father of the baby Tiffany is carrying, and according to her, I may never know. However, if swallowing my pride to raise another man's baby is what it takes to keep my wife, and put me in the governor's seat, then that's what I'll do. I just pray she comes back to me.

Raquel Turner-Cosby

I'm your mother. It felt so good to finally say those words aloud, after having rehearsed them for over 30 years. Years through which I'd only imagined what it might be like to one day meet my daughter. A daughter who proved to be like her mother in so many ways, and now I'll be able to teach her how to be shrewd in business as well.

Tiffany may claim to have never cared about my existence, but I saw that misstep and that glint in her eye when I revealed who I was. No longer did she need to feel abandoned by a mother who never wanted her. I'd wanted her all along. And now sitting here in Danbury Federal Prison, I'm not worried about my future or hers because I've done my due diligence to protect us both.

As for my son-in-law, Mayor Skinner, I know she loves him, but I've made sure that my daughter will never need him or any other man. What role she plays in his life and mine is solely up to her, but eventually she'll return to us both; she won't have a choice.

For the few years that I'm away, that scoundrel, Lou Mendels will see to it that every month I receive pictures of my family. He's already sent me holiday pictures from the City Hall tree lighting ceremony, but he turned me down when I suggested he follow Tiffany to Paris.

Suffice it to say, I realize I no longer need to be the woman on top, because that title undeniably belongs to my daughter.

Made in the USA
Middletown, DE
07 March 2023

26244132R00234